unperfect souls

mark del franco

ACE BOOKS, NEW YORK

THE BERKLEY PUBLISHING GROUP
Published by the Penguin Group
Penguin Group (USA) Inc.
375 Hudson Street, New York, New York 10014, USA
Penguin Group (Canada), 90 Eglinton Avenue East, Suite 700, Toronto, Ontario M4P 2Y3, Canada
(a division of Pearson Penguin Canada Inc.)
Penguin Books Ltd., 80 Strand, London WC2R 0RL, England
Penguin Group Ireland, 25 St. Stephen's Green, Dublin 2, Ireland (a division of Penguin Books Ltd.)
Penguin Group (Australia), 250 Camberwell Road, Camberwell, Victoria 3124, Australia
(a division of Pearson Australia Group Pty. Ltd.)
Penguin Books India Pvt. Ltd., 11 Community Centre, Panchsheel Park, New Delhi—110 017, India
Penguin Group (NZ), 67 Apollo Drive, Rosedale, North Shore 0632, New Zealand
(a division of Pearson New Zealand Ltd.)
Penguin Books (South Africa) (Pty.) Ltd., 24 Sturdee Avenue, Rosebank, Johannesburg 2196,
South Africa

Penguin Books Ltd., Registered Offices: 80 Strand, London WC2R 0RL, England

This is a work of fiction. Names, characters, places, and incidents either are the product of the author's imagination or are used fictitiously, and any resemblance to actual persons, living or dead, business establishments, events, or locales is entirely coincidental. The publisher does not have any control over and does not assume any responsibility for author or third-party websites or their content.

UNPERFECT SOULS

An Ace Book / published by arrangement with the author

PRINTING HISTORY
Ace mass-market edition / February 2010

Copyright © 2010 by Mark Del Franco.
Cover art by Jaime DeJesus.
Cover design by Judith Lagerman.

ISBN: 978-0-441-01838-3

ACE
Ace Books are published by The Berkley Publishing Group,
a division of Penguin Group (USA) Inc.,
375 Hudson Street, New York, New York 10014.
ACE and the "A" design are trademarks of Penguin Group (USA) Inc.

PRINTED IN THE UNITED STATES OF AMERICA

10 9 8 7 6 5 4 3 2 1

To Paul,
who knew when to listen and when to kick my butt

"Connor is an engaging character with a real heart and a sense of humor that humanizes him to the reader. The world that he lives in is well constructed and easy to sink into. I also find it incredibly refreshing to read [about] a male protagonist when so much paranormal fiction is dominated by female protagonists. Del Franco has created the perfect hero for the modern age." —*BookFetish*

"Enthralling urban fantasy . . . Mark Del Franco provides a spectacular paranormal police procedural."
—*Alternative Worlds*

"[A] fast-paced ride through the Weird side of town . . . Rob Thurman and John Levitt fans will want to check out this urban fantasy series." —*Monsters and Critics*

"One of the most compelling aspects of this first-person detective series is the evolutionary track taken by its damaged yet persistent hero. Del Franco continues to enhance the backstory relationships between secondary characters while laying out a gritty, compelling mystery. In the hands of a talent like Del Franco, murder, revenge, and attempted world conquest add up to urban fantasy at its best."
—*Romantic Times*

"Damaged druid Connor Grey is back in his third mystery, which ramps up the magical action considerably . . . lots of snarky characters to keep things fun." —*Locus*

Praise for

unquiet dreams

"A tale filled with magic, mystery, and suspense . . . *Unquiet Dreams* is a well-written story with characters that will charm readers back for another visit to the Weird."
—*Darque Reviews*

continued . . .

"*Unquiet Dreams* is an urban fantasy wrapped around a police procedural, and that makes for a fast-paced, action-packed novel . . . a great new urban fantasy series."

—*SFRevu*

"A solid adventure filled with unique characters and plenty of fast-paced suspense."
—*Pulp Fiction Reviews*

"It's back to the Weird for the second chapter in this striking first-person druid-detective series. Del Franco's clear and textured voice ensures that readers [invest] instantly in characters and story. Waiting for the next installment will be tough."
—*Romantic Times*

"Readers who like a mystery as the prime plot of an outstanding fantasy (think of Dresden) will thoroughly be entertained and challenged by *Unquiet Dreams*. This is a great new series."
—*Genre Go Round Reviews*

"Mark Del Franco is a master at combining modern fantasy with crime detective mystery. Fans of either genre are sure to find a good read in *Unquiet Dreams*."
—*BookLoons*

Praise for

unshapely things

"A richly detailed world . . . It will pull you along a corkscrew of twists and turns to a final cataclysmic battle that could literally remake the world."
—Rob Thurman, national bestselling author of *Trick of the Light*

"Masterfully blends detective thriller with fantasy . . . a fast-paced thrill ride . . . Del Franco never pauses the action . . . and Connor Grey is a very likable protagonist. The twisting action and engaging lead make *Unshapely Things* hard to put down."
—*BookLoons*

unperfect souls

1

The water cut off in the middle of my shower. Irritation settled over me as I suspected the mayor and the police had taken another drastic step to isolate the neighborhood from the rest of the city. When you lived surrounded by barricades and security patrols, a little paranoia happened to the most optimistic person—and I wasn't that person. As I toweled off soap and shampoo, reason crept back in. Even if the mayor of Boston blamed the local population for the recent catastrophes plaguing the city, shutting off basic utilities would be a recipe for disaster. I chalked up the situation to either a building-management problem or a water-main break. That was the point at which Murdock's number lit up the caller ID on my cell. Murdock rarely called during the day unless I was helping him on a case. When he convinced his bosses to consult Connor Grey, it wasn't likely to be a pretty situation.

In the Weird, the bad stuff went down at night. People fought. They screwed up. They died—sometimes by accident, sometimes by their own hands. And murder happened, too, more frequently in this end of town than any other. That's why the neighborhood had the reputation it did. One of the reasons anyway. As a detective lieutenant with the Boston P.D., Murdock tried to contain the worst of it.

When the problems spilled into fey territory, Murdock called me for advice. I didn't mind. I needed the money. Despite having limited abilities these days, I was still a druid. I knew the foibles of most kinds of fey—understood their abilities, their politics, and their perspectives. Even after a hundred years of coexistence, humans had trouble understanding what motivated even fairies or elves to do the things they did, let alone all of the vast subspecies of fey. There was no denying that manipulating essence caused all kinds of trouble. But, it wasn't "magic" like the non-fey thought. It was a system. It had rules. It could be understood. And Murdock wanted to understand it.

I flipped open the phone. "I'm guessing this isn't a social call."

Murdock's low chuckle prickled in my ear. "Oh, I don't know. We can always go for a beer after and guess where the missing head is. You'll probably want to shower first, though."

"I just had half a shower, and now there's no water," I said.

"I've got plenty of water for you. Summer and B Street. Can you make it?"

"Be there in a minute." I closed the phone. The intersection was a brisk walk from my apartment. By "brisk," I meant "frigid wind that would be in my face no matter which direction I faced." The neighborhood of the Weird was bounded by water—the harbor to the east, Fort Point Channel to the north, and the Reserve Channel to the south. Several long avenues stretched from one end to the other and acted like wind tunnels. Winter was the worst for it, making December my least favorite month, even if it did have Yule.

I put on a gray hoodie and a knit cap, then my leather jacket—the streamlined, padded one, not the old biker. I had lost the biker jacket in TirNaNog a few weeks earlier. Since I might have accidentally destroyed the Land of the Dead in the process of escaping it, I couldn't complain too much about the jacket. TirNaNog was weighing on my mind a lot lately. Briallen, one of my former mentors, tells me I brood too much and blame myself needlessly. Easy for her to say. She didn't apparently destroy another entire dimension that finally opened after being blocked for over a century.

A blast of cold air greeted me on the street. Of course. I bunched my hands in my jacket pockets, hunching forward as I walked. Clouds covered the sky, a flat white expanse that threatened snow but refused to deliver. When tourist brochures called Boston a walking city, they never mentioned winter.

I cut the corner to Old Northern Avenue into more wind. To the north, the financial district's skyscrapers clustered along the edge of the harbor, hard exteriors of glass and brownstone and steel that stared down on the Weird as if they didn't quite approve of the jumble of warehouses and failed office buildings that sat across the channel.

The Weird was a neighborhood of the lost and forgotten as much as a place where people escaped whatever passed for their lives elsewhere. Sometimes that was a good thing, a fresh start in a place that challenged them to get their acts together. Sometimes it was a bad thing, a sad end for people ground down by circumstances beyond their control. It was where I lived and hoped and dreamed, like so many others did.

Anyone with a dream of leaving the Weird would be sorely disappointed these days. A series of fey-related disasters had led the city to clamp down on the neighborhood, declaring travel curfews for those who lived there—but not, of course, for those who visited—and instituting road-blocks to keep people inside—but not, of course, anyone who lived elsewhere. Never mind that the local population had little to do with the essence-related meltdowns that had nearly destroyed the city of Boston. As far as humans were concerned, essence manipulation was magic, magic came from the Weird, and magic was destroying their comfort-able way of life.

Anyone with a passing experience of the local scene would have noticed how things had changed. Morning—even late morning—had never been the busiest time of day along Old Northern Avenue. Except for a few diner-type storefronts that served breakfast, the shops didn't even open their doors until nearly noon. Yet police cars were stationed every few blocks along the street, and the bridge had a roadblock. Overhead, black-clad Danann fairy agents from the Guildhouse flew sweeps from rooftop to rooftop, the morning sun glittering off their chrome helmets. Secu-rity was even tighter at night, at least along the main drag. Martial law was on everyone's lips, and not in an admiring way unless one was on the other side of the channel.

I expected to find Murdock on the corner of Summer and B, and with all the police cars, I almost gave a pass to the B Street Headworks. The yellow police tape across the front door drew my attention back. The building had started out life as a machine-shop warehouse long before the mysterious Convergence that brought the fey folk from Faerie into modern reality. By the early twentieth century, the warehouse had been abandoned. It remained shuttered as the neighborhood began to attract elves and fairies and every other species of fey that couldn't find a home else-where. That was when the trouble started.

There's a reason sewers smell the way they do. Down

in the Weird, there were even more. Things get flushed, dumped, drained, dissolved, and discorporated, and end up in a noxious stew percolating and meandering its way under the street to the treatment plant across the harbor. The Fey Guild helped the city of Boston install ward baffling in the main lines all over the city to capture potions and spells made with essence that found their way into the sewer system. The old building found new life as a headworks to collect anything charged with essence before it ended up in the harbor.

It wasn't a perfect solution. Every once in a while, someone's porcelain went flying and landed on the news. Of course, everyone blamed the Weird because that was where the headworks was, but the fey lived all over the city. Just because they looked and smelled nicer on Beacon Hill didn't mean they didn't use the services of the water department.

I flashed my newly minted Boston P.D. identification pass. If anyone looked closely, they'd see that, one, I wasn't a Boston police officer, two, it was a tarted-up travel pass to and from the Weird and, three, my hair was not at its best the day they took my picture for it. Murdock pulled a string or two to get it for me. Being the son of the Boston police commissioner helped that way. Of course, if Commissioner Scott Murdock knew I had the ID, he'd blow a gasket. He's never liked me much, and since I've inadvertently been involved in every recent catastrophe, I was even lower on his list than usual.

The B Street Headworks was one of those places I passed, maybe paused to admire the Richardson Romanesque architecture, but otherwise without giving much thought to it. I had no idea what I had been missing. A wall of glass met me inside, large panes stretching floor to ceiling and the length of the building. Essence didn't travel well through glass, so the wall served as a protective barrier against what happened on the other side. And on the other side was an infernal wonder. Huge iron pipes snaked and twisted through a wide-open space filled with enormous stone cylinders. Conveyor belts rose and fell through a maze of smaller pipes. Steam rose from vats and release valves, hazing the lighting to misty gray and sallow yellow. Catwalks serviced the three-story height. Solitary fey in all their strange and beautiful-scaled and feathered and oddly colored skin glory lounged against the railings.

Solitary fey didn't fall neatly into any of the major species categories. The Celtic and Teutonic fey each had their own varieties, and the Weird was home to most of them. Scorned and feared for their appearances and odd abilities, it didn't surprise me that so many worked one of the most thankless jobs in the city. They peered down at a group of police officers clustered near one of the large conveyor belts on the main level.

The stench hit me as I let myself through a glass door. My body shields activated, patches of near-invisible hardened essence that protected me from essence attacks and reduced the effect of physical ones. They had covered my entire body once, and I could turn them on and off at will. Now they were fragmented, the result of an essence fight that had destroyed most of my abilities and left a black mass in my brain that hurt like hell whenever I tried to use what remained. I could still activate the shields, but doing it on demand was painful. Perversely, they reacted on their own now, which didn't hurt as much but ratcheted up my anxiety until I could figure out why they had gone on.

As I walked to where Murdock stood with the other officers, my essence-sensing ability kicked in. My vision filled with streams and clouds of light, the machinery and pipes glowing in multicolored hues of essence. The B Street Headworks acted as a giant filter, pulling essence out of the water and sewage before it reached the more mundane headworks that sifted garbage out of the system. The way some of the essence resonated with indigo and violet indicated a nasty brew that was probably what had triggered my body shields in the first place.

Murdock wore a B.P.D. parka instead of his usual camel-wool long coat. To the amusement of several workers, the police officers had face masks on. Murdock glanced up from a trough that ran the length of the room. The top of the trough was covered with a glass lid that had quartz wards embedded in it to control the essence inside.

"Hope you haven't had lunch," Murdock said. A putrid stew filled the trough, murky gray water covered with an oily slick. Things floated in it, some of it unrecognizable, but way too much perfectly identifiable. Strands and eddies of essence flickered, more than the natural ambient essence all organic things had. Things intentionally infused with essence pooled in the water, precisely what the B Street Headworks was designed to filter. Unfortunately, one of those things was a male body. He bobbed on the surface, his brawny, naked torso slicked with black grime. His suede trousers had snagged on a seam in the trough, and he pivoted lazily against the side. To up the horror quotient, his head was missing.

"This has to be one of the most revolting things I've ever seen," I said.

Murdock raised an eyebrow. "One of? I don't think I want to ask."

A flash of pink in the dim atmosphere caught my attention. Stinkwort walked along the tiny edge of another trough fifteen feet up, peering into its contents. For a diminutive fairy who topped out at twelve inches tall, a one-inch-wide path was not a problem. Stinkwort preferred to go by the name Joe, for obvious reasons. I've known him since before I could walk and talk, so I tended to think of him by his real name. "Where the hell did he come from?"

Murdock followed my gaze to Joe. "He likes odd smells."

I nodded. "It's why he likes your car."

"And your apartment," Murdock said.

"Touché, my friend. A lie, but touché."

Murdock gestured at the body. "We haven't found the head. The plant manager says this is an essence trough for outflow from the gross-material filter. The body shouldn't have come through unless it had some kind of essence charge on it. That's why I called you."

I leaned forward. Druids had receptors in the nose and eyes that sensed essence in ways no one understood. My essence-sensing ability had become heightened in the past few months, far beyond the ability I'd had before the accident. My vision sensing was more acute, too. I didn't have to be near something now to sense essence—I could see it. The essence coming off the body explained why it had ended up in the trough. The corpse radiated differently than normal essence. The filters must have had a fail-safe to kick out anything they didn't know how to categorize. "He's Dead, Murdock."

Murdock pursed his lips and nodded slowly. "Excellent deduction, Connor. I wasn't sure what to make of the missing head."

I laughed at the dry tone in his voice. "Seriously. He's Dead, as in TirNaNog Dead. You've got a dead Dead guy."

A few weeks earlier, the veil between the world of the living and the dead opened on Samhain, the holiday that the non-fey world called Halloween. Under any other circumstances, that would have been cause for celebration, since none of the veils between here and Faerie had opened in over a century. But things went wrong—seriously wrong—and the veil slammed shut. When that happened, the Dead from TirNaNog who happened to be on the living side of the veil became trapped here. They were supposed to vanish at daybreak. They didn't.

Murdock's face went flat. The Dead were not his favorite topic. He was raised in a Roman Catholic home. Mass on Sunday was not a chore for him, but a duty and desire. Fitting the Dead into his worldview was becoming more and more difficult for him. "Why would someone kill a Dead guy?" he asked.

I shrugged. "For all the same reasons someone would kill the living. When you've got an axe to grind against someone who died, I imagine the temptation to kill him is pretty high when you catch him walking around again. Especially since you can do it over and over. The Dead regenerate the next day. Which brings me to this guy. Whoever did this wanted him to never come back. That's why the head is missing. Since the head is where the fey believe the soul abides, if you remove the head, you acquire the power of the soul, and the Dead guy can't regenerate. I'd get as much info off the body before dawn as you can. Without the head, it's going to discorporate into its elemental essence and vanish forever."

Murdock looked even less pleased. Resurrection outside his Church was not something he liked to discuss either. "How am I supposed to find a motive for killing a Dead guy who might not have even died this century?" he muttered, more to himself than to me.

Joe fluttered down and landed on the trough. He peered through the glass at the body, twitching his nose and shaking his head. "I think he died two and a half hours ago."

"You can sense that by looking at him?" Murdock asked.

With a sage expression, Joe pointed. "Of course. See? His watch stopped. It's probably not waterproof." A murmur of chuckles rippled through the nearby officers. Murdock cracked a smile. Joe was fascinated by clocks and watches, mostly because he didn't see their point.

"Are you going to ask the Guild to look into this?" I asked.

Murdock scratched his nose. "Not enough reason, not with everything else going on. They've already said they take no responsibility for any Dead from TirNaNog unless they become a threat to the city."

"Well, at least that makes their position clear for a change." The Fey Guild theoretically handled fey crime in the city. It failed, mostly owing to politics and indifference. If you had money or any kind of power, they were right there for you. If not, you didn't get farther than the lobby—especially now, when the Guild had its hands full trying to keep the local human population pacified in the wake of recent controversies. Their usual lack of interest in the Weird had become intense interest—the negative kind. With the mayor and governor pointing their fingers at the Guild, the Guild looked for someone to take the blame and pointed several rungs down the ladder at the Weird. The Dead weren't even on the ladder.

An officer stepped closer to Murdock. "They've cleared the main intake. No head. They can isolate this channel, but they need to get the rest back online."

Murdock nodded. "Tell them okay. And call Janey Likesmith over at the morgue and tell her that Connor Grey says we've got a dead Dead guy. She'll need to work fast. Make sure you say dead twice like that."

Janey was a Dokkheim elf and the only fey person who worked for the Office of the City Medical Examiner. She didn't have much support down at the OCME, but these days she was the last hope for fey murder victims the Guild abandoned. She was sharp and intuitive. I doubted we'd get very far on the body, but if there was anything to know, she'd find it.

Murdock raised an eyebrow. "I hear there's plenty in the budget to control crime in the Weird at the moment. You want in on this?"

I stared down at the body. If another Dead guy did the

deed, I didn't know if I cared all that much. The Dead had their own rules that the living didn't understand. But if the killer wasn't Dead, that meant a nut job was running around the Weird, and we already had too many of those. "Yeah, I'm in."

A long screech went up as machinery restarted. The air shifted, its foul odor changing to a new foul odor as water rushed through pipes. Conveyor belts rumbled to life with a metallic rattling, and a heavy static tickled along my skin as essence filters resumed their work. Two men in headworks hazmat suits approached the trough, body shields hardened and augmented as they lifted the glass to retrieve the body.

A shimmer of essence scraped across my mind, signaling that someone fey was about to use a mental communication called a sending.

He's not the first.

My gaze swept the catwalks. The solitaries who had been watching had returned to work. No one made eye contact with me, and I had no idea which direction the sending had come from. Solitaries didn't trust many people, authority figures least of all. I may not be a member of the Guild anymore, but people knew I used to be one of its best druid investigators.

Whoever did the sending didn't trust me either.

2

The wind slapped me in the face as I stepped out to B Street. I backed out of the way as two men from the OCME hustled a gurney through the door. Squinting against the sudden light of the noonday sun, I inhaled fresh cold air. Only a few police cars remained, the interest level dropping once the word went out that the dead guy was nobody interesting.

Hey, handsome. This time the sending was smooth and familiar and brought a smile to my face. I recognized the sender's body signature bound up in the message. Up the street, a black car idled at the curb, its exhaust coiling vapor into the air.

I slid into the passenger seat. "Hey, gorgeous."

Despite the intense heat in the car, Tibbet wore her favorite red hat and gloves with a fur-lined tawny suede coat that almost matched her skin. She knew what looked good on her. She leaned across the seat and kissed me, her lips soft and lingering. She smiled when she pulled away. "I find you in the oddest places these days."

Amused, I settled against the headrest. "Me, too. How've you been?"

She pulled onto the street. Her smile faltered, but she kept it. "It's been rough. I had a bad week in October, but bounced back."

She didn't need to say more. Tibs and I went way back. The Guildmaster's house, where she lived and worked, had been attacked in October, and Tibs had held off the intruders alone. She had to shed her docile brownie nature to do it and went full-blown boggart in the process. Going boggart was like a mania for her kind, and depending on how deep they went into it, recovery from the transition took some time.

"Am I right in guessing that you didn't just happen to be in my neighborhood?" I asked.

From Summer Street, she drove into the city. "He asked to see you."

"In broad daylight? The Old Man must not care about appearances anymore." Manus ap Eagan had been Guildmaster of the Boston Guildhouse all my life and then some. Tibs had worked for him a lot longer than that as far as I knew. She served a number of roles for Eagan, from driver to assistant to legal advocate.

Tibs compressed her lips, her eyes tearing up. I brushed her hair over her ear. "Hey! I was joking."

She shook her head. "I don't think it's a joke anymore, Connor. He's bad. He's had a parade of people coming through the house against Gillen Yor's orders. I don't like to think what it means."

Eagan's wasting disease had baffled everyone for over a year. Danann fairies were among the most powerful fey beings, and they didn't get sick like other species. That High Queen Maeve hadn't replaced him was testament to his abilities to lead. That she moved Ryan macGoren onto the Guildhouse board of directors sent the message that she was waiting for the right moment.

"Why me?" I asked.

Tibs inhaled deeply to still her visibly rising emotion. "He was arguing with Nigel. I didn't like the sound of his voice, so I went in to stop it. As I entered, Nigel was saying to Manus that things could not be more black-and-white, and it was time to decide. The boss looked at me and laughed. He said, 'The Wheel of the World turns the way It will. I could use Grey, Tibs.'"

I exhaled sharply through my nose. Nigel Martin was my old mentor. We'd gone our separate ways after the loss of most of my abilities, and the relationship had slid further downhill ever since. "What did Nigel say to that?"

Tibbet glanced at me. "He said a fool for a fool's errand."

I chuckled. "Sounds like Nigel hasn't changed his mind about me."

As Tibbet drove into Brookline, she tickled my ear with a red-gloved hand. "I haven't either."

I grabbed her hand and kissed it. When Tibbet and I were together, it was sometimes about comfort, sometimes about convenience. It was always mutual. I don't think I would have called it love back then, but I thought we loved each other now—a truer, former-lovers-who-get-along kind. Not the kind of thing I had going on with Meryl Dian at the moment, which was all passion and frustration and, yeah, hotness. And unexpectedness. "I'm not the man I was."

A reflective look came over her as she turned through the opening wrought-iron gate to the Guildmaster's house. "No. But you're more so."

The gates closed behind us. Tibbet guided the car through the tall cedars that lined the drive. Manus ap Eagan's house loomed above an expanse of dead lawn. In the stark December light, it sat forlorn and faded, its facings of brick and shingle worn white and ashen.

Tibbet pulled up to the front steps. "Left at the top of the stairs, last door on the right. He's waiting."

I tapped her nose. "Thanks for the lift."

She grinned. "See you later, handsome."

"Later, gorgeous."

I let myself in the house. Despite windows at its north end, the grand entry hall had an air of twilight about it, the clerestory windows above casting sharp beams of white sunlight through shadow and dust. I climbed the wide freestanding staircase to the right, its banister curving around the hulking stuffed mass of a real Asian elephant, a trophy from Eagan's less-enlightened days. In the middle of the flight of steps, the portrait above the fireplace on the opposite wall came into full view. High Queen Maeve stared at me, eye level. A shiver of recognition ran over me. I never knew how true-to-life John Singer Sargent had captured the bitch until I met her.

Met her was an overstatement. We had come close to each other not long ago, in our minds, if not geographically. Her coal black eyes held no warmth, either then or in the painting. Her sharp-planed face showed the commanding personality she was. She had to be in order to hold the Celtic fey together after Convergence. Her strength kept her adversaries—particularly the Teutonic fey led by Donor Elfenkonig—in check.

I despised her. For all the good she served, she valued life by a strange set of criteria skewed to the strong and powerful. Nothing else mattered. Only I knew she had sabotaged one of her own underQueens, a Danann fairy named Ceridwen, and risked the lives of everyone in Boston to save her own skin. I hadn't told anyone—yet. As far as the High Queen knew, Ceridwen kept her secret and remained faithful until her death.

But I knew, and I wouldn't forget. I had no hope of challenging one of the most powerful beings on the planet. But somehow, when the time was right, I would expose her for what she was and make her suffer if I could. People died because of her. She had to be held accountable for it.

The upper floor had the soft, hushed quality of a house with too many empty rooms. As I reached the end of the hall, muffled voices intruded into the silence. The last door on the right wasn't Manus ap Eagan's study but his bedroom. He lay propped on several pillows, his wings spread flat and wide to either side. A bare glimmer of essence flickered in their gray gossamer, startlingly feeble for a powerful Danann like Eagan. Nigel Martin sat in an oversize leather club chair to the left, his imperious academic face touched with annoyance. Normally, Nigel maintained a calm air about himself, a cultivated look designed to give his emotional moments more impact. Opposite him, a tall, dark-haired druidess leaned against the bedpost, her head tilted to emphasize the flirtatiousness in her smile. A long mohair sweaterdress managed to show off a body to go with the flirt. Her eyes widened briefly when she saw me enter. I took it as a compliment.

Eagan appeared worse than when I had seen him two months earlier. His long dank hair clung to his pale face, his sunken eyes shadowed. He grinned, a vulpine slash that would have unnerved anyone who didn't realize he was ill. Reports of his declining health were far from exaggeration. He hadn't been in the Guildhouse for any length of time in more than three months and had reduced his activities long before that. "Grey! Come in. I've been provoking Nigel all afternoon and was running out of ideas. Can you carry on for a bit while I take a nap?"

I stopped at the foot of the bed. "Nothing would please me more, Guildmaster."

Eagan's eyebrows shot up. He started laughing, but then coughed from deep in his chest. The druidess placed a hand on his shoulder, but he shrugged it off. Wiping his mouth with a handkerchief, he smirked at Nigel. "I'm not sure he's joking, old friend."

Nigel kept his eyes on Eagan. "Yes, well, Grey's thought process eludes me as well these days."

I pursed my lips. "Really, Nigel? After you took a shot at me, I would think my thoughts about you would be fairly obvious."

Eagan's smile broadened. "You shot at him? Why, Nigel, you've been demanding I take you into my confidence all day, and yet only now I'm finding out you attempted to murder one of my staff. How utterly hypocritical of you."

Nigel met my eyes, his expression unreadable. It could have been anything from regret to indifference. "I make no apologies. The disaster he caused was a result of my failure. And he's not a Guildsman anymore, Manus, as I've reminded you many times today."

Nigel was my strongest supporter once upon a time. When I lost my abilities, I realized I had been nothing more than a powerful tool to him. I checked my anger, though. I was a guest in the Guildmaster's house. Causing an argument would be bad manners. Nigel was another person on my list to deal with when the right time and opportunity presented themselves.

The druidess cleared her throat. Manus smiled. "Excuse my manners, Grey. This is the High Queen's Herbalist, Moira Cashel."

"Pleased to meet you," she said.

A little too pleased, I thought. "Connor Grey."

Eagan slowly adjusted his position on the bed. "Since Gillen Yor's slipped his leash, Maeve's worried I'm not being cared for properly, so she sent her gardener to take a look at me. Moira thinks she can put the flutter back in my wings."

Gillen Yor was High Healer in Boston and not one to take orders from anyone. I allowed myself a small smile at Eagan's playful leer. "I'm sure you will find your patient challenging."

She laughed, a musical, charming laugh that oozed insincerity. "I'm sure I've had worse."

Eagan shifted his eyes toward her conspiratorially. "Yes, I've seen Maeve when she's in a mood. Perhaps your charms will play better with me."

She placed an overly familiar hand on his arm. "You have enough charm for the both of us, Manus. I have only my skills to offer."

Eagan smiled up at her. "Run along then and find someone to help you make a daisy chain or something we can play with later. The mere thought of your ministrations is already making me feel I will rise to the occasion."

She tapped his arm like he was a naughty boy. "I will be unpacking my things. Don't exert yourself any more." She flashed me a big smile as she left in a smooth, gliding gait.

"Can we get on with whatever your game is, Manus?" Nigel asked.

Eagan chuckled. "Look who's talking games, you old crow."

"Why is Connor here?"

Eagan grinned. "Because I like him. He irritates people who need irritating—present company included."

"Um . . . thanks?" I said.

Eagan used a fresh handkerchief to wipe his forehead. "Let me bring you to the present, Grey. Nigel here has tendered his resignation as my acting Guild alternate so he can go off and do whatever it is he does when he disappears. He wants me to appoint Ryan macGoren as Acting Guildmaster."

Nigel leaned against the armrest of his chair. "Letting him run the Guild while you recover will please Maeve. You know that, Manus. MacGoren is being groomed for great things."

MacGoren was a player, an aggressive one. Eagan, I knew, didn't trust him to answer the phone without a hidden agenda. Eagan's amusement dropped. "Not by me, he isn't. Maeve can groom whomever the hell she wants, but she knows damned well the underQueens and -Kings won't confirm someone I don't support, and if I don't recover, as you seem to have overlooked as a possibility, I won't have my successor picked for me. In fact, I'm not conceding I'm dying, so this is all smoke and mirrors."

"Whether you're dying or not is not the issue, Manus," Nigel said. "The Boston Guildhouse needs strong leadership. You do not have the physical constitution to face the current crises."

"Keeva macNeve would make a better choice," Eagan said.

"She's indecisive and inexperienced and not, I should add, an underQueen," Nigel said.

"Which means she will think before she acts a helluva lot more than macGoren will," said Eagan. I laughed aloud. I couldn't help myself. Eagan nodded. "You see my sense of play," he said.

Nothing would irritate macGoren more than to be passed over, especially by someone with a lower rank in the Guild—with whom he'd been sleeping. Keeva would be beyond ecstasy to move into a position she wasn't ready for but undoubtedly thought she deserved.

"We're letting macGoren run the business end of things anyway, Manus. You're being petulant," said Nigel.

"What do you think, Grey?" Eagan asked.

I slid my hands in my pockets and stared down at the floor. "The idea of Keeva as Acting Guildmaster is only slightly less frightening to me than macGoren. Given that choice, I would do nothing until someone better came along."

A sly look came over Eagan's face. "You see, Nigel. That's why I wanted Grey. He has a unique ability to think outside the box."

Nigel stood. "If something happens to you and there is no successor, you will throw the Guild board into chaos."

Eagan smiled sweetly. "Then the High Queen's Herbalist has an enormous responsibility in not letting something happen to me, don't you think?"

"I have done my best to advise you, Manus. I have business elsewhere," Nigel said. He nodded, a bare courtesy, and walked stiffly out the door.

Eagan waited until the door closed before laughing. "I do love throwing wrenches in his plans."

"What are his plans?"

Eagan shrugged. "Nigel has plans within plans within plans. He's off to Ukraine or Russia or some such. That's why Maeve sent her spy to replace him."

That was interesting. "Nigel spies on you for Maeve?"

"To a point. He tells both of us enough to keep him close but not enough to trust him fully."

"Then why did you have him as your alternate at the Guildhouse?" I asked.

Eagan showed his trademark self-satisfied grin. "Because I knew the last thing Nigel Martin wanted was to be Guildmaster. Why do you think he lets macGoren run the day-to-day operations? Nigel, at least, is one knife that I knew wasn't pointed at my back."

Eagan struggled into a seated position and waved his hand toward a large vase on a nearby dresser. "I have a flask in that vase."

I reached into empty space. "Empty."

He pointed at the bookcase next to the dresser. "Try behind the Bible. Tibbet won't touch it."

I slid the large volume out and found an antique silver flask behind it. Danann fairies had a weakness for alcohol to the point of addiction. I didn't know if Eagan was an alcoholic, but he liked his whiskey. I handed him the flask. He took a deep draft and handed it back. "I'd offer you a glass, but the house staff will tell Tibbet if they find it."

I took a swig. "Sounds like you have spies all around you."

Eagan chuckled. "Indeed, I do. It's the nature of my life. Which brings me to why I asked to see you."

I held the flask out, but he waved his hand back toward the bookcase. I hid it again. "I had a feeling you didn't need my advice on a political decision."

Eagan smiled. "Don't underestimate yourself, boy. I actually do like the idea of doing nothing. Right now, though, I need information. The human civil authorities are closing ranks against the fey. I need to know what their thoughts are, what they fear, and what they're planning to do about it."

"Why ask me? I'm not privy to that stuff."

"Leonard Murdock is the son of the police commissioner," said Eagan.

The statement didn't exactly rock me back on my heels. Eagan lived in a world of intrigue. For all his comments about Nigel's plans, he had more than a few of his own, and exploiting resources was second nature to him. "Murdock's a friend."

Eagan nodded. "I'm not asking you to do anything you aren't comfortable with, Grey. I'm saying if an opportunity arises that might allow you to pursue a line of inquiry, that you take it. If you learn something in a way that doesn't violate any of your moral qualms about loyalty and friendship, then you might feel the need to share with me what you hear."

I raised an eyebrow at him. "And why might I do that?"

A languid ripple flowed through Eagan's wings, a sluggish movement that revealed how weak he was. "Because I see beneath your attitude, Grey. You don't like the Guild. You don't like Maeve, but you still care what happens to the fey. You even care what happens to the humans. You could have walked away from the recent catastrophes, but you stayed. Because you care. Nigel's a fool for thinking that's worthless."

I pursed my lips. "I'll think about it."

Eagan closed his eyes and nodded. "Of course, you will. That's exactly what I want. You may not do what I want, but you will do what you think needs doing. So far, that's worked in my favor."

"Really? How?"

He laughed, low and raspy. "Because we're not all dead, are we?"

I chuckled. "I guess that's as good an answer as any."

"Damn right. Tibbet will give you a way to reach me."

"What if I decide not to do it?" I asked.

Eagan shrugged. "Then you don't. Part of what I'm relying on is your judgment, Grey. It's an issue of trust for both of us."

I nodded. "Okay."

Eagan's smile broadened. "It was a pleasure to see you."

I bowed cordially. "And you, sir."

I walked the wide expanse of carpet to the door. Eagan called my name, and I paused at the door. He fussed with the covers on the bed, not looking at me. "When you see your friend Murdock, you should ask him with whom he's been sleeping," he said.

3

House staff threw me curious looks as I paused outside the Guildmaster's door. Whatever his intention, Eagan's comment amused more than angered me. Implying anything about Murdock didn't cut much ice with me. I knew where I stood with him. He told me what he wanted to tell me, and we were comfortable with that. Occasionally, my curiosity got the better of me, and I pried. Murdock was a big boy. He ignored it.

I descended the stairs into the shadowed grand hall. Maeve glared from her portrait, influencing events from across the ocean. She was like one of those giant planets that smaller satellites scurried around. Most large planets were big balls of gas if I remembered rightly.

On the bottom step, movement near the fireplace caught my eye. Moira Cashel strolled across the hall, the provocative smile she'd worn in Eagan's bedroom still on her face. "Will you be coming to the Solstice party?"

The major highlight of the fey social calendar was Eagan's Winter Solstice celebration. When I was a top agent for the Guild, my attendance was a given. The last couple of years, my invitation seemed to have been lost in the mail. "The hall doesn't look like a party's going to happen."

She stopped a few feet away, her hands clasped behind her back. "Oh, I heard the staff talking. It's planned. Will you be coming?"

I smiled politely. "I'll have to see."

She moved closer and ran her hand along the lapel of my coat. "I seem to remember a young man who liked parties."

I glanced down at the hand on my coat. "Excuse me?"

Her eyes shone with amusement. "Oh, come now, Connor. Don't tell me you don't sense me in your memory."

With closed eyes, she rose on her toes and kissed me. Surprised, I stumbled back against the elephant. "What the hell, lady?" I said.

She threw her head back and laughed. A chill went up my spine as the sound stirred an old memory. Her face blurred and shifted, her dark hair lightening to a pale brunette, and her face narrowed. "Don't tell me you don't remember Amy, Connor."

She held her hands on her hips, an old familiar smile twisted into a smirk.

I wasn't buying it. "What kind of game is this? Who the hell are you?"

She released the glamour and resumed her real face and former dark hair color. Cashel chuckled. "I'm sorry. I thought you'd get a kick out of the surprise. It really is me, Connor, Amy Sullivan. Actually, Amy Sullivan was really me. I couldn't believe it when you walked into that room."

I frowned. "Forgive me, but you don't think I believe for a minute that Amy Sullivan was the Queen's Herbalist."

She giggled. "I wouldn't believe that either, now that you mention it. I wasn't the Queen's Herbalist back then, silly. What can I do to prove it to you?"

I shrugged. "Nothing. This is some game Maeve is playing."

A crease formed on her forehead. "What interest would Maeve have in you?"

I moved toward the door. "Now I'm really not believing you. When you report back to Maeve, tell her I said nice try. Insulting, but nice try."

I yanked the front door closed behind me. At the bottom of the steps, Tibbet waited in the car. I strode down and got in.

Tibbet put the car in gear. "What happened?"

"Do you trust Eagan?" I asked.

She rocked her head indifferently. "He tries to manipulate me constantly and sometimes succeeds, but, yeah, I trust him."

"Why?"

She glanced sideways at me with a wry smile. "Because more often than not—way more often—his instincts are right. I've known him a long time, Connor. He can be a frustrating man, but I wouldn't have stayed if I didn't believe in him."

"How do you know when he's lying?"

She shrugged. "I assume he is and go from there. It's easier that way. Fewer disappointments and, honestly, more fun. Are you going to tell me what happened?"

"Eagan implied I shouldn't trust Moira Cashel. When I ran into her on my way out, she claimed she was someone from my past," I said.

Tibbet considered. "Are those two things mutually exclusive?"

"No. But if she really is the person she claims, then I'm not sure whether I should believe her or Eagan."

Tibbet nodded. "Who is she claiming to be?"

"A woman I knew when I was younger."

Tibbet merged the car onto Storrow Drive and wound

along the edge of Back Bay to reach the expressway. She'd lived in Boston a long time. On the map, the route might look ridiculous, but it was the fastest way to the Weird. We slowed as the traffic on the elevated struggled out of the merging of three lanes.

Tibbet smiled comfortingly. She rubbed my thigh. "Connor, I'm not going to ask who she was to you, but if you're worried about memories being destroyed, don't be. They're your memories. If Moira Cashel is this person she claims to be, that doesn't mean she gets to destroy who she once was to you."

"But if Eagan is right, maybe she had an ulterior motive for coming into my life then," I said.

Tibbet coasted off the elevated down to Atlantic Avenue. "Did something bad happen?"

I chuckled. "No. The opposite, actually."

"Then let it be. Brownies have an old saying: 'Don't go bogey until you have to.'"

I narrowed my eyes at her. "Is that a real saying?"

Tibbet snickered as she pulled the car to the curb in front of my building. "Yes. It sounds more dramatic and true in Gaelic. But you get the point, don't you?"

I nodded. "Yeah. You're right. I've got enough to worry about without getting all anxious about something this old."

"Good!" She withdrew a flat round stone from her inside coat pocket. A tingle of essence itched my palm as I took it. "It's a calling ward. Say my name, and I'll come pick you up," she said.

I slipped the stone in my jacket. "Can't I call your cell?"

She grinned. "Anytime. But if you have something for the Old Man, use the stone. It never drops calls and doesn't depend on area coverage."

I kissed her just below the ear. "See you, gorgeous."

She ruffled my hair. "Later, handsome."

Tibs and I have never had an argument. We had a strange and wonderful random relationship. We didn't seek each other out, but we didn't avoid each other. We never criticized each other, but always knew the right thing to say at the right time to move the other along in a decision, not necessarily the one either of us wanted to make. We used to have incredible sex until we stopped. Seeing each other always prompted smiles.

And yet, as she drove away, I realized that for the first time since I'd known her, she had said something that wasn't true. Not that she lied. But I knew memories could be destroyed. Mine already had been. I had blank spots. I thought the memory loss started with the damage to my abilities two and a half years previously, but an old friend recently mentioned something from earlier than that, and I had no recollection of it. It made me uneasy. It meant there might be more things I didn't remember that I didn't have the slightest notion I'd forgotten.

I remembered Amy Sullivan, though, and the memory brought a smile. I remember seeing her for the first time in a store, lost in thought as she stared at something on a shelf. She was older than me—much older—but that was part of her appeal. She was a woman, a beautiful woman, and when I spoke to her that first time, she became the first adult woman who didn't dismiss me as a child, who treated me like the man I thought I was. She opened a world to me that my mentors didn't. Couldn't, precisely because they were mentors. Amy taught me things about life, and I didn't understand that until much later. I thought I was in love, and I thought she was, too. I realized afterward that it was something less than that for both of us, yet something important in a different way. When she disappeared without a trace, I was devastated, but even that made me smile in hindsight. Amy taught me that learning wasn't just about knowing, but growing. Maturing. And the gift she left me was understanding that life had a lot more to offer me than I ever imagined from reading books.

Which brought me back to Moira Cashel. If she was Amy Sullivan all those years ago, nothing sprang to mind that hinted at a hidden agenda back then. If she was playing mind games with me, it worked, but probably not in the way she intended. It wasn't like she thought I'd trust her because she was Amy. If she was Amy, revealing that she lied to me years ago and oh-by-the-way happened to be a current member of Maeve's court was not the way to endear herself to me now.

Of course, I couldn't ignore the Guildmaster's role in all of it. Eagan typically knew more than he let on and never made a move without a calculation. He wanted both Nigel and Moira to see me at the house and me to see them. Whether I wanted to be or not, he'd put me in play.

My various mentors taught me many different things, but they all agreed that the first move in avoiding a trap was recognizing that a trap existed. The second was deciding whether to step out of the trap or turn it on whoever set it. But first I had to figure out whose trap it was and whether it was for me or someone else.

4

Snow crystals pelted against my face as I hustled down Old Northern Avenue. The street had started life as an industrial service road, and it still was. That made it wide and open to accommodate trailer trucks and other large vehicles. Which meant it was one big wind tunnel connecting Fort Point Channel with the Reserve Channel. Whichever way the wind blew, it blasted its way down the street.

A bank of clouds had descended on the city as night fell. We hadn't had a real snowstorm yet, but in New England storms weren't as much a question of when as how much. The tiny ice particles whirling about weren't real precipitation but a condensation of harbor and channel air that was still cold and annoying.

The Avenue met Congress Street at a vague boundary between the commercial end of the street, where fey folk also lived, and the industrial end, where people worked. I had seen more than a few fistfights along these sidewalks, more so in recent days.

Tainted essence floated through the Weird, the residue

of a major spell that had gone wrong earlier this year at a place called Forest Hills. The Taint was the last thing the neighborhood needed, yet was the one thing it seemed to have in abundance. When fey folk came in contact with it, the damaged essence provoked their worst aggressions. In the Weird, that made bad things worse, especially with the stresses caused by the police crackdown.

The Taint avoided me. Something about the dark mass in my head made it recoil. Like the cloud that curled around me near the end of Congress Street. In my sensing ability, the green essence with black splotches looked like a dirty wave. It didn't touch me.

The Weird comes alive at night. It's when most of the neighborhood plies its trade, either legal or not. I've never been a morning person, so it suits me. After I got back from Eagan's place, I put the word out that I was interested in the dead body at the headworks. That meetings often get set up in bars suits me fine as well, so when Meryl Dian came through with a connection, Murdock and I made plans to meet her at one of my regular haunts.

Congress ended at a small side street with no name that leads to a soot-stained door with a "Y" painted in the middle of it. Yggy's started out life as a tavern long before Convergence. Some claimed the place had a certain air of otherness even before the fey arrived. Whatever the truth of it, the bar had been in continuous operation for over a century and appealed to a rough-and-tumble crowd that occasionally wanted a drink without worrying about a knife in the gut. I nodded to the coat-check girls who guarded an empty cloakroom. People used the coat check to ogle the girls and not much else. If you crossed someone at Yggy's, the last thing you had time for was picking up your coat as you ran out the door.

By midnight, patrons filled the seats at the large square bar, and only cramped standing space remained. The crowd spilled onto the unused dance floor while a cluster of regulars worked the pool tables. The place smelled of old cigarette smoke and beer, wet clothing and a singed-fabric odor that was the essence-fire equivalent of gunshot residue.

My essence-sensing ability made it easy to find a human signature at Yggy's, but I didn't see Murdock. Humans were welcome—everyone was—as long as they weren't tourists, gawking tourists, or gawking tourists with cameras. The clientele consisted mostly of fey folk. That was one of the attractions of the bar—the one place in the Weird, if not the entire city, where the fey could gather on neutral territory.

Behind the bar, Meryl Dian flipped glasses and poured shots. Apparently, in addition to her talents as archivist extraordinaire, formidable druidess, and scathing intellect, she knew how to sling booze. Even if she weren't on center stage, it would have been hard to miss her in a black leather bustier and black jeans. Plus, she had let her hair grow to her shoulders. Red. This week. A bright red, a hue short of fire truck.

A gust of cold wind rolled in as the door opened and closed, and I sensed Murdock before I saw him. His dark eyes swept the bar, assessing the layout and the patrons. "Meryl need to moonlight?" he asked.

"You never know with Meryl," I said.

I didn't know which was stranger. Finding Meryl bartending at Yggy's or Murdock wearing a Red Sox hoodie and jeans. He downright looked like an average Southie guy. Last time I brought him to Yggy's, he wore clothes that screamed police officer. Our friendship started out as a way for him to understand the people who lived where he worked. While the fey tended to accept people despite appearances, they also reacted accordingly. Cops were not their best friends down there. Murdock was starting to get it.

A tall wood-ash fairy from one of the minor Irish clans paused in front of us with two glasses on a tray. She handed me a Guinness and a glass of seltzer with lime to Murdock. Meryl caught my eye as she rang up a sale and nodded toward the back of the room. Murdock and I threaded our way through the crowd and found an empty booth near the pool table. He took the corner because he liked to face the room whenever he was in a bar.

I plucked the stir straw from his nonalcoholic drink and tossed it at him. "You're not on duty."

He pulled the napkin from under his glass and wiped up a few spots of moisture on the table. "Technically, no. But it's not a bad habit."

I sipped my beer. Perfect temperature, not too cold or warm. "I like my bad habits."

Murdock shook his head. "You do not. You rationalize them."

Meryl arrived with her own Guinness and dropped into the seat next to Murdock. "That was fun."

"Making a little extra money for the holidays?" Murdock asked.

She grinned. "Just flexing some old muscles." She dropped her eyes to his clothes. "I didn't know Brooks Brothers sold jeans."

He feigned insulted disbelief. "Hey! They're Levi's!"

She wiggled her shoulders. "Oooo, trendy! Was your Members Only jacket in the wash?"

Murdock tilted his brow toward me. "Some help here would be nice."

I laughed. "Not me. I get in enough trouble with her."

Meryl nudged him with an elbow. "You should let me trick you out with some clothes, Murdock. Shake up your image a little."

He sipped his seltzer. "I have enough image problems at the moment."

"Your father again?" I asked. We had Police Commissioner Scott Murdock to thank for the aggressive curfews in the Weird. He pushed for them, and the mayor jumped.

Murdock slipped the napkin back under his glass. "He wants me to transfer to Back Bay."

Meryl pursed her lips. "Not a lot of murder in Back Bay."

"Exactly. He wants me out of the Weird. It's undermining his image," Murdock said.

"What are you going to do?" she asked.

He shrugged. "I'm here, aren't I?"

I let it drop. Talking about his father was a touchy subject at the best of times. Murdock had caught the backlash of a spell a few months ago and somehow ended up with the fey ability to produce a body shield. It wasn't something he'd shared with his father, as the commissioner hated the fey. The way things went between them, I guessed he wouldn't tell him for a long, long time.

"Is your friend coming?" I asked Meryl. Meryl knew more people in town than anyone. How she juggled her impressively busy social life with work was a mystery to me. After telling her earlier about the sending I had received at the headworks, she offered to connect me with a contact in the solitary community.

She sipped her beer. "Oh, he's here. He's being careful. Yggy's makes for strange bedfellows, but people still speculate about who talks to whom in here." She leaned out of the booth, then back. "He's coming."

My essence-sensing ability did the looking. Essence sensing worked as a field around the body, so fey folk that have it literally can see behind themselves. Through the clutter of signatures, I recognized one moving toward the booth. A moment later, a solitary named Zev sat next to me. He was a friend—or maybe just an acquaintance—of Meryl's, another in a series of mysterious connections she had the habit of making with unlikely people.

Zev could never hide his place as a solitary in the fey world. His ochre skin had ripples and seams like tree bark, and black spiny growths dangled from his head like thick dreadlocks. White irises gave him an unnerving stare that I'm sure he used to great effect. Truth be told, he wasn't the oddest solitary in the Weird, even with those eyes.

He cracked a smile at Meryl, stained yellow teeth that almost matched his skin tone. "Hey, M, good to see you behind a bar again."

"Yeah, those were the days, huh? You remember Murdock and Grey?" she asked.

He tilted a bottle of Bud to his lips. "Yeah. Last time I was in a bar with them, the place exploded."

"That was Meryl's dancing," Murdock said.

"I seem to remember some hip-shaking from your direction," I shot back.

Zev shifted his eerie white eyes between us. "We here to joke or talk about what's going on?"

I leaned farther into the corner of the booth. "Okay. A corpse was found at the headworks. When I was there, someone threw me a sending that said he wasn't the first victim. Since so many solitaries work there, we were hoping you might know someone willing to talk."

Zev shrugged. "I think an anonymous sending answers that question."

I glanced at Meryl. "So, why are we here?"

Zev brought his attention to Murdock. "Why is *he* here? Cops aren't doing anything down here these days except picking up Guild body bags."

Murdock didn't hide the annoyance on his face. "You don't know everything that's going on. Police follow orders and do the job they're told to do."

Zev twisted his lips. "I doubt you know everything either. What I know is that when the Guild isn't pounding heads, someone else is cutting them off. I watched a solitary get stabbed to death by a Dead guy right in front of a cop, who did nothing."

"You know about other beheadings?" I asked.

He took a deep swig of his beer. "Rumors, mostly. People have disappeared. So many people are in hiding, it's hard to know who's missing and who's just scared. My friend Sekka is missing."

"The giantess chick from Bavaria?" Meryl asked. Zev nodded.

"Could she have taken off?" Murdock asked.

Zev shook his head. "Not Sekka. People looked to her for protection. She stood up to the Dead, and now she's gone without a word."

He was about to say more but paused and cocked his head to the side. The sound in the room tapered off, the loud chatter of people at the bar fading away. A bubble of silence spread from the far side of the room. People watching the pool game looked up as others wandered away from the bar. In the gap left behind, a Dead elf dressed in an old-fashioned cloak and cap came into view. He watched the reaction around him with a faint smile that looked more nervous than amused.

Meryl pursed her lips. "My guess is the elf farted."

Behind the pool table, a door swung inward. All eyes swept to the back of the room. If there was one thing unusual to see in Yggy's, it was the door to the office open. Heydan's tall, wide body filled the doorframe. He's run Yggy's for as long as anyone can remember. No one crossed Heydan. It was hard to say what kind of fey he was—tall enough for a Teutonic giant, but his essence resonated differently, something more organic or primal, like a forest or a lake.

He waited until everyone focused their attention on him. When they did, he moved with a grace that belied his size. The halogen lights gleamed across his bald head, shadows throwing into relief the high-ridged bones that bulged under his skin from his temples and back around his ears. People said Heydan didn't come out of his office because he could hear everything he needed to from inside. With a head like that, I believed it.

He stopped opposite the Dead elf and rested his hands on the surface of the old wooden bar. His deep-set brown eyes examined the elf as if he were a piece of produce. No expression showed on his pale, stern face as he lifted a hand in a gesture that took in the room. "This is Yggy's. All are welcome. No steel or stone, no staff or stench of essence. Words may start things here, but fists end them elsewhere. All are welcome who abide. Do you abide?"

For all his status as Dead, the elf paled with fear. He laid a hand across his heart and bowed. "It would be my pleasure, good innkeeper."

"I am not an innkeeper. I watch and listen. Tell your brethren all are welcome who abide," Heydan said. Without waiting for a response, he retraced his steps. He hesitated when he drew even with our booth and looked at me. An eyebrow twitched as he broke his gaze. He glanced down at Meryl, a brief smile breaking his firm face, and he caressed the top of her head as he passed. The office door closed behind him with an audible click. The room broke into a babble of sound.

We all stared at Meryl. She pursed her lips. "I suggest no one else try that," she said.

Zev made a sharp noise in his strange lump of a nose. "Even the one who watches allows the Dead to roam."

"That's what he does, Zev. He watches," said Meryl.

Curious, Murdock craned his head toward the office door. "What is he watching?"

Meryl shrugged. "I have no idea, but he doesn't let anyone interfere."

"The Dead are doing the beheadings," Zev said, returning to what we'd been discussing before the Dead elf showed up. "They've been hanging at the old Helmet. They call it Hel now."

"The corpse we saw was a Dead guy. Why would they kill their own?" I asked.

He shook his head. "Death is a game to them. I don't care what they do to each other. But now they're going after solitaries, and the police and the Guild aren't doing anything about it. No one misses solitaries."

"How many, Zev?" I asked.

He leveled his white gaze at me. "How many do you need?"

I frowned. "It makes a difference in how to approach an investigation, Zev. Get the chip off your shoulder."

"Four that I know of."

Meryl downed her beer. "The Dead are playing the same games they played in TirNaNog. Dying is an inconvenience if you just wake up again the next day. I think we're seeing a power struggle."

"Why do you think that?" I asked.

She twirled her glass. "The missing head. Someone's playing for keeps. Without the head, the Dead can't regenerate."

With a smug look, Zev hunched over his bottle. "We don't have to hide from someone who can't regenerate."

I had a feeling that what decapitation meant to the Dead wasn't news to Zev. "Sounds to me like some solitaries have figured out a way to level the playing field for themselves," I said.

It didn't bode well for anyone.

5

Meryl didn't come home with me, which wasn't always a given. Probably a good thing, considering that Eorla Kruge, the Teutonic representative on the Guildhouse board of directors, projected herself into my dreams that night. I knew it wasn't an ordinary dream because the vision was wrapped in Eorla's body signature. Damned surprising to have a beautiful elven woman appear asking me to come see her, especially when she'd neglected to wear clothing. I can't say it wasn't arousing.

I stared at the meager collection of clothes in my closet. It seemed only courteous to dress up a little more than normal. Eorla's status as elven royalty played only a small role in the decision. She knew I wasn't thrilled about monarchies and wouldn't expect full court regalia from me anyway. Where some people—like my former Guild partner Keeva macNeve—reveled in the antiquated system, Eorla was more indifferent to it all. Still, she was a business-woman, so worn-out jeans with holes in them weren't appropriate. A clean pair of black dress slacks and a black turtleneck would work.

I left myself plenty of time to get to the Consortium consulate in Back Bay, so I could take the T instead of a cab. The Boston subway system wasn't the fastest in the world, but it worked, and I didn't have to tip anyone. Money was still not my best friend. At least, it neglected to show up when invited.

Copley Square was bustling with shoppers. December brought a gift-giving holiday to the fey as well as humans. Which meant it was the time of year when people argued over whose holiday first included decorated evergreen trees or whose deity laid claim to an actual birthday and on and on and on. Me, I liked exchanging sweaters. Boston is too damned cold in the winter.

Not far outside the square, a tall, slender statue of Donor Elfenkonig, the Elven King, guarded the Teutonic Consortium consulate on Commonwealth Avenue. The Teutonic fey may have respected their warrior-king, but they also feared him. Donor's rule was driven by dominance over his competitors and opposition to High Queen Maeve at Tara. For years while I worked for the Guild, I spent time in counterintelligence against his operatives.

A vapor of pale essence drifted off the statue and floated in the direction of the Guildhouse across town. I never noticed it before. It was so subtle I doubted many other fey could see it. It wouldn't surprise anyone, though. Once upon a time, the statue had included a niding pole with a cursing spell. The horse skull at the top of the staff was long gone, but everyone assumed the curse still existed. Throwing bad vibes at each other was standard procedure for the Guild and the Consortium.

Uniformed elves guarded the doors and sidewalk in front of the building. A month earlier, they had stood guard inside the lobby, but after the rioting on Boston Common on Samhain, everyone had beefed up their security. The Guild and the Consortium worried about the growingly antagonistic human population as much as they did each other.

A guard challenged me by blocking the path to the doors.

"Connor Grey to see the Marchgrafin Kruge," I said.

The Marchgrafin Eorla Kruge was without a doubt the most powerful elf in the city. Since the death of her husband, she had become a formidable presence on the board of the Guildhouse, irritating Manus ap Eagan in general and Ryan macGoren in particular. Her status as a highly connected elf within the Teutonic Consortium weakened her ability to make effective change in the Guild because they didn't trust her, but she managed to sway a vote or two.

I sensed a flutter in the air that indicated the guard had done a sending. "You are not on the appointment calendar," he said.

"Tell the Marchgrafin's secretary that I am here. I have a feeling she will see me."

After another flutter in the air, he stepped aside. "Proceed."

The other guards watched with suspicion as I entered. Inside, four more guards surrounded me and escorted me to the elevator. No one spoke. Elven swordsmen were not the warm and cuddly type. On the third floor, they led me to a closed door. More flutters in the air, more sendings. The lead guard opened the door and stepped aside.

I had been in the same receiving room once before. Last time, it was empty except for a few chairs. Now, a library table covered with documents sat in front of the lit fireplace. Eorla worked at the far end of the table. She glanced up as I entered, her dark almond-shaped eyes glittering with the power of a long-lived fey. She appeared to be in the prime of her life, though, with her dark green fitted jacket showing off a trim figure and her upswept ebony hair emphasizing the smooth line of her neck.

An ancient elf in a black robe leaned on a staff, the quintessential pose of a Teutonic shaman. His long, pointed ears flexed back when he saw me. We had never met, but you couldn't spend much time at the Guild without learning about Bastian Frye, the Elven King's most trusted advisor. By his reaction, he knew who I was, too. Despite being kicked out of the Guild, I felt a measure of pride that I had caused him a headache or two over the years.

By the fireplace, a dwarf wearing ornate court attire perched on a chair. He lowered a document and peered at me over the top of his reading glasses.

I bowed. I wasn't a fan of monarchial protocol, but in Eorla's case, I didn't mind. She didn't demand it out of form. I gave it to her out of respect. "Marchgrafin Kruge, it is a pleasure as always."

She smiled. "Mr. Grey, the pleasure is mine. Since my husband's death, I have reclaimed my original title, Grand Duchess as well as the Elvendottir family name. Do have a seat."

I passed the chair nearest me and took the one to Eorla's left. Frye's posture stiffened noticeably. "I had a dream about you," I said.

She nodded. "I apologize for the unorthodox method of contact, but I required the utmost security."

"Unorthodox" wasn't the word I would have used. "No apology necessary. Dreaming of you was not a burden."

The dwarf clicked his tongue loudly as he whipped his glasses off. Eorla murmured a chuckle. "Let me introduce you to Brokke, my cousin's dwarf."

Brokke replaced his glasses roughly on his nose and lifted the document he had been reading. "I am no one's dwarf."

"And that is Bastian Frye, my cousin's assassin," she continued.

Frye barely nodded. "I am the king's first counselor, sir."

Eorla clearly enjoyed the moment. "I asked you to come, Mr. Grey, because I have received word that Bergin Vize would like to see me."

Bergin Vize had become the bane of my existence. When I was a lead investigative agent with the Guild, I attempted to arrest him for terrorist activities more than once and failed. The last time we fought, he somehow destroyed both our abilities. I held him responsible for that and a lot of other things, including the events that led to the destruction of the gate to TirNaNog and the current clampdown on the Boston fey. His actions led to the problems. "That sounds like an ideal way to bring him into custody."

She pursed her lips. "Yes, therein lies my dilemma. While I do not condone his activities, I cannot help feeling responsible for him in a way."

"How so?" I asked

"How so, *Your Royal Highness*," Brokke spat.

Eorla didn't look at Brokke. "Ignore him. I raised Bergin Vize as my own son."

If I had been standing, I probably would have fallen over stunned. "I had no idea."

She nodded slowly. "You see my problem. I have an obligation to him of safe harbor, yet I have an obligation to the law as well."

"Why does he want to see you?"

She leaned back in her chair. "For my protection, of course. If I speak with him, I may discover what has driven him to such ends; but the moment I do, I will be obligated to protect him. That will put my cousin in a very difficult position, to say nothing of my own standing on the world stage. My question to you is, will it be worth it?"

Frye approached the table. "I object to this conversation, Your Royal Highness. It is improper for you to consult with this . . . Celt on matters of security to the crown and your person."

"I know, Bastian, but I also have an obligation to Mr. Grey that you will never understand. Remain silent," she said.

Bergin Vize had personally tried to kill me twice and indirectly several times. I wanted him imprisoned or dead so much I could taste it. I took a deep breath. "Someone once advised me to let the Wheel of the World determine his fate. I offer the same advice to you."

A quick smile came to her face as she tapped the arm of her chair in thought. "Excellent advice indeed. I believe I shall take it."

"Your Royal Highness, I must . . ." Frye began.

She glared at him. "You 'must' nothing, Bastian. I told you to remain silent. Brokke, ask your questions before I change my mind."

The dwarf slipped off his seat and bowed. "As you wish, Your Royal Highness." He moved closer to the table, removing his glasses again. "I advise the king, druid. His Royal Majesty is concerned that I could not discern the recent events in your city. You are the common connection to all of them."

Dwarves had the ability to see into the future by scrying, which involved infusing water with spells. The talent wasn't exact, more a sensitivity to likely outcomes. The future changed as events progressed. Some people thought they could influence coming events by knowing the possibilities. I didn't doubt they could nudge a thing or two, but no one I knew ever truly predicted the future. "Is that a question?" I asked.

He pursed his lips. "Are you a diviner, Druid Grey?"

Druids and dwarves had a long-running pissing contest when it came to who predicted the future more accurately. When we were being honest, the ability seemed to be roughly equivalent between the two. Of course, no druid or dwarf admitted that to the other. "I once had some talent for scrying and trance. No longer."

"Have you tried?"

My impulse was to tell him to mind his own business, but my ability problems had become common knowledge. Given that he was in the same room as the Elven King's master spy, he probably already knew the answer anyway. "Not in two years. The last time was just after my . . . accident . . . when I lost my abilities. I ended up unconscious for a day and a half."

Despite losing my abilities in the duel with Vize, my essence-sensing ability had gone off the charts. Every time I thought it couldn't get any more acute, it did. Brokke was using his own sensing ability to examine me. It was subtle, even delicate, and not typical of the skill of dwarves. I imagined he didn't become a king's advisor because he had average talent.

"How damaged are your abilities?" he asked.

Just because he knew more about my situation than he probably let on didn't mean I had to make things easier for him. "Why do you want to know?" I asked.

He started to speak, then clenched his jaw. I had a feeling Brokke was not used to being questioned. "A druid with damaged abilities can be a dangerous thing."

"You could say the same thing of an elf. How's Vize these days?"

Brokke narrowed his eyes. A sending fluttered through the room. Old Ones—the fey who lived in Faerie before Convergence like Eorla, Bastian, and Brokke—didn't normally show evidence of using sendings. I had no idea who had spoken to whom, but Brokke seemed to be one end of the conversation.

Frye shifted his staff into the crook of his arm. "Druid Grey, the Elven King is very concerned about your involvement in the recent catastrophes in this city. His Highness is not pleased that his people are being implicated as well. You invite more scrutiny by your reticence."

I frowned. "So, just to be clear here, should I be taking that as some kind of threat?"

Eorla made a show of tilting her head toward Frye as if she wondered, too.

"I mean only that you might find yourself answering questions you may not care to," he said. "The Elven King is not the only one concerned. Should you find yourself in particular difficulties, I am authorized to assist you."

I fought off a look of surprise. I still didn't know if I was being threatened. "I'll keep that in mind."

Eorla waved her hand dismissively. "Enough. I wish to speak to Mr. Grey alone. I will send for you when I am done."

"I do not think it wise to remain alone with this druid," Frye said.

Eorla arched an eyebrow. "For me or for you?" Frye compressed his lips rather than answer. "You are dismissed. Both of you."

They bowed and moved down the length of the table.

"Bastian?" Eorla said. She held up a fist, palm toward him when he paused. With an abrupt opening of her hand, she muttered a short phrase in Old Elvish. Bright green motes of essence shot from her fingers and shattered two ceramic urns to either side of the fireplace. "In the future, Bastian, I suggest you think again before you tune listening wards to eavesdrop on my conversations."

Frye did not meet her gaze but bowed. As he followed Brokke out of the room, Eorla called his name again. "That urn by the door, Bastian? Take it with you and strip the listening ward from it. I rather like that one and would prefer not to destroy it."

Frye removed the urn in question from the bookcase

by the door. He held it against his chest, bowed to Eorla, and backed out of the room. Eorla chuckled. "He tries my patience."

I smiled. "Something tells me you try his a little bit."

She smiled back. "I hope so."

"Why are you telling me about Vize? You know I want him in prison," I said.

She shifted in her seat. "Bastian and Brokke want me to meet with him, but I won't. It irritates them that I spoke to you instead."

"Where is Vize?" I asked.

Eorla arched an eyebrow. "I truly don't know. Bergin isn't why I asked to see you. I have been having dreams about Forest Hills. I want to know if you have, too."

Forest Hills was one of those lovely catastrophes Bastian Frye referred to. A spell created to control essence got out of hand. Eorla and Nigel Martin tried to stop it, but it overwhelmed them. I did stop it, but I couldn't remember how. "I don't remember any of it."

"You remember the staff that was used, don't you? And the runes that were bound to it?" she asked.

I nodded. "That I remember. I saw it before I did whatever I did. The staff held the essence of the oak, and Teutonic runes were bound to it. I don't know what they meant, though."

She gestured to some paper on the table. "Can you show me the runes you remember?"

The spell had damaged essence and produced what everyone called the Taint. The Taint provoked highly aggressive behavior in anyone who touched it. I hesitated as I picked up a pen. I liked Eorla well enough, but we had been uneasy allies at best. I wasn't sure piecing together a dangerously powerful control spell was in anyone's best interest—and helping the Consortium do it could be trouble. Then again, I had never been more angry with High

Queen Maeve, so if something I did caused her a problem, I wouldn't be all that upset. I wrote on the paper and slid it to Eorla. "I remember these four the most. They were floating and revolving around the staff. I'm not sure of their order. I didn't focus on them. "

Eorla added more runes. "I remembered three and dreamed two more. We have some overlap."

I studied the five new runes. "I don't know many elven rune spells."

"It intrigues me that a Celtic staff and Teutonic runes worked together," she said.

I shrugged. "It's just a means to an end, isn't it? Essence is the same either way."

She stared at the runes. "True. Something ancient teases at my memory—a spell I might have seen long ago."

"Why the interest, Eorla?"

She folded the paper and held it on her lap. "A Guild initiative, actually. The Taint still plagues the city. We're hoping to undo the damage."

I sighed. "Good luck. The only person who seems to be unaffected is me, and that's because of the dark spot in my head." Our eyes met in the silence. "Unless you know someone else in a similar situation."

She shook her head. "I haven't spoke to Bergin since before the two of you fought. I have no idea if the Taint does or does not affect him."

I leaned my elbows against the table. "If it's a Guild initiative, why the secrecy?"

She steepled her fingers, the gems on her many gold and silver rings glittering in the firelight. "It's not my secret, but yours. Don't misinterpret Bastian. He speaks truly when he says many people are watching you, Connor. Maeve sent an underQueen to interrogate you after what happened at Forest Hills. Now my dear cousin, Donor, has sent Bastian. When you have the two most powerful fey in the world interested in you, it doesn't go unnoticed by others. The less nervous people are about what you know or can do, the safer you will be."

"What's in it for you?"

She stared at me with an amused look, drawing the moment out. "I don't know yet. But since we are the only two that know we remember some of the runes, I suggest we trust each other, shall we?"

I held my hand out. "You have my word."

Without hesitation, she clasped my hand. "And you have mine. Thank you for coming."

I bowed. "Eorla, it was a pleasure as always."

Out in the hall, guards positioned themselves around me as an escort. They didn't follow me more than a few feet out of the building, but I felt their eyes on my back the rest of the way down the block.

I didn't doubt for one minute that Eorla would throw me to the wolves if it suited her purpose. We played an interesting hand together to our mutual benefit. I had held back one of the runes I remembered. I'm sure she had, too. Until we knew we could trust each other—really trust each other—that was how the game was played. I agreed with her assessment of my position. I was caught between High Queen Maeve and the Elven King. It amused me that it wasn't until I lost my abilities that I came to the attention of the movers and shakers of the world. Once that happened, I needed all the allies I could get, and Eorla Kruge, Grand Duchess of the Elven Court, was not a bad one to have.

6

The answering machine was blinking its little red light when I returned from the consulate. The usual collection of pointless messages droned out. I used my cell phone for people I knew and wanted to talk to. The apartment phone handled the solicitors and the bills. I gave them the courtesy of listening before deleting and ignoring. The last message surprised me.

"Hi, Connor Grey. I don't know if you remember me, but this is Shay. I need your advice on something. If you could stop by 184 A Street later this afternoon, I'd appreciate it. I think I might have a problem."

Shay was hard to forget. When I met him, I thought he was female. I'd never met a guy who looked so much like a woman—and an attractive one at that. He flirted with me outrageously—and with Murdock and with anyone who came within ten feet of him.

I never learned his whole story, but he'd had a hard life. Like so many other kids, he thought he'd find a place to call home in the Weird. He did, too, but probably not the one he hoped for. Most people didn't aspire to turning tricks for a male clientele who were into the transgender scene. As if his luck weren't bad enough, he got himself tangled in a serial killer's murder spree and lost his boyfriend. I didn't think there was a chance I would be forgetting Shay anytime soon.

The address on A Street was near the old Gillette razor plant, a short stretch of warehouses that had been converted to working lofts where painters and jewelry artists tried to stand out by living on the edge of the scary neighborhood. Boston artists were a world of their own. New York was not so far off but was a different scene entirely, more competitive, more commercial. More New York. Boston was about the art and, yeah, the money, but Boston artists had an earnestness about them that you usually see only outside the expensive cities.

I huddled in the doorway of the building address Shay gave me to avoid the cold, stamping my feet to keep the blood flowing. A slender figure in a full-length white down coat appeared at the corner. A lock of jet-black hair escaped the round hood fringed with glossy fake fur and waved in the air. I didn't need to sense Shay's essence to know it was him. The wind pinked his face as he walked carefully down the sidewalk. When he saw me, his Cupid's-bow lips curled into a smile, and he raised a mittened hand, more acknowledgment than wave. "Sorry. Work ran late."

To my surprise, he pulled a key out of his pocket and unlocked the door. Surprise because last I knew, Shay lived in a squat up on Congress Street.

I followed him up steep, wide stairs. "You live here?"

He shifted lightly mascaraed eyes to me. "I have a studio."

We trailed down a long, high-ceilinged hall with thick, wide-planked floors showing the wear of a century of work. New walls had been constructed to divide a once-open manufacturing space into a warren of small rooms. The odor of thinner, oil paint, and solvents permeated everything. Shay let us through a plain white door that had a yew wreath hung on it.

To the left, a wall ran thirty feet without interruption from the door to a set of windows. Paintings, prints, and other artwork covered every available inch. Nine feet to the right, a large freestanding sink stood next to a homemade wood counter with a two-burner hot plate on it and a small refrigerator of the type that students used in dorm rooms. Two tall bookcases formed a bed alcove in the middle of the narrow studio.

"I never knew you were an artist," I said.

Shay removed his coat in a whirling motion and hung it among others on a rack by the door. He wore snug blue jeans and a thigh-length charcoal gray sweater. Twisting his lips, he made an exaggerated and amused pout. "You never knew me, period, Connor."

I smiled. "Does anyone?"

Resting a delicate hand on his hip, he tilted his head. Eyes roved up and down, examining me as if I were merchandise. Maybe I was. I really did not know Shay. "You cut your hair. I like it short. Makes those lovely blues stand out more."

Shay's flirting irritated the hell out of Murdock, but I found his brashness utterly amusing. This slender boy, with his stunningly feminine face, had more balls than men twice his size. Shay spoke his mind when he chose to. "You've moved up in the world. Still working?"

He filled a small teakettle and put it on the hot plate. "Not how you mean. I work full-time at the Children's Institute now. The pay's not great, but I can afford to live here."

When I first met Shay, he was working the streets. He never was arrested for prostitution, but anyone in the profession knew it was a matter of time. It was good to hear he had gotten out of the life before it was too late for him. Back then, he volunteered at the Institute, where he cared for Corcan macDuin, a mentally disabled elf who became inadvertently involved in a murder case. "How is Corky?" I asked.

Shay smiled. "Amazing. After what happened, his mental capacity improved. He's reached the mentality of a teenager since midsummer. You should come by and see him. He talks about you."

"He does?"

The kettle whistled. Shay poured two mugs. "You saved his life. He likes to tell the story of the hero with the shining sword."

I was about to thank him when something ticked up in my sensing ability. At the far end of the studio, hidden from view by the bed alcove, an essence moved. It hadn't been there when we'd come in. Before I said anything Shay looked toward that end of the studio. He was human but claimed to have some kind of fey sensitivity. He might. Or he might have timed the arrival of whoever was in the studio to make it look that way. For all his naïveté, manipulation was another of Shay's skills.

"Who's back there?" I asked.

He handed me a mug. "That's what I wanted to talk to you about. You saved my life, too, but I think it delayed the inevitable."

He led me around the bed alcove to a cramped living room with a small couch and two overstuffed chairs. A large black dog—large in that way that made people stop and gape—sat on the couch and stared at us. Shaggy, glossy coat, massive head and jowls. The kind of dog that, even though an owner claims it is very sweet, you suspect might enjoy kittens for breakfast.

I sipped my tea. The dog wasn't alive. Its essence resonated like the Dead from TirNaNog, but something was off about it. "That's a Dead dog, Shay. Do you know what I mean?"

Shay held his mug with both hands. Resigned, he nodded. "I thought so. He started following me right after Samhain. He seemed to like me, so I brought him home. He wasn't eating when I left food out, so I thought someone else must be feeding him. Then I found out the Dead were in the Weird, and I thought, what the hell, maybe there are Dead animals, too."

"I saw some pretty strange ones on Samhain," I said.

Shay frowned. "I have a feeling this isn't a normal Dead dog, Connor."

He put his mug down and pulled the drapes across the windows. Darkness blanketed the room except for a red glow. Every hair on my body stood on end, and I sloshed tea on the floor as I stepped back. The dog's eyes burned like embers. "Holy shit, Shay!"

Shay swept the drapes open, and the red glow vanished. He crossed his arms and stared at the dog. "It's a hellhound, isn't it?"

Hellhound. Cu Sith. Cwn Annwn. The dog went by various names in various places. Sometimes it was white furred with red ears. Sometimes it was a big, freaking black dog with glowing eyes. Its purpose remained the same everywhere. If it came for you, it came from the land of the Dead, and it meant you were going to die. "I think so," I said.

"I'm going to die," he said.

The dog opened its mouth and panted. "I don't know," I said.

Shay didn't take his eyes off the dog. "Liar."

I don't know which was creepier, the dog's presence or Shay's calmness. "Shay, nothing is what it was. The Dead are trapped here, so maybe the dog is, too. Maybe it reacted to the fact that you brought it home. Dogs respond to kindness, right? It's still a dog."

"His name is Uno," he said.

"What?"

Shay gave me a wry smile. "I thought it was a joke at the time. He had only one head, so I named him Uno."

"The three heads are from Greek myth, not Faerie," I said.

Shay sat in an armchair. "That's the joke, isn't it? I came up with the name based on something that didn't exist. Only, the joke's on me. It's a hellhound, and I'm going to die."

"Stop saying that," I said.

Shay shrugged. "That's the only way it goes away that I've ever heard." He pursed his lips. "Actually, it sort of gets rid of you."

"This isn't my area of expertise. Let me look into it," I said.

Shay stared into his tea mug. "Funny thing—I dreamed of Robyn the night the dog appeared. Robyn would have tried to do something about it showing up, but there was nothing he could have done. He couldn't stop his own death."

I poked him against his leg with my boot. "Will you stop? Robyn died trying to do a good thing. He loved you. I thought he was kind of a jerk, but he loved you."

Shay leaned his head back and laughed. "The two of you had something in common. He thought you were a jerk, too."

He looked back at the dog. "I just thought of something, Connor. If Uno came for me, maybe I'll get to see Robyn again. I never had much faith in Christianity. Maybe TirNaNog is where I'll end up."

I didn't have the heart to tell him that the reason the Dead were roaming the Weird was because TirNaNog might not exist anymore. "Yeah, maybe, but as far as I'm concerned, I didn't save your ass last midsummer for you to end up dog food."

Shay chuckled. "Now you have something else in common with Robyn: promising to protect me when you know you can't."

"I'm not listening to any more of this. I'm going to find out how to get rid of this guy," I said.

Shay shifted closer to me. "I don't think I can ask for more than that, but don't feel bad if you can't. It's not your fault."

"I'll find something, Shay," I said.

He took the cold tea from my hand and walked me to the door. "Thanks, Connor. Maybe some revelation is at hand for me, no? Maybe it means something important. I bet not every human gets to have a hellhound in their living room, even in the Weird."

"Be careful, Shay. I'll get back to you."

Shay amazed me. I didn't think I could do anything for him. I had never encountered a hound from TirNaNog, but all the old tales ended the way Shay said they did. Whoever the hound came for, died. If he was doomed, the least I could do was try to help. I wasn't really big on abandoning people to fate. My life would be a lot easier if I were.

7

The early-morning cold remained, the sky a stark white with the threat of snow. When I'd arrived home the previous night, I spent the evening outlining research ideas for Shay's dog problem. Which, of course, led all too easily to late-night Internet surfing on topics that had nothing to do with hellhounds. Which, more of course, I should have known would lead to an early-morning phone call from Murdock asking me to meet him since I had barely gotten any sleep. He told me to wear clothes and boots I didn't care about, so I wore the oldest pair of jeans I owned and an extra layer of sweatshirt.

I walked the three blocks to the location Murdock gave me. Trucks barreled down Fargo Street, whipping sand into the air. Near the corner of Cypher Street, large blue utility vans emblazoned with MASSACHUSETTS WATER RESOURCES AUTHORITY on the side blocked part of the intersection. MWRA workers placed cones and portable metal barricades around an open manhole. Wearing jeans and an old Red Sox jacket, Murdock stared into the hole in the street. I

assumed he had borrowed the jacket from one of his brothers because I could not imagine Murdock keeping a stained
piece of clothing. His new casual attire was amusing me.

A sewer worker banged on something in the hole below
us. "Please tell me you asked me to dress like this because
we're going hiking," I said.

He chuckled silently. "No such luck. The MWRA gave
us an idea of where the body at the headworks might have
gone into the system based on the time on the broken
watch. Turns out the tunnel he came out of has only two
feeder pipes. This is where they meet."

I slouched. "We're going in the sewer."

"Yep. It's a possible crime scene."

The worker banged some more. "What's he doing?" I
asked.

"Scaring away the rats."

"Great."

Joe burst into the air in front of the detail officer direct-
ing traffic. The guy ducked like a giant insect was attacking
him. "Am I too late? Did I miss anything?" Joe asked.

Murdock watched him flutter around the manhole. "Just
in time, Joe."

Joe showing up at two different crime scenes was a little
too coincidental. "How the hell did you reach him? I can't
get him to show up anywhere on time."

Murdock withdrew a small clear bottle from his pocket.
Motes of yellow light danced inside. "He gave me a bunch
of these."

Glow bees. They were concentrations of essence that
absorb voice sounds. Messages became imprinted on the
essence, which homed in on the recipient when released.
They worked best with strong body signatures—like the fey
had—and since Murdock's signature was hyped enough to
create a body shield, a glow bee would be easy for him to
use. Humans loved to play with them although cell phones

worked a lot faster. The sewer worker climbed out. Murdock gestured. "After you."

I shook my head. "I believe it's your case, Detective. I'm a consultant here."

Murdock placed one foot on the ladder. Joe zipped in ahead of him. The worker handed me a flashlight, and I followed them down. A cast-iron pipe ran through a low, square tunnel. The pipe took up most of the space, and we crouched against a brick wall. A dull odor filled the air, not overwhelming, the tang of chemicals and dankness. "It doesn't smell as bad as I thought," I said.

Murdock swung his own flashlight toward the end of the tunnel. "That's because this part's sealed. The catch basin is up that way."

"Excuse me while I get a*head*!" Joe said. His squeal of laughter trailed down the tunnel as the pink glow of his wings dwindled into the distance.

Murdock shimmied sideways along the pipe. I flicked the beam of my light at his feet, then behind me. I'm not a fan of rats sneaking up on me. "Don't you guys have crime-scene people to do this?"

Murdock cleared his throat. "Short-staffed. They said they don't look for crime scenes, they investigate them. Besides, they can't do what you do."

True. When I climbed down the ladder, my sensing ability got immediate hits, mostly dwarves, several anomalous ones that meant solitaries, and the distinctive signature of the Dead. The Dead felt different than the living. Their signatures had a dulled aspect to them that distinguished them from living ones. "Too many to sort in this area."

Murdock pushed forward. "I don't even want to think about so many people down here."

The body signatures faded the farther we moved from the manhole. Homeless squats appeared under the pipes, faint shimmers of essence indicating they had been used a while ago. The distant sound of water reached my ears at the same time as the stench that I expected to find in a sewer. Joe's pink essence appeared and reappeared, closer now. He was either popping in and out of sight or passing in front of an opening.

"I'm down to five body signatures, Murdock. Two dwarves, a Dead fairy, a solitary I don't recognize and, I'm not sure, but I think it might be a Dead human."

"Human? I thought there were no humans in Faerie," he said.

I ducked my head under a ceiling beam. "No humans came here from Faerie during Convergence. That's different. There were humans in Faerie who lived and died. Whoever I'm sensing died as a human in Faerie."

Murdock stopped. "We're here."

The pipe continued a few more feet, the end suspended over a wide catch basin filled with water. A dozen feet across it, another pipe entered from the opposite direction. Fetid water trickled out of both pipes. Joe circled in the air, examining the debris floating in the water. Murdock would have killed me if I knocked him into it, no matter how accidentally. I was very tempted, I was.

"See anything, Joe?" Murdock asked.

His eyes glowed with excitement. "It's essence soup."

Essences smeared into each other, reds and yellows dominating with streaks of blue and green. Here and there, the pale essence of the Dead twisted on cast-off garments and, yes, indications of body fluids. My head buzzed with the mess, the dark mass pulsing against my skull.

A wet, hollow sound filled the air with a rumble and a rush. I grabbed Murdock's sleeve. "Better step back."

We retreated a few feet into the tunnel as a gout of black-slimed water gushed out of the pipe. As if triggered by its companion, more water spewed from the opposite pipe. The pipe continued dropping a steady stream after the nearer one slackened. The catch basin sloshed as water fell and kicked up debris from the bottom. The water level rose and spilled into a culvert on one wall between the two pipes. The rancid smell of sewage and rotten garbage thickened. The stench had a texture to it that clung to the back of the throat and made it impossible not to gag.

In the midst of the swirls of essence, something pale floated, a void of essence. It rolled up and sank, then rose again. Wet hair spread across the surface, spreading the weight of the thing it was attached to. It bobbed, and dead white eyes stared up at us.

"Jesus," Murdock muttered as he played the flashlight on the face.

"That is one big head," Joe said.

The body found at the headworks was one of the Dead. This head, however, didn't have the signature of one of the Dead. It rolled, its face rising out of the water.

"That's not the head we were looking for," Murdock said.

"I think we just found Zev's friend Sekka," I said.

8

As the cramped space around the catch basin became crowded with the arrival of the medical examiner and more MWRA workers, Murdock and I shuffled along a ledge to the opposite outlet pipe. The sewer workers fitted a temporary flexible pipe to the end of the outflows to bypass the basin, and pumps had been brought in to drain it. The medical examiner had the unpleasant task of fishing the giantess's head out of the water.

Joe wandered around the edges of the space, swooping down whenever he saw something interesting. Interesting, in this case, was everything from a sodden stuffed bear to things that did not bear scrutiny.

"A headless body and bodiless head that don't match," Murdock said.

"I hate to say it, but if Zev's attitude was any indication, there's going to be more of this," I said.

Murdock shook his head. "With multiple perpetrators."

Joe wandered between us and flew up to face level. "Um . . . guys? If I, say, noticed a crack in a wall in a tunnel and a cold, creepy draft came out of it and it smelled like three-day-old lasagna, would you, um, want to know about that?"

Murdock and I exchanged glances. "You invited him," I said.

"Show us the crack, Joe," Murdock said.

Joe turned around and lowered his loincloth.

I tilted my head back with a grin. "You so walked into that."

Murdock shook his head with a half smile. "I did, I did. Okay, what I meant was, where's the crack in the tunnel, Joe?"

Joe's eyes went wide. He turned around again, lowered his loincloth, and bent over. My laugh drew confused and annoyed stares from the MWRA workers. "Murdock, please don't ask him what three-day-old lasagna smells like. I've had enough bad odors today," I said.

Laughing wildly, Joe shot into the tunnel behind us.

Murdock reddened from laughing. "I can't believe I fell for that. Twice."

"Never accept glow bees from strange flits, my friend," I said.

"So, you guys want to see what I found or not?" Joe called out.

He hovered next to the pipe, his wings lighting the space with a pink glow. Murdock cocked an eyebrow with me. "I've learned my lesson. You go first."

I sidestepped along the pipe a few feet and looked where Joe pointed. Behind the pipe, bricks were knocked out from floor to ceiling, leaving a dark gap. I shined my light in but saw little beyond the opening. "He's not joking, Murdock."

Murdock slid next to me. We leaned on the cold cast-iron pipe and aimed our flashlights. The gap led to another tunnel, more rough-hewn, but clearly not natural. The

Weird was built on landfill, so if a tunnel existed, someone had dug it. Faint hints of essence trails ran into it, the ambient remainders of body signatures. More than one person used the gap.

"He wasn't lying about the smell," said Murdock.

We both recognized it. Once you knew what it was, no one forgets the rancid smell of body decomposition. If we hadn't been in the sewer, it would have been overpowering. Something was dead and rotting in there. "We've got another crime scene, Detective Murdock."

Murdock glanced at me from under his brow. "Is that your way of saying I'm going first again?"

I stepped aside, then followed as Murdock ducked under the pipe and squeezed through the gap. The passageway was molded from the surrounding earth with supports made from random material—car bumpers, scaffolding, old timber, granite blocks—holding the opening stable. My body signature tingled against my skin. A few months earlier, troll essence had bonded to me, and it had never gone completely away. I've had a sensitivity to troll work ever since. "The earth and stone were shaped by a troll using essence, Murdock."

Murdock's flashlight beam was lost in the distance. "We didn't fare so well last time we encountered a troll. Maybe we should call the Guild."

I rubbed my hand along the wall, dirt and stone particles clinging to my body essence as the troll residue attracted it. "It's old work. I think the troll who made it is long gone. The only fresh body signatures I'm getting are dwarves and solitaries."

He leaned his chin into his shoulder and called it in on the radio. "Let's check it out," he said.

"Now?"

His face was shadowed when he looked over his shoulder. "I've got a gun and a body shield."

Murdock's body shield existed in my mind as a curiosity and a failure. On an earlier case we worked together, he had become caught in the backlash from a major spell. When he recovered, he could create a body shield stronger than most fey body shields. No other abilities had manifested, though, and he remained human to my senses. The shield's existence fascinated me because I had never seen something like that happen to a human. It also made me feel that my own lack of ability had prevented me from protecting him, and I wondered what the change in him boded for the future. "This is the part of the movie where I think, 'Why the hell are they going in there?'" I said.

He walked up the tunnel. "And this is the part where I say, 'What could possibly go wrong?'"

Joe flew between us. "And this is the part where I wonder if there will be cookies and whiskey when we're done."

Where the sewer had the chill of winter, the air in the tunnel had the tang of steam heat, the faint odor of wet metal and rust. The temperature shifted, warmer and damp, but not hot. A hundred feet in, the troll-worked walls gave way to a wide concrete space with bricked-over archways along one side. The stench of death grew, as did what appeared at first to be homeless squats—piles of clothes, shoes, glasses, pocketbooks. Someone had gathered the items like to like. We passed a mound of cell phones, then a stack of briefcases, and piles and piles of magazines.

At the end of the concrete passage, we found the first skull. Joe spotted it, his keen eyesight picking out the yellowed bone amid a stack of hats. "Murdock, there's an awful lot of stuff down here. We should call for backup," I said.

Murdock squatted in front of the skull as if he were going to question it. He shined his light in the direction we had been walking. "I think I see stairs. This looks like a sealed-off basement."

"We're in the Weird, Murdock. Basements are either abandoned or you wish they were."

We went to the foot of the stairs. Rusted metal steps led up to more darkness, concrete-skimmed walls crackling off to show the brick beneath, paper trash covered in sooty dust lining the sides of the treads. "Up or back?" I asked.

Murdock stared into the darkness of the stairs. "Back. We need to have this whole place secured."

"I found a body!" Joe shouted.

We swung our lights toward him. Halfway back in the basement, Joe's essence illuminated a pile of clothes against the brick wall. As we retraced our steps, my sensing ability picked out a null spot below him, an essenceless void. Our lights exposed a small woman propped against the wall, ashen-faced, her dark hair long and greasy. Her skin pulled tightly over her bone structure, as though she had no fat, her prominent face bones in stark relief to the wells of her closed eyes and open mouth. She didn't look like she had been dead long.

"There's a head in her lap. I think it's the one you're looking for," Joe said.

As he lowered for a closer look, something stirred around the null zone of the body, a purple-black essence forming in my sensing ability where none had been a moment before. The strange haze coalesced into thick ropes undulating in the air a foot or so above the body. "Careful, Joe. Something's there," I called out.

As he reached for the sword that he kept hidden against his side, an essence strand shot at him, and the woman's eyes flew open, revealing deep black pits with no whites. She hissed with a thick rasp.

Joe yelped and popped out of sight. *Kill it! Kill it! Kill it!* he sent from wherever he had vanished to. He materialized behind us. "It's a *leanansidhe*. Kill it!"

Murdock's body shield flared in dense crimson around

us as he pulled his gun. The woman flattened herself against the wall, pressing her head sideways and staring at us with her eerie dark eyes. "What the hell is that?" Murdock said.

"Holy shit, get out of here, Joe," I said. He popped out.

Thick purple strands of essence burst out of the *leanansidhe* and burrowed into Murdock's body shield. He grunted and staggered into me. I grabbed him by the waist and pulled. The strands tightened and pulsed, fighting against me.

"Shoot it!" I shouted.

Murdock moved in a daze, his arms flailing. He dropped his flashlight. The gun went off, the shot ricocheting into the darkness. A strand of purple essence dove at me, spearing my chest with cold, sharp pain. The dark mass in my head flared, and I screamed.

The dark mass moved inside my head, plunging downward with a hot, burning surge. A spike of black light ripped from my chest and coiled around the purple essence, leaping along the strand and wrapping around the *leanansidhe*. Murdock fell from my arms as the darkness yanked me forward. The dark spike lifted the *leanansidhe* and slammed her against the floor. She screamed and released her essence, the purple strands retracting wildly into her body until she became a strange null void again. The thing in my head sucked the black spike back inside me.

Gagging, I fell to my knees. Both flashlights lay on the floor, illuminating dust in the air. A growled panting came from the darkness. I shuffled on my knees and retrieved a flashlight, playing the beam along the wall until I spotted the *leanansidhe*. She winced when the light struck her, but held her ground in a crouch. "My apologies, my brother. Forsooth, I did not know the prey was yours," she said.

"He's not my prey," I said.

She chuckled, revealing slick, blue-tinged teeth. "Yes, yes, my brother, I've played that game. Spool it in with hope and comfort. 'Tis sweeter in the final strike, no? Pray, bring me a sip of this one before it fades. I've never tasted the like before and would savor it again."

I slipped a dagger from my boot. "I don't know what you're talking about. Stand up slowly and keep your hands where I can see them."

She jutted her chin out and stretched her head toward me, her nostrils quivering as if she were scenting me. "Ah, you are young, my brother. Denying what you are will change nothing. You will reach from without or die."

"I said stand up."

"Peace between us, my brother. I leave you to your prey." She scuttled backwards and vanished into the wall.

"Stop!" I ran forward. At the bottom of a blocked archway, missing bricks formed a hole. She had escaped to the other side of the wall. I crouched and saw nothing but more darkness. The opening was too small for me to follow.

Joe flashed into sight high above, then flickered out in less than a breath. A moment later, he reappeared, sword out and ready. "Is she gone?"

I hurried over to where Murdock lay prone. "Yeah, she's gone."

With an anxious look, Joe flew over Murdock. "Is he dead?"

I checked his pulse. "No. Backdraft from the attack."

Murdock lay on his side. Joe settled onto his shoulder and flashed a sphere of essence into him. Flits weren't healers, but they had a knack for enhancing the healing process. Murdock shook his head like someone had thrown cold water over him.

I helped him up. "Easy, let your head settle."

His hand jumped to his holster. "Where's my weapon?"

Joe pointed. "It's bending over there."

Metal warped essence and screwed around with spells. All fey sensed it, and flits had a keener sense than most.

Because they teleport using essence, not being sensitive to metal could have fatal consequences.

Murdock picked up the other flashlight and found his gun. "What happened?"

I leaned against a wall. "This is the part where I say I told you so."

Murdock leaned against a support and took a deep breath. "What the hell was that thing?"

"A *leanansidhe*. It's a nasty solitary that feeds on living essence. Apparently, you were tasty," I said.

He trained his flashlight beam along the wall. "That is undoubtedly the creepiest thing that's ever happened to me."

I played my own flashlight around us, illuminating more piles of clothing and shoes. "They're parasites. I didn't even know we had one in the Weird. It looks like she's been down here a long time."

"I guess we found our killer," he said.

I pulled my jacket around me as a chill wind blew from somewhere. "Maybe not. *Leanansidhes* aren't physically strong, but they're sneaky. She wouldn't risk a physical confrontation, and the Dead guy at the headworks was big. She's probably been picking off homeless people down here when they're sleeping. I bet she found that head down here somewhere."

Murdock wandered to where the head lay discarded on the floor. A look of disgust ran over his face. "What the hell was she doing with it?"

I shrugged. "Not sure. It might have something do with the ability of the Dead to regenerate. Meryl said they can't come back without their heads. Maybe there's an essence thing going on."

Murdock stepped back from the head. "Well, counting that skull over there, we have three murder cases to close now, and that thing's our primary suspect. We need to find her."

I ran the light over the hole through which the *leanansidhe* had escaped. "It won't be easy. People hunt them, so they're good at hiding. From the look of it, I'd say this one is old, so she's experienced. Plus, now she's more dangerous because she's been discovered."

Murdock crouched at a distance from the wall and tried to see into the hole. "Is it okay to bring investigators down here?"

I followed his gaze. "Yeah, I think so. There's safety in numbers, even for humans."

He stretched. "She had no problem going after the three of us."

I nodded. "Flits are composed mostly of essence, so she was stronger than Joe on that level. In fact, flits are ideal victims because of that. She probably wasn't worried about you because you read human even with your body shield, and, um, I don't think she realized I was here at first."

"Why not?" The play of shadows on his face made his curiosity seem sinister.

"I'm not sure. Last time I saw Gillen Yor, he said I'm not reading true druid anymore. Maybe she couldn't read me." Even though he was High Healer at Avalon Memorial, my case was a challenge for Gillen. Since he hadn't able to figure out what the dark mass in my head was, I didn't have much hope anyone else would.

I didn't want to tell Murdock what the *leanansidhe* had said. A *leanansidhe* calling someone a brother was like a serial killer calling someone a hunting buddy. Not the company I wanted to be included in. They were the fey bogeymen. Bogeywomen. I had never heard of a male one.

"The Guild should handle this," he said.

"I agree, this time more than ever," I said. Given the Guild's usual indifference to all matters related to the Weird, it might not care all that much about a *leanansidhe* with some heads in a basement. On the other hand, an agent might want the challenge of the hunt. *Leanansidhe* were rare. That was about the only good thing about them.

Joe popped in over our heads. "Did you stab it?"

I tilted my head up at him. "No, she got away."

He slid his sword back into its scabbard and rubbed his hands together. "All righty, then. Now about that whiskey."

I swept my flashlight beam along the wall. "I think we've earned it. I have some Oreos at the apartment, too," I said.

He shivered as he peered at the dark hole where the *leanansidhe* had escaped. "Screw the cookies."

9

Joe and I spent the rest of the evening drinking, a not uncommon activity for the two of us. Despite his intentions, he did clean me out of cookies. Given the number of crumbs lying around the apartment, I would swear he had used them as Frisbees more often than food. After puzzling over the *leanansidhe*, a fey neither of us had encountered before, our conversation turned to the casual chatter of old friends. It was a nice change of pace from all the recent drama, although the hangover in the morning reminded me that our alcoholic camaraderie had its downside. A hot shower beating down on me helped lessen the effects.

For about the tenth time after drying off from the shower, I examined my chest in the bathroom mirror. The smooth skin showed no sign that hours earlier something dark and ethereal had sliced out of me like a knife. My mind could not reconcile the pain it generated with the lack of evidence of its manifestation.

The dark mass in my head caused me physical pain. I felt the shape of it, sometimes like a smooth orb, sometimes like a sphere of blades. MRI scans showed a shadowy blur, but it appeared to have no physical substance, as if it was a visual manifestation of a metaphorical concept.

Despite all the access to modern medicine and technology that never existed in Faerie, no one understood the dynamics of the interface between physical bodies and essence manipulation. It was, in that sense, magic—an occurrence of something powerful, even miraculous, yet unexplainable. Whatever was wrong with me had to do with that mysterious connection. I had a damaged interface, something unseen in Faerie because no one in Faerie ever fought over a nuclear-reactor pool. Bergin used an elven ring of power when we fought at a nuclear power station north of Boston. The best Gillen Yor could guess was that some kind of feedback occurred between the ring and the reactor, and destroyed my ability to tap essence.

In the last month, something had changed. The thing in my head reacted to outside events. It moved in response to essence intrusions. When essence entered my body from outside, the darkness retaliated against it. It wouldn't let me use essence, and it wouldn't let essence touch me. I didn't want to think it was conscious, and instead hoped that it was some kind of autonomic response. For it to be aware would be like living with a virus or a parasite. If that was true, it was taking something from me in return. What that was, I didn't know and didn't want to think about.

The skin showed no sign of the black shadow's exit and return. My chest felt sore, not the acute soreness of a wound but the more general pain of a fall. The thing inside me had expelled the *leanansidhe*'s essence. It had done something like that before. When I was attacked by the Dead a few weeks ago, the darkness came out of me like a thick smoke, an amorphous haze with no definition, that absorbed their essences. Now, though, this thing seemed to have a more defined shape and purpose.

Idly, I traced my fingers along the tattoo on my left forearm. Another mystery. It wasn't really a tattoo. A silver filigree that once decorated a spear decided it preferred being under my skin instead. A delicate pattern of branches wove around each other to form a mesh from my wrist to my elbow. The silver had been forged as part of a spell that bound essence into the metal to perform a very specific function: to allow travel across the veil between here and Faerie. The old stories simply called the resulting talisman a silver branch.

Only, like so many other things since Convergence, it didn't work the way it was intended. At least, it didn't only work that way. It did help me get into TirNaNog through the veil and back again. It also seemed to do the opposite of the dark mass in my head. The talisman tattoo absorbed essence and became powerful in its own right. A number of times, it actively struggled against the dark mass for control of surrounding essence. I had no idea what it was intended for or how to use it. And, like the dark mass, it didn't seem any more inclined to help me gain access to my lost abilities.

My damaged abilities were my problem, but the *leanansidhe* was another issue altogether. Whatever she was doing beneath the streets of the Weird, she was provoking some serious pain. The Guild had to help this time. Which meant an in-person appeal to Keeva macNeve.

I slipped on my boots and put the daggers in their sheaths. The left one was for my old faithful, a steel blade that had served me well for over a decade. It had seen a lot of action in more than one rough-and-tumble case when I worked at the Guild. I kept it cleaned and polished, but it would show bloodstains under analysis. Briallen ab Gwyll had given me the knife in my right boot. She taught me the druidic path during my teen years before turning me over to Nigel Martin.

Last spring, when she gave me the dagger, she was cryptic about it as a gift as well as as an object. It was old and powerful, laced with spells and inscribed with runes. I tried to piece together what they meant, but they were beyond my knowledge. The best I figured out was that powerful wards protected it, and that protection often extended to me when need be. Except, I didn't know how it did that. Like the darkness in my head, the blade seemed to work for its own purposes sometimes—even turning into a sword once.

I pulled on a hoodie sweatshirt as lining for my old leather jacket. I had lost my padded leather one in Tir-NaNog and missed it every day the past few weeks. Winter had settled into Boston with bitter winds and early dustings of snow.

I headed out the door, and from the end of Sleeper Street, I cut over the Old Northern Avenue bridge into downtown proper. It was the fastest way out of my end of the neighborhood. At a hundred years old, the bridge was one of the oldest steel-truss bridges in the world. The swing mechanism even worked, so that at high tides, boats could sail up the channel. People admired it as a piece of old Boston even if they didn't like the Weird beyond it. Artists painted and photographed it all the time, the four spans of crisscrossing steel making for interesting shapes and shadows. Late at night on a summer evening with the wind kicking up, it hummed and whistled and moaned. In December, I wanted to get off it as quickly as possible. It always felt colder than anything around it.

A typically Boston juxtaposition greeted me at the other end. On one side of the channel sat the Weird, home to a century's worth of architecturally interesting masonry, then the bridge with its classic erector-set beams, which led smack into the chaotic tangle of asphalt and concrete intersections in the financial district, surrounded by smooth, impersonal skyscrapers. Say what you would about the Weird, but someone was ten times more likely to get mugged at midnight on Summer Street in the business district than on Old Northern at two in the morning.

Despite the cold, I walked through the financial district, then Chinatown, then the theater district. The subway was not the direct route to the Guildhouse and didn't let off particularly near it anyway. Being chilled waiting in a subway tunnel was little different than being chilled walking. Besides, I was in no hurry to be underground again.

The forbidding presence of the Guildhouse loomed over Park Square. The winter sun bleached the gray stone almost white. Danann security agents circled above the many towers and turrets, while brownie guards moved along the ground perimeter. After the riots of the previous month, everything remained on high alert. A chain of Guild petitioners waited in the cold on the sidewalk. They formed a long, sinuous line that stretched around the far corner. For security, the lobby had been put off-limits to the general public.

Under normal circumstances, I would have challenged the guards and the receptionists for the fun of it. Not so long ago, being barred entrance galled me, but lately, that wasn't mattering to me so much. I wasn't the Guild investigator I once was. I was okay with that. Being a Guild investigator didn't appeal to me anymore anyway. I called Keeva macNeve on my cell.

"I'm downstairs and need to talk to you," I said, when she picked up.

"And if I say no?" she asked.

"No games, Keev. I'm not in the mood."

"Fine. I'll tell them to let you through."

As she hung up, nearby brownie guards shifted positions, and two led me inside. They escorted me in silence up to the Community Liaison floor and left me in the reception area. The young wood fairy behind the desk stared at me with her pale green eyes as if she had never seen a druid before. I didn't wait for her to say anything but went down the hall to Keeva's office.

Keeva was typing aggressively at her computer but threw me a brief glance. I sat while she finished, then she turned to me with a sly smile. "I have to say I'm impressed you came in here."

I smiled cordially. "That's high praise coming from you."

She shook her head. "You do realize the entire building went on alert when you walked in?"

"I'm flattered."

She snorted. "Yes, I guess you would consider it flattering that people are afraid you'll cause an interdimensional meltdown."

I grinned. "And you're not?"

She shook her head again. "I know better, Connor. You don't have any other ability than to attract disaster. What do you want?"

"I found a *leanansidhe* in the Weird," I said.

She arched an eyebrow. "Oh? I thought you were dating that Meryl Dian person."

I frowned with amusement. Meryl was not Keeva's favorite person. The feeling was mutual. "I'm serious. You should send someone down."

She sighed. "There you go again, telling me how to do my job. We're stretched thin with all the new security. Frankly, if we've got a *leanansidhe* down there, she'll probably save us from arresting a few people."

"That is so not funny," I said.

She shrugged. "Connor, the solitaries are coming out of the woodwork. I get daily reports from Commissioner Murdock about them. I never realized we had so many in Boston. They've become incredibly aggressive."

"That's because the Dead are killing them. They're defending themselves."

She rubbed her neck. "And whose fault is that, I wonder?"

I pulled in my chin. "Are you really going to lay that on me? I stopped whatever was happening on Samhain. If I hadn't closed the veil, we'd have a bigger problem than the Dead."

Keeva looked doubtful. "Let's see: an underQueen of Faerie died, your old partner Dylan died, several dozen fey and humans died in the rioting, you destroyed a possible way back to Faerie, and, oh, by the way, the Dead of Tir-NaNog are roaming the streets of Boston. Next time you feel like helping, Connor, stay inside whatever bar you're in and resist the impulse."

I slouched in the chair. It sounded pretty awful when she put it like that, but, really, it wasn't my fault. I'm pretty sure it wasn't. "Don't change the subject. I can't believe I told you there's a *leanansidhe* out there, and you're not itching to hunt it down yourself."

A conflicted look came over her. "I'm too busy. If I can, I'll get an agent to help your buddy Murdock for a day or two, but no guarantees."

"Busy? It's a *leanansidhe*, Keeva. You can't tell me you're not concerned or interested."

She pursed her lips. "Is there anything else, Connor?"

Keeva's body signature rippled. I tapped my essence-sensing ability and sensed a thin layer of additional essence around her. "Are you wearing a glamour, Keeva?"

Her eyebrows drew together. "It's rude to look at my essence without permission."

"You *are* wearing a glamour! I've known you for years, Keeva macNeve. I know what your body signature looks like. Why are you wearing a glamour?"

She became decidedly uncomfortable. "I don't want people asking me about my health, Connor. I'm here to do my job, not answer questions about my body signature."

I leaned forward, concerned. Genuinely. Keeva and I didn't agree on a lot of things, but I didn't hate her enough to wish her ill. "Are you all right? Have you seen Gillen Yor?"

She pulled herself in toward the desk. "Connor, I said I didn't want to talk about my health. Yes, I'm fine. Yes, I've seen Gillen Yor. My condition is no one's business and doesn't affect my ability to do my job. Next subject."

She had taken some serious essence hits in the last few months. I had walked in on her exam at Avalon Memorial a few weeks earlier and seen the damage. Danann fairies were strong—incredibly strong. I thought she'd be recovered by now. "Does macGoren know?"

Ryan macGoren was powerful, but essence sensing was not an ability Danann fairies worked well. They could do it with physical touch—and I assumed he touched her, since they had been a couple for months—but if he wasn't looking for something and Keeva didn't want him to know, she would have no problem hiding it from him.

"That's even more off base. If I promise to send someone down to the Weird, will you drop it?"

"Okay." Keeva's temper was short normally, but she was more on edge than usual. Actively helping the human police force against fey people couldn't be sitting well with her. Keeva might enjoy the privileges of her position, but she was still fey and took pride in that.

I changed the subject. "Any idea when this curfew is going to end?"

"That's Commissioner Murdock's call. The Guild board supports his decisions."

"And you agree with it?" I asked.

She sighed with impatience. "I don't have to agree with it. Ryan is Acting Guildmaster, and I act under his direction. It's the job."

She didn't say she agreed with it. "Since when is Ryan Acting Guildmaster? I didn't hear he was named."

She shrugged. "He is in everything but name. Eagan hasn't gotten around to making it official."

I was tempted to tell her he wouldn't be getting around to it anytime soon, but I had irritated her enough. Besides, I got what I came for—a quasi promise to deal with the *leanansidhe*.

I stood. "Well, good luck to him if that's what Eagan decides. I'll let you get on with black-booting the Weird now."

"You're an ass, Connor," she said, as I stepped out the door.

I deserved that. "Seriously, Keeva, are you okay?"

She nodded. "Yes. I'm fine. I'll let you know if anything happens with the *leanansidhe*."

Downstairs, I paused under the portico in front of the Guildhouse. If I wasn't mistaken, a crack was forming in Keeva's unmitigated support of Guild policy. She had spent her career climbing the ladder by agreeing to the right things with the right people. Not vocally supporting Commissioner Murdock's curfew was unusual, and she knew I would pick up on it. Then again, as time went on, I thought she was becoming less careful with what she said around me. She told me once that my credibility was so poor, no one would believe me if I repeated what she said. I hated to admit it, but she might have a point.

As I looked up at the sky to see if clouds were rolling in, I noticed the empty expanse of the portico ceiling. The gargoyles that usually clustered were almost all gone. With the extraordinary amount of essence expended on Samhain, they were migrating up to Boston Common, and since the Taint still floated around the Weird, many more were down there, leaving the Guildhouse oddly bare. I wondered what the roof of the place looked like. The heaviest concentration of gargoyles gathered up there.

I pulled my collar up and walked through the gauntlet of brownie security. For over a year, I had wallowed in despair over whether I'd ever work at the Guild again. In a few short months, my thinking had changed dramatically. I had changed. The place had become alien to me. Despite all my disagreements with the Guild, I didn't know whether that was a good thing or not.

10

I retraced my route back to the Weird, turning off a bridge early to enter Southie. By the time I reached the Rose Rose, snow had begun to fall, and my toes became numb. I waited for Meryl in a back booth, enjoying the heater under the table as it warmed my feet. If Yggy's was the bar in the Weird where fey from across the spectrum gathered to be among themselves, the Rose Rose was where the fey and humans met on neutral ground. People went to the Ro'Ro' to relax and have a good time.

Meryl swept through the front door, bringing in a shower of snow with her. People at the tables nearest the door eyed her with irritation. She ignored them as she made a direct line for my table. "You look tired."

I pushed a glass of Guinness toward her. "I had a busy night."

She tapped my glass and sipped. "You didn't visit when you were in the building today."

Meryl ran the Archives in the subbasements of the Guildhouse. The basements were dark, stone-lined, quiet, and filled with stuff most fey didn't even know existed. As Chief Archivist, she got to play with everything. I usually took any opportunity to visit her when I was in the Guild-house. "With all the security watching my every move, I didn't have the energy for the hassle. You missed me, didn't you?"

She nodded. "Yeah. My afternoon was boring. Watching you get dragged out of the building would have broken the tedium."

I crumpled a napkin and tossed it at her. "Nice to know I'm entertainment for you."

She grinned. "That's what would have happened, you know. As soon as you entered the building, they doubled the guards on the elevators. They're watching us. See the cute couple behind me drinking umbrella drinks? Low-level druids with Danann security on speed sending."

I laughed and sipped my beer. "Ya know, I thought I saw them on Old Northern this morning. Why the spying?"

Meryl slowly shook her head. "Don't be dense. The Guild's assessing its next move after Samhain. They let me back to work because they can't figure out if I did any-thing wrong. You, on the other hand, they saw challenge an underQueen who was investigating you, then she died. Why do you think Nigel went to Tara?"

"I thought he was going to Russia?"

Meryl leaned back. "Eventually. I couldn't find out what that's about, but he's stopping at Tara to see Maeve."

I caught the server's attention and ordered another round. I stared in the dregs of my beer. "Meryl, let me ask you something. I'm having this odd moment where I sit here, an unemployed druid with damaged abilities who can barely pay his rent with a disability check, and yet, the High Queen of Tara seems to be oddly nervous about me. Am I suffering from delusions of grandeur, or is that really true?"

"Well, both. I thought that goes without saying," she said.

"Seriously, please."

She wrapped both hands around her glass. "I think you're a victim of circumstances. You're right: You're pretty much washed-up as a druid of any ability. Most fey, never mind the High Queen, would be expected to ignore you as inconsequential."

The server dropped two more pints on the table, and we ordered food. I took a deep gulp of my beer. "Okay, this is encouraging so far," I said.

She smirked. "But you can't deny that some pretty strange and powerful events seem to be sucking you into their paths. Maeve's a strategist. If she thinks you might be some kind of power locus—despite your lack of ability— she's going to want to exploit that."

"Over my dead body," I said.

Meryl shrugged. "That might work in her favor."

"What about Bergin Vize? He was involved in at least two of those events. Why isn't she after him?"

Meryl gave me a look of disappointed amusement. "How you ever got a reputation for being a brilliant investigator I cannot fathom. Think about it, you idiot. Do you think it was coincidence Keeva macNeve was assigned the Castle Island case? She's a bitch, but she's the best agent the Guild has now that you're gone—*and* she captured the perpetrator. He only escaped because someone else screwed up. Do you think an underQueen was sent here because Maeve's main concern was you and the Taint or the fact that Bergin Vize was moving an army through TirNaNog?"

She was right. I hadn't thought of it. "What about Forest Hills? Vize wasn't involved in the Forest Hills event."

"As far as we know. That spell was created through a combination of Celtic druid lore and elven rune spells. Don't forget—I was helping Nigel with his rune research.

We never did find out who supplied the elven aspect of the spell. It could have been Vize. Suborning high-level Guild officials and attempting to destroy Maeve's access to essence has his fingerprints all over it. She's watching him, too, Grey. Don't think for one minute you're her only concern. Maeve's sandbox is a lot bigger than yours."

I feigned a pout. "I think you just pointed out the delusion of grandeur part."

She drank. "Without breaking a sweat, my friend."

"So, I'm a power locus."

"Maybe. Maybe not. Maybe Vize is. Maybe his destiny is bound to Maeve's and yours to his. That doesn't make you bound to Maeve. Destiny may be transitive, but that doesn't mean you're the most important link in the chain."

"What if you're wrong?" I asked.

She shook her head. "I didn't say I was right. I'm poking holes in your assumption that Maeve's interest in you is an either/or proposition. You could be a much bigger problem for Vize than you are to Maeve."

I nodded. "Eorla Kruge said something like that to me once."

"She's a smart lady. Maybe too smart. She requisitioned the rune research I did for Nigel," Meryl said.

"She's trying to reconstruct the runes on the oak staff," I said.

Meryl twisted her lips in thought. "I don't know if I like that."

"If it means the end of the Taint, yeah, it's a good thing," I said.

"What if it means she re-creates the spell that destroyed Forest Hills?"

"I don't believe that's her goal," I said. "She had the opportunity at Forest Hills to take control, and she rejected it.

I believe her when she says she wants peace. It's why her husband died."

She sighed. "I always have a hard time believing people with noble causes. It usually means someone's gonna die."

"Dying can be noble," I said.

She made an exaggerated shiver. "Yeah, that's what nobility turns into—the rationale for every authoritarian regime I've ever seen."

"Anyway, I wanted to ask you something about the decapitation murders."

Meryl leaned her elbows on the table and propped her chin in her hands. "Severed heads and dinner. Who said romance is dead?"

I leaned forward, lowered my eyes, and dropped my voice to a husky whisper. "Wait until I tell you about the rotting bodies Murdock and I found in the sewer."

She closed her eyes and sighed. "Oh, Grey, I think something's happening to my naughty bits. Tell me more, please."

I tapped her nose. "You are a whack job."

She picked up her beer. "That makes you a whack-job chaser."

"You said the Dead can't regenerate without the head, right?"

The server gave me an odd look as she placed our dinners in front of us. Meryl plucked a fry from my plate. "Honestly, it's conjecture. Good conjecture, but still conjecture. In TirNaNog, the head didn't matter. The Dead were in the Land of the Dead. No matter how they were killed there, they reappeared the next day. Here, though, if you killed someone fey and kept the head separate from the body, you denied them entrance to TirNaNog. That much I know for sure. Under the current situation, TirNaNog is closed. No one's getting in. When someone Dead dies here, they regenerate here. So, by taking the head, I think the Dead can't regenerate here. Make sense?"

"I think so," I said.

"We can test it," she said.

"How?"

She shrugged. "Let's kill a Dead guy and see what happens."

I considered the idea. "Is it better to use a sword or an axe to behead someone?"

"Sword. A nice big one."

I tapped the edge of the table without looking at her. Meryl had access to all kinds of artifacts at the Guildhouse, including weapons.

"Can I borrow one?"

She stole another fry. "Sure."

I nodded in deep thought. "Okay, after dessert, then. I want to behead someone tonight if you don't mind bringing me a sword."

"Okay."

I sprinkled salt on my burger, tossed the tomato aside, and closed the bun. I took a big bite and stared at Meryl. She stared back. She ate a chicken finger. I put a solemn look on my face and chewed mechanically.

"You're serious," she said. I nodded.

"Wow," she said.

I smirked. "Gotcha."

Her jaw dropped, then she laughed. "You did, you jerk."

I hooted and clapped. "It's about damned time, I did."

Embarrassed, she shrugged. "Yeah, well, too bad you don't have witnesses."

I shook my head laughing. "I think your theory is right. In fact, I think we can test it. We already have a beheaded body and its head."

"You found the head of the sewer guy?" she asked.

"Yeah. We found a *leanansidhe* who was having it for lunch."

She frowned and rolled her eyes. "I am so not falling for that."

I grinned. This dinner was going to be deeply satisfying.

11

Meryl took off on one of her none-of-your-business eve-nings. I had a hard time understanding if our seesaw re-lationship was a game or a reality. Either way, it was very Meryl. She liked keeping me off-balance and, considering my history with relationships, that maybe wasn't a bad thing. It made me pay attention, kept me curious and, dam-mit, interested. And she knew it. The one message Meryl gave me loud and clear was that she had a life without me, and giving that up was solely on her terms. I was cool with it because she allowed me my time alone, too.

Meryl's absence was for the best anyway since later on Murdock and I were hitting the morgue now that we had both the head and the body of the Dead guy. Until it was time to leave, I scoured my library for whatever I could find on hellhounds, but I didn't make much headway with Shay's dog problem. Despite plenty of references in my personal library, twentieth-century texts added nothing new about them because the hounds hadn't been seen since Convergence. A hellhound was what it was. You saw it; you died. I was convinced, though, that with it trapped outside of TirNaNog, its harbinger-of-doom status had to be compromised. With no Land of the Dead for anyone to go to anymore, what was the doom?

Lost in thought as I watched a plane take off across a dark sky, I jumped when the apartment buzzer went off. Murdock was picking me up so we could go down to the morgue and try the experiment with the decapitated Dead guy. I hit the intercom. "Hey, you're early."

"Are you really so poor you live in the Weird?"

Moira. My first impulse was to not respond. "Who gave you my address?"

"I've lived at court for years, Connor. I know how to get an address when I want one."

"What do you want?"

"To talk. You left so abruptly the other day, and I don't understand why," she said.

"There's nothing to talk about," I said.

"Maybe *I* have something to talk about," she said.

When it came right down to it, Moira Cashel was trouble, one way or another. Either she was Amy Sullivan and her interest in me was sincere and she had no idea of how I had become entangled with High Queen Maeve despite her current connection to Maeve, or she wasn't Amy and it was all a ruse for Maeve to lay some kind of trap for me. Despite what Tibbet said, I didn't want Moira wrecking my memories.

"Are you there?" she asked into my silence.

I had to know. Whatever Maeve's strategy was, I was intrigued that I was still enough a part of it for her to dig into my past. "Okay, I'll meet you."

"I'm downstairs. Can I make it to the front door without being mugged?"

I snorted. Of course she was downstairs. "I've got a meeting. You can have until my ride shows up," I said. I buzzed her in and went out to the hall. She came up the stairs directly to the top floor without having asked where my apartment was. It didn't surprise me, but if she thought she was hiding that she knew about my current life, she was awfully sloppy. Wrapped in a full-length fur coat, she stepped onto the landing.

"Wearing animal fur is frowned on in the States," I said.

She paused at my door, a deep frown on her face. "I'm beginning to wonder if this bitter, angry person is the same happy young man I used to know."

I rolled my eyes and gestured into the living room. Which was basically the room we were already in. My apartment wasn't big enough to get lost in, not when the kitchen and the living room were essentially the same place. Even more cozy since it was where I slept, too. "So, what is it you want to talk about?"

She looked troubled as she unbuttoned her coat and sat in an armchair. "I almost don't know. Believe it or not, Connor, after we met, you changed my life. At the time, I thought it was for the worse, but after all the emotion and drama died down, things were not as bad as I feared. I thought it would be interesting to get reacquainted, see the man you've become."

I crossed my arms. "I don't believe you're Amy Sullivan."

She cocked her head, a willing smile on her face. "What can I do to prove it to you?"

"Explain why you're here."

"I told you. I came to see if I could help with Manus."

"No, I mean what else does Maeve want you to do here?"

Her eyebrows drew together. "Nothing but heal Manus ap Eagan. I was ordered to find a cure or confirm there was none."

"Why?"

She looked startled. "Because he's dying."

"Why would Maeve care? Eagan threatens her. Her pet macGoren is waiting to make the Guildmaster's office his own."

Moira stared at me with troubled confusion on her face. Her expressions did remind me of Amy, even without the glamour. "You seem to misunderstand some of the politics of court, Connor. Eagan's dying does not help macGoren's bid for the Guildmaster position. Anyone the High Queen installed against Eagan's wishes would be fought by the other underKings and -Queens. She can't afford to lose their support. She needs Eagan alive and answerable to her, or he needs to resign his position with an appointed successor. All Maeve wants is clarity on the situation."

I leaned against the kitchen counter. "Interesting analysis for a Chief Herbalist."

Spots of color rose on her cheeks, and she compressed her lips. "Connor, I live and work at Tara. If you think that means I spend my time pressing flowers into books, you are naïve."

"Where did Amy and I meet?" I asked.

She answered quickly. "Flanagan's market."

"Where was I living?"

"With Briallen ab Gwyll. You were staying with your parents that weekend. Your mother sent you to the store."

"Who spoke first?"

"You did. You asked me whether I liked the crackers you were holding. You were a terribly obvious flirt."

"What happened next?"

Moira looked down at her hand. "You kissed my hand. It was very sweet. Then you asked if I would like to have a cup of tea with you sometime. I said yes, thinking that would end the flirtation, but you asked to go right then. So we did."

"Was it raining or snowing?"

"Neither. It was supposed to rain. I left my umbrella in the shop."

She knew all the right answers—even the umbrella, which I had forgotten about. I went back later to find it for her, but it wasn't there. "You could have gotten those answers from the real Amy Sullivan."

She nodded. "You're right. You're absolutely right. But if I weren't Amy Sullivan, would I know what it felt like to meet this brilliant young man at the beginning of his career who was so excited and nervous to start training with Nigel Martin? Would I know how lonely I felt and how that young man made me want adventure again? Would I have turned my life upside down because of him and left Boston in shame?"

That gave me pause. Amy stopped coming to see me, then disappeared. "What do you mean 'shame'?"

Moira looked away from me and gazed out the window. "My husband found out."

I moved to the open door of my apartment. "Amy Sullivan wasn't married."

She stood. "I was, Connor. You didn't know everything about me. You didn't even know where I lived. I lied to my husband about many things, and he threw me out. It was a blessing, though. I wasn't made for married life. I went back to Ireland and the Druidic College and never looked back."

"Until now," I said. The vestibule door downstairs slammed shut, and I heard someone walking up the stairs.

She shook her head. "Not even now. Maeve knows nothing about my past as Amy. She sent me here to do a job. I have no intention of letting my husband or anyone else know Amy Sullivan has returned. I thought the Wheel of the World had given me a fortunate turn when you walked into Eagan's house. You were a secret in my old life, and I thought we could be friends again because no one here would ever connect Moira Cashel and Connor Grey. I guess I was wrong."

"You're damned right. If it will help, tell Maeve I believed you, but I wasn't interested."

The footsteps on the stairs were louder as Moira moved toward me. She shifted into the Amy Sullivan glamour and caressed my face with a gloved hand. "Do you believe me, Connor?"

I didn't answer for a moment. She looked like Amy—even smelled like her. It would have been nice to think it was her. But Moira Cashel was a member of Maeve's court, and Amy was a part of my life that had nothing to do with all the twists and turns that life had taken. And I didn't want her to be in it now. "It was over twenty years ago, Moira. It doesn't matter anymore. Leave it alone. Leave me alone."

She searched my face, a hint of moisture in her eyes. "The Wheel of the World turns differently for all of us, Connor. I don't know where It's taken you, but you aren't the person I remember."

"Neither are you," I said.

As the footsteps came closer, Murdock's body signature registered in my sense. By the quick tilt of her head, Moira sensed him, too. Moira dropped the Amy glamour before he reached the last flight. He saw the open apartment door and paused on the final steps. His face looked intrigued when he saw Moira. "I can come back," he said.

"Moira Cashel, this is Detective Lieutenant Leonard Murdock," I said.

Moira stepped into the outside hall and gripped the stair rail.

Murdock nodded. "Ma'am."

Moira moved to the head of the stairs as Murdock reached the top step. Our conversation had upset her. She paled as Murdock passed. "How do you do?" she said in almost a whisper.

With his back to her, Murdock frowned at me. "Fine, thanks."

"Thanks for stopping by, Moira. It was interesting," I said.

Her eyes shifted back to me. Without another word, she descended the stairs. Murdock watched over the railing.

"I'll be right back," I said. I went into the apartment and grabbed my coat. I checked that I had my cell and wallet, then pulled the apartment door closed. Murdock continued looking down the stairs as I locked up. I didn't hear any more footsteps. "What are you looking at?" I asked.

He had a pensive look on his face. "Nothing. Everything okay?"

Murdock preceded me down the stairs two steps ahead. "I think a certain homicide detective was worried about me."

"No, I wasn't," he said.

I laughed. "Oh, you got out of your nice warm car and walked up five flights for the hell of it? Sure, you did."

He smirked over his shoulder. "I saw the town car downstairs with diplomatic plates. It wouldn't be the first time you ran into trouble with the Guild."

"And it won't be the last time," I said.

"Who was the woman?"

"I'm not really sure. She's trying to cure whatever's killing Manus ap Eagan and is claiming to be someone I knew when I was starting out."

Murdock pulled open the vestibule door to reveal the first few flakes of another snowstorm. In the dark, his car actually looked good for a change. No town car was in sight.

"Do you believe her?"

I shrugged. "Nope. Mostly, I think she's a spy from the Seelie Court."

I sat on a nest of napkins on the passenger seat while Murdock jogged to the driver's side. He pulled out onto the street. "She had dinner with my father the other night," he said.

"Really? Curiouser and curiouser."

He nodded. "My father asked me to pick him up at a restaurant. They came out together."

"How the hell do they know each other?" I asked.

Murdock shrugged. "He said she was Guild business."

I pursed my lips. Eagan said she was a spy. Despite her claims otherwise, Moira Cashel was up to something more than ministering to a sick Danann. "I know it isn't like me to worry about your father, but I would tell him to be careful around her."

He smirked. "Will do, concerned citizen."

"Interesting coincidence," I said.

"Small world," he said.

"Yeah, with small people in it."

12

The Office of the City Medical Examiner was a long name
for a sad place. At night, it was even sadder, a brick building
perpetually clothed in gray twilight on a desolate stretch of
road. It was open twenty-fours a day, seven days a week.
Death made its own appointments, and the city morgue
waited like a patient suitor for a date.

In the cool basement, steam rose from Murdock's coffee.
He leaned against a counter, not looking like he'd been up
all night. The accident that boosted his essence had boosted
his energy levels, too. Not that he needed it. Murdock's
stamina was legendary. As a police officer, he had spent
more than enough time on dull surveillance, which came in
handy for him since he'd been watching Janey Likesmith
and me work through the night. Occasionally, we needed
an extra pair of hands, but for the most part he watched.

The OCME handled all the deaths in the city and trans-
ferred major fey cases to the Guild only at the Guild's
request. As the lone fey staff member at OCME, Janey
worked the rest. All of them. She had to pick and choose

which ones to give more attention to than others. Who the decedent was or who they knew or how much money they had in life didn't matter to her. Producing the best examination results did.

Janey was a dark elf, a member of the Dokkheim clan. The dark elves acknowledged the Elven King, but most of them went their own way in the post-Convergence world. They had never been strong enough to challenge the Teutonic court, but they were skilled enough to have influence over it.

We met on a case together not too long ago. She impressed me with her skills and even temper. The politics of Convergence held no interest for her. Like a child of immigrants, her parents' stories of the old country—in her case, Elven Faerie—were stories, nothing more. She understood where she came from, but she also understood that Boston was where she was. She had no desire to re-create the past or find a way back to it. She focused her energy on the here and now, trying to help the fey and humans live together.

We worked on opposite sides of an examining table. Janey's deep brown hands moved with careful skill as she realigned her side of the glass case. On each side of the table, narrow strips of quartz supported glass panels around the decapitated body from the sewer. The body itself lay on one long pane.

We had spent most of the night tuning the stones—turning them into wards—so that they could receive an infusion of essence. The process was one part skill and one part luck. Getting one stone to work in conjunction with another was easy. Getting several to do it depended on understanding the natural contours and densities of the stones so that essence would flow like a smooth current through all of them. It was like aligning a series of magnets of various strengths so that they would all stand up but not reject each other's shifting polarities.

"I think if you tighten the brace on your side, we're done," I said.

She twisted the wing nuts in front of her. The glass plates shifted into place along the side of the table. Janey flicked a strand of her nutmeg-colored hair around the delicate point of her ear. "Perfect."

"We can put the head in now," I said.

Murdock stepped aside as Janey opened a cooling locker. She didn't pull out the drawer but reached in and lifted the head out. It had seen better days. Bloated skin indicated time spent in the water, and missing pieces of flesh evidenced the natural process of sloughing and banging around in sewer pipes. Without a trace of revulsion, Janey carried it to the table and placed it gently inside the box. "How close to the body should it be?"

I shrugged. "I don't think it matters that much."

She shifted it closer to the neck stump and stepped back, peeling off her gloves. "Okay, now the lid."

Murdock put his coffee down. He grabbed one end of the second large glass pane we had, and I took the other. We lifted, and Janey guided it over the table as we lowered it onto the standing walls.

Essentially, we had created a huge glass ward box around the body. Where metal bent essence and sent it in unanticipated directions, glass absorbed and dissipated it into the ambient air. I loved the irony that something so fragile could defeat something so powerful. Janey smiled in satisfaction. "This is amazing. I will have to call Ms. Dian later and thank her."

"Well, this wouldn't have been possible if you hadn't put the body in a ward box in the first place," I said.

When the Dead regenerated, the body vanished and reanimated somewhere else the next day. Meryl had lots of theories about why—everything from appearing where they died, to where they felt safe, to more complex theories about essence sinkholes or concentrated focal points. Since we worried that we might regenerate the body but not know where it went, Meryl came up with the idea of a barrier spell on a large ward box as a way to prevent the Dead guy's essence from going anywhere.

Janey discarded her gloves in a hazard bin. "I preserve body essence for evidence as part of my routine. I wasn't sure it was going to work with a Dead person."

"The *leanansidhe* must have done something similar. There's still significant essence in the head," I said.

Janey checked her watch. "We have some time until dawn. I'd like to show you something from my examination of the body."

We followed her up the hall to her lab room. The layout looked the same as the last time I had visited, but the instruments on the two tables were more sophisticated. The city budget didn't allow for much in the way of fey-related diagnostic tools. A little enforced guilt toward Ryan macGoren and the Guild helped buy a few things. Janey handed me a small glass box—a miniversion of the one we had built in the morgue. Inside the box, a wafer of quartz glowed with essence. "I made an imprint of the Dead victim's essence for the files. Notice anything?" she asked.

The essence glowed with the vibration of the Dead body in the next room, the dull ochre signature of a Teutonic berserker clan. Splotches of a vibrant green with black mottling mingled in his essence. "The Taint."

Janey retrieved the box and examined it under an essence magnifier. "It's bonded to his essence."

"And if it affects the Dead the same way as the living . . ." I said.

"It reinforces their baser instincts. When the Dead die, they're coming back as killing machines," she finished. She slid the boxed wafer inside a marked envelope and placed it in an evidence drawer in a large wall cabinet.

We returned to the examining room and spread around the table, Murdock and I on opposite sides. Janey stood at the foot of the ward box and placed her hands on the corner quartz strips. She looked at me. "Ready?"

"As we're ever going to be," I said.

In the guttural dialect of her clan, she chanted the soft words of a rejuvenation spell. Normally, such a spell worked to boost someone's energy. Janey had made a few tweaks to it to encourage the essence to mimic whatever it came in contact with, which would be crucial in a situation where the residual essence in the dead body was nearly gone. Pale green essence flowed from her fingers, seeping into the stone strips. It flowed along the edges until the box's entire frame glowed. As the essence penetrated the stones, they flashed once with the charge, and Janey ended the spell.

No one spoke. Janey checked her watch again as my gaze slipped to the clock on the wall. Dawn would arrive in moments. Murdock had his hands in his pockets and was staring down at the floor. He said little when I explained the process we were trying, and it didn't take much deduction to understand why. Retrieving a body from the dead—a soul, in his mind—flew in the face of his religion. Maybe even spat in it.

"Something's happening," Janey said.

The Dead man's dull, yellowed essence seeped out of his chest and forehead. The two spots hovered like mist over his skin, tendrils of essence spreading up from the chest toward the neck and spooling down from his head over the chin. They met at the gap in the neck, coiling and merging into a collar of soft light. More essence welled out of his body, thinning over the corpse in a sheet. Whatever the volume of essence he had when animate, it had diminished after the decapitation. The *leanansidhe* probably absorbed some as well. As if sensing another source, the haze sent tentative feelers out of the sides of the body. One by one, they found the stone frame that Janey had charged with essence. The feelers drew down the essence charge into the body. With renewed energy, the body essence pulsed and thickened, enveloping the body in a cocoon of light.

Janey hopped back a step when the head rocked. A dirty, hazy yellow essence clustered at the neck. The head swayed. Essence pooled in puncture wounds in the face and gathered on the various injuries on the torso. The charged-stone frame of the ward box faded to dullness. The haze around the body swirled and undulated, then contracted and vanished into the skin.

The berserker lay whole, no sign of the decapitation, no torn and rotted flesh. Janey stared, her lips parted in amazement. The Dead man's eyes opened. Janey gasped, and Murdock stepped closer, his hand on his gun. The berserker looked at me, then at Murdock and Janey. Confused, he pressed his hands against the box lid, his fingertips whitening against glass.

"Let's open it," I said.

Murdock helped me to lift the top off and put it aside. The Dead guy grasped the edges of the ward box and sat up. He assessed the three of us with suspicion. In a burst of energy, he leaped up and out of the box. I grabbed Janey as she stumbled into me. As the berserker landed on the floor, he let loose a flying kick. Murdock's body shield bloomed around him and took the brunt of the blow.

I hustled Janey into a corner. The berserker strode toward Murdock, his own body shield rippling with essence that made his skin expand. The berserker swung, and Murdock ducked. He lost his balance, and the Dead man closed in on him. I jumped him, but he sent me sprawling away like I was a fly on his back. I landed hard on my side, my fragmented body shields taking some of the impact. Not enough. My side hurt like hell.

Angry, I jumped on the berkserker's back again, wrapping my arm around his neck. He grabbed my forearm with thick fingers, squeezing against the muscle. The tattoo on my arm flashed with a white light as it drew on my body essence. The pressure from the berserker's grip vanished, but my head felt light with the sudden drop in my body essence. My hold on his neck slackened, and he wrenched my arm away, flinging me against the wall.

Murdock came up out of his crouch and hit the guy in the gut. The berserker staggered, and before he could recover, Murdock followed through with a left to his jaw. He tripped sideways, throwing his leg out again, aiming for Murdock's abdomen. As Murdock twisted sideways to avoid the hit, the hair on the back of my neck rose as I sensed an essence charge behind me. Confused, I pivoted on my heel, ready to fight, then checked my motion.

Janey stood with her fingers pointed like a gun. A bolt of dark green essence shot from her outstretched hand and hit the berserker. His head snapped forward, and Murdock hit him with a right cross to the cheek. The berserker fell.

As she jabbed with her fingers at the air above him, Janey chanted pinpoints of yellow light into existence. They sparkled and burst, scattering a web of glowing strands that spun and fell in a net. It settled over the berserker and became a binding spell that cinched his arms to his sides. Annoyed, I backhanded him hard across the face and reared back with my fist.

Murdock grabbed my arm. "It's cool. It's cool," he said.

I rubbed at my arm. The tattoo had released the essence back into my body as soon as the berserker had let go, but it was sore. "Sorry. Are you all right?" I asked.

Murdock arched an eyebrow at me as he shook his fist loose. "Yeah, I'm glad I wasn't holding my coffee."

I took several breaths to calm myself. Janey had retreated to the other side of the room. "Where the hell did a nice girl like you learn an elf-shot spell like that?" I said.

With hands on hips, she kept her eyes on the berserker. "My mom. She doesn't like me walking around at night alone in this neighborhood."

Janey attracted the berserker's attention when she spoke, and he asked her in German where he was.

"He's confused," Janey translated. "He doesn't understand why he's here. He's never woken up in a place he's never been before."

I understood German, but for Murdock's benefit I let her translate. "Who is he?" I asked.

The berserker stared at me while Janey translated. "His name is Jark, son of Ulf," she said.

I crossed my arms. "Ask him how he died."

Janey bit her lower lip. "He said, 'Which time?'"

I resisted the urge to wipe the sarcastic grin off his face. "The last time, please."

He shrugged. "He says it was a solitary named Sekka. A *jotunn* who hates the Dead."

Murdock and I exchanged glances. "That's whose head we found in the sewer, Janey," I said.

"How'd she lose her head if she took his?" Murdock asked.

By his reaction when Janey asked him—his pleased reaction—Jark hadn't known Sekka was dead. He evaded Janey's questioning at first, enjoying her frustration before giving up a tidbit. "The last thing he remembers is the giant attacking him and a brief pain as she swung a sword at his head. He says the last thing he saw was the Hound, so maybe the Hound killed him."

"And why would the Cwn Annwn want to kill you?" I said to Jark.

He chuckled as Janey translated. Janey blushed at his response. "He says he wasn't killed by a dog."

She didn't mention the part where Jark called me a string of unflattering names reflecting my stupidity, asked why a woman would want to know so much about death, then he had hit on her. "Who is the Hound?" I asked.

"He says 'no one knows and no one wants to know. The Hound hunts the living and the Dead.'"

By the look on his face, Jark was lying. He was probably already planning his revenge. I caught Murdock's eye. "Can we hold him?"

He cocked an eyebrow. "For a while. Legal status on the Dead is a mess."

Jark turned this way and that as he followed our conversation. I pulled Janey aside. "Not, obviously, that you can't take care of yourself, but I don't want to leave you alone with him. Is there an officer in the building, maybe more than one?"

"Sure," she said. We walked with her to a phone by the door and listened while she asked for security. She replaced the receiver. "They'll be right down."

Murdock abruptly walked out. "I'll be outside."

Janey watched him leave. "Is he okay?"

I shrugged. "I'm not sure. He's a Christian. I don't think any of this is sitting well with him."

She rubbed her arms as if to warm herself as she looked across the room at Jark. "I can't say I blame him. I didn't grow up with the Dead appearing on this side of the veil. I thought those were just stories."

"At least they were stories that fit your religion," I said.

She nodded. "I guess. It's funny. Despite my job, I don't think about death much on a personal level. My people die by accident or murder. I don't have—I don't know, a connection to it in the same way humans do. Maybe that's why they fear us, Connor. Even death isn't an end for the fey."

I nodded at Jark. "I don't think that's what the fey expect when they do die."

"It's probably why the solitaries are fighting so hard.

They used to have an idea of what came after death. Now it's a mystery," she said.

I hadn't thought of it that way. She was right. With Tir-NaNog closed to the Dead, no one knew what happened to the fey when they died. It hadn't hit me because I wasn't a target. For all my fears about a shortened life span because of the dark thing in my head, I hadn't been confronted with the visceral realization that death might be an end and an end only.

"Thanks for this, Janey. Our friend here might have given us something solid to follow up," I said.

She crossed her arms. "No, thank you. This has to be one of the more fascinating things I've seen here. I'm not used to my cases sitting up and talking to me."

I smiled slightly. "With any luck, this will be the only one."

Jark's anger had subsided to confusion. He was only . . . animated . . . because we intervened. He had no idea how close he had come to an eternal nothingness. If the *leanansidhe* had drained the remains of the essence in his head, if we hadn't brought his head and body together, he wouldn't be sitting in bindings, wearing nothing but a towel, and wondering what the hell we were talking about.

"Maybe this is what Convergence brought the fey here for, Janey—to experience an end to all things they knew and give them the humans to help them cope."

"I hope that's not true, Connor. I hope it's the opposite— that humans can learn the value of thinking beyond their finite lives. The Wheel of the World keeps turning no matter what. It doesn't stop when we die. If there's one thing the fey and humans have in common, it's that neither of us knows why things happen they way they do."

"Amen to that," I said.

She laughed.

Murdock waited outside with the car running. How he had managed to get newspaper all over the passenger seat in the short time he'd waited there was beyond me. I tossed it all in back.

"You okay?" I asked, as he drove down Albany Street under the highway.

"Yeah. I needed some air."

"I wonder if we can count this Jark as an eyewitness to his own murder," I said.

"Does it matter anymore? He's not dead, and she is," he said.

The fey certainly managed to produce entertaining legal puzzles. "Well, we still have Sekka's murder to deal with."

He nodded. "At least we have a lead without having to do another resurrection."

"The animosity between the solitaries and the Dead is going to become a problem with the Taint involved."

He drove over the Broadway bridge into Southie. "I've been warning my father things are spiraling. Some community activist pressured the mayor's office about it, so they agreed to the neighborhood meeting. My dad doesn't think it's worth the trouble."

"Then what is he doing to reduce the tension?"

Murdock shrugged. "Leaving it to the Guild, I guess. You know how my father is, Connor. The more the fey screw up—especially down in the Weird—the happier he is. He'd like nothing more than for the entire neighborhood to disappear."

A sinking, guilty feeling hit me. Murdock and I talked about his father all the time because of the political issues he was involved in. After what Manus ap Eagan asked me to do, suddenly the discussion felt like information pumping. It was, in a way, but not for Eagan. I had been meaning to tell Murdock about my conversation with Eagan. I knew

Murdock well enough that the longer I held off, the more annoyed he would be with me. "Eagan tells me you're dating someone."

Murdock chuckled in surprise. "The Guildmaster talks about my social life?"

I shook my head. "Actually, no. He thought if he told me you were sleeping with someone, and I didn't know, I would resent it and would wheedle information out of you about planned police actions against the fey and funnel the information to him."

Murdock's jaw dropped in a half smile. "What?"

We cruised down to Old Northern Avenue. Out of habit, we both scanned the sidewalks to check out the action. "No lie. Eagan's worried your father's playing him for a fool."

Murdock flicked an eyebrow up and down. "He probably is. Nothing my father likes more than putting one over on the Guild."

I laughed. "Yeah, that's about the only thing your father and I have in common. But Eagan might have a point. This thing brewing between the solitaries and the Dead is bound to make someone look bad. It's too much of a legal tangle not to."

Murdock pulled up in front of my building. "Are we surprised? The jurisdictional issues are so messed up that nothing's being handled. Just to spice things up, with all the gang deaths in the last couple of months, there's a power vacuum on the streets. You know it's going to get worse before it gets better."

I slumped against the door. "You know what I really want to know?"

Murdock frowned with curiosity. "What?"

"Who you're sleeping with."

He laughed. "No comment."

I didn't care who he was dating. Curious, sure, but at the

end of the day, Murdock told me what he wanted to tell me, and that was okay. I respected him enough to accept what he decided. He's done a lot for me in the two years that I've known him, not least of which was save my life. If anyone deserved some slack from me, it was him.

I punched him playfully in the arm. "Jerk."

13

I spent the day catnapping and reading, my curiosity about
the *leanansidhe* prompting more reading and Internet surfing. Everything I knew about the *leanansidhe* filled one
small volume on my bookshelf. Internet searches picked up
no reliable primary references. Few *leanansidhe* existed,
and those that did spent their lives hidden and alone. By nature, they were not forthcoming, never mind social. Their
reputation was too well-known for them to live openly. By
all accounts, they absorbed the essence of the living. As
with most legends, the whole truth lay beneath hyperbole
and falsehoods. If the only essence the *leanansidhe* survived on was living essence, their presence would be determined quickly. Just look for the dead, essenceless bodies.

Yet they managed to survive. I was willing to bet that
the *leanansidhe* sought other essence resources. Those
who survived encounters with them were probably unique
situations. As Joe likes to say "kings and queens" about
things like that, meaning "yeah, that's one version, but the
reality smelled worse and was usually boring."

It wasn't enough. Failure to learn more drove me out into the night. The chronic lack of progress in understanding what had happened to my abilities frustrated me—and created situations that put lives at risk. Janey and Murdock could have been seriously injured by Jark—or worse. I hadn't thought through resurrecting a Dead man with Taint in his body essence. I failed to protect them because I had no abilities to use against him. No matter what people said about using the abilities you had instead of wishing for ones you didn't, the berserker couldn't have been stopped without essence abilities. Abilities I didn't have anymore.

The *leanansidhe* knew something about the dark mass. I had seen it, and the thing inside me had reacted to it. It was in her, too, at least something very much like it. For the first time since my accident, I had something that looked like a clue as to what was wrong with me. I had to know if it meant anything. I had to know if the *leanansidhe* knew something.

Over two years the dark mass had been in my head, blocking my abilities. Over two years of mistaken diagnoses and dead-end treatments. My healer Gillen Yor was at a complete loss. My friend Briallen's eyes showed more fear every time she examined me. No amount of ibuprofen stopped my chronic pain.

And it was getting worse.

The thing inside me was escaping, for lack of a better word. Whatever it was, it was attracted and repulsed by essence. If essence threatened me, it reacted to protect me, and when it did, it devoured the essence. When a group of the Dead recently attacked me on Samhain, the dark mass absorbed them. I hadn't really understood that at the time, but it was the only explanation under the circumstances. The only person who seemed to know what it was, was one of the most reviled beings known to human and fey.

Brother. She'd called me brother.

Inside the warehouse, my breath steamed in the shaft of light from my flashlight. Despite the many doors and hallways, the basement door was easy to find. The building had been empty so long that dust on the floor was evolving into dirt. I followed the recently disturbed path that the crime-scene investigators had made. The trail ended at a large door with rusted and dented sheet metal nailed over it. It opened with the whine of metal on metal and exposed stairs going down. The corrugated metal steps rang dully beneath my boots as I descended.

I swept my flashlight beam across the sealed-off basement. The categorized piles had been removed, then tagged and bagged in evidence lockers at police headquarters. All the clothing, the hats, the shoes—everything the *leanansidhe* had picked off her victims—were being sorted and scanned, compared to missing persons reports, maybe analyzed for DNA. Phone calls would go out to doctors and dentists. If anything matched a file description, a police officer would have to make that long, slow walk to the door of the next of kin. With the volume of material I saw, it was going to be a long while before the police processed everything. A lot of cold cases were going to be closed. This being the Weird, a lot of unanswered questions were going to result, too. Not all the missing are missed.

The crime-scene team had enlarged the hole the *leanansidhe* had escaped through. A bone-chilling draft wafted over me from between the jagged bricks. Silence filled the utter darkness beyond. Why the section had been sealed off wasn't obvious. The columned space inside was devoid of the usual abandoned equipment or stock supplies left by long-gone businesses.

Body signatures from the investigative team lit up in my sensing ability, two fey signatures mixed in with about a dozen human. Keeva macNeve must have sent someone from the Guild. Probably to cover her ass. If the *leanan-*

sidhe went after humans, she'd have a hard time explaining she knew it existed and did nothing.

The team had scoured the basement. Individual trails branched and overlapped throughout the room. The far wall was another bricked-over section. Other than the *leanansidhe*'s bolt-hole, I found no other openings. *Leanansidhes* weren't stupid. It was no coincidence Joe had found her lying on the floor near an escape route, and she wouldn't let herself become trapped if someone followed her. An exit had to be in the basement somewhere.

I turned off the flashlight and allowed my sensing ability free rein. The investigative team's residual signatures brightened. Down the center of the room, directly from the bolt-hole if I judged the angle right, their signatures masked a thin layer of violet essence, the faint trace of the *leanansidhe*'s body signature. At the far end of the basement, a thin purple haze splashed up against the solid brick wall. I turned on the flashlight.

The wall showed no breaks. The *leanansidhe*'s essence danced on my fingers like static when I touched the surface. She had hidden her exit with a strong-yet-subtle masking ward. Frustrated, I slapped my hand against the wall. The dark mass in my head clenched, and my hand slipped beneath the surface of the bricks. That wasn't supposed to happen. Masking wards were keyed to specific essences for access, usually the spellcaster and whoever else the 'caster allowed. The *leanansidhe* wouldn't have keyed the wall for me, never mind known my essence well enough to do it without me.

I pressed at the bricks. The dark mass in my head danced in short pulses of pain as my hands sank below the surface. A pit of anxiety formed in my stomach. The *leanansidhe* must have set the ward to something she thought unique to herself. The dark mass was the key. I felt open space on the other side of the wall. I stepped forward, a pounding in my mind as I passed through the ward. I stumbled into the other side and took deep breaths as the pain settled.

A narrow section of basement mirrored the one that Murdock and I had found. A sense of pain permeated the air in this one, the echoes of long-past deaths. Tragedy lingered in spaces, the emotion of the moment seeping into the surroundings like a memory stain. It was the *leanansidhe*'s dining room. People died there, drained of their essence to feed another's hunger.

Ignoring the emotions vying for attention, I searched the area. Another staircase led to the warehouse above, but an avalanche of dirt and trash blocked access. No one had used it for a long, long time. At the other end, a door was shaped in the stone wall, more handiwork of the troll who had made the sewer tunnel. The *leanansidhe* must have taken over the space after the troll left or died. More likely, she had used the troll to create the tunnels and killed it when the work was completed.

I hesitated. No one knew where I was. I had no abilities to defend myself, and I was about to seek out a monster. I found assurance in the fact that the *leanansidhe* had tried to absorb my essence and failed—an irony that the one fey with no abilities to defend himself was the one fey she apparently couldn't feed on. I crossed the threshold.

The smooth earthen tunnel led down, the *leanansidhe*'s signature strong enough to be evident even to a normal sensing ability. The path twisted and turned, branched and widened. I walked through at least a quarter mile of turnings before I found a series of chambers. I hung back from the entrance to a furnished room.

Warmth radiated against my face. That was it as far as welcome went. The chamber was a living room of sorts, if a room buried three floors beneath the ground could be considered living. A generation's worth of furniture filled the space, old sofas and bookcases, tables and chairs. A many-joined extension cord trailed from the ceiling, providing electricity for a glass-shade lamp by a reading chair. A book lay open on the table next to it.

Welcome, brother. Enter and be at peace.

I pressed flat against the wall, my dagger out of its sheath and in my hand without a conscious thought. Sendings don't have directional indications like sound. The *leanansidhe* had to have me in her line of sight to know I was in the room. "Where are you?"

A fluctuation in the air passed over me. Definitely someone moving in the room. Some fey can cloak themselves, but I didn't know it was an ability the *leanansidhe* had. *Come, brother. Make peace. There is no blade at your throat.*

I flinched from the brief icy touch of steel against my neck. A soft chuckle came from the middle of the room. The air rippled, and the *leanansidhe* appeared, crouched on an old Persian rug. In her outstretched hand, she held a dagger. She grinned through matted tangles of hair and opened the hand wide to let the dagger fall. "You see, brother? No harm from me for such as we."

She eased back as I entered.

"You keep calling me 'brother,'" I said.

She moved behind a table stacked with books, her pale, stained hands caressing the covers though she kept her whiteless eyes on me. "Kin or akin matters not between us. We touch the Wheel the same."

"I'm not like you."

Her large dark eyes shifted to my dagger. "Aye, 'struth. I could not touch such a thing as that. Lay it aside, brother, and rest in my home."

"And leave myself unarmed? If you violate the rules of hospitality, to whom shall I complain?"

She rubbed long fingers down her face, watching me out of the corners of her eyes. "Keep it, then." She vanished and reappeared at my side. "It will avail you naught." She vanished again and peered at me from behind a tall grandfather clock, clutching the edges of the wood with cracked gray nails. "Unless I will it."

She vanished again. I tracked her with my sensing ability and pressed the knife to her chest as she tried to slip around me. "That's close enough."

She dropped her masking glamour to reveal a surprised and frightened face. Thrusting her hands up, she bowed her head and sank to the floor. "Spare me, brother. I seek only kinship."

"I'm not here to kill you," I said.

She looked up at me through a tangle of hair, suspicious, yet curious. "I have no quarrel with you either, my brother. Shall we sit, then? I should like that."

I motioned her away with the dagger, and she scuttled along the floor to an armchair. Curling up in its corner, she pawed at one eye as I eased into the opposite chair. She shoved her hand into a tattered pocket. She withdrew her hand, clenched around something. Tentatively, she reached across the side table and dropped a battered piece of bread. "I have not flesh nor fluid to offer, but crusty things can stem the pangs of hunger."

She was trying to follow the old rules of hospitality, even if the bread had a couple of colors on it that I didn't usually associate with freshness. "I'm good. Um. Thanks."

We observed each other. At least, by the shifting of her unsettling black eyes, she was doing the same thing I was. Such a small being to inspire such a lot of fear. She was barely half my height but had the ability to take down the strongest of fey. Except for her emaciated head, the only parts of her body visible outside layers of clothing were her thin arms and grimy ankles.

I closed my eyes a moment. If I continued the conversation, I was committing to something, or at least admitting to it. I was seeking help from a *leanansidhe*. I took a deep breath. "You said we touch the Wheel the same. How do you touch the Wheel?"

She threw her hands over her face. "We touch the outside from within, and the Wheel turns."

I frowned. "If you think I believe you can turn the Wheel, you're wrong."

She screeched with laughter and scrambled up the side of the chair. "No one turns the Wheel, brother. It turns and turns, and we touch It where few dare to know. Not all who ride the Wheel ride the Wheel."

"You're lying. Even the Dead ride the Wheel the same as everyone else. It's the Wheel of the World," I said.

She tangled her hands in her hair. "Ah, stupid druid, sees the surface and sees nothing more. The Wheel is a wheel on both sides."

The idea landed on me in stunning realization. I had spent my youth in study of the druidic path, learning from my mentors. The test of a true follower of the path was an intuitive understanding of what came next, the ability to move beyond receiving knowledge to attaining it on one's own. We called it secret knowledge, the knowing of the Wheel in a fundamental way. I left my training years ago and stepped off the path for personal gain, but every once in a while, I was granted a flash of insight to the nature of the Wheel. I laughed in my throat at the realization the *leanansidhe* handed me. "There are two sides to the Wheel."

She squealed as she dropped to the floor and clutched my knees. "You see, my brother! You see the within and without, and the Wheel lies between."

I clenched my jaw at the wave of body odor she emitted. "Show me how you touch the Wheel," I said.

She gasped in excitement, clutching her hands to her cracked lips. Those dark orbs whirled in their sockets, searching. In the blink of an eye, she vanished, surprising me with her speed. Seconds later, she returned, walking through the door and cradling something in her hands. She knelt in front of me with a rat that fought to escape, its sharp claws scratching her hands. "Shhh, shhh, shhh, little thing. Rest and receive," she crooned.

Deep violet essence coated her hands. Tendrils formed, lines of purple light that burrowed into the rat. The rat froze in some kind of paralysis. With a moan of pleasure, the *leanansidhe* brought the filthy rodent to her cheek and closed her eyes. More tendrils waved out of her face where the rat touched skin. They pulsed with light, and the rat flinched as its essence seeped away. Something moved within the *leanansidhe*, something dark and impenetrable. It reached up from within her essence and sapped the rat's essence.

I flinched as the dark mass in my head shifted. The vision in my right eye faded as pain stabbed at it. Pain from within. Something black leaped out of my face, an indistinct line of darkness that burned. The *leanansidhe* screeched and fell back, holding the rat toward me. "Yes, yes, brother, it is yours! Yours! Druse did not mean to take it from you."

I fought the pain, pressing my body essence against it. My left forearm burned with the effort, the swirls of my strange tattoo giving off an uncomfortably pleasurable cold burn. The dark thing inside me recoiled, and I gasped. My vision returned to see a dead rat in a filthy hand inches from my face. By force of will, I didn't slap it away. "Keep it," I said.

The *leanansidhe* shook the rat. "No, yours! 'Sokay, 'sokay."

I turned my head to the side. I didn't know the ramifications of taking a gift from a *leanansidhe*, even if it was only a rat. I wasn't interested in finding out. I stood, and she fell back.

"I said keep it." I stumbled toward the door.

"No! Stay, my brother! You see the truth of it now! Stay with Druse, and we shall aid and comfort each other. Druse will show you the way beyond the pain to the pleasure of the Wheel," she called out.

My head pounded beyond a migraine. I held my aching arm against me as I retraced my way in the dark, not thinking of anything but escape. Without the flashlight, I followed the path in my memory, bumping into walls and tripping over changes in levels of the floor. Passing through the masking ward in the warehouse basement, the dark mass in my head gave me one more kick and stopped spiking.

I ran the rest of the way—across the basement, up the stairs, and through the warehouse. The door slammed against the outside wall as I shouldered through it. I landed on my knees on the snow-covered sidewalk and threw up in the street. A wave of dizziness swept over me, and I fell into the blessedly cold snow. My face pressed against it, the icy shock of it soothing the pain in my head.

A light flashed rose against the snow in the dead white night. "Really, Connor, this throwing up in the gutter is a bad habit."

I tried to talk, but a retching sound came out. Joe grabbed at my jacket collar. "Connor! What's wrong?"

He flew up, pulling me into a seated position. "I'm okay," I said.

He hovered in my face. "Screw that, you look like day-old shite. Your essence is . . . I don't know what it is. It's rippling like a wave."

I got my feet under me and forced myself off the ground. Joe grabbed my coat to steady me. "It's stopping," he said.

He didn't have to tell me. The dizziness receded as I took a great gulp of air. "I'm fine. Just didn't expect that to happen."

Joe whirled around me. "What to happen? Where the hell have you been?"

I laughed. "Hell might be one answer."

He leaned closer to me face and sniffed. "Are you drunk?"

I didn't want to discuss what had happened. Joe can be overprotective, and I didn't want a scolding. I started walking. "Yeah, I am. I must have taken a wrong turn or something."

"But what was going on with your essence?" he asked.

I shrugged. "Maybe alcohol poisoning? I feel fine now. Honest."

He twisted his lips doubtfully. "You're sure."

"I'm sure."

He spun around in the air. "So—let me tell you about my night." I let him chatter on. It was a good distraction from the strange emotions I was having. He talked all the way back to my apartment, a tale of drinks, song, a short wrestle with another flit, an amorous encounter, and more drinks. Joe did know how to have a good time. His busy night was a fortunate coincidence. It didn't take much trying to get him to go home, so I could be alone.

Inside my building, I hit the elevator call button. The old cage was slow as hell, but I was so tired that I didn't want to climb the stairs. I heard a clicking sound, but the elevator didn't move. I peered into the shaft. It was stuck in the basement. I sighed and walked up.

I wanted to reach inside my head and scrub my brain. My gut feeling was right. The *leanansidhe* had recognized the darkness inside me. Recognized it because it was inside her. I saw it beneath her essence, the black, hungering thing that reached out for the rat's essence. My eye ached in memory of it. Whatever was inside me responded, wanted what the thing inside the *leanansidhe* wanted.

The idea revolted me. What the hell had Bergin Vize

unleashed when we fought almost three years ago? Maybe unleashed inside both of us? He was damaged, too. I saw that when I met him in TirNaNog. Did he struggle with the same darkness? Did he feel the same frustrations and pain? I hoped to hell he did. If he weren't so intent on destroying the Seelie Court—hell, destroying the world—none of this would be happening. How someone raised by Eorla Kruge could become so twisted baffled me.

My essence-sensing ability jumped as something moved in the apartment. The security wards hadn't gone off, but something was there. Several wards were keyed to alert the Guild, but considering their more-intense-than-usual annoyance with me lately, whether anyone would show up these days was a good question. The wards wouldn't stop a truly powerful fey person, but they would slow him down long enough for me to figure out how to protect myself.

Both daggers were out and in my hands in seconds. The dagger that Briallen gave me felt heavier than usual, and a few runes on the blade glowed a soft yellow. I peered into the living room, and every hair on my body bristled at a faint red light in the room. Two glowing eyes stared back. I turned on the reading lamp.

Uno's massive head tweaked to one side in curiosity. He relaxed and dropped his jaw, his thick, dark tongue flapping out the end of his muzzle to the rhythm of his panting.

"Okay, you can't be good news," I said aloud.

I picked up my cell phone. Shay answered on the first ring. "Say 'Hi, Dad,' if you're in trouble."

"You don't strike me as the daddy type, Connor," he said.

Relief swept over me. I never knew what Shay was going to say. I don't think he did either. "Is Uno with you?" I asked.

"I was debating whether to call you so late. I heard a bark and woke up, and he's gone."

"He's here."

"He's there? You mean your apartment?"

"Drooling at the end of my bed as we speak," I said.

"Don't worry about that. The drool disappears at dawn. What do you think it means?"

Uno dropped to the floor and lowered his head between outstretched paws. "I don't know. Has anything odd happened to you recently?"

There was a chuckle. "I can't believe you just asked me that."

Shay's daily life was pretty damned odd. "Okay, odder than usual."

"No. What about you?" he asked.

When I saw Uno, I assumed something had happened to Shay. Until he asked, it didn't occur to me that the dog could have appeared because of me. "I had a strange night."

I heard a soft clank of metal on the other end of the phone, then water running. "Do you want to talk about it?"

Shay was less than half my age, and here he was offering me a sympathetic ear. I wanted to laugh, but didn't. He was being sincere and concerned. The kid was sweet, too naïve and too worldly, all at the same time. I worried about people like Shay in the Weird, people on the edge who could fall with the slightest nudge. Shay was dancing near that edge when we first met, but he seemed to be finding his way to safer ground. Except for Uno. "No, that's all right. I'll work it out on my own."

"Call me if you change your mind."

"Will do," I said.

"Connor . . . does this mean I'm not going to die?"

He said it so quietly and matter-of-factly, it pulled at me. I hadn't considered what he must have been going through. Given that I now had a hellhound lying on my living-room floor, I had a feeling I was going to find out. "It'll be all right, Shay. Call me if you need me."

He didn't answer right away. "Thanks . . . um . . . you, too."

I closed the cell. Uno held eye contact with me, calm and steady, long past the point any other dog would have perceived a threat. He didn't. He stared with a gaze that said he knew damned well who would look away first. As a hound from Hel whose job it was to suck the souls out of the living, I guessed not much threatened him.

After several minutes, neither of us had moved. I gave in for what was left of the night. I was drained and tired and not up for vying for supremacy with a supernatural dog. Uno remained where he was while I went through my going-to-bed routine, turning off the light in the study and setting up the coffee for the morning. I sat on the futon, removed my boots, retrieved the spelled dagger from its sheath, and tucked it into my headboard. I leaned on my knees and looked at Uno. "I suppose if you were going to devour me, you would have done it by now."

The tufts of hair above his eyes twitched, and he let loose a loud chuff. I reached out and touched his head. He slumped over on his side and wagged his tail. I scratched at the back of his neck, and his tail thumped on the floor. "Just so you know, Uno, petting a soul-sucking hound from Hel is pretty much an unsurprising end to today."

I peeled off my clothes and slid beneath the covers on the futon. When I turned off the lights, the room filled with the red glow from Uno's eyes. I stared at the ceiling.

Not the least bit surprising.

14

Within a few minutes of another early-morning call from Murdock, I was picking my way across an access road overlooking Fort Point Channel. The constant winds off the harbor solidified the snow into dirty banks of gray ice. Tall frozen hills from snowplow deposits ringed a parking lot owned by the Gillette Company. Even with sturdy boots, the thin skin of ice on the ground made walking a challenge. I had to struggle my way to the police cars clustered along the channel side.

Gillette was always referred to as being in South Boston. The razor manufacturer had employed a lot of local people over the years and for a time boasted about its Boston-based status, but no one wanted to be associated with what happened around the plant, never mind brag that they lived next to its parking lots. Maybe when its workers lived in Southie, it was a true part of the neighborhood, but these days it was the outer edge of the Weird, more a barrier for the residential area next door than a part of it.

Emergency vehicles gathered in an empty section of

the lot. Beyond them, a number of solitary fey loitered on the seawall by the channel. Seeing that many solitaries in broad daylight made me uneasy. Solitaries don't like being seen, especially by humans, especially by law enforcement. Forest species with their rough-bark skin and leaf-like hair rarely mingled with the stone-skin denizens of the underground world. Even a few water fey hung over the wall from the channel, their hair rimed with ice. Their odd appearances made them de facto suspects for crimes committed nearby. It was racist, it was unfair, but it was the way it was. They stayed out of sight, worked night shifts, and tried to live their lives without being hassled. Pretty much like everyone else. A group of solitaries, and an odd group at that, hanging around a crime scene signaled something different was happening.

Officers in winter gear stood inside a ring of crime-scene tape. Murdock wore his camel-hair coat and flat ear-muffs that rode around the back of his head. The wind off the channel brought a flush to his cheeks and nose, but he didn't look particularly cold. A body lay on the ground in the center of the group. A big body.

I ducked under the yellow-and-black tape. A few faces in the group frowned or looked away. The Boston P.D. doesn't like working with the fey, but I thought I had earned a little respect within their ranks in the last year. "What have we got?" I asked.

"Headless female body," Murdock said.

I eased my way between two officers, who gave way grudgingly. Murdock's description pretty much covered it. The body was about six feet long without the head, clad in a simple wool tunic and leggings, and wrapped in a long, soiled leather coat that clearly had been exposed to water. My sensing ability picked up faint traces of her body signature. "She's a match to the head from the sewer. It's Sekka," I said.

Pinned with a long nail to the coat, a sheet of paper flapped in the breeze. The medical examiner held it down a moment. It read: Jark.

"Is that supposed to be some kind of warning?" Murdock asked.

I shrugged. "Or an accusation. Let's check out the peanut gallery."

Murdock followed me to the seawall. A few solitaries slunk away as we approached. I didn't worry about them. The ones who slip off when the police approach are usually petty criminals looking to avoid a hassle. The ones who stand their ground are usually the bigger fish who look forward to antagonizing the law. This group was different. They had the look of curious bystanders rather than low-lifes. I wanted to know if that curiosity tipped into vested interest. By the time we reached the wall, half the group had dispersed.

"Anybody here see anything?" Murdock asked.

"Her name was Sekka," someone behind me said, one of the tree folk. Tall with brown bark skin and tangled mossy hair. In the dry winter air, he had the odor of dampness and earth.

"How do you know it was her?" Murdock said, gesturing at the little matter of her missing head.

The solitary looked at the body. "I knew her. Those clothes are hers. She's been missed. Word is the Dead were after her."

"Anyone in particular?" asked Murdock.

Eyes shifted to the ground or the horizon, anywhere but at us. One of the merrows from the harbor pointed down. Female merrows didn't speak much, preferring to use their bodies to communicate. More than a few people have drowned trying to understand them. I leaned over the wall. At low tide, the channel sank over a dozen feet, exposing the foundation stones of the wall. A sewer overflow pipe jutted over the water. "Did you see someone come out of there?" I asked.

The merrow nodded, her wide, dark eyes like pools of sadness. No surprise there, although coming out of the sewer made a nice connection to where we found the head.

"Was it anyone you knew?"

She gazed at the hard gray water. "It is the one we call the Hound of the Dead. He hunts the Dead."

Someone gasped behind me, and one of the solitaries made a hissing sound. Whoever this Hound was, he was doing a pretty good job of scaring the hell out of people. "Sekka wasn't one of the Dead," I said.

"No, but I saw him drag her body here," she said.

"Did you see where he went?" Murdock asked.

The merrow subtly bowed her head, fear creeping into her eyes. *Behind you,* she sent.

I crouched on the ground, pretending to examine footprints. I pivoted on the balls of my feet to look behind me, as if I were following a trail. On the opposite side of the parking lot, a cloaked figure stood in the alley. He was too far away to get a precise read on his essence.

A solitary's mossy hair swayed with a shake of his head. "You don't find the Hound. He finds you."

"Yeah, well, I'd like to talk to him about that," Murdock said.

"Then ask the Dead. They probably know where he hides, just like they know they can kill us without worrying about being punished."

"Not true," said Murdock.

The solitary looked over our shoulders. "Tell that to Sekka."

We all looked at the victim. The medical examiner had corralled some officers to help lift her body onto a gurney. Murdock turned back to the dwindling group on the wall. The merrow had slipped away. "There's a community meeting about the murders tomorrow night. Spread the word that we need help," he said.

The solitary shook his head. "It won't make a difference. No one cares."

"We do," I said.

The solitary sighed. "That's a comfort."

He walked off with his friends.

"I think we were just insulted," I said.

Murdock leaned over the wall to exam the overflow pipe. "Yeah, I get that a lot these days."

We walked back to the crime scene as the body was loaded into the examiner's van. "Take a nonchalant look behind you," I said.

Murdock glanced over his shoulder, then back at the activity by the medical examiner. "He was over there when I arrived. Been on his cell phone the entire time. Think it's this Hound?"

I stood. "The merrow as much as said he is. Looks like he's in a chatty mood."

As we approached, the cloaked man turned and walked up the alley.

Murdock broke into a run. "Boston P.D.! Stop where you are!"

He didn't stop. We followed, slipping on icy patches. Murdock pulled ahead of me, his body shield glowing a faint red. He'd been practicing with it again. It not only protected him but also had some sort of strength booster. At least, that's what I was going with as I followed his back, because without abilities, I was definitely a stronger runner than he was.

"I said stop, dammit," Murdock shouted.

The alley turned ahead, a corner building making an L-shape at the end of the block. The building cut off my line of sight as they sprinted ahead. I stumbled after them into a dead-end run blocked by a fence and a massive pile of debris.

The Hound swerved, propelling over a stack of wooden pallets into the air. He grabbed the bottom of a fire escape and swung over the railing. As he climbed, Murdock mimicked the move. As I closed on them, I put on a burst of speed and reached for the last rung of the ladder pull. I missed and fell hard, my body shields coming on too late to soften the fall.

Above me, the Hound balanced on a rail of the fire escape, watching Murdock climb toward him. He jumped, sailing across the alley to the opposite building's fire escape. Without pause, Murdock leaped after him, his coat flaring out behind him like a cape. They climbed again.

I scrambled to my feet, hoisted myself onto a dumpster, and climbed onto the fire escape. Three stories above, Murdock and the Hound leaped across the alley to the next building. I ran along a catwalk, then up the next set of fire-escape stairs. The Hound sailed past me on his way across again. Climbing again, he backtracked, with Murdock close behind.

I reached the roofline and swung over the parapet. Below, they crossed to my side, and I dropped down to pin the Hound between us before he was high enough to leap again. Halfway up, he spotted me and charged back toward Murdock. A flight above Murdock, he dodged through a broken window and vanished into the darkness of the building. Murdock reached the opening before I did and ran in.

My sensing ability tracked the blazing red of Murdock's essence in the darkness. We pounded down a long hallway of gaping doorways and graffitied walls. The Hound raced ahead, his dark silhouette flashing in and out of my line of sight as Murdock closed in. The hall ended ahead in a shattered hole where a window used to be. The Hound jumped. Murdock launched out after him, shouting as they disappeared from view.

I reached the opening. The Hound dangled in the air, swinging himself hand over hand across a tension wire to the next building. Not far below, Murdock hung from a bent streetlight, his hands grappling with ice-slick metal. He kicked his legs up to wrap them around the arm of the lamp, but his coat tangled around his feet. He jerked back, losing the grip of one hand.

My mind raced. He was too far for me to reach, either from the building or from the ground three stories below. A loose phone cable hung next to me against the building. I yanked it free and knotted it around a drainpipe. "Catch!" I shouted.

Murdock grabbed the flung cable with his free hand. I spiraled the slack around my arm, dropped to my ass inside the hallway, and braced my feet against the edge of the opening. "Come in feetfirst and kick off the building."

As he twirled the cable awkwardly with one free arm, his other hand slipped off the light. Murdock fell, the cable a sinuous line of black against the white ground. The line pulled taut, biting into my arm as Murdock hit the end. Then the cable snapped, and Murdock plunged in a spread-eagle free fall.

"No!" I shouted.

I tore down the stairs, slamming into the walls as I fought my way at a full run. A broken door blocked the exit, and I ran at it without stopping. Rotted wood gave way as I burst through it and sprawled into the alley.

Murdock lay on his back, arms flung out, in a shallow crater of snow and jumbled ice. His chest heaved, his breath a cloud of steam. I stumbled to him across the ice. He curled to a sitting position as I reached him. Relieved, I helped him up. He leaned one hand against a wall, gasping. I hunched over, holding my knees, trying to catch my own breath. Murdock smirked through heavy breathing. "Why'd you let him get away?"

I grinned back at him, then shook my head and laughed.

"Gods, are you okay?" I said when I recovered.

Murdock stretched and grimaced. "Yeah, the body shield came in pretty handy."

"That was insane."

"Did you tag his essence?" Murdock asked.

I shook my head. "I didn't get close enough."

Murdock covered his disappointment by brushing at his coat. It didn't help the rips and tears and the rust smears. "I'm billing the city for this one."

The tension wire that the Hound had used was anchored next to a fire escape and a window on an abandoned building across the street. I didn't see which way he went. "He's gone," I said.

Murdock nodded with an exaggerated motion, and we walked up the alley. The large dark shape of Uno sat at the turn, watching us approach. He trotted out of sight.

"Did you see that dog?" I asked.

Murdock looked behind him, in the wrong direction. "Where?"

Uno was hard to miss. Murdock thought I had enough problems without him thinking I was hallucinating. "It must have been a shadow," I said.

When we reached the corner, Uno wasn't visible anywhere. He left no paw prints in the snow.

15

I didn't know what to make of Uno. When I told Shay I would look into the whole hellhound thing, it was an academic issue. Motivated by concern, sure, but academic. Now that I had seen the dog without Shay around—and Murdock hadn't—it had suddenly made itself a more personal issue.

Murdock remained at the scene in the parking lot. I returned to my apartment, feeling winter settle into the bones of the city. The stark slivers of sky between buildings threatened snow. Harsh sunlight cast sharp shadows, the sudden change of white light to black shadows causing afterimages to flash in my vision despite my sunglasses.

A black car idled at the end of my street, an elf in Consortium livery waiting beside the rear door. As I approached, he opened the door and revealed a lone figure seated in back. Eorla leaned forward. Surprised, I slipped in with a gust of cold air.

"What brings you down here?" I asked.

"Aren't you pleased to see me?" Eorla asked.

"It's always a pleasure to see you," I said.

She threw a slight sideways glance at me, a thin smile on her face. "You flatter me often. Is it courtesy or mockery?"

I tilted my head. "Is sincerity so hard to believe?"

She chuckled. "Not in my world. Not always. You don't have a reputation for respect."

I shrugged. "I don't think that's accurate. Respect is a two-way street. I might respect someone's authority, but they don't get to keep it if they don't earn it. The fact that you're a Marchgrafin or a Guild director means less to me than the things you do and the choices you make."

She laughed. "Is the fact that you neglect to mention I am Grand Duchess supposed to prove your point?"

"Not really. I don't know why you're called that, so it's not really relevant to me."

She arched an eyebrow. "What if it is relevant?"

I smiled playfully at her. "Prove it."

She settled into the corner of the seat. "I assume you don't know elven history. The title is mine by right of birth. My father was Elven King before Donor. He died when Donor's father challenged him. They killed each other. Since I was an only child with the error of being female, the nearest male heir succeeded to the crown."

"You should have been queen?" I asked.

She pursed her lips. "Not by the custom of my people. When I married, I took the title Marchgrafin to show the world I considered my husband Alvud an equal partner. Now that he is gone, I have resumed the title Grand Duchess to send a different message. Convergence changed the rules of our world, Mr. Grey. Donor Elfenkonig would do well to remember that."

"And you wonder why I like you . . . Grand Duchess," I said.

She laughed aloud. "And I, you. I have something I need

to do and hope you will accompany me. It shouldn't take long."

"Not a problem," I said.

A sending fluttered in the air, and the driver pulled away from the curb.

"How is your Taint research going?" I asked.

She folded her gloved hands loosely together. "Interesting. I am acquiring an understanding of how the Celtic and Teutonic spells worked together. It's fascinating, actually. We tend to view the two modes as separate and distinct, but there are fundamental overlaps. I will show you, if you like."

"I would."

A moment of comfortable silence. "Bastian Frye wants to meet with you."

Whatever the errand, I couldn't help wondering if this was the point of Eorla's appearance. "Why?"

"If I know Bastian—and I do—he had a hand in what happened in TirNaNog. The Elven King would not have made such a blatant military move against Maeve, but Bastian would have manipulated the opportunity."

"He's working with Vize, then," I said.

Eorla pursed her lips. "I'm sure they have contact. In fact, I know they do, but it's through layers of deniable channels. If Bergin is doing something Bastian approves of, I am sure paths get smoothed when possible."

"And why should I help them?" I asked.

She glanced at me with a slim smile. "You don't have to, but it presents an interesting opportunity. Bastian adores secrecy. If I were you, I would suggest a public meeting. It will irritate Bastian and drive Ryan macGoren to distraction when he receives word that you met."

Impressed, I nodded. "Tell him it's a date, then."

"He will be pleased with me that I persuaded you," she said.

When I first met Eorla, she said she used her skills best in the political arena. She wasn't kidding.

The car turned onto Harbor Street. Plywood covered the windows of the building in the middle of a row. A smaller piece of wood had been fitted over the glass door. In a few short months, graffiti had found a home on it, much of it lamenting the closing of the place. The sign across the front, faint beneath a rime of frost, read UNITY. Eorla's husband, Alvud Kruge, founded the place as a drop-in center to help area kids get off the streets. It was where he was murdered, his body hacked to pieces. Eorla stared out the window.

"Why are we here?" I asked.

Eorla didn't turn. "You don't seem to know much of elven history. Do you know much of our religion?"

"Not particularly. Most of what I know is related to how elves manipulate essence."

She leaned closer to the window to peer up at the building. "Yes, the outward manifestation of power always impresses. I am talking about matters of the soul, Mr. Grey. When at last we leave our bodies, we leave a sign of ourselves behind for a time, a bit of the soul, if you will. That is what my people believe. That is what I believed.

"But when I last saw Alvud's body, there was nothing there, no last thought or emotion. It saddened me that my husband did not leave a final remembrance, and saddened me further that my faith was misplaced. I have had a difficult time these last months with no husband and no faith."

I clasped Eorla's gloved hand. She returned the pressure lightly. It was not the first time she shared her grief with me. I don't know why she did, but Bastian Frye and Brokke didn't strike me as sources for heartfelt sympathy.

She turned from the window. "You likely know of these decapitation murders in the Weird, yes?"

Change of subject, then. "I've been helping the Boston police with them."

"I overheard a chance remark among my security staff recently. I was not made aware of the full details of my husband's murder."

Not a change of subject, then. Because of his high profile, the Guild investigated Alvud Kruge's murder. I never read the final report. Murdock and I found his body at the murder scene. Kruge's body was savaged, blown apart by essence. The force of the attack decapitated him. We found his head embedded in a wall.

"I'm sorry you had to hear that, Eorla," I said.

She withdrew and folded her hands in her lap. "I understand the impulse to protect my feelings, but I wish I had known."

"I'm still confused by why we are here," I said.

Beneath her outer calm, I felt her emotions rising. "You were the only one who saw what was behind my husband's murder. I think it is fitting for you to see the final resolution of his death."

With the prompting of a soft sending, the driver trotted to Eorla's side of the car. Even though I overlooked Eorla's royal privileges, on an embarrassing level, I enjoyed watching Teutonic Consortium agents being used as footmen. They tended to be pushy and arrogant types, so watching them taken down a peg or two was entertaining. Plenty of people felt the same way about me. I joined Eorla on the doorstep of the store as she withdrew a key from her pocket.

"Please wait outside, Rand," Eorla said. He hesitated but withdrew after sendings flew between them.

The place had not changed since the murder months earlier. Cast-off furniture filled the front of the large, dim room, a Ping-Pong table and old metal desks in the rear. After Kruge's murder, it was a crime scene. It didn't look like anyone had been inside since the police released it. "Is UNITY closed down?"

Eorla reflectively observed the room. "I appointed a manager and moved its offices. I haven't decided what to do with this property."

"You'll sell it?"

She shook her head. "I don't want to deal with Ryan macGoren asking to buy it. He would be inconsiderate enough to try."

MacGoren's desire to turn the Weird into an urban renewal project was one of the reasons Alvud Kruge had ended up dead. MacGoren withheld information from the police, but there wasn't significant evidence that he could have prevented what happened. Being a callous dirtbag wasn't against the law. "I'd like to check the office before you see it."

She pressed her lips together and nodded. Kruge's office was through a large archway. Unlike the front, the room had changed from my last visit. Kruge's body, of course, was gone. When we found him, blood bathed the office in horrific red. Now, somber brown stains marked the walls and floors in the muted remainders of the murder. To the right, a few feet above my head, darker stains smeared the cavity in the wall where Kruge's head had been. His attacker had killed a young man, too, a teenager who was in the wrong place at the wrong time.

I looked over my shoulder at Eorla. "There are dried bloodstains, but otherwise nothing."

She wet her lips. "I have seen the carnage wrought on battlefields, Connor, but thank you."

Despite her boast, I heard a faint intake of breath beside me. It was one thing to see blood and gore. It was another to know it belonged to someone you knew—loved—no matter how old it was. Her eyes went to the cavity in the wall. "That's where his . . . where he was?"

"Yes," I said.

She muttered an incantation. In a smooth glide, she rose

from the floor until she was eye level with the hole. Levitating your own body was difficult, but Eorla didn't appear to need much effort to raise herself. She stared at the opening and chanted.

From the darkness of the wall cavity, warm green essence eased into my sensing ability. It peaked and gathered, slowly revolving. Eorla removed a glove and reached in. The essence flowed over her hand and vanished. She stayed with her hand outstretched, as if waiting for more, a subtle look of surprise on her face. She closed the hand into a loose fist as tears sprang to her eyes. Closing her eyes, she brought her hand to her lips and held it with her other hand. A single tear escaped and rolled down her cheek as she descended.

I gently turned her from the wall. She leaned her head against my shoulder. I wrapped my arms around her and swayed in place to comfort her. She let me, lost in her husband's last memories, which had bonded to the blood in the wall.

"His final thoughts were for the human child, then he said my name," she murmured into my chest.

"He was a good man, and he loved you. You didn't need to do this to know that," I said.

She placed her hand on my coat over my heart. Warmth touched me. The dark mass in my head flexed at the sensation but didn't do anything else.

Eorla took an audible breath. "Thank you."

She adjusted her hat and took my arm. I escorted her back to the car.

16

Bastian Frye wasted no time arranging lunch the next day. I walked into the Ritz-Carlton Hotel late, half on purpose, half that's-the-way-it-is. Taking a cue from Eorla and the Teutonic penchant for order and timeliness, irritating Bastian Frye wasn't a bad way to start.

The restaurant at the Ritz had a storied history. The Boston Brahmins made it the home of the power lunch for decades, a stuffy, pretentious room of white tablecloths and blue glassware. As the city's power structure expanded into the upstart Irish and Italian immigrant populations, the luster of the place diminished until the dining room was a nostalgia trip for granddames and their granddaughters. No restaurant survived on tea and crumpets. Eventually, the hotel owner gave up and leased the space to an elven group, which rebranded the place Feudal, and the power lunch returned, only this time for the Teutonic fey set.

Frye wasn't alone. Brokke sat with him at a corner table. The two made an odd couple—the tall, regal elven court officer and the short, floridly dressed dwarven advisor. They weren't speaking as I approached, but they didn't need to speak to communicate. Neither expressed surprise when I arrived. They stood and extended their hands, an amusingly quaint gesture since we were all armed. At least, I was. I never left home without the daggers, and I had no doubt that a weapon or two lay hidden among the folds of their outfits.

"You remember Ambassador Brokke, Mr. Grey," Frye said.

"Of course. I didn't realize you'd be here."

"I thought Bastian might enjoy my company," he said.

Frye's long sip of white wine covered an expression that looked nothing like enjoyment. "Let's get down to business, shall we?" he asked.

A waiter appeared and filled my water glass. I picked up the menu. "Sure. I'll have the burger, medium rare, and a Guinness." No one was amused.

"We do not serve Guinness," the waiter said.

Figured. I didn't care for German stouts. Too heavy and long on the finish. I didn't think it was a prejudice. "Any draft ale, then."

Frye slid a long finger along his temple as he leaned on an elbow. "Mr. Grey, as I told you, the Guild believes that the Elven King may have been involved in the recent terrorist attack in this city."

"I'm not the best person to explain what the Guild thinks," I said.

Frye nodded slowly. "Indeed. I am aware of your history. My concern is that you may be fostering this idea."

"I have a number of opinions about the motives of the Consortium."

"The Elven King had nothing to do with the event," he said.

The waiter placed my beer on the table. I took a slip. "Really? Bergin Vize gained access to TirNaNog through the Irminsul gate in Germany. I'm sure the Elven King's people don't let just anyone near it, never mind use it."

"I assure you, Mr. Grey, we are investigating the loyalty of the guards," said Frye.

"Let's talk about magical artifacts," Brokke said. Frye's long, pointed ears flexed down in irritation. The two of them obviously disagreed on their meeting game.

I had a feeling I knew where he was going. "Okay."

"A spear was in the Elven King's possession for many years. I wonder how it ended up at the Seelie Court," he said.

I shrugged. "I have no idea. If it's the spear I think you're talking about, the last time I saw it was after Vize killed someone with it," I said.

"Yes, but he received the spear from you," said Brokke.

"Stole it from me is more accurate," I said.

"But if it was bonded to you, how was he able to take it?" he asked.

The waiter returned with our plates. I assembled my burger. "I didn't understand the mechanism of it. If it was bonded to me, it left me when I needed it most."

Brokke pulled at his substantial ear. "Interesting. Where is the spear now?"

"I already answered that question. Your guess is as good as mine. It vanished when I sealed the veil between worlds."

He rubbed his hands against the tablecloth, staring into his lunch. "Lost again," he muttered.

"My turn. Why are you protecting Bergin Vize?" I asked.

Brokke cut his fish, took a bite, and looked at Frye as if he, too, were interested in the answer.

"We are not protecting him. He is in hiding," he said.

"Where?"

Frye's hooded eyes seemed to be assessing me. "My guess would be your own neighborhood."

With everything else happening in the Weird, an on-the-lam terrorist elf would fit right in. "I'll take that as confirmation coming from you. Things are not going well in the Weird, and lately when things are not going well in a big way, your friend Vize is lurking in the background."

"If the events occurring on the waterfront are getting out of hand, perhaps the Guild might be of service," said Frye.

"As you can imagine, that's not reassuring. If he's so unwelcome, why aren't you looking for him?" I said.

Frye curled his lip in condescension. "As long as he does not make a threat to the Elven King, he is not my concern."

"But threats against the Seelie Court and—What are we up to? A few hundred deaths so far?—those don't concern you either?"

"That has not been proven," he said. He shifted in his seat, arching an eyebrow as he withdrew a cell phone from his pocket. "You will excuse me," he said.

As Frye left the table, Brokke leaned toward me. "We have only moments before he realizes the insignificance of that call, Grey. I have something to say to you alone. You know I am a seer. I have tried to see the events unfolding here, but no matter how I attempt it, I cannot see you."

"You're not the first person to tell me that," I said.

He glanced toward the restaurant entrance. "I know. I've enlisted others in the attempt, to no success. I have seen something that I want you to know. Something will happen, and soon, that will affect the Grand Duchess. I cannot see it. That leads me to believe whatever it is involves you as well."

"You know telling me that won't necessarily change the future," I said.

He nodded. "Truth. The future is the land of the possible, the outcome of choices, not inevitabilities. But sometimes those choices narrow to a point of significance. I believe a time is coming when you will have a choice that affects the Grand Duchess. It will cause a profound change in the Elven Court. When that time comes, Mr. Grey, I implore you to consider the consequences for more than yourself."

"I'm not sure if you're insulting me or warning me," I said.

"Neither. I am a seer. I say what I see. What you do with it is your choice. Even now, I feel things shifting, becoming less certain. Remember that royal blood flows in Eorla Elvendottir's veins, and no one wants that kind of blood on their hands."

That startled me. "I'm going to do something that causes her death?"

He shrugged. "That outcome is likelier than I care to see."

"Eorla Kruge is the last person I'd want to see dead," I said.

He tapped the table. "I as well, but the Wheel of the World is a relentless Thing." He placed a pair of workman's gloves on the table. "You will thank me for these someday. I don't know why. He returns." Curious, I slipped the gloves into my jacket. Frye resumed his seat. "Is your presence required elsewhere?" Brokke asked.

Frye picked at his lunch. "It was minor. Mr. Grey, I will tell you this: You are being watched—by the Guild and by the Consortium."

It was hard to miss the obvious elven security at the end of my street or the Danann agents that appeared overhead when I was home. "Tell me something I don't know."

"You are also about to be arrested by the Boston police force," he said.

I dropped my burger. "For what?"

"A substantial list of violations including inciting a riot and murder charges related to the deaths that occurred on Samhain. A movement is under way to involve your federal authorities in a very novel conspiracy-to-commit-treason charge," said Frye.

I pursed my lips. "I seem to have pissed someone off."

Frey leaned closer. "What's interesting is that the Guild is cooperating with the human authorities to the point of advocating your detention."

"Is this a subtle way of telling me you're not going to pay for lunch?" I asked.

Frye smiled, a thin predator smile. "On the contrary, Mr. Grey. I am willing to pay for this and whatever else you need. I am authorized by His Majesty Donor Elfen-konig to offer you asylum with an offer of Consortium citizenship."

It took several heartbeats before I laughed. I couldn't help it. To hear Bastian Frye, the man who ran counter-intelligence activities for the Consortium, the same man I had worked against for years, offer me protection was damned funny. "I'll keep it in mind."

He gave me a sharp nod, either missing my sarcasm or pleased that I didn't reject the offer out of hand. I didn't clarify but let him think whatever he wanted. Keeping someone like Bastian Frye off-balance was not an easy thing.

Brokke perused the menu. "Let's have dessert, shall we?"

I smiled. "Sure. Anything look good?"

He eyed me and passed the menu. "I'll let you pick."

I hate people who can read the future.

17

As I finished my dessert at the Ritz, Meryl texted me to
meet her nearby at a local Guild watering hole. As usual,
she was cryptic, but asked me to slip in the back unseen.
To continue enjoying bars and restaurants, a good rule of
thumb was never to go in the kitchen. The Craic House was
no different than any other place in town. The rear entrance
had the whiff of garbage, spilled beer, and bug juice. Sure,
the Health Department had rules and inspections, but that
didn't mean the cockroaches read the manuals. The kitchen
staff ignored me after their initial glances, as if it were perfectly normal for someone to walk in their back door and
hang around. Guild employees frequented the restaurant,
so maybe they were used to odd behavior.

Meryl strolled in from the front of the restaurant. Over
the clanking and banging of the dish-washing machine and
cooking areas, several guys called out her name. If I were
a different person, the number of men Meryl knew would
irritate me. But then, if I were a different person, I wouldn't
have gotten involved with Meryl in the first place. Besides,

if I did say something, she would wonder aloud why I wasn't worried about the number of women she knew, then tongue-kiss a random stranger to make the bigger point. With Meryl, I either accepted who she was and didn't make assumptions—likely or asinine ones—or she wouldn't give me the time of day. In all fairness, she respected and accepted my past the same way, although pointing out my flaws continued to be one of her favorite pastimes.

She tossed me a laminated ID badge for the Teutonic Consortium consulate with a picture of a security guard. A cool static settled over me from an essence charge on the badge. It was a glamour. The skin on my hands became smoother and paler, and my black jacket shifted to the regulation red outfit worn by elven security.

"How's your elven accent these days?" she asked.

I held up the badge. "Perfect. Is this what I look like?"

She pursed her lips. "You've got a more quizzical look on your face than he does, but it'll get you through the front door."

"And I need that because . . . ?"

She smiled. "Because Eorla Kruge doesn't want to be seen with you."

"And you're running errands for her because . . . ?"

She shot a glance at the kitchen staff. "She wants to see both of us."

I nodded slowly. "You know what that means."

Forest Hills, she sent.

The events of Forest Hills Cemetery, where Eorla's husband was buried, kept coming back to haunt us. Part of the cemetery was destroyed, which was a small price to pay for the disaster that Meryl and I had prevented. The powerful surge of essence that was released, combined with the control spell that started the whole thing, twisted essence and produced the Taint. Meryl and I were a big part of stopping a cataclysmic meltdown, and Eorla played her role, too.

"She's getting close to something," I said.

Meryl shrugged and rolled her eyes in irritation. Forest Hills wasn't something she liked talking about. She felt responsible for some of the deaths that had occurred, to say nothing of being the subject of a Guild investigation that had led to her arrest. The charges were dropped, but people continued pressing her about what she did. Including, apparently, Eorla.

"I don't trust her," Meryl said.

I chucked her on the nose. "You don't trust anybody."

She grinned. "And that's how I've survived as long as I have." She glanced at her watch. "She's expecting you in fifteen minutes. Give me a few seconds head start, then go out the back."

"I can't leave with you?"

She back-stepped and smirked. "Nope. I don't want to be seen with you either."

On the way through the kitchen, she retrieved a bag from under a heat lamp and went out front. I shook my head. Cloak and dagger with fries.

Out in the alley, I adjusted my stride to the stiff rhythm of an elven security guard. Back when I was working for the Guild, going undercover wearing a glamour was a routine part of the job. Going into the Guild undercover was not something I ever contemplated doing. I didn't need to. They were impressed with me then.

Near the Guildhouse entrance, I flashed my badge at three different sidewalk checkpoints. Consortium agents didn't have automatic access to the Guildhouse, but they were extended the courtesy of bypassing the waiting queue during lockdowns. Without an appointment or high-level security badge, they didn't make it past the reception desk, same as anyone else. I breezed through, though. I guessed Guild directors can wave through anybody they wanted.

The Teutonic section of the Guildhouse was in the rear

on lower floors. Not the best location as offices go, but that was the point. While publicly the Guild welcomed all fey in the name of unity, the Teutonic contingent were assumed spies for Donor Elfenkonig. No doubt they were. Guild spies in other places confirmed it.

More badge flashing on the fifth floor earned me an escort directly to Eorla's office. Despite her stature, Eorla kept a relatively modest yet modern office with glass-and-steel furniture—definitely not Guild issue. The window behind her desk shimmered with a spell that displayed a view of an ancient forest instead of the parking lot I knew was outside that part of the building.

To maintain the facade of the glamour, I stood at attention while my escort announced me. Eorla nodded as she typed on the thinnest laptop I had ever seen. The escort passed her my badge. Eorla stopped to look at it, then returned it with a smile. "Thank you. Has the material I requested from the archives arrived?"

"No, ma'am," the escort said.

Eorla made a slight frown. "Please call. I don't want this courier to wait."

"Yes, ma'am." The escort bowed and left.

Eorla continued working as she passed me a sending. *I'm sorry I have to leave you standing there. They'll think it odd if you sit down and odder yet if we close the door.*

A few moments later, Meryl's voice sounded out in the hall. "Look, I don't care if you're the Elven King's nephew or his dog handler, I'm not turning over classified files to a hallway jockey. Tell Eorla, if she wants them, she gets them directly from me. If she has a problem with that, she can discuss it in my office."

Eorla arched an eyebrow and went to the door. "It's fine, Albrin. Let her through. Ms. Dian is very dedicated to her work."

"Hey, Kru-chacha. Nice to see you again," Meryl said

loud enough for the guard to hear, and effectively put herself on their enemies-of-the-state list. The Consortium puts more effort into nothing than formality and strict adherence to royal protocol.

Meryl snickered as she preceded Eorla, who closed the door.

"You are incorrigible," I said.

She grinned as she sat in a guest chair. "And that's my good side."

I sat next to her. "What's the mystery all about, Eorla?"

She leaned back, her eyes shifting between Meryl and me. "I've been reviewing the Forest Hills files, and I believe there are some gaps in the report."

Meryl shifted in her seat. "I sent you everything that was in the files."

Eorla smiled shrewdly. "Of course you did. I don't think either of you believe that my own report contained everything that occurred."

Her admission didn't surprise me. What had happened when she wasn't observed was anyone's guess. Eorla had made a deal with Nigel Martin. That much I knew. In exchange for her help at Forest Hills, she wanted the Guild director position that had been vacated by her husband's death. Manus ap Eagan didn't want it to happen, but after Forest Hills, Eorla was confirmed. I didn't know if anything else happened that she didn't report.

"What do you want to know?" I asked.

"If we share information, we may be able to resolve the issue of the Taint to everyone's advantage."

"And your credit," Meryl said.

Eorla shrugged. "I have no issue sharing credit for it. In fact, you can have it all if you wish. It's more important that the Taint be eliminated."

I smiled. "You're afraid the Guild will figure it out and use it as a weapon."

Eorla shook her head. "Not afraid. I know that is their intention. Isn't fear of Consortium dominance what the fiasco on Samhain was about? The only thing that keeps war from breaking out between the Seelie Court and the Elven King is parity. If I have anything to do with it, both sides will know the answer or neither will."

"Sounds to me like you'll end up committing espionage against the Guild and treason against the Elven King at the same time. Even I make better friends than that," said Meryl.

"Barely," I said out of the corner of my mouth.

The Guild had interrogated Meryl for weeks about the purging spell she used on the Taint. Meryl insisted she didn't know the mechanics of the spell because a powerful fey called a drys actually performed it through her. It wasn't quite possession, more like having a supercharged battery boosting her already considerable ability, with the drys providing direction. I had more than enough experience with forgetting what happened during extreme essence events, but even I suspected Meryl knew a little more than she was telling.

Eorla steepled her fingers. "I'll let history judge that. I've been out of favor before. I will find favor again. That's not the issue. The Taint is."

"Why should we trust you?" Meryl asked.

A slow smile teased at the corners of Eorla's mouth. "By that question, you confirm my belief that you know something."

Meryl frowned a smile. "Maybe it was a rhetorical question. I didn't just fall out of an oak tree, Eorla."

I suppressed a smirk. Meryl might not have fallen out of an oak tree, but at Forest Hills, I watched her fall into one. Literally. One moment, the bark of the tree formed the face of the drys; the next, Meryl jumped into the trunk.

Eorla pulled a small pad of paper toward herself and

sketched a series of runes. Sometimes the act of scribing can activate a spell. Eorla was a pro, though, and broke them into unlikely combinations. For added measure, she smeared essence on the first few to make them resonate differently. She slid the pad across the desk. "Perhaps an exchange of information would make you more amenable. Those are the runes I saw and remember"—she shot me a significant glance—"all of them this time. I believe, Connor, you held back a few as well."

I picked up a pen and drew three more runes. I didn't look at Meryl, but sensed her caution through her stillness. Eorla studied the pad. "It's ancient. It doesn't have the nuance of the spells we use today. It's much more blunt force." She handed me the pad. "Do you see the rhythm of an elven chant in that?"

I saw what she meant. "I don't follow all of it, but, yeah, I see it."

Meryl took the pad from me with a mixture of reluctance and curiosity. She scanned the page, then closed her eyes, nodding as if listening to music. She opened her eyes and filled in a few blank spaces. "I think those belong. The syntax looks similar to Old Elvish with maybe an eastern influence."

Impressed, Eorla nodded as she reviewed the additions. "The runes were bonded to an oak staff. That changed the nature of the spell by combining Seelie and Teutonic modes."

"That was the point," said Meryl, "to control essence the way the two groups use it."

"Why didn't it affect us?" Eorla asked.

"That part's easy," said Meryl. "We didn't drink the Kool-Aid."

Eorla tapped the edge of her desk in thought. "The drugged ceremonial mead never made it to me for the final toast. That doesn't explain Nigel Martin's ability to fight off the spell."

"He was sidelined at the Guildhouse and wasn't at the funeral. He didn't arrive until after the spell catalyzed," I said.

Eorla considered for a moment before bringing her attention back to Meryl. "The drys used you to execute a counterspell, and the control spell collapsed."

"But it didn't collapse," I said. "That's what the Taint is. Damaged essence."

Eorla leaned back in her chair again. "You broke the Seelie aspect of the spell, Meryl. If that knowledge falls to the Elven King, he may be able to reconstruct the control spell, and we may not be able to stop it again. The Celtic fey would be at his mercy."

No one spoke.

"You have nothing to add?" Eorla said to Meryl.

She shook her head. "I don't remember. It wasn't my doing. The drys used me as a conduit."

Eorla arched an eyebrow. "A conduit. I hadn't considered that."

"If you reconstruct the spell, won't that cause the same problem all over again?" I asked.

She titled her head. "I'm not re-creating the spell. I'm reconstructing it in order to understand how to undo it. You saw how much essence was involved—controlling all that essence is impossible for one person. I have no interest in dying."

A knock sounded at the door. I stood for appearances sake. Another elven guard entered at Eorla's response. "Your meeting is beginning shortly, Your Highness."

Eorla gathered up some papers on her desk, slipped them in an envelope, and handed it to me. "Deliver this by the end of the day, will you?"

I bowed and left the room. Meryl met me at the elevator a few moments later. We didn't speak until the doors closed. "I still don't trust her," she said.

"I know. I do. When you do, let me know," I said.

She cocked her head at me. "That's it? No trying to persuade me?"

I smiled. "I've learned my lesson on that score."

She nodded. "Good."

I wiggled my elven ears at her. "Have you ever had crazy elf sex?"

She watched the lit numbers on the panel as they counted down. She punched the stop button. "Not in an elevator."

18

After a day of political intrigue, it made perfect sense, at least in my life, to shift gears and attend a good, old-fashioned neighborhood meeting. Murdock seemed to think it might be interesting, but I doubted it. Neighborhood meetings were usually dog-and-pony shows, a sop to whoever had a problem, where the powers that be got to pretend they cared and were doing something about it. A neighborhood meeting in the Weird was unusual. The people who lived there didn't have the time—or clout—to demand community service or political attention. Not when they were dodging elf-shot and bullets. But enough people had complained that one was arranged, and Murdock felt the need to attend.

Like most of the old buildings in the Weird, the building on Summer Street being used for the meeting was a manufacturing plant for something when it was built. Plate-glass windows lined the street level now, covered with metal mesh. By the sign above the door, someone had tried to turn it into a lighting showroom, "tried" being the operative word. The sign was long faded.

Snow fell thickly as Murdock parked the car opposite the entrance to the old warehouse. The weather forecast hadn't called for anything more than overcast skies, but the clouds had a different idea. Light leaked through the mesh grate from inside, casting striated shadows onto the solitaries who gathered on the sidewalk. Bark-skinned men with tangled hair in mats of dark green or brown stamped their feet in the snow and bunched their hands in pockets. A few ash-colored women huddled together, their coal black hair trailing to their waists. At the next corner, police officers in riot gear leaned against cars and motorcycles. Suspicious and angry eyes from both contingents watched each other in the sallow light thrown by the lone streetlight.

Despite the cold, we moved across the street with a steady gait. Rushing would have looked like we were intimidated by the stares. More solitaries filled the interior of the warehouse. Some managed to snag the few wooden folding chairs set up, but the majority stood and faced a long table—with a very obvious space heater pointed at it. Mayor Dolan Grant and Commissioner Scott Murdock sat with a city councilor, various aides, and a blasé Guild press agent I remembered. Behind them, I was surprised to see Moira Cashel. When we made eye contact, she didn't acknowledge me.

A thin woman spoke waveringly into a microphone about her recent mugging. When she finished, a community activist who worked across the city took the microphone. She didn't look like your typical advocate for solitary fey. With her simple, stylish black suit and long ash-blond hair, she looked more Back Bay than the Weird. "This has got to be awkward," I said.

Murdock gave me a sharp glance. "What do you mean?"

I nodded at Grant. "That's Jennifer Grant, the mayor's daughter. It's got to be pissing him off to have her criticize his administration."

Murdock let his gaze rove over the woman. She was definitely rovable. "I heard they made peace a long time ago. Business is business, family is family."

I poked my tongue into my cheek. "Maybe they should talk to you and your father."

A corner of Murdock's lips dipped down. "I don't think I could contradict him in public."

"Maybe you should," I said.

Bemused, Murdock shook his head. "Let's not go there, Connor."

"And she's just one of many stories like this," Grant was saying. "The Grant administration has to remember that civil rights extend to all our citizens, whether they are fey or human, legal residents or undocumented workers."

The mayor leaned forward. "Thank you, Jennifer. I have complete confidence in Commissioner Murdock. The city of Boston must meet the current problems with strong action, and we are working diligently to protect everyone."

His daughter scowled back at him. "There have been four unsolved murders in this neighborhood in the last two weeks. That is significant, and I have no information regarding a police response that supports the people who live and work here instead of punishing them through negligence."

Scott Murdock tilted his head toward the microphone. He pinned his dark eyes on Grant like she was some kid who had kicked a ball onto his lawn. "'Negligence' is a loaded word, Ms. Grant. The police department is doing everything it can to maintain order under the current circumstances."

Grant straightened her jacket. "Yes, thank you, Commissioner. Speaking of maintaining order, can you or the mayor please tell us under what legal authority the Guild-house is policing this neighborhood?"

From the tight, thin lips on the commissioner's face, he

didn't like the question. "They are auxiliary forces to help handle the unique challenges of this area."

"That doesn't answer my question, sir. What is their legal authority?" Grant asked.

The commissioner looked at the mayor. Dolan Grant pulled the microphone closer. "As you know, Jennifer, our office is responding to several legal challenges on that point. We believe we have full legal authority to draw on the Guild's generous offer of resources until the courts say otherwise."

The crowd broke out in angry shouts while the mayor held up his hands for quiet.

Several people moved toward the microphone. Someone grabbed it and began speaking but was drowned out. A ripple went through the crowd, and it parted to let someone through. Zev stepped up to the microphone, and the speaker backed away. The room quieted.

"When are the barriers around the Weird coming down?" he asked.

"There is still too much unrest to set a timetable," said the mayor.

"People can't get into the city to work," Zev said.

The mayor began to speak, but his press secretary moved in smoothly. "Everyone with a work permit is being allowed through the checkpoints."

"That's bull. It's taking weeks to get those permits. People need their paychecks," said Zev. The crowd shouted its approval.

The press secretary nodded with understanding. "We know there have been delays, and we are working to streamline the process."

"When are the barriers coming down?" Zev asked again. More shouts. I felt a pulse of essence. Someone was amping up the emotions in the room. I stared at Moira, but she gave no indication that might tip it was her. Other fey in the room seemed more intent on Zev than anyone. He held more sway with the solitaries than I realized.

"Let's move on to the next question," the press secretary said.

"That is the next question," said Zev. "And the next and the next and the next until we get an answer. We are being held prisoner in our own homes while the Guild runs through here like storm troopers."

The few people remaining in their seats yelled with the rest of the crowd. The press secretary tried to speak, but her voice didn't carry over the PA system. Someone banged on the table for order, but the crowd wasn't having it. A scuffle broke out near the audience microphone, and it fell over with an angry whine of feedback. The people behind the table conferred among themselves, then stood and filed out behind a row of police officers. Moira slid a languid hand across Commission Murdock's shoulder as she left. The commissioner remained at the table, hands folded with steepled fingers against his lips. He didn't take his eyes off Jennifer Grant. When everyone else was out of the room, he stood and reached for a bullhorn from a nearby officer.

He clicked the siren on the horn a few times, an earsplitting sound breaking through the noise. He held the horn up to his mouth. "This meeting is adjourned. Please clear the room."

The crowd roared as the commissioner handed the horn back and walked away. Another officer hit the siren and spoke. "You have been issued a police order to clear the premises. Please make your way to the exits."

"That was diplomatic," I said.

Murdock sighed and nodded. "That's my dad."

Despite the angry shouts and arm waving, the crowd left the room. Anyone in the Weird the past few weeks knew what happened when police orders were ignored. Outside, the officers in riot gear moved in closer from the corner, their dark uniforms shadows in falling snow. Some solitaries lingered, shouting at the warehouse and the line of police. At the opposite end of the block, the mayor's SUV drove away with a trail of other cars.

Squad cars lined the street, blocking in Murdock's car. We sat inside it watching the street theater escalate. The jeering crowd became smaller as people went home, but those remaining became louder. Tussles broke out. Snowballs were tossed, landing short of the line of police. The police didn't react, even backed up a few times.

On the other side of the street, I saw Shay exiting the warehouse. I hadn't seen him inside. In his long white coat, he struggled to cross the street amid a barrage of snowballs. A solitary stumbled into him and knocked him into one of the tree fairies, who pushed him off. As he focused on his footing, Shay pushed back and walked away. Obviously angry, the ash fairy followed him.

"Looks like I'm cavalry again," I said, and opened the door.

With his hood up, Shay didn't see the fairy charging up behind him. I reached Shay first and took his arm, looking pointedly at the solitary. He stopped in his tracks, glared, and backed off.

Shay pulled his arm away, then smiled. "Oh, hi. Didn't realize it was you. Some jerk just pushed me."

We walked in the direction of Murdock's car. "He was about to jump you."

Shay looked back with a frown. "He's lucky I'm wearing a new coat."

I pressed my lips together to keep from smiling. Shay's tough, but he couldn't hold his own in a fight. He had no problem getting in people's faces, and his boyfriend, Robyn, used to follow through with the physical confrontation. With Robyn gone, Shay was on his own. "You need to be careful, Shay."

He peered at me from under his fake-fur-trimmed hood. "Uno keeps showing up at my apartment. I'm going to die, Connor. I'm not going to do that with my clothes dirty."

Murdock stood outside his car. The squad cars still blocked us in. "Looks like we're here until the crowd's gone."

"Why don't you wait in the car, and we'll give you a ride?" I asked Shay.

Shay examined the backseat through the window and wrinkled his nose at the mess. "Uh, no, thanks. Like I said, this is a new coat. I'll walk. I've got a late shift at work."

Back up the street, the solitary who had pushed Shay hadn't moved on and was watching. "Why don't we walk you a bit?"

"We?" said Murdock.

I flicked some snow at him from the roof of the car. "Come on. You've got better boots than I do."

Murdock grabbed a handful and threw it. "Fine."

With Shay between us, we trudged up the middle of the street. "What did you think of the meeting, Shay?" I asked.

He answered to the rhythm of his breathing as we slogged through the snow. "No surprises. I only went because the Institute asked me to. Some of the clients' relatives have been complaining that they have to drive around the Weird after work. Poor things in their BMWs. They should try getting to the mall from here without a pass."

The snow whipped about us, dimming the light from the few streetlamps. Within a block of the car, mounds of it drifted on the road. The wind howled, a deep, plaintive moan that rose and fell. I pulled my hood down as far as it would go without blocking my vision. We leaned forward with turned heads as the cold crystals pelted our faces. I was beginning to regret the good deed. Murdock was probably ready to kill me. The wind died a moment later. Then it became louder, an eerie wail of voices and the unmistakable sound of howling. As if planned, we all stopped at the same moment. "That's not the wind," Shay said.

I scanned the area. Above us, someone ran along the roofline, too far away for me to sense his essence. I recognized his silhouette, though, and his running style. The Hound was pacing us.

In the swirling haze far ahead, a dark green light smeared in my sensing vision. A cloud of the Taint rolled toward us, billowing and mixing with other essences. The wind brought the sound of keening pierced by screams and shouts.

"It's the Dead," I said.

Something huge and dark moved toward us in a loping gait.

"What the hell is that?" Murdock asked.

The Taint's mottled essence light spread across the road, great billows of snow or steam or fog rolling out from its edges. Shay grabbed my arm. "Run! We have to run."

He didn't need to say it again. With that many people bearing down on us, it was the right call. We turned and ran, or tried to, anyway. Tripping through deep drifts of snow, we staggered our way up the street between boarded-up buildings. The next alley was tauntingly far off.

I threw a glance over my shoulder. The Dead charged up the street, running and jumping through the snow with wild abandon. Dark shapes filled the air, Dead fairies and other things, wheeling in the darkness on ragged wings.

We weren't going to make it. The alley was too far away. I pulled Shay against my side as Murdock's body shield blazed red in the swirling snow ahead of us. Murdock turned, pulling his gun out. For a brief moment, I saw surprise on his face as he lifted his weapon. Then something slammed into my back. Shay and I fell in a tangle, the great black shape of Uno, impossibly huge, pinning us to the ground with paws that threw an emberlike heat. I twisted beneath him, blindly reaching out to ward off his massive jaws. A torrent of snow washed over us. The Taint bent above the dog, and the rampaging Dead swirled to either side of us.

I craned my neck to see Murdock backing away. He turned to run, but a dim shadow on dark wings dove at him and swept him into the sky. The Taint passed on, rolling up the street, leaving the lane between the buildings empty. The pressure of weight from the dog vanished, and I scrambled to my feet.

"Murdock!" I yelled. Retreating screams and howls answered me.

"Leo!" Still no answer. I looked down the alley, but he wasn't there.

"Leo, answer me, dammit!"

No answer. There was no one left but Shay and the black dog.

Murdock was gone.

19

Blood stained the snow in front of the meeting warehouse. Bodies lay crumpled in the gutter. All solitaries. All dead. At the end of the street, police officers huddled in their cars. Motorcycles lay scattered in the snow, some with their lights flashing. No one was outside.

Shay and I stumbled into the warehouse. Pistols and rifles swung in our direction, and Shay grabbed me by the waist from behind. I held my hands in the air to confused shouts of "get out" and "get on the floor."

"Is Detective Lieutenant Leonard Murdock here?" I shouted.

An officer grabbed my arm and shoved me against the wall. "Get your arms out now," he shouted.

I assumed the position. Shay turned a panicked face toward me as an officer pressed him hard against the wall while another fumbled with his oversize coat. "I'm with the Guild," I shouted.

The officer patting me down shouted in pain as a flash of

heat burned against my ankle. "He's armed! He's armed!" he shouted as he fell back with his gun out.

I kept my hands against the wall. "I've got two daggers in my boots. That's it. One of them's spelled. I need Lieutenant Murdock."

"He's not here," someone said.

"Just throw them out with the others," someone else yelled.

I had no idea what was going on. These guys sounded angry and scared. "Call the Guild, dammit! Tell Keeva macNeve that you have Connor Grey!"

An officer pressed the muzzle of his gun against the back of my neck. I closed my eyes. "Let the kid go," I said.

No one answered. I didn't dare move my head to check on Shay.

After several agonizing minutes, someone called over. "He's clear."

The pressure of the gun disappeared. I dropped my hands. Shay huddled against me again. "This is no way to treat a lady," he whispered.

"Are you okay?" I asked. He nodded against my shoulder.

I called Keeva. She spoke before I had a chance to say anything. "Stay with the police, Connor. We're handling this. Don't tell anyone else you're there."

"What the hell is going on?"

Rustling sounds came through as Keeva moved her phone. Muffled voices argued in the background. "It doesn't matter. Listen, don't talk to anyone. I'll be there as soon as I can."

"What the hell is going on?"

She dropped her voice. "I can't talk. We've got missing police officers. Just do what I say. You're better off in Guild custody."

"Custody?" I said.

She disconnected. I stared at my phone. Bastian's words came back to me. I glanced around the room. No one seemed to be watching me. Given a choice between the police and the Guild, I liked neither. I looked out the window. The storm was raging, blinding white snow obliterating the view to the street. I called Meryl.

"I'm at 264 Summer Street. Can you get me out of here?" I asked.

"It's a blizzard out there, Grey," she said.

"Murdock's missing," I said.

"Missing? Like missing missing or not returning your phone calls because he has something better to do missing?"

I told her what happened. "And now I'm surrounded by cops who apparently don't know they're supposed to arrest me," I said.

She sighed. "I'll be there as soon as I can."

Officers watched the storm through the grate-covered windows. The heightened apprehension faded as time went by, but the tension never completely left the room. No one but uniformed officers came inside. Whatever solitaries had been out in the street when the Dead came through were either hiding elsewhere or dead.

"I'm going to need a distraction," I said to Shay.

"I've got a pretty good singing voice," he said.

I smiled down at him. "I'm sure you do. When I tell you to, go to the back of the room and do something to draw attention."

He nodded. "Then what do I do?"

"Stay here. You'll be safe."

His eyebrows went up. "Really? With the guys with the guns that were pointed at me?"

"You'll be fine. This seems to be about the fey," I said.

He pouted as he looked around the room. "Maybe I'll get that guy who groped me to buy me a drink."

I grinned. "See? I'm giving you a dating opportunity."

A deep, low rumble sounded outside. Everyone moved away from the door and windows except me and Shay. A smudge of light appeared, white and yellow. As the noise grew, the lights brightened and separated into flashing roof lights. A snowplow stopped outside, a massive hulk of yellow steel belching steam out its overhead exhaust.

A cool spot formed in my mind and a sending came through. *You going to stare or get in?*

"Showtime, Shay," I said.

He pulled his hood up and wandered toward the back of the room. I sidled toward the door. When Shay reached the table in back, he stooped and picked up the fallen microphone. For a moment, I thought he really was going to sing, but then he let loose with a loud, high-pitched scream. Every head in the room whipped in his direction. I slipped outside.

Snow swirled around me in thick curtains. In the few feet from the door to the truck, I was covered from head to foot. I hopped on the running board of the plow, then jumped inside the cab. Bundled in a thick black cloak, Meryl waited behind the wheel.

"Where the hell did you get this?" I asked.

She put the truck in gear. "Geez, Grey, doesn't anyone owe you favors?"

"I got you out in a blizzard, didn't I?"

"This is you owing me another favor, not you calling one in."

"Where are we going?" I asked.

"To meet Zev. He agreed to have his people look for Murdock."

The truck rumbled along Summer Street in its own bubble of light. The warehouses to either side were barely discernible through the storm, less so as we drove deeper into the Weird, and the streetlamps became fewer. We drove through a trail of essence. The storm degraded what lingered, but I got hits on elves, fairies, and all kinds of solitaries and large animals. "This is the direction the Dead came from," I said.

The dashboard lights threw a pale yellow glow against Meryl's face. "I've been sensing their trail since the financial district. There were a few live ones, but not Murdock's."

"This is my fault. The Dead wouldn't be here if it wasn't for me," I said.

Meryl took a wide turn onto Drydock Avenue in the deep end of the Weird. "No, I'd blame Bergin Vize for that one."

"He led them here, but I trapped them," I said.

She turned onto Harbor Street and dropped the plow. The snow drifted nearly two feet in front of us. "Eh, that's debatable and beside the point. They're here. The point right now is to find Murdock."

"Are we going where I think we're going?" I asked.

"If you guessed the Tangle, you get to go to the bonus round," she said, as we crossed Old Northern.

The Tangle is where the worst of the Weird meets the worst of everything. The original layout of the streets was buried under shifting lanes and buildings that created a maze with no beginning and no end. Bad things happened in the Tangle, from knife-throwing target practice on the unwary to full-blown essence battles. Blood and sadness soaked the streets, the memories of rage and waste. Human law enforcement gave up on it long ago. It had to. If the fey had to be on guard in the Tangle, a person with only a gun and a badge had no hope of surviving.

Tiny streaks of white lightning danced over the truck as it passed through a warding barrier. The engine coughed, and Meryl muttered a shield spell as she downshifted.

The deeper we drove into the area, the more spells pinged against the shield, bursts of essence in green and white across the hood of the truck, streaks of yellow and brilliant hazes of blue and white. The engine whined higher, and Meryl hit the brake. "We need to get out here. The engine can't take any more hits. I don't want to lose it and have to walk home in this mess."

My head started aching. The dark mass in my mind hated whenever someone tried to read the future, and the Tangle was a hotbed for scrying. As I trudged through the snow behind Meryl, I fought off the nausea that welled up. My vision blurred as the pain increased. "I don't know if I can do this, Meryl. There's too much scrying, and I'm getting hit with sensor spells."

She reached out a gloved hand. Her body shield shimmered around her, a faint yellow glow in the thick snow. The essence flowed off her fingers and up my arm. The dark mass flared, sharp little spikes of darkness reacting to the body shield's intrusion. The mass in my head resisted, intent on blocking outside essence. Including me in her body shield wasn't a true interaction of the kind the dark mass resisted—Meryl's shield wrapped around me more like a blanket than a merging of our body signatures. Meryl jerked her head up at me, surprised at the resistance the mass pressed back with. When her shield blocked the emanations from the scryings, the dark mass settled down and didn't attempt to reject her help.

"That was different," she said.

"I think it's overly sensitive to being in the Tangle," I said. I hoped. It was doing a lot of things lately it hadn't done before.

We shuffled through the drifts and wind without speaking. Few people were out in the storm except the usual suspects—fey solitaries with weather abilities who didn't mind the cold and the wind. They ignored us for the most part, though occasionally one of the highland fairies threw an extra gust of wind at us. We circled a block built on a tight crescent, five- and six-story warehouses leaning back from the street. Eccentric additions cast dark shadows over the windows, twisted bricks rising in sinuous lines across the facades, spikes of stone hanging in the air. They radiated with strong currents of essence.

"We're walking in circles," I said through panting breaths.

Meryl focused in front of her. "It's the path. Once more around the block, and we should be there."

We turned for the third time around a slumped pile of stone. Someone had died under it, the pain of their passing gnawing at the edges of my sensing ability. The rear of the warehouses were no better. Death always leaves a footprint behind, one that can take years to fade.

Meryl stopped. We stood on the front side of the block in the middle of the crescent. The center building had changed. A door that hadn't been visible the first two times we passed yawned above us in a white stone carved to resemble oak leaves. Unlike the brick used on the rest of the walls, large blocks of granite in an irregular pattern surrounded the entrance. Clinging to the stones were several *vitniri*, their lupine faces lifting into howls as we approached. Two jumped down from the lintel and barred our way.

The Teutonic *vitniri* were known for their skills at guarding homes. Whether they were humans with wolflike features or wolves with human characteristics was hard to tell. They walked on their hind legs or all fours as it suited them, their limbs ending in rough pawlike clawed hands.

Meryl took off a glove and held out her hand. "I am Meryl Dian. Connor Grey is with me. We are invited."

I took off a glove, too. The *vitniri* on the walls barked and yipped. The two in front of us rose on their hind legs and came closer. They sniffed at our hands and licked our fingers. A few moments of more sniffing, and they backed away. "You may enter," one said, his voice a raspy growl. They scrambled back up the sides of the door.

I resisted the urge to wipe my hand before putting the glove back on. As long as the scent-marking remained, we would be unharmed. By unharmed, I meant not ripped to shreds and maybe eaten. If nothing else, *vitniri* are dedicated watchmen.

Meryl pushed open the door. "At least they didn't pee on me this time," she muttered.

20

Inside, heat and chaos enveloped us. In the flickering half-light, fey of all stripes filled an industrial cathedral of interlocking steel beams and arches. Shouts filled the air with the roaring vibration of cheering spectators. The clank and crash of metal on metal created a shrieking bass line. The air smelled of oil and chemicals, the burnt-ozonelike residue of spent essence and the reek of unwashed bodies. Rhythmic screams of someone in deep pain pierced through it all.

"Cozy," I said.

"You should be here on a busy night," Meryl said.

Half the time I thought Meryl said things like that to emphasize the point that I didn't know everything about her. The other half of the time, I hoped that was true. The reality was I didn't know everything about Meryl, and I never would. It was the nature of the fey to move in and out of each other's lives without knowing who the other person had been a generation ago. Long lives trailed long histories, some good, some bad. The fey either accepted that about each other, or they ended up being alone.

No one paid us any attention as we threaded through the crowd on the main floor. I had been to a few places like it before, underground clubs and safe houses where the persecuted hid to be themselves among their own kind. I loved being part of the fey subculture, but I had the luxury of not needing it. I shared a certain sensibility with the lost and shunned in the Weird, but in places like this, I realized a level of acceptance existed that I would never achieve among the solitaries. I was a druid, an acceptable fey to the mainstream. My face wasn't scarred or scaled, feathered or furred. My skin color fell into the peach to brown spectrum the outside human world understood and accepted.

I brought my own prejudices, too. I recoiled instinctively at times, thought entire species unattractive, or feared people simply by virtue of their race. I could tell myself all I wanted that my attitudes weren't the same thing as the human racism that was based solely, inexplicably, on skin color. All trolls did like their meat raw and weren't particular where they got it. Merfolk occasionally did drown air-breathing lovers in the throes of passion. The fey—all fey—were filled with as many of the vicious as the virtuous. My fears and biases might be more reality based, but they were still fears and biases.

"What the hell?" Meryl swung her pocketbook around to her chest and pulled up the flap.

Joe crawled out. "You really need to clean out your purse."

"It's not called the Bag of Doom for nothing," she said.

"How long have you been in there?" I asked.

He fluttered between us, taking in the sight of the ranks of solitaries hanging in the framework of the warehouse. "Just now. I had to come in tight because of all the security these guys have. Last time a *vitniri* licked me, I licked him back. They've had it in for me ever since."

"Any word on Murdock?" Meryl asked.

Joe shook his head. "I've been looking for him ever since your sending. No dice." He ducked as someone threw a beer bottle across our path. He swooped down, picked it up, and threw it back. "I don't think he's dead," he continued. "His signature vanishes right where you last saw him, Connor. There should have been something for me to follow. Wherever he is, he's masked by something powerful."

The crowd thickened, and we pushed toward the center of attention. The screams grew louder. "There were a lot of Dead."

"They have a knack for hiding stuff," Joe shouted over the noise.

Chains dangled from the ceiling ahead, the heavy-duty kind for lifting machinery. They swayed and tangled as the crowd cheered. Meryl was a foot shorter than I was. I gripped her hand tighter when I saw over the heads of the crowd.

A Dead man hung by his wrists from the chains, both his shoulders dislocated and his feet just touching the floor. By his essence, he belonged to one of the lesser elven clans I didn't know well. By what remained of his clothes and his wild, long blond hair, he was a warrior from a few centuries ago. His shirt and boots had been stripped, leaving his torso and feet bare. Blood trickled down his body from numerous slashes, and thick clots of it matted his hair.

Zev stood in front of him and pressed a knife against his chest. "For the last time, where are my people?"

The elf smiled through shattered teeth. "Go ahead and kill me, animal. I will come back and cut you down before you wake."

Zev sliced the knife against the elf's skin. The guy squeezed his eyes shut and grimaced. "You think so?"

"This is sick." I moved forward.

Meryl grabbed my arm. "Don't interfere, Grey."

"Meryl, I won't watch him torture this guy."

Her eyes lit with warning. "Then don't watch. We're on their turf, Grey. You step in, this whole place will come down on you. Let it be."

Angry, I yanked my arm away and instantly regretted it. Her body shield slipped off me. The dark mass became exposed to the scrying in the air and spiked with pain in my mind. "This isn't right, Meryl."

Meryl put her hand on my back and replaced the shield. "Sometimes, Grey, people don't have a choice in doing what they do. We're here for their help, not to change their ways. This isn't the time."

"It's torture," I said.

She glanced at Zev. "Yes, it is. Can you smell the blood-lust in the air? We're outnumbered. Let it go. He's a Dead guy."

Zev wiped the bloodied knife against the elf's cheek. "Bring the leech!" he called over his shoulder.

The crowd hooted and screamed as it backed away. We didn't move as the circle withdrew and exposed us. Zev noticed, then turned his attention to a widening gap in the crowd. Meryl sucked in air as several elves with bows loaded with elf-shot appeared, the green essence primed and pointed at the *leanansidhe* walking in their midst.

"You weren't kidding about her," she said.

The *leanansidhe* stopped in front of Zev. She came no higher than his shoulder, her whiteless black eyes fixed on the hanging elf. She wrapped her arms around herself and crooned, pulling her tattered and soiled coat tighter.

Zev leaned down and picked up a stained sack. From within it, he withdrew the decapitated head of one of the Dead. He held it in front of the prisoner. "Look familiar, elf? Your friend thought I was bluffing, too. When you see

Jark, tell him we can play his game, too, but we can take it a step further."

He tossed the head at the *leanansidhe*, and she effortlessly snatched it from the air. Zev grabbed the elf by the hair, forcing him to face the *leanansidhe*. "Watch, elf. I know your clan can sense essence. Watch and tell Jark what waits for him if he continues hunting us."

The *leanansidhe* cradled the head. With soot-covered hands, she smoothed back the bloodied hair. The deep purple tendrils of her body essence oozed from her fingers and burrowed into the face. They latched onto the faint remains of essence in the Dead man's head and bulged as they siphoned it off. The dark mass in my head shifted, a strange sensation of hunger that sent a shiver down my spine. My vision darkened, the dark mass rising. The urge to join the *leanansidhe* tugged at me. I held my breath and pushed back at the darkness. It retreated, slowly, reluctantly. The *leanansidhe* moaned softly as she savored the essence, pawing at the face until the head was drained. She dropped it on the floor.

Zev picked it up and dangled it in front of the elf. "Do you see, elf? There is nothing. True death, elf, final and complete. You will live tomorrow, but as you die tonight, think what it would mean if it were your true death. Tell Jark whatever he is seeking, we do not have it. Tell him if he and his brethren do not stop attacking us, the only thing they will find is true death. Tell him in the end, we will drink his soul."

Zev shoved his knife into the elf, directly into the heart. The elf gasped, his chest heaving up. His body went limp and swayed from the chains. Zev raised the knife, clenched in his bloody fist as the crowd screamed its approval. "Leave the body somewhere the Dead will find it," he said to one of the elf guards.

He leaned toward the *leanansidhe*. "Remember our pact, leech, and be ready when we call."

She smiled and bowed, clearly mocking Zev. He was playing with fire and probably knew it. If he didn't kill her when he was done with her, the *leanansidhe* would hunt him down. They both knew one of them would be dead by the end of it. The *leanansidhe* walked away with the elf guard close behind her. When she reached the edge of the crowd, she paused. Looking over her shoulder, her eyes met mine, her fathomless pools of black to my blue. She turned away again, leaving me a sending. *We meet again, brother. That within you calls to me and mine to you. I know you feel it. You will answer it and soon. Thus, we meet and meet.*

21

With the main event over, the shouting subsided, and people wandered off. A number remained watching, curious about the druid who registered little of his own essence and the druidess with brilliant red hair. Joe crawled out from Meryl's hood once he was sure the *leanansidhe* was gone.

Zev wiped his hands on a soiled cloth while two Dokkheim elves lowered the Dead man to the floor. He examined his fingernails. "You don't approve," he said.

"You didn't ask for my approval," I said.

He tossed the rag aside and crossed his arms. "'Struth. But you still don't approve."

I pursed my lips. "I watched you murder someone."

He shrugged. "He was Dead anyway. He'll be fine tomorrow."

I shook my head. "That's a dark road you're walking, Zev."

He gestured to the remaining watchers. "I gave them what they needed."

I snorted. "Bread and circuses, is that it? Read some history, Zev. You may not like where that led."

He fixed his white eyes on me. "The Dead are killing us, Grey, and no one gives a damn. If we don't stand up to them, they will kill us all. They want us truly dead, and the cops and the Guild are just watching it happen."

"The Guild is working on tonight's kidnappings as we speak," I said.

He laughed. "Really? You think so? I've got my people out looking for *everyone* who went missing tonight. Can the Guild say the same?"

My conversation with Keeva chose that moment to remind me that she only mentioned missing police officers. I decided not to share that with Zev. "You're playing with fire and gasoline. You keep pumping these people up like this, you'll lose control of them. Whatever the Guild and the police aren't doing is beside the point."

Will you knock it off? Meryl sent to me.

He nodded dismissively. "And what they *are* doing is the point. They created the situation by boxing us in. With the Dead hunting us down and the law locking us in, we're trapped, Grey. Solitaries live without hope most of the time, but things have never been this hopeless. If giving them hope breaks the chains that bind them, so be it. Let the humans reap our wrath."

Meryl tugged at my arm. "We're not here for a political discussion."

I ignored her. "Sekka is dead, Zev. That will never change no matter how you dress your revenge."

He locked eyes with me. "Jark must pay for her death."

"The Hound killed her," I said.

Zev shook his head. "The Hound saw Jark kill her."

"How do you know that?" I asked.

Zev lowered his eyes. "Let's just say I know people who know people who know."

"So if that's true, then why is Jark afraid of the Hound?" I asked.

"Because all the Dead are afraid of him. The Hound is hunting the Dead whenever they cross the line. He may be Dead himself, but he's not their ally. Jark's lying to get you to focus your attention somewhere else. And if you eliminate the Hound for him in the meantime, even better."

"The Hound killed Jark?" I asked.

Zev pursed his lips. "He's not dead, so it doesn't matter."

"Where can I find the Hound, Zev?"

He gave me a grim smile. "I wouldn't tell you if I knew. Whenever the Dead go on one of these rampages, he's there for us, not them."

His flat white eyes fixed on me with a blank stare. It was one of those moments when one group—in this case solitaries—closed ranks against another—me, who wasn't a solitary. I wasn't going to get any more from him about the Hound.

"Aaaaand, we're not here for this," Meryl interrupted. "What's the situation?"

Zev took a deep breath. "Eighteen solitaries and three cops were grabbed. Six solitaries were killed. The cops were dumped alive not far from the meeting."

I fought down the urge to continue the argument. Meryl was right. Murdock was more important at the moment. "Any pattern to the dumps?" I asked.

He shrugged. "All in the Weird. The cops were dropped fast. Your friend will be fine, Grey. The Dead don't want humans."

"Murdock doesn't read full human anymore." The silence among us was lost in the rising and falling sounds of the solitaries around us.

"Got him!" Joe shouted and vanished.

Joe sensed people at greater distances than I could. It's one of the ways he understands where to go when he teleports. Even with my hypersensitive ability, my sensing range was limited by my physical location. Meryl's, too. But she could do sendings.

"Where is he?" I said to Meryl.

She held her hand up. "Give me a sec." She closed her eyes. "Joe says he's not far. They're bringing him in."

"Who is?"

Meryl paused as she listened. "Callies. They were nearby."

The *cailleacha*, the Scottish clan of winter women. The storm outside didn't feel natural. They had to be the cause. I wasn't going to complain. If anyone knew how to move through snow and ice, they did.

"But he's alive," I said.

Meryl's brow dropped in concentration. "Joe says something's wrong. He says Murdock doesn't recognize him." She put a hand on my chest. "They're here."

The doors on the far side of the floor flew open with a gust of wind and snow. Four tall callies rushed in, half walking, half flying, their long white hair trailing into their flowing gray gowns. They carried Murdock with gnarled hands, clutching his arms and legs.

My head screamed as I left the protection of Meryl's shield. When the callies lowered him to the floor, I pulled him into my arms. His clothing was torn and soiled. Hat, gloves, shoes, and coat were gone. His lips were chalk blue and his skin cold and hard. I searched for a pulse. "I think he's got hypothermia. We have to get him to AvMem." I lifted my face to the nearest callie. "Can anyone fly the storm?"

Meryl knelt beside us and placed glowing hands on him. Her face dropped. "We don't have time, Grey. He's dying.

We need to get him warm now." She pulled off her cloak and wrapped it around us. "We need blankets or coats. Anything. Zev, we need a warm bath."

A callie leaned her aged face down. "The ice was in his heart."

I searched her cragged features. "Can you take the ice out?"

She shook her head. "I withdrew the cold, but I cannae warm it."

A ripple went through the crowd, and a large wash of essence came toward us. Out of the darkness walked a *jotunn*—a ten-foot-tall giant of a man. Without asking, he knelt and pulled Murdock from me. Cradling him in his arms like a child, he placed a wide hand on Murdock's chest. He rocked and hummed. A pool of warm, orange essence welled out of his hand. Joe fluttered down next to them, his pink essence mingling with the giant's and seeping into Murdock's chest.

Murdock convulsed. The *jotunn* held him closer and increased the cadence of his hum. The convulsions settled to a shiver. Murdock opened his mouth, heaving forward with a racking cough that scattered Joe into the air. The *jotunn* eased him to the floor.

Murdock looked around in a daze. "Is this hell?"

Joe swooped down and laughed. "Nah. That's two blocks up on the left. Don't order the chili."

I squeezed Murdock's shoulder. "It's okay. You're safe."

He frowned, pulling Meryl's cloak around him. "Where are my shoes?"

"You lost them somewhere," I said.

He struggled to his feet. Meryl grabbed his arm. "Take it easy. Let your body warm up."

"I want my shoes," he said.

"We'll find some, Leo. We have to get you to a hospital," I said.

"Take me home."

"Murdock, you need to see a doctor."

"I said take me home," he snapped.

I looked at Meryl. "What do you think?"

She stared at him. "He's okay. Let's take him home. We can talk about the hospital in the morning."

I held my hand out to the *jotunn*. "Thank you."

He touched his massive palm against mine and wandered into the darkness.

Zev stood alone near the bloodied, dangling chains. "Thank you, too, Zev."

He nodded. "Remember this, Grey. I helped you and the police. The solitaries are not the enemy."

"I never thought they were," I said. Someone found something for Murdock to wear on his feet, and we went back into the storm. The callies followed, shifting and swaying around us through the snow. Essence ringed us, a pale blue light that pressed the wind back. I don't know why the callies did it for us, but it made walking easier. Murdock tried to shake me off as I supported him, but a few steps later, he leaned on me without argument.

The snowplow sat where we had left it, the protection spell that Meryl had cast almost gone. We bundled inside, with Murdock in the middle. He wouldn't speak, just stared into the night sky. Meryl wheeled the truck around and drove toward South Boston.

"Take a left," Murdock said when we reached Broadway.

"Murdock, you live the other way," I said.

"Just take a left. Please," he said. I looked over his head at Meryl and nodded. She turned left. "Stop here," Murdock said after a few blocks. He gestured at me. "I need to get out."

"Murdock, you had hypothermia. I'm not letting you wander around in the storm."

Meryl peered out her window. "No, it's okay, Grey. Let him out."

I threw her a look like she was crazy. She pointed. In the blur of snow and wind, a brick building stood. I opened my door and helped Murdock out. As we walked around the truck, Meryl remained inside.

"Are you coming?" I called out.

Yeah, that's not going to happen. I'll wait here, she sent.

I put my arm around Murdock's shoulders and ushered him across the street. We walked into the hushed, silent warmth of St. Brigid's Church.

22

First thing in the morning, I called to check on Shay. The cops had let him go when Keeva showed up and confirmed he was human. He was more annoyed that a paramedic played cute with him but didn't follow through with a phone number. The kid killed me. With all the stuff he gets into, he still manages to roll with it.

Murdock didn't return my phone calls. I didn't like that, but I had probably been too insistent about taking him to Avalon Memorial. He hated doctors in general, and if he felt fine, he wanted no part of a hospital. That was his choice, and I had to let it go. That didn't mean I wasn't worried about him. Whether he liked it or not, I was going to check up on him.

Murdock's car was right where we'd left it the night before. I dug it out of a snowbank, which was a welcome respite from thinking about anything. Dig the shovel in. Toss the snow. Repeat. Nicely rhythmic and mindless.

Driving wasn't something I did. Living in cities all my life, there wasn't much need. Sure, a car was convenient, right up to the point when it was stolen or, worse, needed a parking spot. So, I didn't drive, and Murdock's car did nothing to elevate my desire to drive. It was a swamp of trash and papers in contrast to the orderliness of the rest of his life. I guessed he needed somewhere to release his inner slob.

The day after a major snowstorm in Boston was an exercise in dysfunction and denial. Cities, by definition, did not have acres of open space. Thousands of people lived cheek by jowl, sidewalks were narrow strips of concrete with little room for more than three people to walk abreast, and cars weren't tucked off the streets in driveways or garages. In short, snow had no place to go, shoveled or plowed.

Neighborhoods transformed into mazes, narrow paths along the sidewalks, streets turned into valleys between mountainous ridges, and between the two, snowed-in cars formed a barrier of snow and metal and ice. Snowplows left small hills at intersections to be taken away by front loaders. Shoveling out a parked car was an art in itself, the challenge of finding enough places to throw snow without burying someone else in. The day after a blizzard, the snow walls around a single parking space could rise four feet high.

As dawn broke, people grabbed their shovels, while others pretended the storm didn't happen and tried to go about their normal routines. The two sets clashed, some idiot tossing snow on some other idiot who could not care less he was in the way. The parking situation devolved into the haves and the have-nots, with the haves leaving their cars until the next warm day freed them or digging them out with great time and effort, while the have-nots either garaged their cars at exorbitant rates or stalked neighborhood side streets for an abandoned shoveled-out space. Which led to a winter peculiarity of Southie: the kitchen chair in the snow.

Finding a parking space took effort. Digging out a car took effort. When someone in Southie snagged a parking space before a storm and dug it out afterward, a certain ownership to the space evolved. A kitchen chair defined that ownership, perching in the vacated space while the temporary owner ran errands or went to work. The kitchen chair sent the message that someone else had put time and effort into clearing the space, not you. The cardinal rule was: You do not mess with someone's kitchen chair. Violators were subject to snow being shoveled back in, paint scratched, nasty notes, and, for the worst offenders, tires slashed. How long the shoveler maintained ownership was a gray area, but at some point, the kitchen chairs disappeared and the normal parking-space jockeying resumed. The city didn't approve, but a little anonymous dog feces on a windshield deterred whoever agreed with the municipal authorities.

East Broadway was an obstacle course of pedestrians, delivery vans, double-parked cars, and piles and piles of snow. Tempers flared as someone had the audacity to stop her car to allow someone else time to find the least-slush-filled path cross the street. Deliverymen frowned as they climbed over salt- and sand-caked snow. I took my time, unimpressed with the frustrations. People didn't seem bothered by a few decapitations up a few blocks. Not when something important was happening, like missing a yellow traffic light.

A sea of kitchen chairs lined the edges of K Street. I drove down the ice-slick lane until I reached the Murdock house. A thrill of victory and doubt ran through me as I pulled up. In front of the black-shuttered row house stood an empty space with no chair. The spaces in front and behind it were meticulously cleaned and chairless as well. I parallel-parked between the spaces and sat in the car, considering whether I was violating any neighborhood tradition. Three empty spaces in a row—with no chairs—in front of the police commissioner's house could not be a coincidence. K Street apparently had its own subset of unwritten rules. I turned off the engine and lifted a box from the passenger seat.

Salt on the shoveled sidewalk crunched under my boots as I walked up the short steps and rang the bell. A large Christmas wreath with small white bows hung on the door. The cement urn to one side was filled with greens and decorated presents.

Kevin Murdock, an earnest kid in his twenties and the youngest of the family, opened the door. Unlike the rest of his police brothers, he had joined the fire department. He was dressed in his day uniform, his dark hair cut in a buzz. "Hey, Connor . . ." He paused when he saw the car. His blue eyes met mine. "Did you actually drive that trash heap here?"

I grinned. "I've had all my shots."

He stepped back with the classic Murdock smirk. "Get inside before my dad yells about heating the neighborhood."

I wiped my feet on the mat. Row houses were long, narrow buildings, the rooms stacked one behind the other. In the front parlor, a Christmas tree took up the small space near the windows. The house smelled of evergreen and roasted meat.

Kevin gestured at the box. "Can I take that for you?"

I shook my head. "It's for Leo. Is he here?"

He pointed with his thumb at the ceiling. "He's in his room." He picked up a uniform overcoat. "I have to get back to work. Can you tell him to get his ass out of here and get to work like the rest of us?"

I looked up the stairs. "How's he doing?"

Kevin's smiled dropped. "He's okay, I think. A little shook-up. You know him, he doesn't say much, but I think he's okay. He won't tell me what happened."

I smiled. "Then I'll kick his ass out of here for you."

Kevin winked. "Thanks." He patted me hard on the shoulder. "Good to see you, Connor. Merry . . . um . . . holidays."

I laughed. "You, too."

Kevin was a good guy. As the baby of the family, the Murdocks doted on him. Leo was almost twenty years older, so they tended to have a more mentor/protégé relationship than simple brotherhood.

The rest of the Murdock men—Gerry, Bar, and Bernard—were local cops, and their sister Faith had gone the state police route. They all lived at home except Faith and Bernard, who had separate apartments not far away. The coming year looked interesting for them all, with the other Murdock sister, Grace, getting married, and Bernard deciding to run for city councilor. Politics and public service ran deep in the blood.

The commissioner's wife was gone, and while the impression I had was that she was dead, there was an underlying silence about her absence that hinted at tragedy. Despite the sisters, the house didn't have the feel of a woman's presence. It was very much the commissioner's.

Murdock's bedroom was on the second floor. Shifting the box to one hand, I knocked on the slightly ajar door.

"I'll be down in a bit, Kev. You don't need to keep checking on me," Murdock said.

I pushed the door open. "Not Kevin."

From his desk chair, Murdock gave me a tired smile. "Sorry. Kevin's been like an old-lady gnat all morning. Come on in."

He swiveled in the chair. Other than some darkness under his eyes, he looked fine, to the point of wearing his usual work attire—neatly pressed dark pants and a white collared shirt—sans tie. Papers from an open file on the desk were stacked neatly in a row. More files in file boxes lined the wall. All copies of case files.

I placed the box on the foot of the bed and took a side chair. "What are you working on?"

He rotated the chair. "Not really working. Reviewing the nanny case."

Several years ago, a young student from Europe summering in the United States was murdered. She was found in a dumpster, just her torso. The list of suspects was bizarre—a photographer, a panhandler, a rock musician, and a guy who walked his dog while dressed as Superman. The woman's complete remains were never found. Neither was her murderer. That Murdock would decide to read that case was no surprise. Every cop in the city wanted to know what happened to the nanny. "I can't believe I'm saying this, but I'd rather you read one of those romance novels you don't want anybody to know you read."

He smiled and jutted his chin at the box. "What's that?"

I flipped open the top. "This, my friend, was in my building vestibule this morning addressed to me. It's your coat, hat, and gun."

Murdock was on his feet and at the box in an instant. He grabbed the gun and checked it, spun the chambers and sniffed it. Relief washed over him. "It hasn't been fired."

"Neither has your bug," I said.

Murdock pulled the coat out and found the backup gun. Despite what I said, he checked it, too, then locked both guns in his nightstand. "That gives me one less hassle today. I was about to go to the station house and report them gone. What the hell is going on?"

"No one gives up a free gun in the Weird. Someone's being helpful."

He pursed his lips. "Do you think it was Zev's people?"

I shook my head. "That was my initial thought, but it's got Dead essence all over, several signatures."

He sat back in his chair. "That doesn't make sense. They're the ones that grabbed me."

"I don't think they meant to grab you, Murdock," I said. "Zev told me last night that only solitaries were swept up. The patrol officers who got snagged were returned almost immediately."

He swiveled slowly in his seat, then met my eyes. "I talked to one of the guys who was there last night. He said they were ordered to stand down and get off the street."

I frowned. "I can see pulling back if the crowd dispersed on its own, but getting off the street? Who the hell gave that order?"

Murdock glanced toward the door. "I'll find out."

He let the silence hang, his face troubled. Two people could have given the order: the senior officer on-site or the police commissioner. But with a couple of hundred angry solitaries out there, an officer on the street would not have made that call. Murdock removed a black shoe from the box. "They only found one shoe?"

"I guess. What's up with the shoes?" I asked.

He gave me a quizzical look. "What do you mean?"

"You were all upset about your shoes missing last night."

He shrugged. "I don't remember that."

I leaned forward. "What happened, Leo?"

He went to the window. "You drove my car here?"

I tossed him the keys. "The keys were in your coat, so I picked up the car on the way over. Don't change the subject."

He looked down in thought. "I don't think the Dead are really people, Connor. I've been thinking all morning that these Dead we're seeing are some sort of manifestation of our, I don't know, hopes? Fears? I don't think they're real."

"They felt pretty real when they tried to kill us in Tir-NaNog," I said.

He shook his head. "You know I don't understand all this essence stuff, but I've read enough about psychology to know it's possible to see—and feel—stuff that's not real. I've seen crowds panic for no reason except that one person did. Maybe between essence and the Taint and mass hysteria, these Dead folks aren't really there."

"Murdock, I saw you pulled into the air. You experienced it independently of me. How can we both hallucinate the same phenomenon that neither of us ever experienced before?"

He scratched the back of his head. "I don't know."

"I'm no psychologist, but maybe you're having some kind of denial reaction to what happened. Maybe you should talk to someone."

He frowned. "I know what happened, Connor. I don't need a shrink."

"If there's one thing I've seen you do when it comes to the fey, Leo, it's keep an open mind. This isn't like you."

He rubbed his hands against his thighs. "Maybe one Murdock mind is closing and another one is opening."

"I have no idea what that means," I said.

"My father is sleeping with Moira Cashel," he said.

I blinked several times. "Um . . . did hell just freeze over?" He shook his head. "Murdock, I do not believe your father is sleeping with a powerful druidess. He hates the fey."

Murdock snorted. "Sex and hypocrisy go hand in hand, don't they?"

I gnawed at my lower lip, thinking. "Still, your father? I can't wrap my head around it."

"He was evasive the other night. I got curious and followed him when he went out. I thought he was having dinner with her again. He went to a hotel in Burlington. She met him in the lobby, and they went upstairs. It didn't look like he stayed for dinner when he came out."

Burlington was a small town north of the city. Not the

place anyone would look for the Boston police commissioner or the High Queen's Herbalist. "What do you think
it means?"

He shook his head. "I can't even begin to guess."

"Why are you bringing this up? You still haven't said
what happened to you last night, Leo."

He looked out the window again. "Fine. I'll tell you, but
I want your word you won't tell anyone else."

"You don't even have to ask," I said.

He inhaled deeply and sighed. "A green light fell on me
like a wave. Something grabbed me and dragged me into
the air. I felt weightless, tumbling and falling, then rising
again. All kinds of people and strange animals surrounded
me, tossing me back and forth, laughing and screaming. I
thought I was losing my mind. I started to pray. There was
this loud shout, and someone threw me higher. Someone
else caught me. She wrapped her arms around me and held
me up. They say as you die, you see the people who went
before you, welcoming you to heaven."

Murdock paused, looking down at his hands. He frowned
and gazed out the window. "She looked like my mother,
Connor. The woman holding me looked like my mother."

My mind went blank. "Wow. I don't know what to say,
Murdock. You never talk about your mother."

He remained silent for so long, I thought he was going
to change the subject again. "She was killed in a traffic
accident after Kevin was born. My mother was Catholic,
Connor. We had a funeral mass. We buried her. What happened last night leaves me with two choices: Either everything that's been happening is fey essence manipulating
our minds, or everything I believe about God and heaven
and hell is a lie. I'm not going to lose my faith over this.
The one thing I do know? The moment I started praying,
the craziness stopped. I think God sent me a message to
help me keep my faith."

What do you say to someone who has a religious epiphany? It didn't happen? A few months earlier, I met a drys, which druids consider the manifestation of the power of the oak. A demigoddess. I couldn't say it didn't affect me profoundly, that my secular agnosticism wasn't rocked. But I still had my doubts. Reason told me the drys might be just another fey, an extremely rare and powerful one, but fey. Despite my rational mind, the faith I was raised in clouded the issue. I wanted to believe, dammit, but I still preferred to know.

I took a deep breath. "Murdock, I'm not going to disagree with you. That's the whole point of religion, isn't it? That we don't know? I've been asking myself those kinds of things all my life. If you found your answer, that's cool. I don't think my worldview and your faith are an either/or proposition, but maybe you're further along that path than me."

A subtle change settled over Murdock, a release of tension in his body, like maybe he had been thinking I was going to argue with him or didn't believe him. I didn't blame him. For one thing, I'm not shy about my opinions. For another, he probably couldn't help but feel defensive after telling me he thought God saved him from the crazy fey people.

His father was another matter. Leo and the commissioner might try to work out their differences on a lot of things, but the fey were something they would never agree on. Scott Murdock's odd interest in Moira Cashel had to do with more than sex. The question was, which of them was playing the other.

Murdock pulled some folder across his desk. "Let's review the file."

23

Murdock and I spent the remainder of the day alternately discussing why the Dead attacked the solitaries in such a strange manner and why Murdock wouldn't go to Avalon Memorial. Of the two topics, Murdock preferred the former and I the latter. Despite my acute sensing ability, I never had much ability in the healing arts. To my senses, Murdock seemed fine, but I worried. Our work partnership was getting to the point where Murdock's human nature put him at risk when working with the fey, and our friendship was making that harder for me to watch. I felt responsible for his strange acquisition of a body shield. I was afraid of what more might happen to him if I couldn't protect him better.

But Murdock was Murdock. I'd call him stubborn, but that would be disrespectable to what was really his resolve. He assessed situations and made decisions with firm resolution. As far as he was concerned, he was fine, he would be fine, and until something indicated otherwise, he would continue as he was. That didn't stop my anxiety about him. So, when I went home while Murdock went to check in at the station house, I called Briallen ab Gwyll, my childhood mentor and one of the finest healers in the fey world. Without argument, she agreed to an impromptu dinner with friends to see if my fears about Murdock had any foundation.

A light snow fell as I walked up Park Street to Beacon Hill. Against the early-evening sky, white lights glowed along the architectural trim of the old brick statehouse, its gold dome shining under spotlights. Along the edges of Boston Common, multicolored lights filled the branches of old elm trees. The scene had a classic New England charm, except for the darkness on top of the small hill where the war monument used to be, replaced now by a smooth granite pillar, a muted bone white finger against the night sky.

The pillar had once stood in the center of a giant circle of stones in TirNaNog. On Samhain, the pillar ripped through from the Land of Dead, and it remained after the veil between worlds closed. In the chaos of that night, trees were destroyed, leaving the top of the hill bare. Since then, gargoyles had gathered around the pillar.

The city granted the Guild jurisdiction over the site to figure out if it was dangerous. No one was allowed near it, especially fey who were not authorized. Another restriction. The citizen group that maintained the landscaping was pretty ticked off, too.

Briallen lived on Louisburg Square behind the statehouse. The exclusive address had its share of business executives and politicians who called it home. These days, I imagined that they were less than pleased to have a powerful druidess living in their midst. Screw 'em. Briallen had lived there since before most of them had been born and, if anything, kept the place safe from both human and fey shenanigans.

The brownstone let me in. My old partner, Dylan

macBain, was the only other person I knew whom Briallen had spelled free access through her door at any time, and he was supposed to be dead. In a way, I had grown up in Briallen's town house. Even though my family lived three miles away, I spent the majority of my teens on the third floor of her home. She was one part teacher, one part parent, and a big part friend. Even when my life fell apart, she stood by me. I knew she had put herself on the line more than once in my defense, especially lately.

"I'm in here," she called out, as I crossed the threshold.

I left my jacket on the hallstand and went to the kitchen. The wave of warmth from the stove brought the smell of stew. Briallen came out of the pantry with a stack of dishes. "You're early."

She hugged me, then stared into my eyes as she placed her hands on either side of my head. A warm sensation radiated from her palms. After Gillen Yor, Briallen was the most experienced healer in the city, if not the world. Her essence moved inside me, an intimacy I allowed no one else outside a hospital room. I had an uncomfortable memory flash of the *leanansidhe*.

Briallen feathered her essence along the edges of the dark mass in my mind. I winced as it flexed when she came too near, but it didn't react. Perhaps it knew I wasn't threatened by her touching. Perhaps it wasn't threatened, if it was that aware. Briallen withdrew and dropped her hands, rubbing my shoulders with a troubled smile.

"I thought you'd want to talk before the others got here," I said.

She turned away. "It's changed."

"I know."

She kept her back to me as she worked. "It's bigger. I think it's spreading."

"It is."

She didn't speak as she broke some greens for a salad. I

sat on a stool. She finished, wiped her hands with a towel, and held on to the edge of the counter. "Are you in pain?"

"Headaches. Sometimes it's worse."

I slid off the stool and hugged her from behind. She relaxed into me and let me hold her, then looked up at me. She pulled my head down and kissed my forehead. "Okay, enough maudlin. I'm frustrated because we can't figure out what it is. We will."

I smiled. "A little darkness never stopped Briallen ab Gwyll."

She recovered her usual self and pushed me away. "Damn right. Start slicing onions and tell me why you were at the Guildhouse."

Amused, I picked up a knife. I didn't think anything happened within a five-mile radius of Briallen without her knowing about it. "I was reporting a *leanansidhe* Murdock and I stumbled into."

She scrunched her nose. "Ick. I hate those."

Only Briallen would react to one of the most fearsome fey with an "ick." "Keeva said she'd try to get someone to look into it."

"She must be thrilled that Ryan's stepping in now that Nigel is leaving," she said.

"It's not official."

"Is that the official unofficial position that came out of your meeting with Nigel and Manus?" she asked.

I chuckled. "I knew you knew about that. Eagan won't name Ryan. At least, not yet. He wants to drive Ryan and Maeve crazy."

Briallen chuckled. "I enjoy that myself sometimes. In the meantime, stay away from the Guild, Connor. With Nigel gone, I'm the only ally you have left there, and I'm not there enough."

"I haven't thought of Nigel as an ally for months now," I said. Which was true. After I reached the age of majority, I trained with Nigel. He was my mentor and taskmaster. But when I lost my abilities, he abandoned me and took every opportunity since to ridicule me.

She tasted her stew. "He's run more interference than you know."

I scooped sliced onions into the salad bowl. "You mean lately? He tried to kill me last month, Briallen."

She arched her eyebrows. "I've seen news footage of that. Don't be too sure he wasn't putting on a show for witnesses. What happened to that leather jacket you were wearing, by the way? I haven't seen you with it since that night."

"I lost it when I accidentally destroyed TirNaNog."

She pursed her lips. "Pity. You looked quite handsome in it."

"We were talking about Nigel trying to hit me with a deadly essence strike."

Briallen moved the salad bowl to the island counter. "Look, Connor, you know that Nigel and I don't agree on everything, but I don't believe he would hurt you. In fact, if you think about it, his going to Tara will take Maeve's attention away from you."

"Tara? I heard Russia."

She leaned against the counter and sipped her wine. "Via Tara, of course. Trust me, Connor. Maeve isn't going to forget you anytime soon. Between her worries about the Taint and all the deaths here, you need to be careful."

"I'm not afraid of Maeve."

She lifted her chin and smiled. "Good. Just remember that not being afraid is not the same as poking a bear with a stick. Can you get the door?"

The doorbell rang. When I opened the door, Murdock and Meryl stood side by side, each holding a brown-papered bottle. Meryl stamped snow off her Doc Martens. "Guess who tried to give me a ticket for parking in an illegal parking space?"

I cocked my head out the door. "The guy who's parked at the fire hydrant?"

She mock-glowered at Murdock. "The very one. I mentioned it would be a shame if that hydrant broke in this cold weather."

She removed her full-length wool coat. Murdock and I smiled at the same time. Meryl wore a black leather top with long lace sleeves, a short black wool skirt, and fishnet stockings. She caught our expressions and looked down at herself. "What? Are the stockings too much? I wore the violet ones because the pink looked kinda trampy for dinner."

I smirked. "They look fine."

"More than fine," said Murdock.

She rolled her eyes. "Children."

"Hey, you wore 'em. Don't complain if we look," I said.

She took her bottle back, and we followed her into the kitchen. Meryl hopped on a stool and said hello. Briallen, I noticed, barely acknowledged her. The two of them disagreed about things I wasn't privy to. Sometimes I thought it was druidic politics. Sometimes it seemed something more.

Murdock handed Briallen the bottle of wine. She placed it on the counter next to Meryl's. "You look well, Leonard."

"Thank you, Ms. Gwyll. You like French wines, if I remember."

She smiled and brushed her hand down his arm. "Charmer."

She handed off the bottle to me. "If you could do the honors."

Murdock and Meryl teased each other about their parking skills while I hunted down the corkscrew. Briallen laid out the salad bowls, and we took seats around the kitchen island. I poured the wine. I may like my Guinness, but a glass of wine in Briallen's kitchen brought back pleasant memories from my younger days.

Murdock made a curious face as he chewed. "What's this dressing?"

"Vinaigrette, mostly, with a few special things thrown in," Briallen said.

"Don't ask the definition of 'special things,'" I said. Briallen poked my hand with her fork.

Murdock chuckled. "I never know what I'm eating around you people."

Meryl poured herself another glass of wine and leaned on her elbows. "So, Murdock, I heard you're knockin' boots with someone."

Murdock choked in surprise. "Why is everyone so interested in my love life?"

Meryl's eyebrows went up. "Ohhhh! Love life? No one said anything about love."

He twisted his lips in a smirk. "Are we talking about you, now?"

Meryl smiled as she sipped her wine. "No changing the subject."

He shrugged. "All I'm saying is there's a lot of scuffed boots at this table, and they're not mine."

Briallen's brow went down slightly as she parsed his meaning. The on-again, off-again, on-again thing Meryl and I had going was not something I discussed with her. "Hey, isn't this snow crazy?" I said to change the subject.

Briallen nodded as she brought stew to the table. "That was *cailleacha* work if I ever saw it. They stayed away from here, though."

"Maybe they haven't decided whose side they're on yet," I said.

"The solitaries," said Meryl, around a mouthful of salad.

"Oh?" I asked.

She nodded. "They caused the storm. Zev got word that the Dead were going to attack, so he asked the callies to provide some resistance."

"I guess it didn't work," I said.

"It could have been worse," Meryl said quietly.

We avoided looking at Murdock.

"Jark's been released," he said.

I didn't expect that. "How? I thought you said you could hold him?"

Murdock poured himself more wine. "Someone put the word out to let him go. The Dead's legal status is messed up, and the city's afraid of lawsuits."

Briallen shook her head in exasperation. "That whole situation down in the Weird is getting out of hand. It's neglect."

I dropped my fork and clutched my chest melodramatically. "Finally, Briallen ab Gwyll agrees with me."

She wrinkled her nose at me. "It's not your issue to agree or disagree with, Connor. I never said the Guild deals with the Weird appropriately. I said you let it annoy you too much. I've lived a long, long time. There's always a Weird of some kind, and neglect is always the reason it exists."

"So you just accept its existence?" Murdock asked.

She gave a noncommittal shrug. "Not per se. It's a problem to be managed. Acknowledging that it can't be eliminated isn't the same thing as allowing it to flourish or degrade."

"So how would you manage it, Briallen?" Meryl asked.

Their eyes met for a fraction of a second. I knew Meryl well enough to know her flat tone was about disagreement and challenge, like I knew that Briallen's habit of making eye contact then breaking it was a sign of disagreement and dismissal. "By getting people talking to each other," Briallen said.

"In other words, let other people fix it," Meryl said.

Murdock and I threw wary glances at each other. The firmness of their responses was feeling a lot like a prelude to an argument. My idea for us all to have dinner with Briallen was on the brink of spinning out of control. As I tried to think of a way to redirect the conversation, Briallen surprised me by laughing. "You're right, Meryl. It's never been my nature to step in and solve problems. Maybe I'm a bit selfish that way. No one ever tries to solve mine."

Meryl's lips twitched into a smile, and she nodded in acquiescence. "Been there, baby."

"Hey! I think I've helped both of you a few times." They turned their heads and stared at me, that stare that women have like the calm before a storm. "What?"

Meryl leaned over and placed her hand on mine. "Grey? When you make a mess and someone else starts to clean it up and you show up at the eleventh hour to help? You're not really solving someone else's problem."

Murdock hooted. Like an owl, hooted. I glowered at him. "I'm taking that as betrayal of the unwritten male code of brotherhood."

He held his hands up. "Hey, there's an escape clause that says I can get out of the way when a guy pisses off two women at the same time."

I tossed my napkin on the table and crossed my arms. "I hate everybody."

Briallen grinned as she stood and placed both hands on Murdock's shoulders. Meryl narrowed her eyes, then looked at me suspiciously.

"Leonard, why don't you take poor, misunderstood Connor upstairs, and he can make us all drinks?" Briallen asked.

"My pleasure," he said.

We left them in the kitchen and went up to the second-floor parlor. Briallen used the room as a study. When I was a kid, I used to find her sitting by the blue fire that always burned in the fireplace, reading books in languages I didn't know or standing at the window thinking. Next to the window, a small table held glasses and liquor bottles, mostly ports and liqueurs. I flipped some glasses up and sorted through the bottles while Murdock dropped in a chair.

"I'm beat," he said.

I found the always reliable Jameson's and poured a glass. "How'd things go at the station house?"

He shrugged. "It was fine. No one knew I had lost my gun, so I didn't have to deal with that. I told Ruiz I had a headache in the morning, but it was better."

Ruiz was captain of Area B, which covered the Weird. I didn't envy the man having the police commissioner's son on his team, more than one of them, actually. "You lied? That's not like you."

Another shrug. "No one knew what really happened. It would have been a lot of red tape if I gave a full report. It's over. No harm, no foul."

"I told Keeva you went missing," I said.

"Yeah, the old man told me she called. I told him you and I got separated in the storm is all," he said.

I turned back to the table to cover my frown. Murdock was by-the-book. Pragmatic, but he bent rules more than he broke them. "What do you want to drink?" I asked.

"Do you think Briallen has any Guinness?"

"I was thinking maybe we should run down Jark later, see if he has anything new to say," I said.

"And?"

Surprised again, I looked at him. "I thought you didn't like to drink if you were going to be working?"

He smiled. "It's one beer, Connor. That dinner deserves a nice finish."

Briallen was a good cook. "I'll see what she has."

I slowly descended the stairs, trying to decide if I should

be worried about his behavior. Murdock was calm, steady. Honest. The irony that I was worried he was acting more like me wasn't lost on me. Voices from the kitchen caught my ear. I paused on the last step.

"I said maybe you're spending too much time with him, not to avoid him," Briallen said.

"I know what I'm doing," Meryl said.

"I'm concerned," Briallen said.

"And I'm not. It's different this time."

"Do you remember something?" Briallen asked.

"Do you?" Meryl responded.

A long pause followed. The longer it lasted, the more likely one of them would sense me, so I entered the kitchen. "Remember what?"

Meryl shifted on her stool. "What?"

"I thought I heard Briallen ask you if you remembered something," I said.

She waved her hand and picked up her wineglass. "Oh, it's nothing. Briallen and I refuse to tell each other how much we remember of Faerie."

I covered my curiosity by opening the fridge. "I thought you didn't remember any of it."

The fey—the Old Ones—who lived in Faerie before Convergence over a hundred years ago remembered a world far different than the modern one. People like Maeve and Donor wanted to get back to it at all costs. The here-born like me, born after Convergence and never knew the place, were sometimes ambivalent about it. I wasn't, though. I didn't care at all.

Meryl chuckled. "Nice try, Grey."

I faced her with two Guinnesses. "Can't blame me for trying."

Meryl won't tell me if she's an Old One or not. When the fey came through to this reality, their memories were damaged. Some didn't remember who they were. Others didn't remember anyone else. No one remembered what caused Convergence. If Meryl was an Old One, I was having sex with a centenarian. When I thought about it, I waffled between whether that was cool or creepy.

"And Briallen keeps trying, too," Meryl said. "Until she tells me what she knows, I ain't tellin' what I know—*if* I know."

Briallen leaned back against the sink and shook her head. "I know more than she wants to believe."

Meryl smirked. "Back at ya, Bree. For instance, what's the little game you're playing with Murdock?"

Briallen looked at me. "I told you that you shouldn't have invited her."

I shrugged. "He would have been suspicious otherwise."

Meryl waved her hands above her head. "Okay, I'm still here and still want to know what's going on. You weren't very subtle about it, Briallen. That last bit with the hands on his shoulders lit him up like a candle."

"He won't go to AvMem or New England Medical, so I asked Briallen to check him out," I said.

Meryl arched an eyebrow. "And?"

Briallen smiled. "He's in perfect health. Extraordinary health for a human."

I put my arm around Meryl. "I'll be your best friend if you keep this to yourself."

She slipped out from under my arm. "Oh, happy me. Just so you know, Grey, I have my own gynecologist, so don't go doing me any favors."

She walked out, shaking her head.

Briallen pursed her lips. "Are you going to tell him?"

"Not tonight. Eventually."

"And what about you? When was the last time you went to see Gillen?"

"He can't do anything, Briallen. If he had any new ideas, he would have called. He hasn't," I said.

She stared at her foot as she scuffed at the floor. "Within the Wheel are many paths, but only you can find the one you need."

I wanted to tell her about the *leanansidhe*, but she wouldn't approve. Whatever the dark mass was in my head, it was beyond Briallen's knowledge and skill. She'd be concerned if I told her about using the *leanansidhe* to figure it out. Actually, she'd be afraid. I certainly was. But the normal path wasn't helping me, and where I needed to go was not a place Briallen would approve. "And if I don't find my path, it will find me. That's how you taught me the Wheel works."

She caressed my cheek. "It's nice to know you listened occasionally."

I kissed her on the forehead. "Don't worry so much. Things work out eventually. Let's get upstairs before Meryl convinces Murdock to plant whoopee cushions for us."

24

After-dinner drinks wound into the early-morning hours. For a brief time—too brief—the events of the world outside Briallen's second-floor parlor faded behind the softly falling snow. The four of us sat before the blue-flamed fire, laughing and at ease with each other as we talked into the night. Beer and wine and liqueurs flowed, loosening tongues and relaxing muscles. To be trite, it was nice. Nice in the way nostalgia colored our memories or the way a day felt hung in suspension when all the chores and errands were done and there was nothing left to do but curl up and do nothing of consequence. It had been a long time since I'd had the feeling, had it and appreciated it.

But all such times end, time and energy taking its toll, nudging us back to activity and to life. We made our good-byes with smiles and reluctance and ventured into the night. Meryl drove off alone, determined to get some sleep before an early morning at the Guildhouse. Murdock and I, though, decided to make a short pit stop before he dropped me off. A good meal, good drink, and good conversations were great ways to spend an evening, but after a while, memories of murder and unanswered, lingering questions crept back into our minds. It was a good time to visit the Dead.

Murdock pulled up near the old Helmet. The side street off Old Northern was far enough out from the Tangle that the nasty stew of essence down there didn't muck with my head. Panels of cheap plywood painted black hid the original facade of the building, and hundreds of silver or rusted staples littered the surface, the remains of long-gone posters. Weathered advertisements for band dates, club contests, and local services lingered long past their relevant dates. The pitted metal sign above the door bore the ghost image of the last three letters someone had removed from the old bar's name.

We attracted significant looks and stares when we entered. In TirNaNog, if one of the Dead killed a living person, they absorbed the living body essence—the basic life spark—and escaped back into the world. A sort of Get Out of Jail Free card for the afterlife. On this side of the veil, the rules had changed. When the Dead killed someone living here, they didn't return to life. Their essence didn't change. The victim, though, ended up very much dead.

Hel didn't look different from when it was Helmet. Lighting in the wide, square dive ran to blue spots and a flashing dance floor, the better to distract people from seeing much. When the bar was Helmet, the faint odor of damp bodies in cramped spaces permeated an atmosphere of heady sex and drugs. It was amusing to watch who went home with whom at last call.

The change of clientele didn't change the look. Hel even played the same loud dance music, but the new patrons had that sharper edge of menace the Weird was too well-known for. Nobody danced, probably because they had no idea what to make of modern music. Being Dead made it tough to keep up with the latest dance trends.

The most visible change was that everyone was Dead. It was inevitable they'd find a place to gather. That's what bars were for, to bring together the like and like-minded, people who wanted to hang out with others with a shared sensibility, drink, or get laid. Being Dead didn't change any of that. In fact, the Dead had a higher appetite for everything. They all seemed to know each other, definitely drank more than average, and I wouldn't want to compare notes on dating with them. Take away the risk of dying, and everyone was willing to try anything and more of it. Of course, they still got killed, but what was a mortal wound if you woke up fine the next day?

Murdock and I grew up in a city that had embraced the fey to an extent. I didn't think twice when the people around me had wings or pointed ears. The scary solitaries gave everyone pause, but that was the point. Individually, solitaries were odd-looking, misshapen, and unattractive by mainstream standards, but the rest of the fey didn't raise an eyebrow. Until I saw these solitaries who were Dead clustered in a dark bar wearing outdated clothes bordering on costumes, sporting jewelry that went out of fashion centuries ago, and displaying a penchant for physicality not much admired in our more enlightened times.

"Is this job ever going to get easier?" Murdock asked.

"Now what would be the fun in that?" I said.

We eased our way through the crowd. I ordered beer for me and water for Murdock. In bottles. From the end of the bar, we had a clear view of the goings-on. The novelty of our presence wore off among those who had noticed us, and they returned their attention to whatever they were doing before we arrived. For all their strangeness, the Dead acted like anyone else in a bar—laughing, glowering, cruising, drinking, and arguing. Except dancing. Still no dancing.

A woman, a Teutonic norn, leaned over and ordered a drink at the bar. A Dead norn. When druids and dwarves read the future through scrying and dreams, they see patterns and events on a grand scale. A norn's ability sensed what was and what was to be on a more individual level. Our eyes met, then she indifferently watched the front of the bar. The bartender set a plastic cup by her hand. She sipped through the stirrer, staring at us. Her wide brown eyes slid from me to Murdock. "You don't belong here."

Murdock cracked a smile. "Said the Dead girl."

She narrowed her eyes at him, looked at me. "I remember you."

Not the first time I've heard that in a bar. By her dated clothing, the odds that Murdock or I had known her in life were slim. I decided to be polite. "Then you have me at an advantage."

"I saw you in Niflheim."

Niflheim was the Teutonic perception of TirNaNog. I searched my memory, trying to place her, but came up empty. I had spent my time in TirNaNog running away from the Dead and trying not to get Dead myself. Not a lot of time to socialize. "I'm sorry. I don't remember you. I was kinda busy."

Her eyes visibly dilated as she stared. "You're like me. You touch the Wheel."

Murdock and I exchanged glances. He knew what the Wheel of the World was. He got that it was about faith and destiny, but he couldn't bring himself to remove his Catholicism from the concept. Where the fey see a world that Is, Murdock sees the hand of God, especially after the previous night.

"We all touch the Wheel," I said.

She feathered essence over me, and my body shields activated. They were too damaged to protect me from anything, but the norn wasn't attacking. She was curious. I winced as the dark mass clenched. Its rejection of the seers apparently wasn't limited to scrying.

She paled and backed away. "I see no path for you, druid."

"I'm trying to find one," I said.

"Everyone has a path, even if they cannot see it. A norn sees what others can't. If you have no path, druid, that bodes ill for you and everything you touch."

I sipped my beer. "Thanks. I'll update my will."

"What was that all about?" Murdock asked.

"Norns see personal futures. She basically told me I had none."

The crowd shifted, and Jark's vibrant red-orange signature registered nearby. I spotted him sitting in a dark corner. I nudged Murdock. "Let's try not to provoke him any more than we have to. Keep a weapon accessible, though."

Murdock unbuttoned his coat. "Most definitely in here."

Jark held court at a crowded table. He pretended not to notice us, though with all the sendings fluttering around, someone had to have warned him the law was there. The conversation stopped as we sat. The onlookers watched curiously, their eyes shifting from us to Jark and back again. Jark's smile rippled the scars on the side of his face. He lifted a pint of beer and drank half in a gulp, landing the glass hard on the table. He wiped a gray-streaked beard. "What brings you to this place?"

"You can speak English," I said.

He snorted. "The plain of Niflheim holds many men from many places."

"You didn't mention that at the morgue," I said.

"You didn't ask," he said.

"You said the Hound killed you," I said.

The crowd around us shifted. People stepped back or moved away completely. Jark downed a long draft of his beer. "And yet you have not hunted him down."

"Funny thing about that. We heard you're afraid of the Hound," Murdock said.

Jark snorted. "Then you're hearing wrong. Me afraid of the Hound? That's a lie. The Hound hunts the Dead like a snake. He has no honor. He lurks in the shadows and strikes out of cowardice. I don't fear men who won't face me in a fight."

Jark reached for his beer again, and Murdock pulled it away. "Wrong, Jark? Wrong like you admitting you killed Sekka and here you are drinking a beer? Or wrong like you were lying when you said that Sekka killed you?"

Jark lowered his chin and stared. "I would watch your tongue. No one calls Jark a liar."

By Murdock's flat stare, I knew he was about to explode, but antagonizing a berserker was not the way to go. I leaned between the two of them. "We seem to have some wrong information, then, Jark. Maybe you can clear up—"

Murdock interrupted me. "I'm calling you a liar."

Jark glowered. "I said watch your tongue, whelp. You don't know who you're dealing with."

A smile twitched in the corner of Murdock's mouth. "Did you just threaten me?"

Jark drew himself up and puffed out his chest. "I will do more than threaten you, you impudent dog, I will . . ."

Jark didn't get to finish. Murdock's body shield flickered on as he yanked the table out of the way. Jark rocked back in his chair with his hands in the air, the sudden exposure as comical as the surprise on his face. He obviously wasn't used to anyone coming back at him. Murdock grabbed him by his tunic and slammed him against the wall.

Murdock pressed his face in close. "You will *what*?"

Jark struggled, color draining from his face at the realization that the human he called an impudent dog was strong enough to pin a berserker to a wall. "I will have your head for this."

Murdock shook him like a doll. "Really? I'd like to see that. You didn't seem so tough when I beat you down at the morgue. Remember, my friend, if the law doesn't recognize what you guys do, it doesn't recognize what happens to you either. I'm going to tell you this once more. I want the Dead to stop hunting the solitaries. If they don't, I'm coming back for you, Jark, and I'm going to rip your worthless head off again, only this time I'll make sure it gets washed out to sea."

Murdock flung him to the floor. "If one more person dies, start looking over your shoulder."

He straightened his jacket and strode away through the crowd. No one stopped him. Everything had happened so fast, I was amused to find myself still in my chair with my beer in my hand. I chugged the rest of my bottle as Jark sat up. I leaned forward, elbows on my knees, twirling the bottle with two fingers, scanning the crowd. I tossed the empty bottle at Jark, and he batted it away. "I suggest you take his advice. You don't want to make him angry."

I followed in Murdock's wake, enjoying the stunned and fearful looks on the customers' faces. I couldn't blame them. After what Murdock did, I didn't want to see him angry either. He waited in his car by a handicapped ramp. I got in, and he gunned it into the street. "That was impressively ballsy, sir. Did you miss the part where I suggested not provoking him?"

Murdock stared out the window. His body shield flickered as he restrained his anger. "I don't know how things work in Dead People Land, but I'll be damned if I let anyone talk to a cop like that."

"Pull over. This guy's going to rabbit," I said.

"You think he's going to run somewhere?" He glanced in the rearview mirror and made a U-turn on Northern Avenue

I rolled my head toward him. "Leo, you just took down a berserker without breaking a sweat. He is angry right now and wants to do something about what just happened. We need Joe. Do you have any glow bees on you?"

He pulled a small bottle out of his inside coat pocket and held it out to me. Two motes of yellow light danced inside. It was bad enough I couldn't do sendings anymore, but even something as simple as a glow bee didn't work for me. I was able to imprint messages, but they took forever to reach their destination. Humans used them because they were a fey thing and fun, but weak essence made cell phones a faster option. But Murdock didn't have a simple human body essence anymore.

I waved away the bottle. "Your essence is stronger than mine."

He popped the lid and rolled one of the motes onto his palm. Curling his fingers over it, he cupped his hand to his mouth. "Stinkwort, corner of Tide and Oh No. Now, if you can."

Hearing Murdock use Joe's real name sounded odd. But no matter Joe's preference, his real name had an intrinsic connection to him, and that connection was what made a glow bee work. Murdock opened his palm. The glow bee rose, danced in the air, then shot through the windshield. I tried not to feel jealous when pink light flashed in the backseat. A strong odor of alcohol wafted over the seat.

Joe stood on the console, unsteady on his feet. "What's goin' on? You boys got something you can't handle?"

"Hey, Joe. We need you to follow someone," I said.

He put a tough look on his face, then nodded so hard, he lost his balance. He fell face-first into the police radio, hovered up, and hit his head against the rearview mirror. Grabbing the dashboard on the way down pivoted him into the glove compartment. He held a hand out to steady himself. "I'm okay, I'm okay. The seat's a little icy."

"Do you remember the Dead guy from the headworks?" I asked.

He nodded. "Sure, sure. The dead Dead guy without the head in the headworks. I never forget a face."

"He didn't have a face then," I said.

He grinned. "Right, right. I never forget a neck stump either."

I shook my head. "He has his head back, and he's reanimated. Can you track him?"

Joe's eyes lit up. "No problem! Those walking Dead guys stick out like a sore thumb."

"Last we saw him, he was in Hel."

Joe pulled a long face, his eyebrows dropping low. "I thought you destroyed Hel."

"The old Helmet, Joe. Just up the street. And for the record, we don't know if I destroyed Hel," I said.

Joe cocked his head at Murdock and pointed his thumb at me. "I don't know how you understand this guy."

Joe blinked out. Murdock chuckled silently. At least Joe made him lighten up. "Is he too drunk for this?" Murdock asked.

"Nah. He's not even over his threshold capacity yet," I said.

Got him. Drydock Ave, Joe sent.

Murdock pulled onto the street. "Nice work, Mr. Grey."

We turned down Tide Street again, passing Hel. A few people huddled outside smoking and talking. Murdock eased the car to the corner of Drydock Avenue. We faced the Black Falcon terminal, a massive building two thousand feet long. Cruise liners with a few hundred thousand passengers a year calling on the port of Boston docked at the terminal in one of the worst neighborhoods of the city. They never learned that, though. The Chamber of Commerce made sure shuttles and taxis whisked them directly to downtown without their having to soil their experience by seeing the immediate area.

He's crossing to the channel.

Mountains of snow lined either side of Drydock. Traffic down there in the middle of the night was rare. I pointed out Jark's unmistakable figure as he crossed the parking lot in front of the terminal and disappeared behind the building. Murdock drove down the street and stopped before we reached the access road. "Everything's wide open from here. He'll spot us if I make the turn."

He stopped on the dock. I don't see anyone else.

"He's meeting someone," I said.

You know, I'm burning alcohol here.

"Just so you know, Joe's going to make us buy him drinks," I said.

"It'll be worth it if we can stop the Dead," Murdock said.

"Famous last words, my friend. I've seen him drink."

Car coming . . . black one . . . it's stopping, and your guy got in.

Joe flashed into sight between us. "Damn, it's cold out there. I'm sober again."

I looked at Murdock. "I think that's a hint."

"Did you see inside the car, Joe?" Murdock asked.

He shook his head. "You want me to pop in and say hello?"

"Get as close as you can without being seen," Murdock said

"This is sure making me thirsty," he said, and vanished again.

"Oh, yes, this is going to be expensive," I said.

Okay, I'm under the car . . . It's warmer and less windy . . . I'm getting the berserker and a human . . . oh, hey!

Joe reappeared, annoyance across his face. "Okay, what's the joke?"

I twisted in my seat. "What joke?"

"Why'd you pull me out of the bar to spy on the commissioner?"

I shifted my gaze to Murdock. He clenched his jaw. "What did you say?"

The annoyance vanished from Joe's face as he picked up on the threat of anger in Murdock's voice. "Murdock, your father's in that car. This isn't a joke?"

Murdock gripped the steering wheel, glaring out the window. He cleared his throat. "Joe, I want to know the minute Jark gets out of that car."

Joe looked at me in a panic. I nodded, and he disappeared.

"Leo—" I said.

"Don't talk," he interrupted.

I closed my mouth so quickly, I heard my jaw snap. Murdock's essence flickered a deep crimson. His face looked like stone as he stared up the access road. I don't think I have ever felt more uncomfortable in his presence.

"We don't know what this is, Leo," I said quietly. And we didn't. As much as the commissioner didn't like me and I didn't like him, he was still Leo's father. He wasn't above bending the rules, and when it came to the fey, he enjoyed it. But I wasn't ready to make the leap to something more sinister, not without more information. Police used shadowy operatives for information all the time.

He's leaving, Joe sent.

"Get out, Connor," Murdock said.

"Leo, let's leave. You can talk to him later."

"Don't make me ask again, please."

His tone sent a chill down my spine. I opened the door as Joe appeared in the backseat. Apprehensive, he fluttered out the door. I leaned in again. "Call me, Leo." He didn't say anything. "Dammit, Leo, I'm only leaving because it's your da. Say you'll call me."

He didn't look at me. "I'll call you."

He pulled away and picked up speed as he turned onto the access road.

"Come on, Joe. Let's go get a drink," I said.

Before we walked away, Jark reappeared and watched

Murdock pass him. He lingered on the corner, then continued toward me. Behind him, the commissioner's car passed through the intersection, and Murdock followed it.

"What the hell is going on?" Joe said.

"I have no idea anymore," I said.

Jark stopped a few feet from me. "You made a mistake following me."

Joe hovered close to my shoulder, his hand gripped to his side where he hid his sword behind a glamour. "I don't think so," I said.

His gaze shifted to Joe. "Do you think that little thing can stop me from breaking your neck?"

The dark mass in my head shifted like a hand flexing its fingers. It hurt, but in an oddly pleasurable way. I stepped closer to Jark. "Who says I need him?"

Joe moved forward. "Connor . . ."

I held my hand up without taking my eyes off Jark. The dark mass shifted inside me, a warm flush spreading down to my right hand, a burning sensation that kicked my adrenaline into gear. "It's okay, Joe. This could be interesting."

Joe swung around behind me as Jark and I stared at each other. Despite knowing I was no physical match for a berserker, I wanted to wipe the sneer off his face the way Murdock had. The darkness pressed at me and made me feel it would be there at the right moment. I believed it, even if I didn't know why. I wanted to hurt Jark.

Wind whipped with a low groan around the corner of the terminal. Jark's body shields shimmered with deep green and oil-like swirls of black from his Taint infection. A part of my brain observed him change as he tapped his essence, the warning sign that he was going to go full berserker. Even without that, he was big enough to crush me without much effort. I wasn't afraid. More than that—I didn't care. The dark thing in my head prickled down my neck. It wanted Jark, too, and I wanted to see it happen. I lifted my right hand, palm up. A dark spot formed there, a black stain that spread across my skin. "Come on, Jark. Let's see what you've got."

His body flexed and grew as he set his feet in a fighting stance and clenched his fists. A growl sounded behind me, a feral threat I had never heard before from Joe. He landed on my neck and straddled my shoulder, his sword a thin blue flame in his hand.

Jark hesitated, with a look of fear. He stepped back.

With my hand held out, I took a step. "Not so sure of yourself all of sudden, Jark? Are you afraid? Murdock gave you one surprise tonight. Are you ready for another?"

He paled as a familiar essence resolved in place behind me. Uno padded in front of me, hackles up, his teeth bared in a snarl. He pressed Jark back, and they paced each other, step for step, as Jark kept his distance.

The darkness retracted. I shook my head to clear it, like I had awakened from a dream. An odd sensation of disappointment swept over me as Uno stood between me and Jark. The heat inside me subsided. I had no idea what I was thinking. I wasn't going to fight Jark. Even if the dark mass could be controlled, I sure as hell didn't know how to do it, no matter how much it wanted out.

Uno howled. It wasn't directed at me, but chills ran up my arm anyway. The dark thing in my head withdrew, like a predator disappointed its prey was escaping. Uno crouched. Jark shouted, more an involuntary yelp, and ran toward the channel. Uno followed for a few feet, then stopped and barked at Jark's retreating back. He turned and loped toward me.

Joe yanked on my collar as he hovered up. "Let's go! Let's go!"

I pushed him away. "It's okay, Joe."

He grappled with my hand. "Don't you know what that is?"

Uno sat in the snow and sniffed the air. With a soft huff, he ducked to scratch his nose on the ground. He lifted his head, snow speckling his dark muzzle. He was suddenly the least threatening hellhound on the planet.

"It's okay, Joe. I'd like you to meet Uno."

Uno jumped and put his massive paws on my shoulders, woofing at Joe as if he understood what I said. I staggered under the weight as I dug my fingers into his thick fur and scratched.

A terrified smile froze on Joe's face. He laughed nervously. With a flat, stiff hand, he patted Uno on the head. "Nice doggie."

Uno dropped and rolled in the snow. I stared down the access road. Jark was nowhere to be seen. Murdock promised he'd call, and I had to let him play this out his way. I balled my hands in my pockets and started walking.

Joe fluttered around me. "That was kinda awesome. You should keep that dog. I mean, as long as it doesn't suck your soul or something."

"I can barely keep you in Oreos, Joe. I don't think a dog would be a good idea for me."

"Still. You could take it for walks and people would talk to you and be friendly and pretend not to notice you're holding a bag of shite when you run into them. It's a very civilized thing to have a dog."

"I don't think he's that kind of dog, Joe. Let's go find a drink."

Joe flew around in front of me, throwing looks back at Uno. "Yeah, I need about a dozen."

25

In the cold of the empty street, I swayed in front of the warehouse door. The yellow crime-scene tape across it fluttered and shivered in the wake of small puffs of wind, slashes of color across the entrance that warned people off at the same time they lured me closer. A feeling had been building in me all night as Joe and I drank. I had known him all my life, but there were tales I didn't know about him. Dark ones that he hinted at in ominous yet nonchalant tones. He had done things he didn't like to talk about but managed to accept them as part of his history. Whatever those acts were, somehow he remained content with who he was and happy to move on. I wasn't at the point with myself yet. Certainly not tonight, on a bleak stretch of road where I found myself after leaving Joe snoring in a pretzel bowl.

Two kinds of people walked the streets of the Weird in the middle of the night: those up to no good thing and those down to one last thing. Both had the tinge of desperation about them that drove the need and desire to go out in the darkness and accomplish whatever deed necessary to satisfy them. Standing in front of a warehouse door with crime-scene tape across it, I wasn't sure which category I fell in. It was easy to rationalize that my motivations were good, which allowed me to slice open the tape and push open the door. It was equally true that I was breaking the law. Which brought me to that one last thing—I didn't think had a choice.

When I'd faced Jark down by the harbor terminal, I wanted to hurt him. Not hurt him as the side effect of stopping him from committing a crime or hurt him in the process of stopping a fight. I wanted to hurt him for the sake of hurting him. No matter how much I tried to rationalize it, I wanted to hurt him for the pleasure of it. I didn't know if it was me, though. I didn't know if on some suppressed animal brain level I wanted to hurt him, and the dark mass exposed that baser instinct, or if the dark mass, for its own reasons, wanted to hurt him and use me as its instrument.

I had to know. I had to go back to the one person who might have that answer.

The *leanansidhe*'s chamber reflected her sad and solitary life. Dust caked in dark gray on surfaces that weren't touched. Dirt was tracked everywhere, the side effect of living underground and the *leanansidhe*'s indifference to it. The glass lamp's shade speckled the nearby furniture in golds and red. A jumbled assortment of blankets layered a bed in the corner. The stale air held the electric whiff thrown off by a small heater running full blast by the side chair.

The *leanansidhe* had gathered mundane ephemera throughout the room—a bowl of key chains, a box of gloves, stacks of playing cards. They were either trophies of her kills or the by-products of an obsessive-compulsive mind. Haphazard stacks of books covered three tables. No common theme ran through the titles, everything from pulp

detective novels from the 1950s to studies of irrigation sys-
tems in the Midwest. They seemed collected for the sake
of collecting, many soiled with dirt or blood, their pages
swollen from old moisture.

Forlorn. That was the overall impression. The nature of
her existence was depressing. We all played the hand we're
dealt, but when that hand made you a murderer and you
had a modicum of conscious mind, it had to weigh on you.
If it didn't, that made you something less than humane.

Her essence permeated the room, probably the only
place she allowed it to remain, but nothing indicated anything more than a hideout. A lair. The room had a distinct
lack of feyness. No grimoires or spell references, no major
ward stones. Not even a stray wand. It was as if her entire
life was about hiding, with no interest beyond that.

I sat in the same chair that I had the other night and
flipped through a well-thumbed decorating magazine by
the armchair, imagined her poring over it, wondering about
sun-filled windows and flower-stuffed vases. Was she envi-
ous? Perplexed? Or was it a safe way of understanding the
living environment of her prey? Studying their habitat in
order to set a trap for them?

She was watching, I knew. When you fear being killed
in your sleep, you made arrangements to protect yourself. I
didn't have wards all over my apartment building for peace
of mind alone. Even if she wasn't there when I arrived, she
had to have some kind of warning system that her space
had been violated.

"Are you going to watch me all evening?" I asked.

I heard a soft gasp and a chuckle from near the bed. A
hand appeared from a narrow fissure in the wall, and she
peered in at me, her face tentative, yet avid. "You return,
brother."

"I have more questions," I said.

She crept across the floor in plain sight, hid behind one

of the tables, and stretched her neck up above the books. "Druse has questions, too, my brother. Why did you flee so? Shall I bring the rat for you? It is yours. It was always yours. Druse swears this."

The idea that a dead rat was somewhere in the room was not something I wanted to dwell on. "I meant no offense. Please accept the rat as my apology."

She ducked down behind the books and muttered. Hospitality rules among the old fey were complicated. In certain quarters, offering a guest a gift was required and refusing it brought shame. With matters of honor and apology, the same sort of thing happened. When the rules conflicted, things got interesting. I hoped this particular complication would not end up with a rat in my pocket.

The *leanansidhe* moved on tiptoe across the floor toward her armchair, shooting looks at me as if she were trying to slip by without attracting my attention. She huddled in the chair, her legs tucked under her, and fidgeted with the hem of one of the several skirts she wore. Her eyes darted to the open book on the table. She flipped it closed and pushed it toward me. "This is a very good book. Druse should like you to have it, yes?"

I picked it up. It was a computer-programming reference work from 1983. "Thank you."

She clutched her hands to her mouth. "Yes, it's very exciting. You will enjoy it."

I leaned forward, and she leaned back, wary. "Druse . . . is that your name?" She nodded vigorously. "Druse . . . I sense in you something akin to what is in me. Do you know what I mean?"

Her eyes went wide as she nodded. "You are my brother. We share that which the others deny."

"Darkness," I said.

She shook her head. "No! No, no, no . . . not dark. Rich. It is rich in lack."

"Does it have a will of its own?" I asked. The question had been gnawing at me for months. The idea that something alive, maybe even malevolent, was in my mind sickened me. Sometimes the dark mass seemed alive and aware, moving in ways that were more than autonomic responses. Sometimes it seemed to protect itself. Sometimes it seemed to protect me. It prevented me from accessing my abilities yet absorbed essence that was thrown at me. On Samhain, it devoured the essence of several Dead people.

Confused, Druse cocked her head to the side. "It is the Wheel, my brother. The will of the Wheel is the will of the World."

The Wheel of the World. I believed in the existence of the Wheel. It wasn't a faith in the same way others believed in gods. It was an acceptance of a philosophy and understanding of the world. Some people thought of it as fate, the inexorable unfolding of what is meant to be. For me, it was an eternal now—a constant present that moved from moment to moment, becoming the present even as it became the past. In short, shit happens, and you have to roll with it.

I groped for words. "It's not a person."

Druse tangled her fingers in her hair and scratched at her head. "It is the lack. It is the Wheel the others deny."

I pursed my lips. "The others—do you mean the solitaries or people who aren't like . . . us?"

She rubbed at her face. "You confuse Druse, my brother. We all touch the light, but the others, it blinds them to its lack." She pulled her knees up and stared at me. "Only such as we, the chosen of the Wheel, touch the whole of it."

Essence. She was talking about essence, the light of the Wheel, the force that permeates everything. The fey manipulated it. Their ability to manipulate it defined them as fey. But Druse was talking about something else, something other that existed, too. "Can you work this . . . this lack of essence, Druse? Is that what you do? Like the others manipulate essence?"

Her eyes teared. "Oh, my brother, we are kin, we are. Stay with me, brother. We are not like them. We are apart. We shall bring joy to each other here."

Not my first choice for retirement. "Show me what you do."

A joy spread across her face with a slash of gray teeth. She jumped from the chair and tugged at my knee. "This way, brother. First, we reach the safe place. The Wheel is not always kind."

I followed her to the fissure in the wall, which was wide enough for me to step through sideways. On the other side, an empty chamber rose two stories, empty except for a heaving of dark gray bedrock in the center. On the outcropping, an oval ward stone about a foot wide rested, glowing with essence. More traditional obelisk wards ringed the natural pedestal, protecting the ward stone behind a thin barrier field.

Druse approached the field. "You have a bowl, brother, yes?"

"I don't understand what you mean."

She trotted back to me and patted my left arm, clenching my forearm up and down its length. "Here, ah, not a bowl, no. Something different, but the same. Good, good. Nice to carry it in you. Druse should like that. You should show Druse how to make such as this."

The tattoo on my arm tingled as she probed at it through the sleeve. I gently pulled away from her. "Show me yours, Druse."

I bit back a nervous chuckle at the reminder of the "I'll show you mine, if you show me yours" game that children play. Despite wanting to know how her abilities worked, that particular situation wasn't a line I was willing to cross.

She pinched my sleeve between two fingers. Her essence slipped over my arm, not a full envelope, but enough to allow the wards on the ground to recognize me. The dark mass shifted in my head as we entered the contained haze of essence around the stone pedestal. My ears popped from a sudden pressure against the inside of my skull.

Druse trailed around the pedestal, staring at me, waiting for a reaction. On the natural outcropping sat a rough-worked ward stone shaped like a bowl, a rich green color with dark red splotches. Heliotrope, an ancient jasper stone used for a variety of rituals, mostly involving healing and balance. The spots gave it its more dramatic name: bloodstone.

"This is beautiful, Druse. Where did you get it?"

She placed her hands to either side of the stone and rubbed at it. Essence pooled inside, a silvered white that coiled and swirled like liquid clouds. "It's mine, brother. She gave it to me, didn't she? Long ago. She had no need of it anymore. I found it and kept it."

Sounded like an interesting story, rife with contradiction. And beside the point. "What do you do with it?"

She dipped two fingers in and withdrew them dripping with the translucent essence. "Save it to save Druse. In the slack time, the danger time, when they seek Druse, the bowl feeds and nurtures. They will seek you, my brother, and bring you harm. You must hide then, hide and wait and drink from the bowl to live."

I paced around the pedestal, Druse mimicking my steps on the opposite side. "Where does the essence come from?"

"It gives it, it does. Druse gives to it, and it returns tenfold. It is a good thing, no?" she said.

A fine quality piece of jasper that beautiful was worth a fortune. That it was some kind of capacitor and amplifier ward pushed its price off the charts. Something this big could potentially output unlimited essence over time. I allowed myself a small smile. Now I understood what Zev meant the night Murdock vanished. He said to tell Jark the solitaries didn't have what he was seeking. The bowl in front of me was a powerful artifact, the kind that could have only come originally from Faerie. And it was sitting in an unguarded room with a simple barrier field around it. A fey with moderate abilities could collapse Druse's shield. Sekka's body had been found nearby. She must have been guarding it. "You leave it out like this?"

She laughed, a raspy bark of sound. "No one can touch Druse's bowl. Try it, my brother. Try to take it."

I reached out a hesitant hand. A hot burning sensation ran down my right arm from the dark mass in my head, and a cold constriction pulsed through the tattoo on my left forearm. I've learned those are warnings of more pain. Before the silver tattoo appeared, the dark mass in my head rejected external essence and contained my own inherent essence within me. It was why I couldn't touch my abilities. The silver tattoo seemed to want the opposite, hungering for essence and releasing it. Something about the bowl was confusing both of them.

An electric static ran over me when I touched the stone. Nothing more painful than surprise. I put my other hand on the opposite side and tried to lift it, but it wouldn't budge. Not a fraction of an inch. I dropped my hands. "Is it bonded to the bedrock?"

Druse laughed as if I had made an incredible joke. She lifted the bowl off the pedestal with no more effort than necessary for its weight. She replaced it. "Only the pure can take the bowl, my brother, and only the unpure ever seek it."

I frowned. I might not have the best moral record going, but I liked to think I was at least several notches above a *leanansidhe*. "The pure," I said.

She ducked her head, caressing the side of the bowl. "Yes, yes, of course. The pure, the innocent, the chaste, my brother."

Pure and innocent meant one thing, but in the same sentence with the word "chaste," their meanings shifted in one direction. "Are you telling me only a virgin can move it?"

Druse clutched her hands in excitement and brought them to her lips. "You are my brother, my brother. You see true. Druse will protect you in need. Druse will let you use the bowl in need."

My responding chuckle confused Druse, but finding a virgin geasa in a hole in the ground in a modern city was so surreal, I had to laugh. The geasa bans were powerful taboos, hard to create and harder to break. The virgin geasa served many purposes, the least of which a pretty good indicator of how few virgins there were around. In the old days—the real old days—virginity was something lost almost as soon as puberty was gained. I wondered if Druse ever heard of teen abstinence programs. I knew that the failure rate for them was high, but there had to be a danger of at least one naïve teen who didn't know everyone else was lying.

"What does this have to do with the darkness, Druse?"

Her hand trembled over the bowl. Purple essence welled up from within her, coating her fingers. It undulated across her palm, forming bumps that stretched and grew into wormlike tendrils. They waved in the air then dipped toward the essence. Druse closed her eyes and parted her lips as the tendrils drew up the essence. Something moved within her, an oozing behind her essence, a darkness that called to the thing in my mind.

I swayed with a touch of vertigo as the burning sensation in my right arm tightened and stretched. Druse gasped as her darkness touched the silvered essence from the bowl. The essence vanished, enveloped in darkness, no intermediate mingling or change. Just gone.

I clenched my jaw in pain as a sharp blade of darkness pierced my palm. The blade had no substance, a solid shadow that snaked and twined itself around Druse's fingers. The sharp tip cut through her body signature, and a hot pleasure ran through me as I sensed her essence like a flavor in my mind. Druse slumped against the pedestal with a groan. The thing from my hand moved deeper, and the darkness within her rose to meet it. The two modes of darkness touched in a burst of black shadow. I shouted and wrenched my arm away, my silvered tattoo blazing through my jacket as the dark thing whipped back into my hand. I tripped backwards and fell, red and white lights flashing in my eyes.

Druse leaned over me. "My brother?" she whispered, her voice a raspy tremble.

She reached for my face. I shoved her away. "Don't touch me."

She cowered back, an uncertain smile flickering on and off her lips. "It is fine, my brother. The Wheel's touch burns with ignorance at first, but in time it cuts with joy. You are strong, my brother. Druse slept many days after her first touch."

I grabbed the edge of the pedestal and pulled myself up. "What did you do to me?"

Druse yanked at her hair. "Nothing, my brother! You asked to see. We are akin. We touch the light and bring the lack. It is the Way of the Wheel."

I rubbed my arms. They were sore with the pain of heat and cold. "Can it be controlled?"

Druse crawled behind the pedestal and raised her head above the bowl. "The solitaires seek Druse, and Druse must answer. Enough for today, my brother. Return again and learn."

She cloaked herself and vanished. Her essence trail faded into the far end of the chamber where the light didn't reach. She was gone. I examined my hands and found smooth unbroken skin. My sensing ability traced a faded area in the middle of my right hand that wasn't there before. Tiny flashes of silver essence winked here and there along my fingers. Bits of jasper from the bowl had attached themselves to me. In spite of the pain, I pushed my body essence against them, and they sifted to the floor like fine dust.

I backed away, not turning until I reached the room's exit. My chest constricted as I strode away from Druse's room. I wasn't going to be stomach sick this time. As I wound through the tunnels to the exit above, my face burned with a feverish warmth. Yearning desire raced through me, my skin tingling with an almost carnal hunger for more of what happened—to savor and, yes, devour essence as if it were the only thing I needed for sustenance. The sensation of that moment had a kick like a chemical high, only deeper and more profound, as if nothing else would matter if I could have it again. It felt wrong, corrupt. In the cold slap of the winter air outside, I refused to release the shocked emotion hovering inside me. What had happened felt wrong.

I wanted to go back even as I staggered away.

26

All the next morning I nursed the mother of hangovers, the combined effects of alcohol and the flood of essence I had absorbed in Druse's chamber. The pounding in my head left little room to think of much else for hours. As the cloud of pain lifted, I debated calling Murdock, trying to decide if it would be pushing him to talk when he obviously didn't want to, or if he wasn't talking because he wanted me to push. It's hard to read him sometimes. As I sat on the subway train, I checked my cell, scrolling through the caller ID in case I had missed his call. I hadn't.

The train stopped at Boylston Street, and I got out with several students. I lingered behind them as we neared the stairs. When I was sure no one was paying attention, I slipped into the train tunnel. About fifty feet in, the barrier between inbound and outbound tracks ended, and I crossed over to the opposite side. Hopping onto the narrow concrete ledge, I listened to the distant, hollow sound of a train. I had plenty of time before it arrived. At regular intervals, shallow niches opened in the concrete walls, safety spots for transit workers to stand if they were caught on the tracks when a train approached. I reached one shallower than the others and walked into the concrete wall.

The wall let me through, a static resistance running over my body as I slipped to the other side. Feeling along the edge of the first step leading down, I found the small flashlight Meryl had promised to leave for me. I turned the light on and descended the stone stairs. At the bottom, I turned right into a long, narrow tunnel. Sometimes it was lined with bricks or granite blocks, sometimes with bedrock. Few people knew that an entire network of tunnels existed under the streets of Boston. Meryl made sure no one knew about this one, her secret way out of the Guildhouse.

Light appeared ahead, and I turned off the flashlight. The end of the tunnel gave a transparent view into Meryl's office. An archway framed the desk area where she was working, seemingly oblivious to my approach. I knew better. No one sneaks up on Meryl Dian. *We're clear. Come on through,* she sent.

I slipped through another field of static into her office. From her perspective, it looked like I had emerged from a solid wall. I sat in the messy guest chair as she finished reading something on her computer. She swiveled toward me. "Sorry. Minor catastrophe with the network."

"Anything I can help with?" I understood a big chunk of the Guildhouse's computer network from my days helping the IT department build security. Meryl, on the other hand, apparently spent her free time shredding through it with ease.

She shook her head. "It's resolved. We've been getting a lot of intrusion attempts for the last month. MacGoren thinks it's the Consortium, of course. I'm pretty sure it's a bunch of college kids from BU."

With a self-satisfied smile, she turned her monitor so I could see the screen. "Check this out."

I leaned over the desk and skimmed through an agent briefing notice. "Sekka was a Consortium agent?"

She nodded. "I found that in an archived alert file from two months ago. All references to her were wiped from the system the day after you found Jark."

I stared at the screen. "The day Jark killed Sekka. And now you're going to tell me who deleted the files."

Meryl's eyebrows disappeared under her bangs. "Keeva."

Keeva followed the rules. She bent them occasionally, but only when she felt a situation forced it. Or her. Wiping internal files didn't sound like something she would do unless it was so serious, she needed to cover her own ass. Or she was ordered to do it. "They're trying to bury something, and it isn't dead bodies."

Meryl leaned forward. "Here's the juicy part. Keeva hasn't had any assignments related to the Weird. MacGoren has a contained group of agents working down there under confidential directive. Rumor has it that Keeva and mac-Goren have been arguing behind closed doors."

"I told Keeva about the *leanansidhe*. That could be what they're working on."

Meryl shook her head. "MacGoren's boys have been down there since before you found the *leanansidhe*."

I looked down at my hand. The spot where my essence had faded last night was normal again, my body signature intact. I scratched my palm. "Meryl, I have to ask you something. What do you know about *leanansidhes'* abilities?"

She bobbed her head slowly from side to side. "You mean besides the whole soul-sucking thing?" I nodded. She shrugged. "Not much. They're rare. I don't think anyone's studied them much."

"What do you know about the other side of the Wheel?" I asked.

She pursed her lips. "The Wheel is what is, Grey. It's all there is. There is no other side."

"What about beneath the Wheel?"

She opened her mouth to say something, then closed it in thought. "There is no beneath. It's not a wheel like a ribbon. It's a Wheel like a movement."

"You're changing the metaphor," I said.

She shrugged. "Only sorta kinda. There are no sides. There are relative relationships—that's what we mean when we talk about paths—but talking about sides is taking the metaphor too literally."

I shifted in my chair. "Okay, let me put it this way. What's not the Wheel?"

She shrugged slowly. "Nothing. Chaos. The Void. Utter Meaninglessness. Something we cannot define because we can only define things in terms of the known, and what's not the Wheel is so inconceivable we can't begin to describe it."

"You sound like you're quoting something."

She smirked. "You sound like you made a deep knowledge leap."

I nodded. "Which is why it makes sense to me, Meryl. I think the thing in my head is outside the Wheel. That's why no one understands it."

She tilted her head. The moment lengthened while a cryptic expression passed over her face. "What does this have to do with the *leanansidhe*?"

"It was something she said."

Meryl licked her lips. "You didn't mention this before."

I shrugged and failed to look casual about it. "I didn't think of it."

She narrowed her eyes. "You found her again, didn't you?"

We had grown close in the past few months, closer than I would have guessed. Despite her insistence that we weren't a couple or seeing each other or friends with benefits or whatever I wanted to call it, we had made connections that friends without didn't have. I could lie. She might believe me. But if I lied, and she knew it, I would damage whatever the hell it was that we did have. I took a deep breath. "Yeah. I had to know what she meant when she called me 'brother.'"

Meryl frowned. "It's a *leanansidhe*, Grey. If there's one thing I do know, it's that they're liars. They have to be to survive. She's playing with your mind. The thing in your head has an explanation, and the answer is within the Wheel of the World. It has to be, by definition. If it's within the Wheel of the World, it's part of the Wheel of the World, not outside It."

I closed my eyes and rubbed them. Even as I did it, I knew it was to hide the fact that I was embarrassed. "She made the dark mass in my head move, Meryl. She showed me how to let it free and it felt wrong and it felt amazing. I used to be afraid it would kill me." I opened my eyes. "Now I'm just afraid of it. I'm afraid of what it makes me want to do. I'm afraid it's not really making me feel that way and is just exposing something wrong inside me."

Meryl came around the desk and sat on my lap. She wrapped her arms around my head and pulled me to her chest. My stomach did a little flip as the dark mass pulsed from being near her strong body essence. She tilted my head up by the chin. "Listen to me, Connor. You were one of the biggest assholes I've ever worked worth. That was then. If you were in danger of some weird-ass darkness in you coming out, it was before this thing happened to you, not now. Not from what I've seen. You might be caught up in some shit lately, but if I thought for one moment there was something seriously whacked about you, you wouldn't be here."

I leaned my head against her shoulder. "I hope you're right."

She scrubbed her fingernails through my hair and hopped to her feet. "I am. Besides, in any given personal relationship, I have to be the crazier one. It's a rule. Now, let's go have lunch."

I stood. "I want to go talk to Keeva and see if I can find out what's going on."

Meryl rolled her eyes. "Yeah, she loves to confide in you."

I pushed playfully at her shoulder. "Hey, don't underestimate me. I know someone who never thought she'd confide in me."

She looked at her watch. "Okay. Go. If you're not back in fifteen minutes, I'm getting takeout."

I took her hands, leaned down, and kissed her. She kissed me back with no games. I tousled her hair. She punched me.

Since I wasn't officially in the building, I used the freight elevator, which was accessible in the basement but the call buttons on the upper floors were disabled. Which meant no guards riding them for routine security. The added benefit was it opened near Keeva's office, so I could bypass the floor receptionist as well.

Keeva looked up from her desk when I knocked, and I immediately got her narrow-eyed, compressed-lipped suspicious look. "I don't remember guards locking down the building. How'd you get in?"

I sat in her guest chair. "Nice to see you, too. How are things going?"

She didn't change her expression. "Busy."

I nodded. "Good, good. How's Ryan?"

Her frown deepened. "Busy."

I looked around the office, then brought my gaze back to Keeva. "You're still wearing a glamour."

She leaned back. "Why are you here, Connor?"

"I have a proposal for you. I have a piece of information you might find helpful. In exchange, I need a favor."

She smiled. "It would have to be some very good information."

I smiled back. "Is it a deal?"

She shook her head. "You know better than that. I'm not going to obligate myself without hearing the whole story."

I nodded. "True. That's smart, of course. How about this, if you use the information, you don't have to do the favor if you think it isn't equitable."

She grinned. "This should be interesting."

"I know what Sekka was hiding."

As Community Liaison Director, Keeva saw all open case reports from the Boston P.D. She twisted her lip in dismissal. "Why should I care about a routine murder case?"

"Because it wasn't routine, and I know you know that. Sekka was a Consortium agent, and macGoren has people trying to find what she had."

She arched an eyebrow. "Go on."

"I know where it is."

She swiveled her chair in a small arc. "Assuming this is accurate, and I'm interested, what's the favor?"

"I want you to capture the *leanansidhe*," I said.

Her suspicious look returned. "You're not telling me everything. Assuming what you say is true about the Guild's interest in Sekka, capturing the *leanansidhe* pales in comparison. Why are you offering something so important for something so not important?"

"Honestly?" I asked.

"Honestly," she said.

I took a deep breath. "Because the *leanansidhe* scares the hell out of me, and I don't have the power or ability to bring her in. I'm afraid of what will happen to me if she's left running free."

Keeva's jaw dropped in surprise. "Whoa! When you said 'honestly,' I wasn't expecting . . . *honesty*."

I laughed. "Yeah, well, that's how much I need you to do this, Keeva. In fact, to make it even easier for you, the *leanansidhe* has what Sekka was hiding. It's in her cave." I picked up a pen from her desk and pulled a sheet of notepaper toward me. "This is where she's hiding."

I handed Keeva a rough map of the tunnel route from the abandoned warehouse. She stared down at the scribble, then at me. "Do you want to tell me why you're so scared?"

I smiled. "Do you want to talk about your glamour?"

She tossed the map on her desk. "Assuming your theory is correct—and I'm *not* saying it is—I'll take your request under advisement. You need to leave now. I don't want anyone seeing you in here if you're not officially in the building."

Keeva and I had a long history, not all of it good. We both had egos, and we had clashed often when we were partners. But at the end of the day, I thought we believed the other would do the right thing. Not necessarily what both of us thought was the right thing, but the right thing in some respect. Now, though, this gulf existed between us that I didn't think we could bridge anymore. She worked for an organization I no longer believed in. I worked outside the chain of command in a way she couldn't condone. And that was okay with me. She had a career to think about. If I didn't think someday we'd see eye to eye, I wouldn't have bothered talking to her. I gave her a wink and left without argument.

As I rode the freight elevator back to the basement, relief and regret fought in my stomach. The urge to make another visit to the *leanansidhe* bordered on overwhelming. Asking Keeva to do something to take that option off the table was the right thing to do. I didn't like how the *leanansidhe* made me feel precisely because I liked how she made me feel. Keeva could get the *leanansidhe* into the Guildhouse, a controlled environment. Maybe then Briallen or Gillen Yor would have something to work with. If the *leanansidhe* held the key to the dark mass in my head, I would rather that someone other than her turned it.

27

The ring of my cell phone startled me out of a dreamless sleep. After leaving the Guildhouse the previous afternoon, I had gathered my resource materials and holed up in my living room in a fruitless quest to figure out a way to get rid of Uno. Squinting against the light in my living room, I pushed aside the nest of books that surrounded me as I groped for the phone. Uno rose from the floor at the foot of the bed, a physical reminder that my research had gone nowhere, the dry, academic prose of many of the books lulling me into a bored stupor. The dog vanished as my hand closed on the phone, probably fading off to Shay's apartment again.

"I need you," Murdock had said.

The man didn't return my calls all day and night, then rang me at five o'clock in the morning like it was a perfectly normal time for either of us to be awake. Granted, I spent more of my waking hours in the middle of the night than most people, but I was surprised Murdock was up that early—so early that I had to take a cab down to the morgue to meet him because the subway wasn't open.

I went around the back to the back of the OCME. The building was open twenty-four hours, but the main door was locked before 6:00 A.M. The loading dock, though, remained open for business twenty-four/seven. Dead bodies didn't much care about regular office hours.

A morgue in the middle of the night is exactly how you imagine it would be. Dim atmosphere, cold light, dark corners, empty corridors, and dead bodies in freezers. Under normal circumstances, I would write off the notion of a dead person leaping out of a darkened room as the product of an overactive imagination. Boston after the Samhain catastrophe, though, made the idea not only plausible, but even likely.

The bright light from the cooling room cast a stark blue beam into the dark basement hallway. When I reached the door, Janey and Murdock looked at me with relief and irritation. They stood on opposite sides of an examining table—a large examining table—with Sekka's body laid out on it. Her head had been placed above the neck.

"I'm glad you're here. I've been trying to talk sense to him for an hour," said Janey.

"What's going on?" I asked.

Murdock rested his hands on his hips. "I was thinking the best way to find out if Jark was telling the truth about the night he died was to ask Sekka."

I joined them at the table. "You want to reanimate her."

"Exactly," he said.

I opened my sensing ability and looked at Sekka. "I think we're too late for that. Her body essence is long gone."

"Well, then, where is it? You keep saying the Dead are here because TirNaNog is gone. If that's true, where are the dead solitaries going?"

I shook my head. "I don't have an answer for that, Murdock. But I do know that there is no more essence in this body, and without essence, there is no reanimation."

Janey crossed her arms. "I already told him Jark killed Sekka."

That surprised me. "He's an eyewitness to his own murder. How do we refute that he said she killed him?"

Janey gestured at Sekka's body. "Physical evidence. Jark left here with a city-issued coverall as clothing. He didn't want what he was wearing when he died."

"I don't blame him. It did go through the sewer," I said.

Janey nodded. "But that didn't wash out the DNA evidence in his clothes. I tested it. They were soaked in Sekka's blood and his own."

I pursed my lips. "You're suggesting he couldn't have Sekka's blood on him if she killed him first."

"Right."

"But if she was near him when she was killed, her blood could have gotten on him if she was close enough."

Janey nodded again. "True. But if she killed Jark first like he said she did, she'd have his blood on her. It's virtually impossible to decapitate someone and not get blood on you. I checked everywhere. The only blood on Sekka is her own. The blood on Jark is hers and his."

"He killed her first," Murdock said.

"Which leaves the Hound," I said.

Murdock stared down at Sekka. "You're sure this won't work?"

I shrugged and looked at the clock. "Yeah, but we can wait until dawn if you want."

He nodded. "I'd like that."

Janey and I exchanged a bewildered look. Murdock usually deferred matters of the fey world to me. He never disputed the things I told him. For someone who had been dragged out of bed in the middle of the night, Janey seemed a lot more understanding than I was. As the only fey person on staff at the OCME, Janey was used to humans making odd requests and ignoring her expertise.

"Okay. We're here, so we might as well," I said.

Another twenty minutes would decide the issue either way, and waiting was a small thing compared to contributing to Murdock's anger and frustration. I didn't see the need to get into an argument about it.

"You want to tell us what's going on, Murdock?"

He spread his hands over the body. "Let's see what happens. I need to see what happens."

"Okay," I said.

The clock ticked off the minutes as we waited in silence. Murdock stared at Sekka's body like it was going to reveal something important to him. Maybe it was. He didn't like the whole reanimation thing, didn't like the questions about his faith it created. Yet now he wanted to make it happen.

Dawn arrived. Sekka lay still, no sign of movement. No sign of essence. Murdock continued staring as Janey checked her watch. "It would have happened by now," she said.

Murdock had a strange look on his face, at once relieved and frustrated. A polite smile flickered on and off his face as he looked at Janey. "I'm sorry. I had to take the chance."

Janey pulled a sheet over the body. "Don't apologize. Part of my job is research. We answered a question."

We didn't speak as we left Janey to close up the lab. Murdock pulled out of the parking lot and into early-morning rush hour. We crept along the access road to the highway, waiting to cut over to the Southie side of the channel.

"Are you going to tell me what that was all about?" I asked.

"My father ordered the stand-down the night the Dead attacked the neighborhood meeting," he said.

I nodded. "I thought so. I didn't want to say anything because I thought you might think I was being cynical."

"You are cynical. It gets worse. He as much as admitted he's letting the Guild operate with no oversight," he said.

"Why the change? He never likes the Guild to get the upper hand," I said.

"They persuaded him that the issue was critical. The solitaries are hiding something the Guild wants. In exchange for allowing them in to get what they needed, the Guild offered to take care of the solitary leadership."

I turned my head toward Murdock in disbelief. "Are you telling me your father—the police commissioner—took out contracts on fey people?"

Murdock grunted. "I asked the same thing. My father said the Guild assured him it meant the solitary leaders would be taken into legal custody. Then he said, of course, if someone dies in the attempt, it serves the same purpose. He smiled when he said it."

"What does Sekka have to do with this?" I asked.

He glanced in the rearview mirror as he cut across the traffic lane. "She knows who killed her. We make an arrest, we expose the whole damn scheme."

"You'll expose your father, too," I said.

"He'll survive. That's the point of their plan, Connor. It's set up so that everyone can deny what's going on."

"So why bother?"

Murdock smiled. "Because it will stop. I don't care what game the Guild is playing. I never have. I just want the killing stopped."

"So, we're back to square one, then. Sekka didn't reanimate," I said.

He pulled up in front of my apartment building. "Maybe not." He gave me a sly smile. "So, who's the Guildmaster sleeping with these days?"

I chuckled. "That's funny. That's very funny."

I pulled the sending stone out of my pocket. The palm of

my hand tingled as my body signature interacted with the ward spell on it. I held it near my mouth. "Hey, gorgeous. I have something for the Old Man."

Her voice floated softly out of the stone. *I hear you, handsome. I'll let you know when a car's ready.*

28

As luck would have it—my luck anyway—my request to see Eagan fell on the same day as his annual Winter Solstice party. When Tibbet called back and told me Eagan thought the party would be a convenient cover for the meeting, I tried to beg off and arrange another time. Eagan wouldn't hear of it.

It had been over three years since my last invitation to the party. Three years ago, I was a sought-after party ornament. I realized after I lost my abilities that's what it really was all about: who could get the prize guest. I was riding high then, solving big-time cases, the go-to guy for advice, and the role model for a career on a rocket. Any host who snagged me with a party invite could bask in my coveted reflected glory. Receiving Eagan's invitation to the Solstice party put me on the must-have list for everyone else's events. Getting dropped from his list had the opposite effect. No one wanted to preen over last year's favorites, and now I was not even that.

The cedar-lined driveway to the Guildmaster's mansion

was a postcard-perfect Yule scene. The car headlights reflected off the snowbanks to either side, and the soft crunch of tires rolling over the snow-softened pavement evoked a warm nostalgia for winters past. At the top of the drive, the cedars ended, opening to the wide vista of the front lawn, a meadowlike expanse of untrodden white velvet. A soft yellow glow lit the windows in the house with telltale flashes of blues, pinks, and yellows from flits dancing in the air.

Dozens of cars and a few limos lined the drive, where brownie security guards jockeyed them into place. They cleared the front as my car approached, and the driver stopped at the front steps. Someone opened the rear door for me, and I got out of Eagan's official Guildhouse limo. Eagan wanted people to notice me arrive and had used his own car to send the message that he had invited me. Whatever his reasons, he wasn't bothering with subtlety.

Despite the cold, the front doors were flung open to the outside, framing the party within. People danced and swayed and flew in the grand hall. Enough greenery had been brought in to create a forest. Cedar and fir garlands adorned the doorways and ceiling cornices. Branches were twined around pillars and woven through the balustrades of the staircase leading to the second floor. Sprays of mistletoe hung from the enormous chandelier, and white roses overflowed from tall crystal vases. On the upper balcony overlooking the room, an orchestra played traditional Yule music with flutes.

Tibbet found me before I left the vestibule. She wore a floor-length dress in maroon velvet, her hair in a tangle of long, thin braids with amber crystals threaded through them. She wrapped her arms around me, spinning us both in a circle as we kissed, before pulling away with a huge smile on her face. "You look dashing, sir."

Her words made me feel better about my outfit. Gone were the days of high-end designer fashion on a regular

basis. I was wearing a deep violet silk jacket that I had
had for years. I was actually surprised to discover I still had
it. Most of the good stuff had gone long ago to consign-
ment shops. A simple black shirt and pants finished off
the outfit. People don't notice old black unless they look
more closely than they should anyway. I couldn't not smile
at Tibbet. "And you, my love, look more gorgeous than
ever."

"Promise me we will dance later?"

I slipped my arm around her. "If you promise it will be
something slow."

She rested her head on my shoulder. "Or we can just
stand like this and be the envy of everyone else."

I kissed her temple. "Thanks, Tibs. You always say the
right thing."

She smiled up at me. "Get yourself a drink and mingle.
Manus is holding court by the fireplace. He said to tell you
he'll meet you upstairs later."

I smiled. "Okay."

She did a little twirl away and pointed at me as she slipped
back into the crowd. "And we will dance, handsome."

The bar was set up under the stuffed elephant. Around
me, glances slid away before I made eye contact. The fast
fall from grace meant a long climb back up, and three years
was nothing in the fey world. I had made matters worse by
not wanting to climb in the same direction again. It was
still uncomfortable to be snubbed.

I lingered near the back of the hall in a recessed alcove
by the French doors, watching Eagan greet his guests. Even
though he was near a roaring fire, he had draped a blanket
on his lap. Despite his pale and gaunt face, he seemed to
be enjoying himself. I didn't begrudge him the opportunity
to be fawned over. He didn't leave his house for months at
a time anymore. I certainly didn't envy him the apprehen-

sive looks people gave him, like he was going to die any moment.

"I never pictured you as a wallflower," someone said next to me.

With all the fey folk in the room, keeping track of body signatures was pointless. I hadn't realized Moira Cashel was standing near me until she spoke. "I'm waiting to speak to someone."

Moira was decked out as only the rich fey could be. She wore a midnight blue gown shot with white crystals and an evening wrap of gossamer-thin white cloth. More jewels glittered on pins in her hair—true diamonds and sapphires. A glamour completed the outfit, a soft, gauzy halo of golden light that made her look like she floated in a cloud of sunshine. There was no denying she looked incredible or—for that matter—that she knew she did. She sidled closer. "If only it were me," she said.

I glanced down at her. "What do you want, Moira?"

She lifted a champagne glass to her lips. "I think the moment you could do something for me passed in your apartment, Connor."

I chuckled. "Yes, well, if you need a good lay, I'm sure you can find someone else here."

She gave me a tight smile. "Bastard."

I shrugged. "You're not the first to call me that, so I'll ask you again. What do you want, Moira?"

Essence rippled as her face shifted to Amy Sullivan's softer jawline, and her hair lightened. "A piece of the past, Connor. A piece of me that I'm afraid doesn't exist anymore. Can you look at this face and feel nothing?"

"Oh, I feel something all right, just not what you intend. I'm going to walk away if you don't stop using that glamour," I said.

Tears—real ones, I think—sprang into her eyes. "Why?

Because I'm destroying some kind of delusion you had by revealing that perfect Amy Sullivan was more than you knew? That she was a woman with a life and a home that you knew nothing about? That she was in pain, and you appeared at the right moment?"

"I did not seduce you," I said.

A cold light crept into her eyes. "We seduced each other, Connor. You may not have been a man yet, but you weren't a child either. You knew exactly what you were doing."

I shook my head and laughed in disbelief. "If you were a man, I'd knock you on your ass for that. You know nothing about what was between me and Amy. You're just a manipulative creature from Tara working for an egomaniac who's afraid that I know she's responsible for what happened here on Samhain."

She seemed genuinely taken aback. "What are you talking about?"

I stepped closer to her, forcing her to step back against the wall. "Maeve abandoned us to save her own precious skin, and if not for me, this entire city would have died, too. So spare me the feeble little guilt trip about who I slept with years ago. If you really are Amy, then you made your bed and, yeah, you slept in it. And if you want to get in bed with Maeve now, you'll suffer the consequences. I don't give a damn, and I sure as hell am not going to fall for whatever game you're playing now."

Tears flowed free. She slapped me across the face. "You are a bastard."

I frowned. "Yeah, well, maybe you helped make me one."

"What the hell is this?"

Moira gasped and extinguished the Amy glamour. Behind us in a formal tuxedo, Commissioner Scott Murdock looked more angry than I had ever seen him. He wasn't looking at me, but at Moira. "Commissioner, I'm sorry if—" I began.

"Shut up, Grey." He shoved me aside and grabbed Moira by the arm. "I asked you a question."

"Scott, I—" she began.

He shook her. "Scott, is it? Scott?"

I pulled at his coat. "Commissioner, I can explain."

He dropped his hand, then grabbed me by the shirt and pushed me against the wall. "What game do you think you're playing with me, boy? Is this another Guild game to make me a fool?"

I'd seen the commissioner angry before, even angry at me, but this came out of the blue. "Excuse me?"

Moira grabbed his arm. "Scott, stop it."

"I think stopping this is very good advice, Commissioner." Tibbet's voice was low and sharp. Behind her, two brownie security guards waited with polite expressions on their faces.

The commissioner released me with a shove. A few guests had noticed the commotion but were pretending they hadn't. Tibbet tilted her head down and toward one shoulder as if listening to something behind her. "The Guildmaster requests that you join him in his study in a few moments, Commissioner. My assistants will provide you with whatever you need in the meantime."

Scott Murdock adjusted his jacket. "Tell Eagan I'm leaving. I will speak to him tomorrow."

Tibbet clasped her hands at her waist. "I respect that desire, sir. However, I believe it will take some time to retrieve your vehicle, and I am sure you would not wish to break protocol and neglect to thank your host while you wait."

The commissioner set his jaw and glared at Moira. "Get this . . . person away from me, then."

Tibbet nodded with a smile at Moira. "Please wait in the back hall until I arrive, will you?"

Moira had gone pale. "Do extend my regrets to Manus, but I believe it best I retire for the evening."

Tibbet's smile tightened. "This is the Guildmaster's house, Cashel. Your presence is not a request."

Tibbet took my arm and led me through the great hall. She smiled as we eased our way through the crowd and toward the fireplace. A servant was helping Eagan to his feet.

Are you okay? Tibbet sent.

"Yeah, I'm fine. I have no idea what that was about," I said.

Manus is furious. It's not good for him. Please try to keep him calm, she sent.

"I will," I said.

We followed Eagan and the servant into the back hall. Moira waited there, but Eagan ignored her as we passed through double doors that the servant opened. Moira wouldn't meet my eyes and looked like she wanted to escape.

The servant helped Eagan to an armchair by the lit fireplace. The study had a classic décor of dark wood, expensive leather couches, and stained-glass lamps, and miles of bookcases filled with books on subjects both fey and human. As the servant adjusted the blanket on Eagan's lap, the old man brushed him away. "That's enough. If you and Tibbet will wait outside please."

Tibbet gave me a significant glance as she left to remind me what she had said. I squeezed her hand. Eagan leaned back in the corner of the chair and shook his head. "It's never dull around here. There's a flask behind that curtain over there. Could you get it for me?"

I went to the window he indicated and found a small glass flask on the floor hidden by the brocade drapery. "Who the hell hides all these flasks for you?"

He grinned around the neck of the bottle, then wiped his lips with the back of his hand. "That's a secret. And speaking of, I assume you have something to report?"

I nodded. "How familiar are you with the crackdown in the Weird?"

A cryptic look spread over his features. "I get reports."

I spun an antique globe on a stand near the wall. "Are you aware that the Boston P.D. has turned over all security to Guild agents?"

"Out of political necessity, I had to allow Guild agents to act under civilian authority. The Boston police are powerless against the fey. You know that," he said.

I nodded. "Some of their actions are going beyond the law—civilian or Guild. Complaints to the police are referred to the Guild and complaints to the Guild are ignored."

A sly smile slid onto his face. "I know you, Grey. You've been complaining about that for some time."

I shrugged. "I've been complaining about neglect. This is different. The Guild agents down there are actively breaking the law. They're encouraging a turf war between the solitaries and the Dead. It's going to explode if they don't back off."

Eagan frowned. "And the Boston police are involved?"

I glanced at him. "Human officers have been ordered to stand aside and let the Guild do what it wants. I personally saw Commissioner Murdock meet secretly with a leading perpetrator among the Dead."

Eagan rubbed at his chin. "What do you make of it?"

I smiled at him. "If you ask the Guild, they're acting on your orders."

Eagan chuckled softly to himself. "And when there is blood on the ground, macGoren can blame me and gain the support of the solitaries at the same time. How much time do you think I have?"

I shrugged. "I think it's reached a crisis point."

Eagan hummed to himself. "It seems I may have to put in an appearance downtown and shake things up a bit. I had hoped to spoil their plans once they had Vize in custody, but I suppose I can adjust."

I didn't know how to respond to that. "What does Vize have to do with it?"

Eagan leaned his head back, his eyebrows raised in thought. "Everything, of course. The solitaries have been hiding him for Bastian Frye. MacGoren is using the Dead to find him, particularly a miscreant named Jark. Matters seem to have gotten out of hand. I didn't anticipate the human police colluding with macGoren. An excellent move on his part, though he seems to have overplayed it. That's always been macGoren's flaw—his unwavering surety in the perfection of his plans."

My feet felt rooted to the floor. "I can't believe you let this happen."

Eagan shrugged. "I didn't *let* anything happen. The whole point of a black ops program is in its unprovability. I couldn't stop it unless I knew the identities of macGoren's agents, and that I was still working on. Unfortunately, Jark killed my inside agent before she could expose them."

Jark killed his inside agent. The statement sank in with a sense of disbelief at what I was hearing and what it meant. "Are you talking about Sekka?"

Eagan barely suppressed a look of exasperation. "Of course, Grey. Why do you think I called you in the first place? When Sekka disappeared the same night Jark's body turned up, I wanted to keep tabs on your investigation."

I shook my head with a touch of anger that I had completely missed the connection. "And you had Keeva bury the Guild notice that Sekka was a Consortium agent to keep her Guild double-agent status secure, didn't you?"

He tapped his knee in acknowledgment. "And had the damnedest time getting her to do it."

"You used me," I said.

He managed to look indignant and amused at the same time. "I most certainly did not. You took on Sekka's murder case before I spoke to you. I gave you a complete choice in the matter. I merely covered my bases."

I laughed. The man amazed me. "You're right. I take it back."

He grinned. "I'll have to deal with this tomorrow. Something tells me the commissioner is in no mood to discuss his failings tonight." He gestured at the door. "Now, tell me. Why have two of my guests felt inclined to lay hands on you?"

"Moira I insulted. I have no idea what the commissioner's problem is."

Eagan chuckled again. "I should chastise you for being a rude guest, but that minx has been spying on me for weeks. She's quite the amateur. I expect better court intrigue from Maeve. She disappoints, she does."

I bowed my head. "I apologize anyway."

He acknowledged it with a nod. Eagan might have been pleased I had annoyed Moira, but he still liked the niceties of protocol. "Let's see what they have to say for themselves," he said.

A weak sending fluttered in the air, and the doors opened. Moira entered first, her expression firmly angry. She glared at me as she moved to the side of the room and bowed extravagantly toward Eagan. "You have my deepest apologies, Guildmaster. I was provoked in the situation. Allow me to make it up to my host."

Eagan hummed. "I've already spoken to Mr. Grey and will deal with him as fitting. I will think on your apology. Stay a moment, will you, Moira? I would like your presence while I speak to my other guest."

Moira bowed again as the commissioner strode in without acknowledging either of us. Tibbet closed the doors behind him. *I will be right outside,* she sent.

"What do you want, Eagan?" the commissioner asked.

Eagan put on a tolerant smile. "Pray, have a seat, Commissioner, and let us sort through this disruption of my house."

"I apologize for involving you in a personal matter. I'm leaving now. Thank you." He turned and stopped short, obviously making eye contact with Moira over my shoulder.

Eagan didn't change his expression. "I appreciate that, Commissioner, but I believe you owe an apology elsewhere as well."

The commissioner's gaze shifted to me. "I'll be goddamned before you get an apology from me, Grey."

Eagan spoke to the commissioner's back. "I will be the judge of that in my own home, Commissioner. What is the meaning of this?"

Moira stepped forward. "This is all a misunderstanding, Manus. We should not take any more time from you."

Eagan rocked his head against his chair. "I don't think so, Moira. I invited Grey here, and both of you laid hands on him. I am not pleased."

The commissioner stepped toward me. "Where do you think you're going with this? I will cut you off at the knees, you miserable piece of shit."

"I have no idea what you're talking about," I said.

He grabbed the lapel of my jacket. "I am going to ask you one more time: What little plan did the two of you come up with?"

Eagan struggled to his feet. "Unhand him now, Commissioner."

Moira pushed herself in front of me, forcing the commissioner back. He didn't let go. I reached up to pry his hand away. Moira shoved him back. "Knock it off, Scott. He didn't know," she said. Only she used Amy's voice.

The commissioner backhanded her across the face. "Don't you dare use her voice," he said.

The door opened behind me as Moira fell back into my arms. In the blink of an eye, Tibbet was in the center of the room. Her eyes were huge, and her fingers elongated and tipped with claws. She didn't speak, but I felt sendings fluttering in the air. Tibbet went to Eagan's side and gently forced him back into his chair.

"What the hell is going on here?" Eagan said.

The commissioner faced Eagan. "She's betraying you, Eagan. Setting you up to take a fall and using me to do it."

Moira moved toward the commissioner, her body shield flickering around her as a bitter, angry glint sparked in her eye. "He's lying, Manus. Scott Murdock has been blackmailing the Guild to force his political agenda down in the Weird. He's been taking money to let Guild agents operate in the Weird without human oversight. I've been trying to convince Ryan macGoren it's a trap. He's going to let you take the fall when things get out of control. This man hates us, Manus. He hates all the fey. It amuses him to get paid to watch them kill each other down in the Weird, all because once upon a time, his pride and ego were damaged by a woman."

"Stop using her voice," the commissioner said through gritted teeth.

Moira's face shifted, a ripple of light and color cascading over her. Amy's face resolved into focus. "It's my voice, Scott, and I will use it. You're not going to silence me ever again."

"You are not her," the commissioner said.

Moira laughed, an unattractive sneer on her face. "Oh, but I am, Scott. I would have been satisfied to watch you lose your precious reputation, and no one had to know why except you. But you had to make a scene. So finish it, little man. Tell them what I did to you and what you did to me."

Blood drained from the commissioner's face as he began to tremble. "Shut your mouth."

Moira shook her head. "Never again, Scott." She tilted her head toward Eagan. "This man put a gun to my head and threatened to shoot me and my children if I didn't leave, Manus. He was so horrified that he had married a fey that he was willing to commit murder to hide it from the humans."

The floor felt as if it shifted under me, as the reality of what she said sank in. "Holy shit," I whispered.

"You bitch," the commissioner said. A gun appeared in his hand before anyone registered his movement. Tibbet came forward as I yanked Moira back. Eagan shouted.

The gun went off.

The flash blinded me. The crackle of essence-fire burned in the air. Something slammed into my face, a searing hot blow beneath my right eye. Pain lanced through my head, then a wash of cold ran down my body. My knees collapsed. Fluid filled my throat as I fell. I coughed a spray of blood into the air. I tried to inhale but choked as more blood entered my lungs. I couldn't move. I couldn't feel anything. I couldn't breathe. My vision blurred. The room spun in a smear of color and

everything

went

white

29

White.

Sound stopped. The music. The shouting. Gone.

Whiteness filled my vision with nothing to break the relent-lessness of it. I coughed, feeling blood in my throat, hot blood welling out of my mouth and down my face. Blood ran into my ears, across my chin, down my neck.

Above me, the white simply was, as if the air itself was color. Or no color. As if nothing else existed except the white. I lay on the ground, if there was ground, on something. The firmness of it pressed against the back of my head, but no-where else. My head rolled to one side of its own accord, blood pouring out of my mouth. I wanted to sit up, to stand, to reach up and touch my face, but my body did not respond. Numb. I was numb. Paralyzed. Gods, I can't move myself.

Everything was white. I have been here before. This is where it started. Or ended. I don't remember which.

Everything around me is white. I lie on my back, star-ing into a nothingness of white. I am here again. This place. Above me, I see two vast shadow shapes. Powerful shapes speaking with words I do not understand. They move closer.

Bursts of color flare in my vision, fireworks against the white, fading to darkness. More, then more, the darkness closing on me, like the slow closing of my eyes. My mind, like my eyes, closing, like my eyes blinking. Like my mind blinking.

My mind blinked.

I jerked my head up, feeling like I had passed out. People surrounded me, staring at me. Some I recognized, and some I didn't. Their faces held a multitude of expressions—fear and horror and sadness. Then the screams began.

My mind blinked.

Dylan swims up into my sight again. My head hurts with a ringing as loud as a clock tower. I hold my hands to either side of the knife, not touching it. Blood blossoms on his shirt, deep red blood against a deep red shirt. He doesn't move. He stares at me and stares at me and stares at me. Terror in . . .

My mind blinked.

They move closer and resolve into people. A man, yes, a man and woman. Their vast shadow shapes are a wash of gray against the white. Huge and tall, he's taller, but she . . . she is . . .

My mind blinked.

Briallen looks at me in surprise, glowing in the white, a golden Briallen in a sea of white. She lifts her hands, something in her hands is moving, swaying with essence in a rainbow of color.

My mind blinked.

Briallen looks at me in surprise and rushes toward me as I lean over Dylan.

"Tell me what to do." I hear myself. I hear myself and I hear fear.

My mind blinked.

I stand on a plain, white grass waving against a white sky. It's not winter, pray, what is this new madness? Where have I come? I turn in place, searching, searching across the plain, searching about the standing stones, but Maeve is not there. Was she? What is this place?

My mind blinked.

. . . the one who leads. He follows, reluctant in his step. The blood fills my mouth, burns in my chest, and I cannot breathe anymore. I try not to breathe. I do not want any more blood in my lungs. Try not to.

They stand over me, huge figures, white on white, then faint wisps of essence coursing over them in pale, pale color. He looks at me with a storm in his eyes, and she . . . she is beautiful. She leans down, leans a long way down, her hand outstretched, reaching down. She touches my chest and the pain . . . stops.

"What are you doing, Mother?" he asks.

She straightens up, so far up and away, her face a light of glory. She stops. Everything stops. I stop. Everything . . .

My mind blinked.

Vize is running. Everything is white. I am running. Everything is white. He looks over his shoulder at me. He looks determined . . . or crazed . . . I can't tell. Everything is white. One minute we were facing each other, and now everything is white. He stops. He looks surprised. There is someone lying on the ground. Something about him is familiar. Everything is white and there is no ground. There is someone lying in the white. Everything . . .

My mind blinked.

"I can't do this, Briallen," I shout.

Briallen kneels by me. Something is not right. Or different. She doesn't look right. She reaches out but stops.

"You must. I can't," she says.

I close my eyes and see white and something black, far, far away. Black like a seed in the white. Briallen sings and then she screams and then I know what to do.

My mind blinked.
My mind blinked.
My mind blinked.

. . . stops. Everything stops. Even me.

"Thinking," she says.

"You interfere with the Wheel of the World," he says.

"I am the Wheel of the World. So are you. So is he. So are we all. The all of it is one," she says.

He leans toward me, ranks of hair cascading down, wild and wind-wet. "He seems familiar to me."

The light of her face moves with her nod. "He is and was and will be."

He withdraws, a slow receding of immensity, but I can see his face. "I know what you are thinking," he says to her.

"Tell me, then. I do not know," she says.

He laughs, something deep, a rumble from the deep that sounds like time.

My mind blinked.

Vize looks feverish. "It must happen this way. You must let it happen."

"I won't let you," I say.

He looks frightened yet determined as I reach toward him.

He recedes.

My mind blinks.

"He's dying. That is the Way of the Wheel," he says.

"I am here. That is the Way as well," she says.

He laughs again. "Yes," he says.

"Yes," she says.

My mind blinks.

My hand reaches out for the staff.

My mind blinks.

My hand reaches out for the knife.

My mind blinks.

My hand reaches out for the ring.

My mind blinks.

My hand reaches out . . .

My mind blinks.

She extends her hand again, down, down, down, it comes, glowing with light, with essence, with her. My hand reaches out for her hand. We touch. Sensation returns. I scream and

everything

                    goes

                                        white

30

I wrenched forward and coughed, spitting blood into my lap. Spots of light flashed across my eyes, red and white and black. Moira gasped, backing away from me in horror. Her hair had come loose on one side. Blood speckled her white wrap, which slipped from her shoulders to the crook of one arm. I wiped at my mouth, and the back of my hand came away covered in blood.

The commissioner lay facedown at my feet, his arms thrown forward. Beyond him, Tibbet crouched over Eagan where he slumped on the floor against the chair, slack-jawed, chin curled into his shoulder, arms gathered limply in his lap, hands palm up.

I gathered my feet under me. "What the hell happened?"

Tibbet rose with tears streaming down her face. She threw herself into my arms. "I thought you were dead."

My gut tightened at the sight over her shoulder of the commissioner. Faint wisps of smoke curled from his damaged and sunken eyes, a telltale sign of essence shock. Scott Murdock was dead. "Gods, Tibs, did I kill him?"

She shook her head against my chest. "Manus did it. He won't wake up, Connor."

Eagan's essence smoldered within him fainter than it had been. He wasn't dead. "He used whatever he had left, Tibs. He's alive, though."

A pounding on the door sounded. Tibbet lifted her head and grimaced through her tears. I kissed her forehead, leaving a bloody lip print. I blotted it off with my sleeve. She closed her eyes and took several deep breaths, smoothing her dress as she did so. She opened her eyes, still wet, but clearer and sharper. With an upward tilt of her chin, she approached the door and opened it partway to speak to whoever was on the other side.

I wiped at my chin, coating my fingers in more blood. Pointlessly, I looked for something to wipe my hand with, then settled on the front of my jacket. The silk was ruined anyway. "Where is all this blood coming from?"

Moira gathered up her wrap and came closer, lifting the end of the garment to wipe at my face. "Scott shot you in the face."

I pushed her hand away, taking hold of the white cloth myself. She let it slip off her arms. I bunched it into a usable rag and wiped at my face and neck. "I think I'd know if I were shot."

Moira focused on my face and the movement of my hands, her forehead smoothing in surprise. "You were. That's part of your jaw on the floor. I would swear you were dead. Do you have some kind of self-healing ability?"

The bloodstain on the floor did have pieces of something in it. The idea that it was pieces of me seemed inconceivable. I wasn't wounded. I was covered in blood "Why did you do that to him?"

Without the slightest remorse, she gazed at the commissioner's body. "Why did he do it to himself?"

"You made him believe you were Amy Sullivan."

One corner of her mouth turned down. "Murdock, Connor. I was Amy Sullivan Murdock. He believed it because it's true. I suppose a husband would know his wife before her lover does. He really did put a gun to my head, you know. I wanted him to suffer for that and for taking away my children. This was too easy for him."

"Leo went to your funeral," I said.

She met my eyes. "You're a detective. Go investigate. If anyone was in that casket, it wasn't his mother."

"I still don't believe you."

She sighed. "I don't care, Connor. He had me followed all those years ago. He knew who you were. Your youth saved you then. I'm surprised he didn't shoot you long before now."

A conflicted look passed over her face as she stared down at Scott Murdock. "I did love him then, you know. That surprised me more than anything. He was a strong and attractive man. I knew he hated the fey, but my heart ruled my head, and I didn't want to lose him. So I said nothing and married him. I never intended any of this to happen, Connor, but I didn't deserve what he did."

I frowned. Her story kept getting better all the time. "If you expect me to say 'boohoo,' don't hold your breath."

Tibbet allowed six brownie servants into the room and closed the door again. "Bring him up the back way. I have Dananns guarding the upper floors."

They lifted the old man with care, shifting and folding his wings gently around him. Tibbet let them through a door at the back of the room.

"The police are arriving," she said.

Moira went to the door. "I will be tending Manus."

"Stop right there, Cashel," Tibbet said. "I am barring you from his presence. Once you deal with the police, you will be escorted to your rooms to retrieve your possessions. They are being packed as we speak. You are no longer welcome in this house."

Moira drew herself up in a classic court hauteur. "The Queen's Herbalist does not take orders from a servant."

Tibbet strode toward her with a predatory grace, her fingers elongating as she edged toward her boggart nature. I followed, ready to pry them apart if necessary. She stopped inches from Moira. "Listen carefully, Cashel. You will leave this house on my orders. Maeve is far away, and I am very, very near. Do not think for one moment you can best me in the house of Manus ap Eagan, underKing."

Moira didn't completely back down, but the truth of what Tibbet said penetrated. "As you wish, then. Maeve will hear of this."

Tibbet nodded once sharply. "As will all the underKings and -Queens. Now, go."

Moira slipped out the door. Tibbet's eyes glowed with a fierce yellow light. She touched my face. "Gillen Yor is on his way. Are you okay?"

I took her hand in both of mine and kissed it. "All I remember is the muzzle flash and a sharp pain, then waking up."

She examined my jawline. "It was horrible, Connor. After the commissioner shot you, a bright flash came from your body. When you sat up, I thought I was seeing something I only wished to see."

"I'll let Gillen look me over. Right now, we have an international disaster on our hands," I said.

She gave me a crooked smile. "My hands, handsome. It's my job. If there's one thing I'm good at, it's damage control."

"You are good at more than that. You and Manus would not have stayed together all these years otherwise," I said.

She smiled more fully. She paused, her eyes shifting as she received a sending, probably several under the circumstances. Her eyes came back to mine. "Leonard Murdock is here and one of his brothers . . . Gerard? . . . Yes, Gerard. I need to be out there." She moved to the door. "You can stay here tonight. I can protect you from what's coming for a while."

"I'll think about it," I said, as she slipped out into the grand hall.

I reached down and closed the commissioner's eyes. His sons didn't need to see the damage. Guests clustered outside the door, shock and excitement on their faces. The music had stopped long ago. Police officers marched in, Leo and Gerard pushing to the front. My chest ached at the pain on their faces. When they reached me, I held my hand lightly to Murdock's chest. "He's on the floor. He was essence-shocked. I don't think he even knew what hit him."

Gerard muscled in front of Leo. "Let me through, dammit."

I let them pass and followed another four officers inside. They closed the doors. A strangled sob came from Gerard as he stood with hunched shoulders. Leo knelt on one knee and checked his father for a pulse. He knew what essence shock looked like. His hand fell away slowly, and he stared at his father as the other officers spread around the room. He rose, and Gerard clung to his lapel, shaking it with his fist. Murdock hugged his brother close as he shook with sobs. Our eyes met.

"You've got blood on you," he said.

"It's mine. He . . . I was shot," I said. It didn't seem like a good time to tell them their dead father shot me.

Gerard whirled around. "Who did this?"

"Manus ap Eagan. He's in a coma," I said as neutrally as possible.

Gerard's face became redder. "I want to see him. I want to see the bastard. Where is he?"

I lightly put my arm across his waist as he tried to pass. "Give yourself a minute, Gerry."

Leo hugged him from the side, his body shield flickering. I gently squeezed Gerry's arm, then dropped my hand. Murdock closed his eyes and touched his forehead to his brother's.

Paramedics and more police entered. The medical examiner hovered in the background like a carrion crow. I didn't know the Chestnut Hill police, but they were a lot more professional in a fey situation than I was used to. Maybe because Chestnut Hill had a lot of fey folk—a lot of rich fey folk. One of the officers moved me to a couch on the far side of the room and began to interview me. He asked several times if I were injured, confused by all the blood on me. A paramedic made me take off the jacket, convinced I was in shock and bleeding profusely somewhere. I didn't blame them. I was uninjured, yet soaked in my own blood.

The interview was thorough. It helped that I was a druid. Between my inborn talent for instant recall and my understanding of what the police needed to hear, it went quickly under the circumstances. I did not hide the fact that Manus killed the commissioner. There was no need. Eagan's essence signature saturated the commissioner's body. When his body arrived at the morgue, Janey Likesmith would have no difficulty registering it. Besides, the Guildmaster was acting in my defense in the confusion of the moment, though why he used so much essence I didn't understand.

The real aggressor in the room was dead.

31

I waited on the second floor of the Guildmaster's house. At either end of the hall, Danann security agents guarded the stairs. The Guild and police had locked down the entire property while the local police went through the list of guests and released them one by one. Commissioner Murdock's body was long since gone. Ryan macGoren had arrived shortly after the first responders, along with the mayor of Boston and the governor of Massachusetts. They spent time behind closed doors in a meeting room downstairs, emerging hours later with grim faces.

Tibbet came out of Eagan's bedroom, and we hugged. As a fey, she could count on a resilient physical constitution, but that didn't prevent deep worry lines from forming around her eyes. She idly rubbed my arm. "I've had a room prepared for you upstairs."

I adjusted some of her braids away from her forehead. "I've been thinking about that, Tibs, and decided I should go home. Eagan had his reasons for keeping a public distance from me. I don't think he'd want me here. You have enough to deal with anyway without me complicating things."

"Are you sure?" she asked.

"I'm sure," I said.

A commotion at the top of the main stairs drew our attention. Several police officers—Leo and Gerard among them—were arguing with the Danann agents. I trailed after Tibs as she rushed toward them. Halfway down the flight of stairs, Barnard and Kevin Murdock waited with intent, angry faces. Davis Jones, the Superintendent in Chief and the commissioner's second-in-command, gestured for the officers to step back as Tibbet approached.

"I need to see the Guildmaster," Jones said.

"This has already been discussed. The Guildmaster is in a coma. You need to coordinate any further inquiries through the governor's office and the Guild," Tibbet said.

"I would like to confirm that he's really in a coma." Jones leaned his wide, imposing frame between the guards and toward Tibbet.

I knew that type of thing didn't work on Tibbet. To prove my point, she calmly pressed the Danann agents to the side and moved closer. Tibbet is tall for a brownie, but she had to look up into Jones's face. "I am the Guildmaster's attorney. My client is unavailable." She relaxed her stance and placed a sympathetic hand on Jones's arm. "It's been a long night, Davis. We all need to rest."

Jones dropped his voice. "I've got angry men, Tibbet. They want to know why he's not under arrest."

"I'm going in there," Gerard Murdock said. He pushed past Jones, but a Danann agent stepped in front of him. Leo pulled him back.

Gerard was not in the best frame of mind. I needed to do something for the Murdocks. "Tibbet, will you let Leo through?" I asked.

She considered my request and moved aside. Leo

stepped between the guards, and I escorted him down the hall. "How are you holding up?" I asked.

"Barely. They're already rumbling about diplomatic immunity," he said.

"That's expected, Leo. That's why I thought you should see Eagan's out of it. People will know you're not using political games for a cover-up."

I opened the door to the bedroom. The pungent odor of burning herbs hung in the air. Gillen Yor chanted under his breath as he leaned over Eagan's still body. A mix of druid and brownie assistants worked quietly behind him. On the opposite side of the bed, Briallen moved into the pool of light from the lamp on the nightstand. I hadn't known she was there. She immediately stopped whatever she was doing and hugged Murdock. "I'm so sorry, Leonard," she whispered into his ear.

He cleared his throat. "Thank you. What's his status?"

"Critical. His wasting disease had already compromised his health, and the expenditure of essence almost depleted what was left. He might die," she said.

Eagan's ashen skin pulled over a shrunken frame. His wings—normally large and lit with the powerful reserves of essence of a Danann fairy—curled dim and opaque like swaddling around his body. I had seen something similar before. Briallen once showed me a dead flit. When fairies die, their wings eventually close around them like a cocoon. Eagan was on his way out.

"Why did he do it, Briallen? Why did he kill my father?" Murdock asked.

Briallen studied the dying fairy. "We have to hope he wakes up, Leonard. Maybe it was instinctive. Maybe he couldn't control it because of what's wrong with him. I don't know. If nothing else, Manus is a shrewd politician. I cannot imagine why he would have intentionally caused an international incident of this proportion."

Murdock nodded, a tiny muscle on his jawline twitching. He pulled his hand out of his pocket and handed me his keys. "Can you get my car? It's in the driveway somewhere. I need to get my brothers out of here."

He left us standing at the foot of Eagan's bed. Briallen held her hands up to me. "May I?"

She placed her hands on either side of my face. I closed my eyes as a warm surge of essence flowed through my skull. The dark mass in my head didn't even react but sat like a pinpoint of pressure deep in my mind. Briallen released me, her face troubled.

"You have new bone in your jaw and new teeth, if I'm not mistaken," she said.

I remembered the sensation of cold washing over my body after the pain of the gunshot. "I think I was paralyzed, too."

Briallen crossed her arms and compressed her lips. "The dark mass is smaller, almost as small as it was last summer. Do you think it healed you?"

I rubbed my hand over my face. "I don't know. Sometimes it feels like it's trying to kill me, and sometimes it seems to keep me alive."

She rested a hand on the footboard of the bed. "What do you see in him? Your sensing ability is more acute than ours."

The mass in my head normally didn't care if I used my sensing ability, but its low, steady pressure pulsed as if to draw attention to itself. The druids moved in auras of gold and green, the brownies in a more subtle amber. Eagan should have glowed brighter than all of us, except perhaps Gillen and Briallen. Instead, a dim white spark smoldered in his chest and head, casting a shadowed wash of light through the rest of his body. A haze threaded through his aura, speckles of darkness like pinholes in his body signature. I withdrew.

Gillen jerked his head up from the mortar and pestle he had in his hand. "What did you just do?"

I startled. "Nothing. I just looked. He's on the edge of death."

Gillen peered at Eagan. "His essence dimmed for a moment. Do it again."

"Gillen, I don't want to hurt . . ." I began.

"I said do it, you idiot. I'm the doctor, not you," he snapped. Bedside manner is not Gillen's strong point.

I pushed my sensing ability to interact with Eagan's body signature. The pinpoints of darkness blurred, and I jumped out. "Holy shit."

Gillen frowned. "I never made the connection."

Briallen looked from one of us to the other. "What is it?"

I took a deep breath and exhaled. "He's got whatever I have. The dark thing is in him, too."

Gillen shook his head. "It's more subtle than yours, and all throughout his body. Until he expelled so much of his own essence, I didn't even see it. Which means he's probably going to die because I don't know what the hell it is."

"What do you want me to do?" I asked.

Gillen shrugged. "Leave. You seem to be making it worse."

Thunderstruck, I stepped back. "Do you think I . . . ?"

Briallen hugged me. "Don't say what I think you're going to say. It isn't true. You need to go home and get some sleep."

I left the room in a daze and wandered down the back stairs. I didn't know the layout of the house and ended up back in Eagan's study. Crime-scene investigators blocked the entrance. One of them took pictures of the disconcertingly large stain on the rug from my miraculously healed wound. I went out a door to the back hall and exited the side of the house.

I found Murdock's car and started it. Before I had a chance to process what happened, Murdock opened the passenger door and got in.

"You want me to drive?" I said in surprise.

"Yeah, let's go before someone else talks to me," he said.

I guided the car over the thin sheet of ice that had built up on the long exit drive. Murdock dropped his head back and closed his eyes. Joe flashed in and leaned over the seat. We exchanged glances but didn't say anything, the heater fan making the only noise.

I drove through middle-of-the-night empty streets, the faint sounds of ambulances and police cars echoing through the city. An occasional lone pedestrian waited at a crosswalk, prompting idle curiosity about what someone would possibly need to do out in the cold and snow in the dead of night. Except for a few streetlights, nothing delayed us from Chestnut Hill to Broadway Bridge into Southie.

"How the hell did this happen?" Murdock's tone was soft and hurt.

I put my hand on his shoulder. "I don't know, Leo. It's fucked."

"But why did he even pull his gun?"

I crossed an intersection and parked the car on the edge of a curb. "Leo, I want you to hear from me what happened before you read the report. First, believe me when I tell you, Moira Cashel is a manipulative liar. If there's anyone to blame for this, it's her."

"What does she have to do with my father?"

I told him. All of it. About what she said and what his father said. About Amy Sullivan. I didn't tell him things she said that I didn't share with the police about the commissioner taking bribes. Let her make a public accusation. By the time I finished, Murdock had his hands clamped firmly over his face.

"She's a liar, Leo. Remember that," I finished. He shook his head, and I realized he was crying. I didn't know what to think anymore, but at that moment, I refused to believe Moira Cashel was telling the truth—about anything. "It's not true, Leo."

He wiped his face with his hands and let out a deep sigh as he stared out the window. "This is my fault. If I hadn't called you in on the case, you would have never gone to Eagan."

"No. If it's anyone's fault, it's mine. I didn't go to Eagan, he called me. He knew Sekka was hiding Vize, and Vize wouldn't be here if it wasn't for me. It's my fault, Leo. If I had done my job right three years ago, Vize would not be on the loose today."

"Vize didn't make my father pull a gun," he said.

"Cashel was planning something anyway, Leo. She wasn't going to stop until your father was disgraced. This is some Guild trick."

He shook his head. "No, no. It's my fault. I argued with my father about his meeting with Jark. He admitted he was letting it happen, Connor. He liked seeing the fey tear each other apart. That's when I confronted him about her. And then I told him about me, Connor. I threw it in his face that his son had a fey ability. I told him about my body shield. I primed his anger at the fey, and the last words I spoke to my father were angry. It's my fault."

"Dammit, Leo. Don't let her do this. Don't let whatever Maeve and the Guild are planning do this to you. That's what they want."

He covered his eyes as the tears flowed again. "I can't fix this."

I grabbed him by the back of the neck and pulled us together. He broke down when I did, sobbing into my chest as I rocked him. Joe crept from the backseat and draped himself on Leo's shoulder. "Let me take you home, Leo. You need to rest."

He shook his head against me. "I can't go back there to-night. I can't face them. I can't be who they need right now."

"They're your family, Leo. They love you."

He kept shaking his head. "I can't do it tonight."

Joe picked up his head. *I know a place.*

32

Only in the Weird will a bar let you sit quietly in the corner wearing a bloodstained jacket and drink yourself blind. Of course, Joe would know such a place. It had no name or windows or, for that matter, respectability. A neighborhood guy by the name of Carmine ran a number of places like it—hidden, quiet, and invitation-only. The music was killer blues, the smoke was thick, and the dancers came in all shapes, sizes, sexes, and species. A vaguely sweet scent filled the air, an aromatic happy drug that skirted close enough to legal that the law let it slide. It helped patrons focus on their beer and their dates and numbed the ache of whatever drove them to such places.

When we first walked in, I thought it was a bad idea. The next day would be tough on Murdock, between the press and the funeral arrangements and being the rock of the family. Joe deduced the situation better than I did. He said Murdock needed the breathing room and would crash before he became too drunk. He was right. Once the liquor started flowing, the waves of emotions sapped his strength, and he was done in a little over an hour.

As dawn neared, a small sober part of my brain convinced me to put Murdock in a cab home. Joe went along for the ride, convincing the driver to skip the fare in exchange for some flit karma. I watched the broken taillights of the cab coast away and stumbled through the mounds of snow. If Murdock was half-asleep by then, I wasn't. Mental images continued flashing through my mind: the commissioner's gun going off, Moira Cashel's bitter face, Eagan slumped on the floor. The commissioner dead. Scott Murdock was dead. The idea staggered me so much, and yet it paled next to whatever Leo was feeling.

"And for what?" I said. My own voice startled me as the close-in buildings amplified it. I wasn't prone to talking to myself, but everything that had happened pissed me off.

I'd lied to Murdock. I needed to tonight, needed to help him believe for a few more hours that his father was a good man. I never liked the commissioner because he always—always from the beginning—had treated me like crap. And I never knew why until now. I lied to Murdock because the truth was so appalling I didn't want to admit to it.

I believed Moira Cashel.

It wasn't her uncanny Amy Sullivan glamour or the pitch-perfect voice or even the small, trivial facts she knew about how I had met her. A skilled fey with the right information mimicked things like that all the time. I didn't put it past the Guild to play with my mind that way for some gain.

But tonight had changed my thinking. The look on the commissioner's face as he pulled the gun convinced me. No one pulled a gun over such stupid and obvious lies, at least not someone like Scott Murdock. But he did because he believed her, and he believed her because she wasn't lying. She had betrayed him as Amy Sullivan and had suckered him as Moira Cashel.

Scott Murdock was taking bribes. It was the only explanation for how the Guild was getting away with what was happening in the Weird. He had cut some deal with Ryan macGoren for some mutual benefit.

He was dirty.

I had slept with his wife.

"Danu's motherfreakin' blood," I said.

Uno appeared in the road.

"What the hell do you want?" The dog cocked its head as I walked around it. He reappeared in front of me.

"Leave me alone, dammit." I went around him again, then walked backwards. "You're a lousy harbinger of doom, you know that? I got shot in the *face*, and you didn't even bother to *show up*."

He loped around me and stopped again, dodging as I tried to pass. "Go away, dammit. Go bother Shay."

I shoved him with my leg. He stumbled sideways with a snarl that rose into a bark, then he vanished. I circled in place, waiting for him to come back. A cold wind swept down the street, but he was gone. "Good," I muttered.

The dark mass in my head shifted, and I pressed the heel of my hand against my temple. I laughed. I practically kicked a hound from Hel, it ran away, and the worst I had to show for it was a headache. I pulled my jacket tighter, the flimsy silk doing little to warm me.

My memory skipped to Eagan's bedroom and the faint dark haze in his essence. It was and wasn't like mine. I couldn't see mine in a visual sense, but I could feel it and had seen MRIs of it. It was a dense thing, a black concentration of shadow at the base of my skull, pressing right on the old brainstem. From what I saw of Eagan's condition, the darkness was more a dull haze.

I turned the next corner, and the damned dog was back. Uno shied before I took another step, then faded away.

The dark mass blocked my abilities, but Eagan didn't have that problem. Clearly. Gillen Yor thought the haze was responsible for his weakness. My dark mass devoured essence, but Eagan's seemed to just drain it away.

I stopped. I had seen that before. I had seen the darkness drain off essence like it was feeding on it. The *leanansidhe* did it on demand. She might not know what it truly was, but she wasn't dying from it, and it wasn't blocking her abilities. She knew how to use it.

Uno appeared, sat in the middle of the sidewalk, and barked once. I frowned. "If you're only good for stopping muggings, go back to bed, you stupid mutt. It's ten degrees, and the only things out here are me and you."

He faded. Insulting mysterious beings from the Land of the Dead was a defense I never knew worked. It didn't work with Jark, but I guessed it did with dogs.

I cut through an alley. Petty street crime goes down in the winter, and the Weird was no different on that score. The damned cold bothered murderers and thieves like anyone else, so I wasn't too worried. Besides, I wasn't joking with the dog. I wasn't stupid. I had my sensing ability ticking away. No one was out, especially not by a section of abandoned warehouses where they weren't likely to find anyone to mug.

I slowed to a stop. In the gray and white of the street, a bright orange sticker stood out like a flare. The crime-scene warning on the warehouse door. The one I slit open. I looked up and down the street for anyone. Empty. Uno flashed into view at my side but disappeared before I fully looked at him.

Did he herd me there? Could he hear my thoughts? Did he know I was thinking about the *leanansidhe* or sense that I was about to? The possible connection between my dark mass and Eagan's haze had simmered in the back of my mind all night. Could Uno know that? Or did I lead myself to the door, my subconscious pushing me there because of what I was thinking, the sensual pleasure I got from using the dark mass's abilities bubbling up in some mental center of desire.

I didn't care. I was there, and the creature in the tunnel held a key to possibly saving the Guildmaster's life. I hadn't heard from Keeva. I didn't think I would now, not after what Moira said. There was no way Ryan macGoren wasn't involved in her game, and Keeva wasn't likely to do me any favors over her boyfriend's objections. The *leanansidhe* was going to be down there. I pushed aside the thought that I was rationalizing going inside. No law said I couldn't learn something that might help Eagan and get off on the feeling at the same time.

The door popped open easily. Between the cold and the walk, the edge of my drunk was blunted by the time I reached the walled-off basement. Uno took care of the rest. He appeared near the back wall, suddenly there in the dark, and let out a howl that shook the walls. Adrenaline surged through me at the sound, burning off the rest of the alcohol in my system. When I reached the hidden opening in the wall, the dog was gone.

I hesitated. Maybe the dog was trying to warn me off. Maybe I wasn't as secure against the *leanansidhe* because of the thing in my head as I thought I was. I pushed the thought aside. The dog was messed up, a lost Dead animal with no more purpose, twisted like any other Dead fey. How could it portend my journey to TirNaNog if there was no TirNaNog anymore? It should have shown up at Eagan's when I apparently died and was reborn, but it didn't. I walked into the tunnel.

The dark mass pulsed in my head, a throb of pressure against the back of my eyes. I flushed with warmth despite the cold in the tunnel. The air rubbed against my skin, an itchy pleasure of temperature difference. My peripheral vision narrowed as the dark mass moved, and I navigated the tunnel by instinct and memory.

The *leanansidhe*'s room was a shambles. Books scattered across the floor where they had fallen from overturned tables. Burn marks seared the fabric of the armchair Druse used, and her reading lamp lay shattered next to it. I sensed nothing, no essence, the dull, sterile aftermath of the *leanansidhe*'s ability. At the back of the room, a white-and-silver essence glow drew me to the fissure in the wall.

Druse hunched over the bloodstone bowl in the chamber. No barrier field prevented me from approaching; the ward stones that generated it lay broken on the floor. The dark mass shifted, a burning sensation down my neck moving with the slow ooze of hot metal. My tongue grew thick with anticipation, a physical reaction to my desire for essence. Or the dark mass's desire. The difference between what I wanted and what the dark mass wanted blurred in the light of the bloodstone bowl.

Druse lifted her head, her eyes half-closed in a stupor. Her essence field shimmered in shades of purple, thick, pulpy tendrils of light hanging from her face, their tips silver with fading essence as she absorbed it. Her lips lifted in a lazy smile. "Ah, my brother, come, taste, and sup with me. I feel the need within you."

Speech refused to come. Something pierced my right hand with exquisite pain. Something pierced my chest with exquisite pain. Something pierced my cheek with exquisite pain. Dark essence snaked out of me, hungry darkness that danced in ropes of darkness. I stumbled against the bedrock pedestal beside Druse and drank, strands of darkness dipping into the ward stone, eclipsing the essence. Blood pounded in my temples, a steady, sensual rhythm that reverberated throughout my body, my chest filling as I inhaled through blood-gorged lips.

Druse touched me—with her hand, with her essence—a languid caress on my forehead. "Yes, my brother, surrender to the need, let the desire guide you. It's not pain, is it? It's the pleasure in the pain, yes?"

Her face pressed near mine, her eyes luminous with excitement, and I smiled. I understood her, the pulsing dark things slicing out of me, pulsing with rich essence, a pleasure that demanded payment. My skin shivered, every pore alive with feeling, with need and desire. My face grew hot, blood rushing through me in waves, prickling my skin to life, arousing me like nothing I had ever known.

Druse whispered in my ear—words, sounds—I was no longer sure. Her essence pressed against me, bulbous tendrils worrying at my face, my eyes. They pressed inward, and I gasped as they cut through, cut through and merged with my own, coiled around my darkness and my need and . . .

. . . yes yes I feel us we are us and the essence is ours and the want and the need and the same so good so strong so much so more we need more yes more the bowl empties and still we want and still we need and and and still there is more always more we need the prize the treasure the hidden gem we do not need to save it now to cherish it we need it now we want it now we reach for it now . . . oh myself my brother . . . oh there yes there yes it is there oh yes oh yes oh yes here it is so rich so lush we must have it must have it all drink of it take it all in the more the more we will have more and find more and more and . . .

Something broke in my mind, and I screamed at the pain. Druse vanished out of my mind like an extinguished candle. I opened my eyes. Dark ropelike lines trailed out of me across the floor, trailing off into the darkness of an exit from the chamber.

"Connor!" someone shouted.

Essence shivered and oozed through the shadow lines, the living essence of someone fey. As it seeped through me, my sensing ability touched it, and I recognized fairy essence.

Someone shook my arm. "Connor!"

I touched the fairy essence through the darkness, Danann fairy essence. Something hit me in the face, jarring the darkness out of the vision in one eye. A haze lifted off my awareness. I shook my head. The dark mass burned with a flow of essence, Danann essence from the next room. I shook my head again. Horrified by what I was doing, I recognized the essence that I was absorbing.

The dark ropes undulated as the silver mesh in my left arm flared and lit with essence. Like the dark mass, the actions and reactions of the tattoo seemed to have their own agenda, one I didn't understand and couldn't control. I shuddered as blades of ice sliced through me, tangling with the streams of darkness from my head. The dark mass convulsed and retreated. The white light from my arm flickered and went out. The backlash of the force and the pain threw me off my feet.

33

Wetness touched my face. I wiped at it, feeling something slick and sticky. I opened my eyes and stared into Uno's fetid, gaping mouth. He barked once softly and sat back on his haunches. The *leanansidhe* lay beside me, blood smeared across her forehead, the bloodstone bowl on the floor by her head. No essence emanated from her.

I sat up and reached for the ward stone. It wouldn't budge.

"Is it dead?" In his long white coat, hood thrown back, Shay stood near the pedestal nibbling at a fingernail.

"Where did you come from?" I asked.

He brushed at dirt and blood smears on his coat. "You know, my friends said I'd never be able to keep this clean."

"Shay!"

Startled, he met my eyes. "What?"

I stood. A heavy pounding filled my head. The dark mass moved like a restless sleeper at the base of my skull. "How did you find me?"

He looked down at Uno sitting beside him. "He forced me outside and chased me down the street. I thought he was taking me to . . . to wherever he was going to kill me."

"Something's screwy with that dog," I said.

Shay moved closer and stared at Druse. "That thing could use some hair conditioner."

I shook my head, too weak to laugh. "Not anymore."

Shay froze, blood draining from his face. "I killed it?"

"What happened?"

He pointed. "It was hanging off your back. All this black stuff was coming out of you. You wouldn't answer me. Then that . . . that thing spun its head around and hissed at me. I grabbed the bowl and hit it."

"What was that black stuff?" Shay asked.

"You don't want to know."

"It was running into that hole in the wall over there," he said.

Memory rose, the darkness pulling in essence, an essence I knew, and gorge rose in my throat at the thought. In two long strides, I reached the exit and found Keeva on the ground. Her pulse beat strongly beneath my fingers, but her essence flickered like a dying lightbulb. Another essence signature glowed inside her, strong and vibrant. Burn marks on her skin and wings showed the remains of a binding spell.

I patted her cheek. "Keeva?" No response. I pinched her.

"Help me get her up," I said.

Shay gave the *leanansidhe* a wide berth. Keeva groaned as we turned her over and pulled her into a seated position. I rubbed her arms. "Keeva? It's Connor. Can you hear me?"

She lifted her head, her eyelids fluttering. "Danu," she whispered.

Relief swept over me. "Keeva, wake up. You're okay."

She opened her eyes, struggling to focus on me. "Connor?"

"Yeah. Don't move. You were attacked by the *leanan-sidhe*. I think she infected you with a parasite or something," I said.

That brought her around. Her hands flew to her stomach. "What do you mean?"

I shook my head. "I'm sensing another body signature inside you. There's some kind of protective shield around it, and I can't see what it is."

"Get me up." She grabbed my shoulder, and we helped her to her feet.

"Maybe you shouldn't move until we know what's wrong," I said.

She swayed. "Get me to AvMem."

"Keeva . . ."

"I'm pregnant, you idiot! Get me to AvMem now."

My jaw dropped.

"Oh, congratulations!" said Shay.

Ignoring him, I draped Keeva's arm around my neck. "Get that ward stone, Shay. I'm not leaving it here."

Easy as he pleased, Shay stooped and picked up the bowl. Supporting Keeva with my other arm, I walked her through the chamber. "What happened, Keeva?"

She leaned against me. "I followed your ridiculous map. You might have mentioned the binding traps."

"Sorry. They weren't there when I was here last time."

"How did you know I was down here?" she asked.

It was hard to decide which made me look worse, the angry drunkenness or the creepy desire that drove me back to Druse. "It's a long story."

Uno bounded down the tunnel ahead of us, circling around back and running off again. He acted more like an overgrown puppy than what I expected in a hound from Hel. Keeva pressed her arm against me. "Do you feel that?"

"What?"

"Something's down here with us. I feel something moving around us. Something malevolent," she said.

I didn't sense anything but Uno. "You mean the dog?"

She cocked her head up. "What dog?"

Shay and I looked at each other. He looked away, sad and resigned. He didn't have to tell me what he was thinking about the dog.

"Another long story, Keev. It's nothing to worry about."

When we reached the walled-off basement, I sensed the remains of a binding spell across the *leanansidhe*'s bolthole. Threadlike tatters dangled from the walls and ceiling. I hadn't been in the right frame of mind to notice them on the way in.

"He wasn't here," Keeva said.

"Who wasn't?"

She forced herself to walk on her own. If there was one thing I knew about Keeva, it was that she was tough. "Vize."

Guilt swept over me. I had been wrong, and Keeva had walked into the *leanansidhe*'s chamber unprepared. "I'm sorry, Keev. I'm really sorry. I thought Sekka was hiding the ward stone. That's what I thought the Guild wanted. I didn't know that you were looking for Vize until tonight. I'm an idiot."

Keeva started up the stairs. "You won't get any argument from me on that score. Why the hell would we care about a ward stone?"

I looked back at Shay coming up behind me as he clutched the stone bowl to his chest. "I thought it was important."

Uno burst out of the warehouse door. The morning sun blinded us after the tunnels. I blinked hard against the tears in my eyes. As my vision returned, I saw essence building up in Keeva's wings.

I pulled out my cell. "You are not flying to AvMem, Keeva."

A challenge rose in her eye, but she checked it. Without argument, she leaned against the building while I called the Guild's emergency line. Keeva held a hand out to Shay. "Let me see that."

He pursed his lips and held out the bowl. "I know you meant it, but let me see that 'please,' right?"

When Shay released it, it slipped through Keeva's hands and hit the ground. She bent to retrieve it, but it wouldn't budge. "What's the trick?" she said to Shay.

He leaned down and picked up the bowl. His finely arched eyebrows drew together as he turned it in his hands. He handed it back to Keeva, and it fell again. I tried to pick it up, but no luck. The three of us must have made an interesting scene as we squatted around a stone bowl in the snow. Shay picked it up again. I took it and couldn't hold it. I stared at it and remembered what the *leanansidhe* had said. "Shay, this is going to be an odd question, but are you a virgin?"

It *was* an odd question. When I met Shay, he was turning tricks on the street and living with a boyfriend. He pretended to have his dignity insulted. "A gentleman would not ask such things."

"Right. That's why Connor would," said Keeva.

I scowled at her. "Funny."

The familiar buzz of large wings moving at speed filled the morning air, and two great shadows swept overhead. Danann security agents wheeled above us and descended. "Are you well, Director macNeve?" one of the chrome-domes asked.

"Take me to Avalon Memorial, please. It's just a precaution," she said. She folded her wings against her back as the two agents slipped their hands into straps sewn into her jumpsuit. "Not a word to anyone, Connor. I'll stop by to kill you after I see Gillen Yor, okay?"

I smiled weakly. "You sound like yourself already."

The security agents flexed their wings and rose on drafts of essence. When they cleared the roofline, they swung around and disappeared. As they left, a movement caught my eye, someone on a roof watching us. The Hound. He ducked out of sight.

Shay stared at the now-empty sky. "She's still kind of a bitch, isn't she?"

Keeva had been less than kind to Shay in the past. When I say less than kind, I mean ignored him like he didn't exist. "She has her moments, Shay."

He picked up the ward stone. "Why did you ask about my virginity?"

I shook my head. "The *leanansidhe* said only a virgin could move it."

Shay gave me a sly look. "There's more than one kind of virgin, you know."

"One kind of . . ." I laughed. "Gods. You've never slept with a woman, have you?"

He rested his chin on upright fingers. "Look at this face, doll. The only girls in high school who wanted to sleep with me were confused lesbians."

"I guess whoever put the taboo on the stone was a little old-fashioned," I said.

He pouted coyly. "I try to be modern."

"Hang on to that for me, okay? And don't tell anyone you have it. The last thing you need is someone coming to look for it."

He pulled his hood up. "Are you going to be all right, Connor?"

I shrugged. "I need to get some sleep. You should, too."

"I don't think I'll be able to do that for a while." He

clutched the bowl to his chest again and started up the street.

"Hey, Shay?" He turned his head, but his hood didn't move. Half his face showed along the edge of fur, a few strands of his long dark hair waving in the wind. "Thank you for saving my life."

He wiggled his nose at me. "Karma, doll."

He weaved down the sidewalk, following a sinuous path of compacted snow. When he was a block or so away, Uno lumbered out from between two cars and followed him.

I checked the roofline again. The Hound was gone. Exhaustion weighed down on me. Thinking about Keeva and Shay—and even the Hound—were just avoidance tactics. I didn't want to think about what had happened down in that tunnel. The thing in my head could be used. I could guide it. It reacted to what I was feeling, and I could use it. Only it seemed to work with aspects of myself that made me feel wrong. And ashamed. The worst part was, that wasn't enough to make me not want to use it.

And that scared me.

34

Meryl was asleep in the middle of my futon when I arrived at the apartment. After hearing about what happened at Eagan's the night before, she had surmised I was with Murdock and had let herself in to wait for me. How she got in with all the security warding, I didn't know, but it didn't surprise me. Very little stopped her when she put her mind to it. Without a word, she wrapped her arms around me and drew me into bed. Exhausted, I slept the morning away. By the time I woke up, the governor had called in the National Guard, and the Weird was under curfew. Meryl and I spent the rest of the day in various stages of undress, lolling about the apartment and watching TV.

The scent of popcorn filled the air. Meryl watched the bag revolve in the microwave while I sat on the edge of the futon annoyed by the television news.

"They're doing the 'Wasn't-Scott-Murdock-a-Noble-Guy?' piece again," I said.

The news had settled on its angle for the life of Scott Murdock. Television station after station outlined the life of a man who walked the fine line in Boston between fey dominance and human accommodation. Parts of it were even true. Scott Murdock was no fan of the fey, but he also knew he couldn't ignore or eliminate them. Helping them, of course, was not on his list. That was the Guild's job, and as long as it dropped the ball, it played right into his political maneuvering. I saw it time and again. Someone could blame the Boston P.D. for its ineffectual approach to fey crime, but its failings always paled in the face of the Guild's indifference.

In the end, he had crossed the line. Why, only he could answer, and that wasn't possible anymore. Maybe the catastrophic events of the last months overwhelmed him. Maybe he realized his contrived failures to protect the human populace had mutated into real ones out of his control. And maybe Moira Cashel pushed him over the edge with her revelations of his past and her revenge for his actions. She seduced him once and seduced him again. That had to suck for him.

The microwave dinged. Meryl juggled the hot bag to the counter, pulled the corners of the bag open, and let out the steam. "Eh, I'm indifferent. Police commissioner in this town is a no-win job. Whoever gets it is going to end up sucking at it one way or the other."

I cocked my head toward her. "Are you defending him?"

She pushed a kernel of popcorn into my mouth as she settled on the futon. "I didn't say I liked him."

I slid back to sit next to her against the wall. "Did I mention the part where he shot me in the face?"

She grinned, watching the television. "Who am I to criticize someone who succeeds where others failed?"

I poked her, and she laughed, sending some popcorn flying as she pulled away. "It hurt," I said.

"Yeah, your poor wallet. The dry cleaning bill's gonna be a bitch."

I ate popcorn off the blanket. "Ha-ha."

She fished in the bag, as if looking for a particular kernel. "Do you think Moira healed you?"

"I was wondering that myself. What I can't figure is why she would."

"Maybe she thinks you'll forgive her and be her boyfriend again," Meryl said.

I tweaked her nose. "Oh, you're in fine form tonight."

She giggled and tilted the bag toward me. "I'm getting bored. We've been trapped in here all day. Anything from Murdock?"

I took a handful of popcorn. "Not since the text." Just one word: Thanks. He probably didn't intend it, but I had been worrying over that one word all day. Thanks for what? Letting him mourn his father? Telling him what happened? Or was it sarcastic, implying I said things he didn't need to hear last night? Was it because I called him a cab? He wasn't one for long, drawn-out explanations, and I was. The difference made us question ourselves. I think.

"You know Murdock. Man of few words," Meryl said.

Man of few words, indeed. I never thought I'd see Murdock like I did the night before—lost and confused. He always kept control of his emotions—even his anger, which could be formidable. To see him so helpless and riddled with guilt hurt me because none of it would have happened if he had never met me. He would have never had a case that involved Vize. It always came back to Vize.

"Can you ask Zev where Vize is?" I asked.

She cocked an eyebrow at me. "Where the hell did that come from?"

I shrugged. "Because Zev knows. The night Murdock disappeared, Zev wouldn't tell me, and I could tell damned well he knew where to find the Hound. I think when Sekka died, Zev took over hiding Vize, and the only other person present when she died was the Hound. Vize is the Hound. That's why Zev wouldn't tell me."

"But you told me the Hound was one of the Dead," she said.

I nodded. "I also told you he had something funky going on with his essence. I'm betting he's wearing a glamour."

Meryl considered the idea, then I felt the flutter of a sending in the air. A moment later, I felt another. "Zev said he's busy," she said.

I snorted and ate some popcorn. "That tells me I'm right. I'll be talking to Zev again."

In addition to all the troubles in the Weird, film crews had descended on the neighborhood, using the commissioner's death as a prism to view the conflicts he was involved in. By midafternoon, a contingent of solitaries rejoicing at the commissioner's death had managed to alienate the general public. I supposed their position was inevitable. Bad timing, to say nothing of poor taste, but inevitable. Solitaries in the Weird had suffered under the commissioner's leadership of the police force. But they did themselves no favors by dancing in the streets over his death.

When the governor called in the National Guard, the situation had gone national. CNN fed live images of tanks and trucks stationed at the Fort Point Channel bridges at Summer, Congress, and Old Northern. The mayor and governor assured everyone they were precautions and would enter the neighborhood only if the situation deteriorated.

I reached for more popcorn and paused. Meryl was wearing an old sloppy sweater of mine with an open neck. A purple spot in her cleavage showed above the collar. I pulled her sweater down a few inches. Near the bottom of her right breast, a red circle of teeth marks showed against purple-and-blue bruising. "Did I do that?"

Meryl tucked her chin and looked down. "Well, I'm not that limber."

I slumped against the wall. "Hell, Meryl, I'm sorry."

She shrugged. "I've had worse. It's a little out of character for you, though."

I was horny as hell when I got back to my apartment and found her sleeping in it. When she woke up, we went at it like rabid cats on a hot summer night. At least, I did. The need was . . . I didn't want to finish the thought. Something in my brain had clicked off. It hadn't mattered who was in my bed. A need consumed me, and I wanted release.

Meryl adjusted her sweater and ate some popcorn. My stomach clenched. "Did I go over the line?" I asked.

She shook her head. "You would have known that last night, if you had. I'm making an observation, not an accusation. Trust me, if I hadn't been having fun, you'd be in the hospital."

I closed my eyes and dropped my head on her shoulder. "Something dark's inside me," I said.

"Something dark's inside all of us, Grey. It's only a problem if we let it too far out," she said.

"What happens then?"

She pushed popcorn in my mouth. "No one shares popcorn with you, except maybe a big burly guy named Bubba. If you're lucky, he'll like butter."

I twisted my neck to look up at her. "You have a knack for being flip and comforting at the same time, you know that?"

She grinned. "It's not a knack; it's a talent."

I rolled up from the futon and opened the fridge. One benefit of having a small apartment is being able to reach for beer practically from bed. "We're low on Guinness. Do you want to make a packie run?"

"Whoa! Check this out," Meryl said.

The local news station had jumped to their helicopter

camera. Black smoke billowed from a building on the far
end of the Weird. The helicopter hovered, moving in a slow
arc to keep upwind from the pall. Thick flames reflected
from beneath, coloring the snow-covered streets a lurid
orange.

I handed her a beer. "That's Tide Street."

She took a swig. "Yeah, tomorrow's *Herald* is gonna
read, 'Hel Burns.'"

As I sat on the bed, a sending hit me so hard, it gave me
a sharp pain. *Get out of the apartment now. They're coming
for you.*

"Did you get a sending just now?" I asked. Meryl
shook her head. "Someone warned me to get out of the
apartment."

"Who?" Meryl asked.

Sendings usually have personality signatures on them,
telltale touches of essence from the person who sent them.
"I don't know. It was stripped. Someone doesn't want to
be known."

"Do you trust it?" she asked.

I drank some beer. "It was pretty strong. People don't
waste that much essence for a sending." I paced along the
foot of the futon. I glanced at the smoke on the TV screen.
"I don't like that it came as soon as that happened."

Meryl slipped to the edge of the futon and leaned down
for her boots. "So, let's go watch the fire. Can't hurt."

I wandered into the study and pulled on a heavy black
wool sweater and a knit cap. My boots were under the desk.
When I leaned in to drag them out, I heard a deep rumble,
and the lights went out. "Should I be freaked out by this?"
I called out.

"Give me a sec," Meryl called back. I carried the boots
into the living room. Meryl was mostly dressed for outside,
but she paused, hand palm up, with a ball of blue light filling the room. Her eyes shifted back and forth as the soft

flutters of sendings tickled my senses. Her eyebrows shot up. "Wow. The power plant blew up."

The old Boston Edison plant overlooked the Reserve Channel, not far beyond where the fire on Tide Street was. It serviced the general area, straddling the Weird and Southie. "Who'd you ask?"

She released the ball of light in order to pull her boots on. "No one. A bunch of people sent."

I retrieved my daggers from the head of the futon and slipped them into my boots. With everything going on outside, being unarmed was not the way to go. Meryl pulled her cloak around her. "You know, sane people don't go for walks after a curfew when the neighborhood is blowing up," she said.

"Yeah, well, sane people don't get warnings to get out of their apartments because someone's coming for them either," I said.

A ripple went through the air, and my ears popped at a sudden release of essence. Meryl pursed her lips. "Um . . . your security wards just died."

I nodded, scanning the apartment with my sensing ability. "All of them. All at once. Let's go."

As I opened the apartment door, glass shattered behind us. Meryl whirled, a wall of essence flaring out of her. The yellow barrier slammed against a Danann fairy climbing in the window and knocked him outside. The sound of running echoed in the stairwell. I leaned over the stair railing, then ducked back into the apartment. "We've got armed brownies coming up."

Meryl held her hands out to either side as she powered a barrier on the broken living-room window and pumped essence into the window wards in the study. "I'm getting Danann hits on the roof. What the hell is going on?"

Basement. Elevator shaft. Now.

"I just got hit with another sending," I said. I rushed back out to the hall. Whoever did the sending was accurate. I didn't have an elevator. I had a shaft. Far below, flashlight beams swept in wild patterns through the cage of the shaft as the brownies ran up. I pulled open the metal gate. The elevator car was in the basement. "Get out of there, Meryl!" I called.

She was at my side in an instant and surveyed the cables in the open shaft. "You're kidding."

I held out my hand. "Time's wasting."

"Hold on." She ran back into the apartment and returned with a pair of canvas gloves. "I saw these on the counter. They'll protect your hands some."

"Thanks." I pulled on the gloves.

Meryl hugged me from behind, one arm over my left shoulder, the other under my right arm. Her body shield flared around us. "Go!"

I jumped and grabbed the nearest cable. Momentum carried our weight across the shaft. "I'm sliding," I said.

"I thought that was the plan," Meryl said to the back of my head.

I relaxed my grip, and we started down. Meryl chanted behind me, and a thick mist billowed around us as she created a druid fog. The flashlight beams of the brownies drew closer. The brownies shouted as the fog obscured their vision. The gloves were coming off, and I grabbed the cable tighter. We jerked to a stop, my shoulders threatening to dislocate. We hung in the fog as a half dozen brownies on the stairs circled obliviously around us. I settled my hands deeper into the gloves when they passed and let go again. We spiraled around the cable the last three floors and hit the top of the elevator. Meryl's body shield bounced us off the mechanics of the lift, and we rolled apart. The hatch on the elevator popped open. Meryl thrust essence-charged hands at the opening.

"Hurry up before they realize you're gone," a deep voice said.

Through the elevator hatch, a dwarf I didn't know stared up at us. I gave Meryl a shrug and jumped. I landed on my feet and held my hands up to break Meryl's fall. I didn't need to. She grabbed the edge of the opening and swung herself through, landing with a lot more grace than I had.

"This way," said the dwarf. He darted out of the propped-open gate, and we followed him through a twisting basement corridor. Another dwarf stood at a door, gesturing us in. We ran through to a sizable room with several couches arranged around a wide shallow bronze vessel of water. A scrying pool. Someone slammed the door shut. "I thought you guys moved," I said.

"That's what everyone was supposed to think," the first dwarf said. He joined his partner in pushing a large bookcase out of the way to expose a short, finished opening in the wall. "Through here. Don't stop until you get to the car."

"Whoa, whoa. Who the hell are you people?" I asked.

The dwarf threw me an annoyed look. "Does this look like a party? Everything you need to know is in the car. Get moving."

We moved toward the opening, but the dwarf held his hand in front of Meryl. "She can't go."

I glared at him. "What the hell? I'm not leaving her here."

"No, go ahead," Meryl said.

"What!"

She nodded. "No, really. I'll be fine. I'll scrub your essence trail and slow them down."

"No," I said.

She turned back to the door. "Just go, Grey. They're not after me. You're going to screw up whoever did this for you. Move!"

I hesitated. The dwarf sighed heavily and pushed me. I fell through the opening, and someone grabbed my arm. I looked back at Meryl's retreating figure. "Get Joe for me, Meryl!"

The bookcase slid back in place. I jerked my arm away. A flashlight clicked on. In the backwash of light, another dwarf smiled at me. "Hey, Grey. Fancy meeting you here."

Banjo turned and walked away. "Will you please tell me what's going on? Is this Moke's doing?" I asked.

Banjo and Moke had helped me out of a tight spot a few weeks earlier. Moke's troll essence was still bonded to me from the experience. "No, he's taking care of one of the bridges. This is just a side job I picked up from an old friend," Banjo said over his shoulder.

He led the way in the dark through some kind of rough tunnel. My sense of direction told me we were somewhere behind my building under the street. "Side job for who?" I asked.

"Whom," Banjo said. We passed through another opening into a dark basement. "You don't need to know. Keeps things safer that way."

"Did you foresee this?" I asked.

Banjo was one of the best seers in the Boston, or at least claimed to be. Dwarves were damned good at scrying. "Parts of it," he said. He pointed to a door. "That's the exit. Car's waiting."

I gave up. My experience with Banjo was that if I didn't pay for his predictions, I wasn't going to get them. I opened the door. "Thanks. Tell Moke I said hi."

"He'll be flattered, I'm sure. Mind your—" I stumbled in a pothole but kept my feet. Banjo shrugged. "Step." He closed the door.

I was in the alley behind the building next to mine. A black car with diplomatic plates idled in the lane. The rear door opened on the passenger side.

"You arrived faster than I anticipated," Eorla said.

35

"The early warning you sent helped," I said, as the driver gunned it up the alley.

Eorla tilted her head. "I sent no warning."

I shook my head in exasperation. "Great. Whatever. What the hell is going on?"

Eorla glanced out the window as we crossed Old Northern Avenue. Fire lit the night sky in several places. "The Guild either overplayed or underplayed its hand. I haven't decided."

"The Guild? That's the Guild in my apartment building?"

She nodded. "Of course. Didn't your security system fail? Who else has the knowledge and ability to do that?"

"Is this because of what happened at Eagan's?"

Eorla placed a delicate hand on my thigh. "Bastian told you before that happened that the Guild was working through legal channels to arrest you. With the unrest caused by the commissioner's death, they panicked that they might lose you."

We slowed as we turned onto Congress Street. Brownie

security guards were marching on a group of elves in the street after curfew. Eorla pursed her lips as she assessed the scene. "Overplayed, I think. They started something with these people and have lost control."

"Eorla, I do not have any idea what you are talking about," I said.

She shifted on the seat. "The Guild was using the Dead to flush out Bergin Vize. The solitaries were hiding him at the power plant."

"Danu's blood, Eorla. Are you saying the Guild blew up the power plant?"

She nodded. "There was an emergency evacuation of the human staff a short time ago. It was an excuse to clear the building, of course. That's when I knew the Guild was moving. They were hoping to capture both of you in the confusion."

"So, the Consortium is kidnapping me instead," I said.

Eorla turned to me with amused insult. "The Consortium has no idea I'm here. I'm helping you move across the board, Connor. You are free to get out of this car anytime you please, but do remember you are free to do that because I made it possible."

Bemused, I shook my head. "Why are you doing this?"

She shrugged. "For the same reason I investigated the Taint. Maeve and Donor are playing a far more dangerous game than I think any of us understand. I truly believe keeping their power in equilibrium is the only thing keeping us all safe."

"So Maeve gets Vize, and I go on the run from her and the Elven King," I said.

Eorla chuckled. "You know better than that, Connor. You tried to capture Bergin for years. I doubt Ryan macGoren can. No, it would not surprise me at all if Bergin is sitting in another car somewhere nearby having this same conversation with someone equally interested in the game."

On Summer Street, the car rocked as people crowded near it. Eorla leaned forward. People filled the street between the concrete barriers on one side and buildings on the other. The car slowed to a crawl. A block ahead, tanks lined the Summer Street bridge as searchlights arced through the sky above them.

"Rand, please send ahead to the checkpoint and see if they can clear a path for us." She leaned back with a sigh. "You need legal help, Connor. Unless you have truly important allies in the Seelie Court, you should consider Bastian's offer."

"You knew about that?" I asked.

"I know more about what Bastian knows than he will ever realize. His major flaw is a chronic habit of underestimating me," she said.

"He's an idiot," I said.

She laughed. "Yes, I've told him so, many times. Do you feel that?"

A faint vibration trembled through the car, a sensation like a large truck or a train passing by. "We're nowhere near a subway line," I said.

On the bridge, National Guardsmen ran for a wall of sandbags on the Weird side of the channel. Danann security agents hovered over the command post on the downtown end of the bridge. The vibration increased to a rumble. The crowd shifted direction as nervous people sidetracked into the nearby alley. The solitaries who had been making their way to the bridge turned and began to run.

"Your orders, ma'am?" Rand said.

Eorla watched with confused interest as people streamed by. "This might be happening to get us through. Let's see if they clear the way."

The car rocked on its suspension and a fracture appeared in the road. Rand backed away, turning the car amid a sea of people. The car bounced as another large rumble filled the air. With a loud snap, the edge of the bridge shifted on its supports. My teeth rattled as the shaking increased. With a roaring rumble, the bridge buckled, chunks of concrete and stone bursting into the air. Soldiers scrambled as tanks slid off the crumbling pavement. With a slow shudder, the bridge collapsed into the river. Essence shimmered over us like a wave front.

"Troll work," I said.

"Congress Street Bridge is gone, too," Rand said. He wheeled the car around in the intersection and turned down A Street.

"Why the hell would trolls destroy the bridges?" I wondered aloud.

Eorla leaned toward her window. "I'm getting confused reports of fighting throughout the neighborhood."

More National Guardsmen blocked the street two blocks ahead. As we approached, essence-fire cut across our path. Rand hit the brakes and spun the car.

"They are not responding to my sendings, ma'am," Rand said.

Eorla's gaze shifted back and forth as she watched the running crowd. "Let's go to the power plant. Guild staff should be present there," Eorla said.

"Guild staff just fired on us, Eorla," I said.

She looked out the rear window. "They're following orders. I'll get us through at the plant."

Eorla's calm reactions impressed me. I supposed they shouldn't have. She was an Old One, an eyewitness to more war and danger than I had ever seen or probably ever would. "You're enjoying this," I said.

She shook her head. "I don't enjoy pointless bloodshed, Connor. The Guild will need to be held accountable for this."

"The Consortium isn't blameless," I said.

She nodded. "True. The Consortium has its own crimes to answer for."

Summer Street became impassable as the crowd changed direction again and streamed back toward the channel. Rand cut through an alley and headed down Old Northern toward the power plant. More fires had sprung up, whether set by angry residents or spread from existing ones, I didn't know. It would be a long investigation when it was over.

"Ma'am, we have a problem," Rand said.

Rand brought the car to a slow stop near B Street. Ahead, Old Northern ran into a gauntlet of fire. From the city's World Trade Center on the left to a series of empty warehouses on the right, flames and smoke filled the air. Fire trucks hung back, but it didn't look like they were going to make much difference if they got through. "Find a way around it, Rand," Eorla said.

Glowing embers floated on the air, wind whipping them in a dance of orange lights. Rand backed the car. A single mote of yellow floated down, then dove toward us. It hit the windshield, popped inside, and plunged into my forehead.

D and Northern. Vize here. Need help.

Murdock. The essence faded with the message, but his body signature was unmistakable.

"Wait! Murdock's up ahead there. We have to go through it," I said.

Rand stopped the car and looked at Eorla in the rearview mirror.

Eorla's eyebrows drew together. "We can't risk it, Connor. We have to go around."

I stared at her. "You said I'm free to go anytime. If we don't go through, I will get out and walk through that fire if I have to."

Her eyes flashed with anger, exposing the temper I knew

she had. She shifted in the seat and leaned back. "Rand, I will bond the car. Drive through when I'm finished."

His expression read disagreement, but he shifted his focus to the fire. Eorla closed her eyes and chanted. Pale blue essence welled out of her and spread through the car. The essence seeped through windows and doors, indifferent to the metal. When it surrounded us from end to end, Rand hit the gas.

We skidded on ice before the wheels caught. The car raced toward the wall of flame and pierced it like an arrow. The car rocked violently in the firestorm, the temperature spiking incredibly fast. Indigo cracks appeared in Eorla's barrier, but she maintained her chanting. In a funnel of burning air, we shot out of the fire into a clear space. Rand slammed on the brakes to avoid hitting a mass of people on the other side.

Eorla caught her breath. "That wasn't as bad as I imagined it would be."

Solitaires and the Dead battled in the street. Essence raked the air, streams and spikes of amber, burgundy, yellow, and white. Green streaks of elf-shot poured in from all sides, and the blue spark of essence bombs flashed and burned. Twisting and turning through the fighting, a sickly green fog with black mottling undulated. The Taint clung to everyone, goading them, boosting their own essences and overwhelming their minds. The malevolent essence glowed in the faces of the Dead, bonded to their body signatures like a second skin.

I flicked an eyebrow up. "I'm afraid to know what you imagined."

36

A fire truck sat on the sidewalk. Several dozen humans used it as a vantage point—firefighters, police officers, and National Guardsmen. When the solitaries were not attacking the Dead, they kept their distance from the truck but took random shots at it. The humans were not shy about shooting back. Whenever anyone came too close, the firefighters directed high-pressure truck hoses to push them back. That would only last until the water ran out.

"Do you see your friend?" Eorla asked.

The sight lines from the backseat made it difficult to see much of anyone. "I have to get out."

Behind the car, the firestorm roared with fury. The night sky lit red and orange with the reflected glow. Eorla opened her door and got out.

"What are you doing?" I asked. "The fire's advancing. Rand, get her out of here."

Rand got out, but Eorla raised her hand. "I'll keep the fire back while you find your friend."

I was about to turn away, when Brokke's words came

back to me. Something was going to happen to her because of me. He was sure of it. "Eorla, you don't have to do that. Get out of here. I'll find my own way."

She smiled. "And I, mine. I want to ensure that you are safe before we part."

"Rand," I said.

"Rand"—Eorla interrupted—"answers to me alone. Go, before neither of us survives this."

She raised her arms and chanted, a fierce neon green essence welling up in her hands. I locked eyes with Rand. "If things go wrong, you make sure she gets out whether I'm back or not. No matter what she says, got it?"

He glanced at Eorla to see if she was looking, then nodded once before I ran from the car. A cluster of the Dead marched up the street as a unit, a mix of fairies and elves shooting their way through the melee. A blaze of red essence flared to my left. Another group was entering the fray. Murdock was leading several officers in. Gerry and Bar Murdock guarded their rear flank. Officers leveled their guns at me, but Gerry held his hand out. "He's okay," he shouted.

I fell in next to him. "What the hell are you guys doing?"

Gerry nodded ahead. "Leo says we have to take down the guy they're protecting."

The fire truck showered water across the path of the Dead. The street was slick with wet ice as I pushed my way through the knot of men. At the front, Leo carried guns in both hands. His body essence flared like a crimson shield that covered people to either side of him. "Leo, the solitaries will kill you if you try to take Vize," I shouted above the noise.

He waved one of his guns. "The Dead guys already have him. Cashel has him."

I ducked my head around him to see through the crowd.

Jark led the Dead fey down the street, knocking aside any-one who got in his way. In the middle of the group, Vize stumbled, his arms bound to his sides with essence bind-ings. Moira walked behind him, holding the bindings like a leash.

"That's even worse, Leo. Cashel can knock this whole group down with one hand," I said.

Determination set in on his face. "Then she'll have to do that. Those two caused this. My father's dead because of them."

Rage poured off him like a vapor. I'd seen that look be-fore on people. It was commitment and anger driven by vengeance, and there was no talking him out of it. I took a deep breath. "Give me a gun," I said.

I hadn't used a gun when I worked for the Guild. I hadn't needed to, but I knew how to use one. Leo handed me a 9mm pistol. He pulled an extra magazine out of his belt and passed it over his shoulder. I checked the slide and sight.

The Dead reached the high-pressure water blast and paused in their march. When they turned to take out the fire truck, they realized we were bearing down on them. Pale essence-fire raked against Murdock's shield. He bounced on his feet but held his ground. The Dead came closer. Someone behind me fired his gun. The shot spooked the others and more shots rang out. Four or five Dead fell in the front of the group. Panic set in as they recoiled from the shots. The fey weren't used to guns, especially the Dead who had never seen one before.

Jark screamed in fury. In a blur of green, he leaped out of the pack and tackled Murdock. Their essence collided in a shower of amber sparks as they tangled on the ground in a knot of flailing arms and legs.

Without Murdock's shield, essence tore through the group behind me. Officers fell, stunned or dead, as the rest scrambled out of the way. My dark mass spiked and scuttled across my mind. An essence strike came at me, bending at the last moment and striking my left arm. My silver tattoo ignited in cold pain and reflected the bolt back into the fighting. The Dead flinched away from me, the Taint in their body signatures reacting to the dark mass within me.

Gerry circled Leo and Jark, tracking them with his gun. Murdock pinned Jark, hitting him with glancing blows as they slipped across the icy ground. They rolled, their essence shields tossing people aside like gnats. Jark grabbed Leo by the arm and flung him. He landed against a car, its door crumpling behind him. Without a pause, Murdock lunged back, clamping his hands on the berserker's neck, his momentum taking them both to the ground again.

Murdock's body shield intensified as he raised his fist and swung. Jark's head snapped to the side. He thrust his hands up and tried to force Murdock off, but Murdock gripped his neck with one hand and hit him with the other. Murdock hit him again. His body shield held us all back. I couldn't stop him. Again and again, he pounded on Jark's face, the Dead man's body shield collapsing beneath the onslaught. Jark let out a strangled scream of anger, his voice trailing hoarse as his larynx was crushed beneath Murdock's weight. Yellow streaks of essence bounced futilely off Murdock's body shield as the Dead tried to help their leader. Jark's arms fell slack to his sides. His head lolled, one eye crushed beneath a shattered cheekbone, the other staring sightlessly. Leo staggered back.

"Someone cut this bastard's head off and throw it away," he said.

The Dead froze in shock at the sight of Murdock standing over Jark's body. The protective circle around Vize crumbled as more of them retreated, leaving only a small contingent around Moira and Vize. Murdock charged into them, sending bodies flying as he lost his footing and fell. Gerry and I rushed after him. As we reached him, Murdock sprang from the ground and knocked aside a lone elf left protecting Moira.

She yanked the bindings on Vize, forcing him to bend back as she twisted him in front of her as a shield. She raised a hand blazing with essence to Vize's temple.

"I'll kill him," she said.

Murdock stopped. Gerry raised his gun. "Go the fuck ahead, lady, and save us the trouble."

She glared at me. "You know this is bigger than they understand, Connor. You know how long we've tried to stop Vize."

I dropped my gun to my side. "You started this, Moira. You're on your own . . ."

His body shield shimmering, Murdock spread his arms out. "Drop your hands and give him to me."

Fury twisted Moira's features. Her face blurred as the Amy glamour settled over her. "You must listen to me, Leonard."

Gerry took two steps forward, his arms straight out as he pointed his gun. "What kind of shit is this?"

"Gerry, listen to me," Moira said.

Leo pressed one hand against Gerry's chest. "Let Vize go," he said to Moira.

"Get that face off!" Gerry screamed.

"You're my children . . ." she said.

Gerry fired.

Moira's head jerked back. As if in slow motion, she reeled over backwards with a deep red mark blossoming on her forehead. Gunpowder spray tattooed her forehead and cheeks—the Amy Sullivan glamour rippling away to show Moira Cashel's true face again. Vize stumbled to the side, his neck speckled with more gunshot residue. Moira's binding spell disintegrated off him. Suddenly free, he tripped, managed to keep his balance, and ran off.

"Get him out of here, Leo," I said. He didn't respond. I

shook his arm. "Leo! Get Gerry out of here before the Dead realize what he's done."

Gerry dropped his gun, his face devoid of emotion. "How the hell did she do that?"

Leo lifted his head as if coming out of a fog and stared at me with red-rimmed eyes. "How did all this happen?"

I gripped his arm. "Leo, listen to me. Get Gerry and everyone else on that fire truck and get out of here."

He looked around in a daze. "There's a fire. They need the truck for the fire."

I slapped him hard across the face. Angry, he grabbed me by the front of my coat. For a moment, he looked like he didn't recognize me. We stared at each other from inches away. "Let it burn, Leo. Let it fuckin' burn."

Reason returned to his face. He relaxed his grip, then gave me a bear hug. I pushed him away. "Go! Now!"

I chased after Vize. His cloak flared out behind him as he ran into the nearest alley. I swept around the corner building and pounded down the lane. The noise of fighting faded behind me. I followed Vize through a whirl of smoke and fire. At the far end of the alley, a shadow detached itself from a building, and someone jumped to the ground. Vize and I both skidded in surprise to a halt. The figure rose from a crouch on the ground and drew a sword. My mind seemed to disengage from thought as I stared at the Hound. I had been wrong. Again. Vize wasn't the Hound. I didn't know who the Hound was, but Vize turned a frantic, angry face toward me, then looked back toward the end of the alley. The Hound advanced on him, sword held high.

I took advantage of Vize's indecision and ran toward him again. As I did, a burst of Danann essence swept above me, and Guild security agents dove from behind. They skimmed over the pavement in front of me, outpacing me. In one smooth motion, they grabbed Vize by the arms and swept him into the air.

I stopped running, facing the Hound. He relaxed his fighting stance and stared at me over the swaddling of a scarf across his face. I was close enough finally for his essence to register in my vision, coalescing into a familiar, yet changed, body signature. My jaw dropped in recognition as he sheathed the sword and leaped into a shattered window in the building next to him. I shouted, my frustration echoing through the empty alley. Gone.

And so was Vize. I had lost him again.

37

With the wail of its siren, the fire truck surged by the end of the alley as I reached the street. Murdock perched on the top of the truck with Gerry slumped against his side. The truck vanished into a billowing cloud of smoke. The Dead and the solitaries continued fighting in a fog of the Taint. I skirted the side of a building and ran back to Eorla's car. Rand kept watch outside. Behind him, the firestorm had abated, a building lying in ruins on each side of the street. I surprised myself with a small prayer of thanks when I saw Eorla in the car. She was okay. I jumped in the back as Rand took the driver's seat. Eorla reached over and held my hand.

"Vize was captured by Guild security agents," I said. Rand didn't wait for Eorla to respond and hit the gas.

A bright pink flash illuminated the interior of the car. Joe shouted as inertia kicked in and zipped him backwards through the car. He hit the rear window and tumbled to the floor as Rand slammed on the brakes. Eorla and I lurched forward. Joe shot into the console between the front seats and fell to the floor again. Seeing we weren't in danger, Rand hit the gas. Joe pushed himself up with a dazed look on his face. "Meryl didn't mention you were in a moving car," he said.

"Where is she, Joe? Is she all right?"

He shook his shaggy head like a dog. "She's fine. She's fine. Some chrome-domes were hassling her at your place, but I put an end to that, I'll tell you. You should have seen them when I was done with them. Actually, you couldn't see them when I was done because they flew off like little baby birds being chased by a . . . a . . . a littler bird, right? A littler scary bird with a sword . . ."

Eorla cleared her throat.

"Joe, this is Grand Duchess Eorla Kruge Elvendottir of the Elven King's Court. Eorla, this is Joe Stinkwort. He's an old friend," I said.

She held her hand out to him. "I am pleased to meet you, Master Stinkwort. You sound most formidable."

Joe managed to stand. He examined her hand suspiciously, then touched his forehead to it. "Pleasure, m'lady. And it's Joe Flit, if you don't mind."

"Where's Meryl?" I asked.

He stepped onto the seat to peer out the window. "I'd say about four blocks ahead."

Over his head, I met Eorla's eyes. "We need to go get her."

Eorla tilted her head. "I don't think that's wise, Connor. The Guild's command center is set up at the end of the bridge. I can assert my rank down by the power plant, but you may end up in their hands if we go back."

I gestured toward the fighting blocking the street. "That's not an alternate route."

"The Oh No bridge is still there," said Joe. "The steel's warped a little, but the trolls couldn't do anything with it."

"Then we'll run the bridge if we have to," I said.

Eorla shook her head. "You're not making this easy."

"I don't care. Tell Meryl we're coming, Joe," I said. He winked out.

Rand chanted in the front seat. A shroud of essence poured out of him and enveloped the car. He shifted his tone, and the barrier spell compressed around the car.

Eorla sighed. "Alvud would be disappointed to see this."

I gently squeezed her hand. Anything I said would be trite to the ears of a widow of a centuries-long marriage. She didn't withdraw her hand, which was enough to tell me I was right. Silence in the face of grief can be as powerful as words.

Something hit the back of the car, and Eorla clenched my hand. The car lifted on its front wheels and skittered forward. Sparks flew across the windshield as metal met pavement. The car slammed down onto the street and lurched to a stop. Rand accelerated, but we didn't move. "I believe the axle's broken, ma'am," he said.

I looked up out the window. "That was a Danann blast. They're shooting at anything."

Eorla opened her door. The fires had not yet spread that far up the street, but fey folk were moving toward us fast. Rand took Eorla's arm as we struggled through sidewalks obstructed by compacted ice and piles of plowed snow. We took to the street to make faster progress.

No one had any reservations about throwing essence at us. The Taint did that, stripped people of their reason and goaded them into baser aggressions. Even fairies and elves unaffiliated with solitaries and the Dead were firing on us. The oppressive pressure on the neighborhood from the Guild and the police had exploded, and the Taint gave license to express bottled-up rage.

The Old Northern Avenue bridge became visible. Haze from the fires shifted in the arcs of searchlights and the flashing lights of emergency vehicles. The patter of gunfire echoed down alleys, but no one armed came our way. Yet. The slow steady bursts of tank gunfire rumbled from the south.

A small figure dressed in black strode down the middle of the road. I didn't need to see Joe's pink essence light swirling around her to recognize her. Meryl didn't change her pace when she realized it was me, but the moment we were close enough, she threw her arms around me. She eyed Eorla up and down. "Your daring escape skills need some sharpening, Eorla. We should do lunch."

Eorla didn't rise to the bait. "Agreed. At the moment, however, we need to keep the rioters from overtaking us and the Guild from arresting Connor."

Meryl looked down the street at the burning warehouses. "On the plus side, with this fire, I'm not chilly anymore."

The smoke haze obscured a clear view of the Old Northern Avenue bridge. "Joe, do some recon ahead, then see if we can get out past Summer Street."

He winked away. And blinked back. "What's recon?"

"The bridge, Joe. See what's happening on the bridge," I said. He saluted and vanished again.

I turned to Eorla. "Can your dwarf friends hide us?"

She shook her head. "The plan was for them to disappear. They're long gone by now."

Meryl grabbed my arm. Back toward the bridge, tanks rumbled out of the alleys and swiveled onto Old Northern. National Guardsmen followed on foot, shielding themselves behind trucks and the tanks as they spread out and took positions across the road. In a matter of moments, hundreds of weapons were pointed at us. Behind, the rioting fey churned their way toward us in a maelstrom of dark green Taint. Solitaries backed toward us as the Dead pressed them toward the bridge. And the guns and the tanks.

"This is going to be a slaughter," I said.

Eorla gazed up at the sky, her eyes narrowing as she stared at the Taint. She faced Meryl. "You know we can stop this."

Meryl frowned. "Do I?"

Calm as ever, as if we were not about to be crushed between competing factions, Eorla casually folded her arms. "You did it at Forest Hills. You collapsed the Celtic half of the spell."

Meryl shook her head. "I don't remember."

Eorla moved closer to her. "That's because you didn't do it. The drys did. You were the means to an end. We can do the same thing here."

"Wait a minute. I thought *I* collapsed the spell," I said.

Eorla shook her head. "I thought so, too, at first, but after examining the runes, I realized you didn't. You grounded all the essence by anchoring it with stone."

"I created a short circuit," I said.

She nodded. "And dissipated the excess essence that the spell had produced. Nigel and I provided a window of opportunity for you to do it. We would have failed if the drys had not collapsed the Celtic side of the spell. She used Meryl as a conduit to channel her counterspell. Even together, Nigel and I did not have the power to hold all that essence at bay and negate the Teutonic half of the spell. We took care of the immediate problem—we held back the essence and gave you time."

She pointed into the vibrant green sky. "The Taint is the remnant of the Teutonic half of the spell. I reconstructed the rune sequence. We can get the rioters under control by removing the Taint from them. I can do that if I stop the Taint."

"That's a big if," I said.

She stared at the approaching mayhem. "I do not think I can live with what might happen otherwise."

"Then use me," I said.

Eorla shook her head. "I do not know what effect your damaged abilities will have. We must use a pure vessel."

My gut clenched. I'd heard the phrase "pure vessel" the night the Taint was created. It was what the drys called Meryl. Everyone else had been touched by the Taint. Meryl moved several feet away from us. "You don't know what you're asking," she said.

"Nothing more than what I am asking of myself," Eorla said to her back.

I didn't say anything. I couldn't. Time after time, Meryl reminded me that I gave her choices that were not choices. I didn't know what I wanted her to do this time. What Eorla was suggesting was dangerous. I saw what had happened when the drys used Meryl as a conduit. It was terrifying. I had no idea what the Taint would do to her.

Meryl came to me, and we hugged. *Promise me you will kick her ass if I die,* she sent. I kissed the top of her head. "Hers won't be the only one," I said.

She inhaled deeply and pushed me away. "Let's do this before I change my mind."

Eorla placed her hands on Meryl's shoulders from behind. She closed her eyes and chanted in Old Elvish, the sounds harsh to the modern ear, but in Eorla's voice, it sounded both soft and mournful. Meryl's skin bleached to white as essence welled up from within, her body becoming sheathed in a vibrant halo. Eorla's cadence shifted, her voice growing stronger with the power of her song. Pinpoints of light appeared, dancing around Meryl like green fireflies. Faster and faster they spun, growing larger with each circuit of her body. They shifted and bent, forming shapes in response to Eorla's voice. They flickered brighter and resolved into the angular shapes of Teutonic runes.

Joe popped back in. "Whoa! What the hell are they doing?"

"I'll explain later. Who's on the bridge?" I asked.

He swooped around me, keeping his eyes on Eorla and Meryl. "It's a war party up there. That Frye guy from the Consortium, macGoren. Lots of security agents from both the Consortium and the Guild. And"—he eyed me significantly—"a bunch of chrome-domes just brought Vize in."

The air vibrated as Eorla pulled more essence from her surroundings and funneled it into the rune spell. The dark mass in my head spiked into a ball of claws as her essence touched our surroundings. My eyes watered as I struggled to hold in the darkness. Moving away didn't help. The desire to touch Eorla's powerful essence burned in my gut. The dark mass moved, spreading inside me, hungering to cross the distance between Eorla and me.

I clenched my jaw, refusing to let the darkness free. It wanted the essence. It wanted Eorla and Meryl. It wanted too much. I pushed back against it with my mind. My left arm flared with cold as the tattoo burned on the surface of my skin. The dark mass didn't retreat, but it paused. I stepped farther back. My stomach churned. I almost didn't care if I did interfere, if I reached out and touched them, touched the luscious reams of essence coursing from them.

A wind sprang up, biting and cold. Essence circled Meryl and Eorla in vibrant streams of green and blue and white. Meryl trembled as the runes swept around her. Her head fell back, the cords in her neck straining against the power coursing through her. The light in her face pulsed and flared and obliterated her features.

Eorla shouted above the rising wind. Clenching the back of Meryl's neck, she thrust her other hand up. A surge of blue-white light leaped from her palm, pure essence fanning across the sky, crackling with power and piercing the clouds of Taint. The rioters paused in confusion as the green haze rippled. The wind rose to a gale, spinning the Taint into a whirlpool of sickly green light. A funnel formed beneath it, dancing in the air like an appendage groping for contact. It lashed like the tail of an angry beast and plunged into Meryl.

The Taint poured down. The funnel sucked it out of the sky and more shreds of green haze gathered from all directions. Meryl convulsed with shock as the Taint coursed through her. Eorla sang higher, her song becoming a roar of power. The Taint surged out of Meryl, along Eorla's arm and flooded her body. The dark mass in my head contracted abruptly. It had never liked the Taint, had avoided it as much as the Taint avoided the darkness. I stumbled toward the bridge but the pain refused to subside. With the amount of essence powering in, no place within walking distance would be far enough.

Everything stopped. An utter silence hung over the street. Eorla and Meryl swayed on their feet. I searched the sky and found nothing but ambient essence. I didn't sense Taint anywhere. They had done it. Eorla and Meryl had done it. The Taint was gone.

Up the street, the fey folk broke into a babble of confusion. I jogged toward Meryl and Eorla. Rand rushed to Eorla's side as she stumbled and fell, and Meryl crumpled to the ground at the same time. I threw myself onto my knees beside her and pulled her to my chest.

"Meryl?"

Her head lolled to the side, her eyes glazed and sightless. I grabbed her chin and turned her face toward mine. I shook her gently. "Meryl? Answer me."

Not a flicker of awareness. I hugged her to my chest and rocked her. "Come on, Meryl. Wake up."

I stroked her face. Her skin was hard and cold. She lay in my arms, deadweight. I sensed nothing from her at all. Whatever made Meryl Meryl was gone. I lowered her to the ground. Eorla's essence glowed like an emerald star as

Rand held her, but her head fell back slack. She lay still and insensate in his arms. He stared at me, stricken.

The Weird was not their home. The solitaries were not their people. Vize was not their problem. Or Moira. They could have walked away. They had wanted to help. They wanted to help me. But I couldn't help them. I couldn't stop the madness. I was useless and now they were—I didn't know what they were. Mindless. Brain-dead. I didn't know.

I lifted my head at the sound of a tank moving at the end of the Avenue. It shifted into place, its gun turret rotating toward us. Another moved forward. More National Guardsmen arrived through the side alleys. They pointed their guns at us.

I rose to my feet. "Stay with her, Joe."

Agitated, he whirled around me. "What are you doing?"

I thrust my hand at him, and he somersaulted out of reach. "Just stay with her and don't argue," I said.

I walked toward the waiting tanks and soldiers, the pain in my head tearing at my mind. Essence light flared on the bridge—powerful Danann and Teutonic body signatures. The power players. The elite. The ones who played games while innocent people died. Something broke inside me, and I shouted in rage.

The darkness answered.

My head exploded with a visceral pain. My vision blurred and faded away into a relentless black field. Essence exploded everywhere into my awareness, every body signature, every nuance, and every mote blazed around me against a black, hungry night. The ambient essence of the Weird crackled and flickered, buildings a pearlescent white, the street a rainbow oil slick of fractured color. Human soldiers moved like soft shadows of azure against the dead null zones of their tanks and trucks. The bridge became defined by its negative space, its steel beams a nothingness of essence that formed a cage for the fey who waited there— blue-white Dananns, amber brownies, the green streak of elves, and yellows and whites and everything between.

The Guild. The Consortium. Safe in the steel nest of the bridge. Safe from the essence-fire of the rampaging solitaries and the Dead. Safe from the collateral damage of their own agents firing on innocent bystanders. Safe from the tanks and the guns and the soldiers prepared to attack on their orders. Safe from the ramifications of their own decisions.

The dark mass surged within me, feeding my anger and need. I let it. I wanted it. I didn't care anymore about what it could do or not do. My chest ached as hot spikes of shadow pierced my skin. Darkness blossomed around me like a pall of smoke. I stalked toward the bridge, toward the waiting tanks and soldiers.

The faint echo of gunfire sounded as if from far, far away. Pinpricks of red-white lights shot toward me, then sparkled and vanished in the darkness. Humans scattered away from me as I approached, their faint blue body signatures fleeing into the distance. The shadows extending from my skin shuddered and coiled, enormous waves pressing against the null void of the tanks. They scattered like leaves before me, the shadows flinging them aside like the nothingness they were.

Essence flared ahead, delicious strikes of light that pulsated in the darkness only to evaporate as they neared me. I savored them, tasted the hot, burning flavor through all my senses, a rush of ecstasy coursing through me as I consumed them. The body signatures on the bridge shifted in place, uncertain hoverings of fear and confusion that heightened my desire. Fear was there. Delicious fear. I wanted them. I wanted them all.

Darkness split my forehead like a blade. A nightness blossomed out of me, long ribbons of it unfurling and slithering in and out of the dull shape of the bridge, wrapping itself around the beams and tension cabling. The body signatures retreated, then stopped moving as the darkness outpaced them to the other end of the bridge. They huddled in the center. Trapped. I had them trapped together, wrapped in an embrace of the darkness.

My mind clenched. The thing in my mind clenched. The long ribbons flexed and yanked. The bridge shuddered and twisted as I pulled, bending and peeling it open like a tangled knot of metal. The channel waters beneath it teemed with shots of essence, water fey and sea creatures fleeing the strands of darkness that waved over them. I pulled at the darkness as it pulled at me.

I reached the bridge. The fey who cowered there surrounded themselves with a shield barrier, thick and powerful. My shadows ripped at it, shredding it layer by layer the closer I got. Their fear was palpable now, delicious and sweet. Satisfaction coursed through me, a deep pleasure that for once the powerful and the strong felt the profound helplessness of the weak and desperate. I wanted them to know what they had done to the Dead and the solitaries. I wanted them to feel the burn of flames tearing through the Weird, the rending of flesh from blades and bullets. I wanted them to know what they had done to us, to all of us. To me. To Meryl.

The darkness—my darkness—slithered among them, snaring their essence, siphoning their power. I moved without thought, watching their lights fade one by one. As the essence around me diminished, another darkness appeared in its midst. Something moved in my vision, something dark and familiar. Insignificant in size, weak in force, but nevertheless there. It recoiled from me and my darkness danced and swirled around it, resisting its presence.

Realization pushed itself into my hunger. Another darkness. Another window into this nameless other that I was setting free. Another mark of everything that had gone wrong since that day we fought and he destroyed my abilities as he tried to destroy the world.

Vize.

Rage rose higher within me. He would not hide among the powerful fey. He would not escape by claiming safe harbor. I wasn't going to let him. I forced the darkness out of me, forced it toward the dark thing in front of me.

I touched his darkness and met the thing within myself.

My mind exploded in a cacophony of pain.

38

A high-pitched tone rang in my head. The dark mass smoldered inside me, a shrunken mote of heat. I lifted my face from hard, ribbed pavement. Pushing myself up, I tamped down my sensing ability to soften its raw sensitivity, but its physical aspects—the nerve endings in my nose and eyes—throbbed with pain.

A hard, cold wind swept up the channel. Black smoke rolled down Old Northern Avenue, obscuring the neighborhood. A tank lay on its side. Another was embedded in the wall of a building. The rest were spread along the sides of the street as if they had been dropped like toys from a child's hand.

Behind me, dozens of bodies lay scattered on the bridge—fairies, brownies, dwarves, elves, druids—even solitaries and the Dead. Their essence guttered inside them like wind-torn candles.

I had done that.

My stomach clenched as I swept them with my sensing ability. Not dead. Depleted, but not dead. I hadn't killed them. The fact that I could have and not given it a second thought when I released the darkness left me with a coldness that had nothing to do with the wind.

Bergin Vize stood, holding his scorched cloak closed with one hand. A burn mark across his knuckles left a red slash that set off the dead black ring he wore. He stared, wet and filthy, a faint light glittering in his eyes. "What were you hoping to accomplish by this?"

"Justice, Vize. And your death," I said.

He murmured a long, low chuckle. "As usual, Grey, you make the rules to suit you, while claiming I transgress by doing so. How convenient for you. How just."

I grabbed him by the front of his cloak. "Do you really think this is the moment to mock me, Vize? Do you have any idea what you caused here?"

He laughed, and I shoved him away. He had no idea and never would. People stirred around us. At the far end of the bridge, Ryan macGoren rose in the air on white-shot wings. He surveyed the damage with a blanched look on his face. For all his talk, I don't think he had the guts to deal with the reality of being a Guildmaster. He floated down and landed beside Bastian Frye. As they approached me and Vize, Brokke disentangled himself from a pile of bodies and followed.

"You should have turned yourself in," macGoren said. He had the gall to look annoyed.

"Really? Would that have stopped you from blowing up the power plant?" I said.

His glance slipped to Bastian Frye and away. "The Dead did that."

I gave him the coldest smile I knew how. "Stick to that story, macGoren. I'm betting not enough people involved died despite your best efforts. They will talk."

Danann security agents appeared in the sky above us and settled down beside macGoren. He gestured at Vize and me. "Take them into custody," he said.

Frye held up his hand. "The Consortium has an interest in these men as well."

MacGoren bowed his head with a smile. "My agents are here now, Bastian. We can sort it out later."

Frye returned the smile. "I believe I am more than capable of handling two damaged fey folk."

Brokke gazed off into the distance, a bemused smile on his face. "Wind's changing."

Frye shifted his eyes to the dwarf, then followed his line of sight to something behind me. The wind had swung around, pushing the smoke to the west away from the burning buildings. Down on the Avenue, a lone figure moved within the gray haze. With her head high and determined, Eorla strode out of the smoke, her essence shimmering a brilliant, pure evergreen. The wind shifted farther to the south, and the fire smoke retreated up the Avenue. More figures appeared behind Eorla, shadowed silhouettes in all shapes and sizes. Eorla threw her hands out as she continued walking, and she sent a surge of essence swirling through the air. A gale rushed off the channel and down the Avenue. The last of the smoke lifted and billowed away, revealing thousands of fey filling the street and the air above it. The Weird was on the march. The Dead and the solitaires, purged of the Taint, moved forward in united purpose.

Eorla reached the bridge and paused between me and Vize. She had changed on some fundamental level. Bright pinpoints of light glittered in her eyes, and her skin gleamed a translucent green. When I had first met her, I thought her power impressive. Now, she radiated essence like no one I had ever met.

"These men are under my protection," she said.

A slight smile creased Frye's lips, while macGoren shifted uncertainly on his feet. Frye bowed and swept his hand toward the far end of the bridge. "I have a car, Your Highness. Allow me to take charge of them."

Eorla gave him a cold smile. "You mistake me, Bastian. I am granting them free passage. They are free to go by my authority."

The smile slipped from his face. "Your Highness?"

She thrust her arm back. "Do you see what is behind me? That is failure, gentlemen, and I will no longer tolerate it. Do you see all those people? They are under my protection, too. All of them. Any transgression against them shall be a transgression against me."

Frye came forward with his hand held out. "Your Highness, you are not yourself."

White light filled Eorla's eyes. "Step no closer, Bastian. I am more myself than ever. I claim these people. Do you hear me? Withdraw the Guild and Consortium forces and your human lackeys, or I will unleash a fury that will shake the thrones of the High Queen of Tara and the Elven King."

"You would incite the Consortium to war against us?" macGoren asked.

Eorla shook her head. "No, Guildsman. Hear me, both of you, and hear me well. I send this message to High Queen Maeve and Donor Elfenkonig: You have failed. You face a new Court. Hear my words and know fear: Eorla Elvendottir shall not abide either of your courts any longer."

MacGoren narrowed his eyes at her. "Be reasonable, Eorla. Look at that rabble. They can barely stand. Do you think you can withstand my forces?"

Eorla tucked her chin and glanced over her shoulder. "Like so many others, you underestimate me, Danann. Look beyond what you see. Set your sights a little higher. I have."

Someone appeared on the roof of the nearest building. As he stepped up on the high cornice of the building, Rand lifted a bow strung with flaming green elf-shot. One by one, other archers joined him, flanking him to either side along the roof. More appeared on other buildings until rooflines all around us bristled with elven soldiers wearing the house insignias of Kruge and Elvendottir.

"Cross me at your peril," Eorla said. She pivoted on her heel and strode back into the Weird. Vize didn't hesitate to follow. I stared at macGoren, flanked by his security agents. True shock and fear showed in his eyes. There was nothing left to say. I walked away.

At the end of the bridge, Eorla waited with Vize. "I am not Maeve or Donor. The old ways are gone. I reject any claim either of you may have of me and make none of you. I have granted you free passage for today. Use it as you see fit and may the Wheel of the World turn in your favor."

She proceeded alone down the Avenue, a tall flame of power. As she approached the gathered crowd, they sank to their knees, rank upon rank bowing before her. All save one. Zev continued walking toward me, carrying Meryl's limp body.

Vize smirked at me. "How's it feel to be a fugitive?"

I punched him in the face.

I leaned my forehead against the cold window, watching the snow swirl into drifts along the riverbank. The flakes fell like pale moths against the dark, a world of white against black blurring to gray. The heart monitor beeped behind me, a soft, regular rhythm that was at once reassuring because it existed and worrisome because it was needed. My breath steamed against window, obscuring my darkened image. A flash of pink in the room reflected in the mirrored surface. Joe hovered over the bed.

"Sorry I'm late," he said to my back.

I moved to the side of the bed. "It's okay. It doesn't matter."

He frowned. "Of course, it matters. Did you think it didn't matter when you were in the same position? You heard me when I was here then. I know you did."

I slipped my hand into Meryl's. "I don't remember."

"Course you don't. We don't remember things. We remember making it through things. So will she."

"Gillen Yor says it's not a coma," I said.

Joe knelt on the pillow by Meryl's head and placed his hands on her forehead. "No, it's not. She's not here."

"Don't say that," I said.

He rose from the bed, hovering next to me. "Talk to her. She will hear you even if she doesn't answer."

I leaned my head next to hers, feeling her warm cheek against mine, her breath a soft touch on my skin. Her hair— her crazy fiery red hair—smelled like apple blossoms. I brought my lips to her ear. "Come back. Please."

I slid my lips to her forehead and kissed her there, long and soft.

"We have to go. The shift change is almost over," said Joe.

I tapped Meryl's nose. Joe blipped out as I opened the room door.

The outside hall was empty. Gillen Yor was keeping the security guard occupied at the far end near the nurses' station. *I'll let you know any change,* he sent.

I strolled away in the opposite direction and entered the back stairwell, where Keeva waited for me. I handed her the white lab coat I was wearing.

"Thank you for this," I said.

She flicked her eyebrow dismissively. "By the time anyone notices the gap in the watch schedule, I'll be in Tara claiming hormone surges must have affected my organizational skills."

"They're going to bury it, aren't they?" I asked.

She nodded. "It's already happening. Cashel and the commissioner went rogue. That's the official story."

"Did macGoren know? Did you?"

She pursed her lips. "I won't speak for Ryan, but, no, I didn't know."

I could have said something sarcastic about her sleeping with macGoren. It would have been justified, but inappropriate. I didn't always understand Keeva's motivations, but right then, she was doing me a big favor. I let it pass.

I glanced down and smiled at her swollen abdomen. "I never said congratulations."

"No, you didn't. In fact, I believe you said I had a parasite. But, thank you," she said.

"How come you didn't want anyone to know?"

She didn't answer immediately, looking at me for a long moment as if deciding what to share. "Dananns don't have children often. It was bad enough Ryan had me on desk duty because he was worried about my health. I didn't want him trying to keep me from working altogether."

"You two have a strange relationship, you know that?" I asked.

She rolled her eyes. "I think that's an insult coming from you."

I laughed, and she shared a grudging smile. "Are you— both of you—going to be all right?" I asked.

She nodded. "The energies at Tara will restore me. Gillen says the baby is undisturbed, but I need rest to make it through the birth."

"I'm sorry. I didn't know what I was doing."

She shook her head. "You never do. Get going before the next shift arrives."

I saluted her as I hurried down the stairs, my footsteps ringing hollowly as I descended. At the bottom of the stairwell, I peered out the exit door to the garage. Nothing out of the ordinary except Murdock's car parked near the door. I slipped into the passenger seat, and he pulled away as the late shift of Danann agents flew past.

"No change," I said.

"A lot's changed," he said.

We spiraled up the garage ramp and into the night. The callies had kept their storm going for a week, a blizzard the likes of which Boston had never seen. The city plowed the streets enough to maintain basic services, but almost everything had shut down to wait out the storm. It was Eorla's gift to the mayor, a way to confine everyone inside and calm the situation without guns or essence-fire.

From where I sat, I couldn't see the heavy abrasions on Murdock's left cheek and forehead. He looked like the man I always knew. He looked like Murdock, not the crazed guy who had beaten a Dead guy to death. The berserker was in a holding cell at the Consortium consulate. Eorla had turned his body over to Bastian before it regenerated. They were no longer strict allies, but that didn't mean they didn't have mutual enemies.

"I should have killed him," I said.

"It wouldn't have mattered," he said.

The car fishtailed down the off-ramp of the elevated highway. Momentum built as the grade steepened. We swung side to side in a growing arc, inching closer and closer to the guardrails on either side. I grabbed the dashboard as Murdock worked the steering wheel like a carnival ride. The view out the windshield became a blur of gray and white as the understructure of the highway whipped past. At the bottom of the ramp, the car shuddered and spun wildly, bouncing on the surface road. Murdock hit the brake. The wheels locked and we did a long, frenetic slide into an intersection. The car stopped beneath a flashing red traffic light. We stared at empty streets, mounds of snow surrounding us.

"Wouldn't be funny if we died in a car accident?" Murdock said. I stared at him slack-jawed as he laughed. When he saw the look on my face, he laughed harder. I laughed, too. We weren't wrapped around a pole, and he was right. It was damned funny.

He eased his foot onto the accelerator and turned down Old Northern. Just short of the bridge, the Boston police and Guild and Consortium security manned a checkpoint. We passed them without incident. Murdock stopped at the bridge.

I didn't move. "Do you blame me for what happened, Leo?"

For a long moment, he watched the snow coating the twisted beams of the bridge. "I don't know how to answer that. If it wasn't for you, it wouldn't have happened, but that's like saying it's your fault. I don't think I can go that far."

I couldn't bring myself to look at him. "I don't know how you don't hate me."

He sighed heavily and ran his fingers lightly over the steering wheel. "You know what's the hardest part of being a Catholic, Connor? Forgiveness. If I can't forgive other people, I can never forgive myself. That's something the fey don't get."

Everything about the fey was about winning and revenge and our own brand of justice. Nothing was ever forgotten. Nothing was ever let go. How did you know the point beyond which justice became revenge? How did you forgive the intentional infliction of pain or the needless loss of life? How did you forgive the unforgivable, especially when the failings were your own? The fey had all these rules for getting along, but they always ended up being the cause for resentment and injury instead of the cure. And yet, despite a history of wasted lives and failed happiness, we still strove to make the world a better place. But in the end, we're flawed—all of us, even the humans. We were all unperfect souls doomed to error. Maybe that was the point. Maybe it was that flaw that made us want more for ourselves, to want to change ourselves into something better. Murdock was right. The fey didn't know how to forgive, and the humans weren't much better at it. And, maybe, we needed to learn before we could build something better.

"So," I said. "Who are you sleeping with?"

He laughed, a natural laugh, the laugh of the Leonard Murdock I knew. "Get out of the car, Connor."

I grinned and gave him a light punch on the shoulder. He'd tell me eventually.

"Thanks, Leo," I said. He didn't respond as I got out of the car. He never says good-bye.

I walked across the bridge. *Vitniri* clung to the intersecting beams above, watching and howling as I passed. Other fey watched, too, hidden and alert, waiting for the Guild or the Consortium or the humans to make a move.

Uno materialized at my side and accompanied me down Sleeper Street, his dark bulk pressing against my leg. I let my hand trail through his thick fur. Next to the door to my apartment building, the Hound leaned against the wall, his cloak wrapped tightly around him and his hood pulled down to hide his face.

With a languid movement, he tossed something at me. I reached out and snatched it from the air. A shoe. Murdock's shoe, in fact. "Tell Murdock I couldn't find it sooner," he said.

He crouched and whistled. Uno bounded toward him like a puppy. The Hound scratched him roughly under the neck. "He was supposed to protect Shay, but I guess he had his own ideas," he said.

As I approached, his essence resolved more clearly in my sensing ability, confirming what I had sensed the night of the riots. "He did protect him. Just like you did, Robyn. I'm sorry I didn't do the same for you," I said.

Robyn stood and waved his hand at the dog. Uno danced backwards from him, then sat next to me. Robyn shifted his hood back, revealing his face. He looked the same, but the angry punk who protected his boyfriend from the dangers of the Weird had been replaced by a confident young man. Shay would be proud. "My death wasn't your fault, Grey," he said. "I was stupid. In the end, it was the best thing to happen to me. I'm not on drugs anymore, and I'm better than I ever was."

"I don't understand how you ended up in TirNaNog," I said.

He shrugged. "The glamour stone I was wearing when I died fused with my essence. At least, that's what my friend Alvud thinks."

"Alvud Kruge?"

Robyn cocked his head. "Yeah, did you know him?"

I shook my head. "Never met him. I wish I had, though."

Robyn pulled the hood up again. "He's cool. He didn't want to come through the veil on Samhain. He said the living have enough trouble without the Dead haunting them."

"Is that why you haven't told Shay you're here?"

He wrapped his scarf around his face. "I wanted to know he was okay. I didn't know I'd get stuck here. If the veil lifts, I don't want to hurt him again by leaving. I came to ask you not to say anything."

"I won't, but he feels bad that you were angry with each other when you died. You might think about that."

His face was unreadable behind the scarf. "I will." He walked away, his green cloak fluttering in the wind, and faded from view as the snow fell around him.

People failed. It was what people did best. We tried and tried and tried to do the right thing, even when it was the wrong thing to do. I failed. I thought of Vize, and a knot of anger formed in my chest. He believed he was doing the right thing. What he failed to see was that anarchy wasn't the solution to Maeve or even Donor. The world was a bigger place than the squabbles of two decaying monarchies. Something new had to happen. Maybe that was what Eorla was trying to accomplish. Or maybe she would end up creating another mess. But whether it was Vize or Eorla, or Maeve or Donor, the Wheel of the World would keep turning as It willed.

All of it was one as far as I was concerned.

For this paranormal investigator,
it's business as unusual…

DEAD TO ME

by Anton Strout

psy·chom·e·try (si-kom'i-tre) n.

1. The power to touch an object and divine information about its history
2. For Simon Canderous: not as cool as it sounds

Possessing the power of psychometry never did much for Simon Canderous, until it landed him a job with New York City's Department of Extraordinary Affairs. But he's not at all prepared for the strange case that unfolds before him—one involving politically correct cultists, a homicidal bookcase, and the forces of Darkness, which kind of have a crush on him…

"Following Simon's adventures is like being the pinball in an especially antic game, but it's well worth the wear and tear."
—Charlaine Harris, *New York Times* bestselling author

penguin.com